P9-DDP-181

Mothers in a Million

Celebrate Mother's Day with Harlequin® Romance!

Enjoy four very different aspects of motherhood and celebrate that very special bond between mother and child with four extra-special Harlequin® Romances this month!

Whether it's the pitter-patter of tiny feet for the first time, or finding love the second time around, these four Romances offer tears, laughter and emotion and are guaranteed to celebrate those mothers in a million!

For the ultimate indulgent treat, don't miss:

A FATHER FOR HER TRIPLETS by Susan Meier

THE MATCHMAKER'S HAPPY ENDING by Shirley Jump

SECOND CHANCE WITH THE REBEL by Cara Colter

FIRST COMES BABY… by Michelle Douglas

Dear Reader,

Mother's Day has been a tough holiday for me to celebrate in the years since I lost my own mother. The first couple of years I didn't want to do anything to acknowledge the day, because it was too painful to be reminded that I didn't have my mom around to call, to talk to, to visit with. I would just ignore the holiday and spend it like any other Sunday.

In the past two years or so I've had a change of heart. I've started to look at Mother's Day as a way to celebrate not just my amazing children but everything that nurtures and fulfills us. The only thing I want for Mother's Day is a trip to the garden center, so I can pick up my spring flowers and spend the day in the garden, weeding, pruning and renewing areas that have been long neglected. Then I can step back and see the flowers bloom day after day, giving me a happy little reminder of Mother's Day for months afterward. To me, it's like a long visit from my own mother when I walk outside and see the impatiens and pansies waving in the breeze. And because my kids have helped me plant and tend them, it gives me some special time with each of them, as well.

I hope you enjoy this mother-daughter story and the special bond that Marnie has with her mom. And I also hope that you, dear reader, have a wonderful Mother's Day and find a way to take a peek at Mother Nature's beautiful gifts each and every day.

Shirley

SHIRLEY JUMP

The Matchmaker's Happy Ending
&
Boardroom Bride and Groom

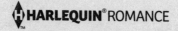

Recycling programs
for this product may
not exist in your area.

ISBN-13: 978-0-373-74241-7

THE MATCHMAKER'S HAPPY ENDING

First North American Publication 2013

Copyright © 2013 by Shirley Kawa-Jump, LLC

BOARDROOM BRIDE AND GROOM

Copyright © 2008 by Shirley Kawa-Jump, LLC

This is a work of fiction. Names, characters, places and incidents are either the product of the author's imagination or are used fictitiously, and any resemblance to actual persons, living or dead, business establishments, events or locales is entirely coincidental.

This edition published by arrangement with Harlequin Books S.A.

For questions and comments about the quality of this book, please contact us at CustomerService@Harlequin.com.

H HARLEQUIN®
www.Harlequin.com

Printed in U.S.A.

CONTENTS

New York Times bestselling author **Shirley Jump** didn't have the willpower to diet, nor the talent to master under-eye concealer, so she bowed out of a career in television and opted instead for a career where she could be paid to eat at her desk—writing. At first, seeking revenge on her children for their grocery store tantrums, she sold embarrassing essays about them to anthologies. However, it wasn't enough to feed her growing addiction to writing funny. So she turned to the world of romance novels, where messes are (usually) cleaned up before The End. In the worlds Shirley gets to create and control, the children listen to their parents, the husbands always remember holidays and the housework is magically done by elves. Though she's thrilled to see her books in stores around the world, Shirley mostly writes because it gives her an excuse to avoid cleaning the toilets and helps feed her shoe habit.

To learn more, visit her website at www.shirleyjump.com.

Books by Shirley Jump

MISTLETOE KISSES WITH THE BILLIONAIRE
RETURN OF THE LAST MCKENNA*
HOW THE PLAYBOY GOT SERIOUS*
ONE DAY TO FIND A HUSBAND*
THE PRINCESS TEST
HOW TO LASSO A COWBOY
IF THE RED SLIPPER FITS
VEGAS PREGNANCY SURPRISE
BEST MAN SAYS I DO

*The McKenna Brothers trilogy

Other titles by this author available in ebook format.

The Matchmaker's Happy Ending

To Mom. I miss you every day.

CHAPTER ONE

MARNIE FRANKLIN LEFT her thirtieth wedding of the year, with aching feet, flower petals in her hair and a satisfied smile on her face. She'd done it. Again.

From behind the wide glass and brass doors of Boston's Park Plaza hotel, the newly married Mr. and Mrs. Andrew Corliss waved and shouted their thanks. "We owe it all to you, Marnie!" Andrew called. A geeky but lovable guy who tended toward neon colored ties that were knotted too tight around his skinny neck, Andrew had been one of her best success stories. Internet millionaire, now married to an energetic, friendly woman who loved him for his mind—and their mutual affection for difficult Sudoku puzzles.

"You're welcome! May you have a long and happy life together." Marnie gave them a smile, then turned to the street and waited while a valet waved up one of the half dozen waiting cabs outside the hotel. Exhaustion weighed on Marnie's shoulders, despite the two cups of coffee she'd downed at the reception. A light rain had started, adding a chill to the late spring air. The always busy Boston traffic passed the hotel in a *swoosh-swoosh* of tires on damp pavement, a melody highlighted by the honking of horns, the constant music of a city. She loved this city, she really did, but there were days—like today—when she wished she lived somewhere quiet. Like the other side of the moon.

Her phone rang as she opened the taxi's door and told the driver her address. She pressed mute, sending the call straight to voice mail. That was the trouble with being on the top of her field—there was no room for a holiday or vacation. She'd become one of Boston's most successful matchmakers, and that meant everyone who wanted a happy ending called her, looking for true love.

Something she didn't believe in herself.

An irony she couldn't tell her clients. Couldn't admit she'd never fallen in love, and had given up on the emotion after one too many failed relationships. She couldn't tell people that the matchmaker had no faith in a match for herself. So she poured herself into her job and kept a bright smile on her face whenever she told her clients that they could have that happy ending, too.

She'd seen the fairy tale ending happen for other people, but a part of Marnie wondered if she'd missed her one big chance to have a happily-ever-after. She was almost thirty, and had yet to meet Mr. Right. Only a few heartbreaker Mr. Wrongs. At least with her job, she had some control over the outcome, which was the way Marnie preferred the things in her life. Controlled, predictable. The phone rang again, like a punctuation mark to the end of her thoughts.

In front of her, the cabbie pulled away from the curb, at the same time fiddling with the GPS on the dash. Must be a new driver, Marnie decided, and grabbed her phone to answer the call. "This is Marnie. How can I help you make a match?"

"You need to stop working, dear, and find your own Mr. Right."

Her mother. Who meant well, but who thought Marnie's personal life should take precedence over everything else in the universe. "Hi, Ma. What are you doing up so late on a Friday night?"

"Worrying about my single daughter. And why she's working on a Friday night. Again."

The GPS announced a left turn, a little late

for the distracted cab driver, who jerked the wheel to the left and jerked Marnie to one side, too. She gave him a glare in the rearview mirror, but he ignored it. The noxious fumes of Boston exhaust filled the interior, or maybe that was the bad ventilation system in the cab. The car had seen better days, heck, better decades, if the duct tape on the scarred vinyl seats was any indication.

"You should be out on a date of your own," Marnie countered to her mother.

"Oh, I'm too old for that foolishness," Helen said. "Besides, your father hasn't been gone that long."

"Three years, Ma." Marnie lowered her voice to a sympathetic tone. Dad's heart attack had taken them all by surprise. One day he'd been there, grinning and heading out the door, the next he'd been a shell of himself, and then…gone. "It's okay to move on."

"So, what are you doing on Sunday?" her mother said, instead of responding to Marnie's advice, a surefire Helen tactic. Change the topic from anything difficult. Marnie's parents had been the type who avoided the hard stuff, swept it under the rug. To them, the world had been a perpetually sunny place, even when evidence to the contrary dropped a big gray shadow in their way.

A part of Marnie wanted to keep things that way for her mother, to protect Helen, who had been through so much.

"I wanted to have you and your sisters over for brunch after church," Ma said. "I could serve that coffee cake you love and…"

As her mother talked about the menu, Marnie murmured agreement, and reviewed her To Do list in her head. She had three appointments with new clients early in the morning tomorrow, one afternoon bachelor meet and greet to host, then her company's Saturday night speed date event—

"Did you hear what I said?" her mother cut in.

"Sorry, Ma. The connection faded." Or her brain, but she didn't say that.

The cab driver fiddled again with the GPS, pushing buttons to zoom in or out, Marnie wasn't sure. He seemed flustered and confused. She leaned forward. "Just take a left up here," she said to him. "Onto Boylston. Then a right on Harvard."

The cabbie nodded.

And went straight.

"Hey, you missed the turn." Damn it. Was the man that green? Marnie gave up the argument and sat back against the seat. After the long day she'd had, the delay was more welcome than annoying. Especially to her feet, which were already complaining about the upcoming three-flight walk upstairs to her condo. She loved the brick building she lived in, with its tree-lined street located within walking distance of the quirky neighborhood of Coolidge Corner. But there were days when living on the third floor—despite the nice view of the park across the street—was exhausting after a long day. Right this second, she'd do about anything for an elevator and a massage chair.

"I said you should wear a dress to brunch on Sunday," her mother said, "because I'm inviting Stella Hargrove's grandson. He's single and—"

"Wouldn't it be nicer just to visit with you and my sisters, Ma? That way, we can all catch up, which we never seem to get enough time to do. A guy would end up being a fifth wheel." Marnie pressed a finger to her temple, but it did little to ward off the impending headache. A headache her sister Erica would say she brought on herself because she never confronted her mother and instead placated and deferred. Instead of saying *Ma, don't fix me up,* she'd fallen back on making nice instead. Marnie was the middle sister, the peacemaker, even if sometimes that peace came with the price of a lot of aspirin. "Besides, if I want a date, I have a whole file of handsome men to go through."

"Yet you haven't done that at all. You keep working and working and…oh, I just worry about you, honey."

Ever since their father had died, Helen had made her three children her top—and only—priority. No matter how many times Marnie and her sisters had encouraged their mother to take a class, pick up a hobby, go on a trip, she demurred, and refocused the conversation on her girls. What her mother needed was an outside life. Something else to focus on. Something like a…

Man.

Marnie smacked herself in the head. For goodness sake, she was a professional matchmaker. Why had she never thought to fix up her mother? Marnie had made great matches for both of her sisters. Oldest sister Kat got married to her match two years ago, and Erica was in a steady relationship with a man Marnie had introduced her to last month. Despite that, Marnie had never thought about doing the same for her widowed mother. First thing tomorrow morning, she would cull her files and find a selection of distinguished, older men. Who appreciated women with a penchant for meddling.

"I'll be there for brunch on Sunday, Ma, I promise," Marnie said, noting the cabbie again messing with the GPS. "Maybe next time we can invite Stella's grandson. Okay?"

Her mother sighed. "Okay. But if you want me to give him your number or give you his…"

"I know who to call." Marnie started to say something else when the cabbie swore, stomped on his brakes—

And rear-ended the car in front of him. Marnie jerked forward, the seatbelt cutting across her sternum but saving her from plowing into the plexiglass partition. She let out an oomph, winced at the sharp pain that erupted in her chest, while the cabbie let out a stream of curses.

"What was that sound?" Helen asked. "It sounded like a boom. Did something fall? Did you hit something?"

"It's, uh, nothing. I gotta go, Ma," Marnie said, and after a breath, then another, the pain in her chest eased. "See you tomorrow." She hung up the phone, then unbuckled, and climbed out of the yellow cab. The hood had crumpled, and steam poured from the engine in angry gusts. The cabbie clambered out of the taxi. He let out another long stream of curses, a few in a language other than English, then started pacing back and forth between the driver's side door and the impact site, holding his head and muttering.

The accordioned trunk of a silver sports car was latched onto the taxi's hood. A tall, dark, handsome, and angry man stood beside the idling luxury car. He shouted at the cab driver, who threw up his hands and feigned non-understanding, as if he'd suddenly lost all knowledge of the English language.

Marnie grabbed her purse from the car, and walked over to the man. One of those attractive, business types, she thought, noting his dark pinstriped suit, loosened tie, white button-down with the top button undone. A five o'clock shadow dusted his strong jaw, and gave his dark hair and blue eyes a sexy air. The matchmaker in her recognized the kind of good-looking man always in demand with her clients. But the woman in her—

Well, she noticed him on an entirely different level, one that sent a shimmer of heat down her veins and sped up her pulse. Something she hadn't felt in so long, she'd begun to wonder if she'd ever meet another man who interested her.

Either way, Mr. Suit and Tie looked like

a lawyer or something. The last thing she needed was a rich, uptight man with control issues. She'd met enough of them that she could pick his type out of the thousands of people in the stands at Fenway on opening day.

"Is everyone okay?" she asked.

The cab driver nodded. Mr. Suit and Tie shot him a scowl, then turned to Marnie. His features softened. "Yeah. I'm fine," he said. "You?"

"I'm okay. Just a little shaken up."

"Good." He held her gaze for a moment longer, then turned on the cabbie. "Didn't you see that red light? Where'd you get your license? A vending machine?"

The cabbie just shook his head, as if he didn't understand a word.

Mr. Suit and Tie let out a curse and shook his head, then pivoted back to Marnie. "What were you thinking, riding around this city with a maniacal cab driver?"

"It's not like I get a resume and insurance record handed to me before I get in a taxi," she said. "Now, I understand you're frustrated, but—"

"I'm *beyond* frustrated. This has been a hell of a day. With one hell of a bad ending." He shot the cab driver another glare, but the man had already skulked back to his car and climbed behind the wheel. "Wait! What are you doing?"

"I'm not doing any—" Then she heard the sound of metal groaning, and tires squealing, and realized Mr. Suit and Tie wasn't talking to her—but to the cab driver who had just hit and run. The yellow car disappeared around the corner in a noisy, clanking cloud of smoke.

In the distance, she heard the rising sound of sirens, which meant one of the people living in the apartments lining the street must have already called 9-1-1. Not soon enough.

Mr. Suit and Tie cursed under his breath. "Great. That's all I needed today."

"I'm sorry about that." Marnie stepped to the corner and put up her hand for a passing cab. "Well, good luck. Hope you get it straightened out and your night gets better."

"Hey! You can't leave. You're my witness."

"Listen, I'm exhausted and I just want to get home." She raised her arm higher, waving her hand, hoping to see at least one available cab. Nothing. Her feet screamed in protest. Soon as she got home, she was burning these shoes. "I'll give you my number. Call me for my statement." She fished in her purse for a business card, and held it out.

He ignored the card. "I need you to stay."

"And I need to get home." She waved harder, but the lone cab that passed her didn't stop. "This is Boston. Why aren't there any cabs?"

"Celtics game is just getting over," the man said. "They're probably all over at the Garden."

"Great." She lowered her arm, then thought of the ten-block hike home. Not fun in high heels. Even less fun after an eighteen-hour day, the last four spent dancing and socializing. She should have drunk an entire pot of coffee.

"I'll make you a deal," the man said. "I'll give you a lift if you can wait until I've finished making the accident report. Then you can give your statement and kill two birds with one stone."

She hesitated. "I don't know. I'm really tired."

"Stay for just a bit more. After tonight, you'll never have to see me again." He grinned.

He had a nice smile. An echoing smile curved across her face. She glanced down the street in the direction of her condo and thought of the soft bed waiting for her there. She weighed that against walking home. Option two made her feet hurt ten times more. *Stupid shoes.*

She glanced back at the misshapen silver car. "You're sure you can drive me home? In that?"

"It runs. It's just got a little junk in the trunk." He grinned. "Sorry. Bad joke."

A laugh escaped her and eased some of the tension in her shoulders, the pain in her feet. "Even a bad joke sounds good right now." No cabs appeared, and that settled the decision for her. "Okay, I'll wait."

Not that it was going to be a hardship to wait with a view like that. This guy could have been a cover model. Whew. Hot, hot, hot. She should get his contact information. She had at least a dozen clients who would be—

You're always working.

Marnie could hear her mother's voice in her head. *Take some time off. Have some fun. Date a guy for yourself. Don't be so serious and buttoned up all the time.*

What no one seemed to understand was this buttoned-up approach had fueled Marnie's success. She'd seen how a laissez-faire approach to business could destroy a company and refused to repeat those mistakes herself. A distraction like Mr. Suit and Tie would only derail her, something she couldn't afford.

The man opened the passenger's side door. "Have a seat. You look like you've had a trying day. And I know how that feels."

She sank into the leather seat, kicked off her shoes and let the platform heels tumble to the sidewalk. The man came to stand beside her, leaning against the rear passenger door. He had the look of a man comfortable in his own skin, at ease with the world. Confident, sexy, but not overly so. A hot combination, especially with the suit and tie. Her stance toward him softened.

"You're right. I have had a long, trying day myself." She put out her hand. "Let's try this again. I'm Marnie Franklin."

"Jack Knight."

The name rang a bell, but the connection flitted away before she could grasp it because when he took her hand in his, a delicious spark ran through her, down her arm. If she hadn't been seated, she might have jumped back in surprise. In her business, she shook hands with dozens of men in the course of a week. None had ever sent that little…zing through her. Maybe exhaustion had lowered her defenses. Or maybe the accident had shaken her up more than she thought. She released his hand, and brushed the hair out of her eyes, if only to keep from touching him again.

The police arrived, two officers who looked like they'd rather be going for a root canal than taking another accident report in the dent and ding city of Boston. For the next ten minutes Marnie and Jack answered questions. After the police were gone, Jack turned to her. "Thanks for staying. You made a stressful day much better."

"Glad to help."

Jack bent down and picked up the black heels she'd kicked onto the sidewalk when she'd sat in his car. He handed them to Marnie, the twin heels dangling from his index finger by their strappy backs. In his strong, capable hands, the fancy shoes looked even more delicate. "Your shoes, Cinderella." He gave her a wink, and that zing rushed through her a second time.

"I'm far from Cinderella." She bent and slipped on the damnable slingbacks. Pretty, but painful. "More like the not-so-evil stepmother, trying to fix up all the stepsisters with princes."

His smile had a dash of sexy, a glimmer of a tease. "Every woman deserves to be Cinderella at least once in her life."

"Maybe so, *if* she believes in fairy tales and magic mice."

She worked in the business of helping people fall in love, and had given up on the fairy tale herself a long time ago. Over the years, she'd become, if anything, more cautious, less willing to dip a toe in the romance pool. When she'd started matchmaking she'd been starry eyed, hopeful. But now...

Now she had a lot of years of reality beneath her and the stars had faded from her vision. She knew her business had suffered as a consequence. Somehow she needed to restore her belief in the very thing she touted to her clients—the existence of true love.

Jack shut her door and came around to the driver's side. The car started with a soft purr. "Where to?"

She gave him her address, and he put the car in gear. She settled into the luxury seat. The dark leather hugged her body, warm and easy. Damn. She needed to step outside the basic car model box because sitting in this sedan made it pretty easy to fall for the whole Cinderella fantasy. It wasn't a white horse, but it was a giant step closer to a royal ride. Having a good looking prince beside her helped feed that fantasy, too.

"I'm sorry for being grumpy earlier. That

accident was the icing on a tough day. Thanks again for staying and talking to the cops for me," he said. "I can't believe you remembered all those details about the driver."

She shrugged. "My father used to make me do that. Whenever we went someplace, he made sure I noticed the waiter's name or the cab driver's ID. He'd have me recite the address or license plate or some other detail. He said you never knew when doing that would come in handy, and he was right." She could almost hear her father's voice in her ear. *Watch the details, Daisy-doo, because you never know when they'll matter.* He'd rarely called her Marnie, almost always Daisy-doo, because of her love for the flowers. Kat had been Kitty, Erica had been Chatterbug. Marnie missed hearing her father's wisdom, the way he lovingly teased his daughters. "Besides, the cab driver had his hands on the GPS more than the steering wheel, and that made me doubly nervous. If I could have, I would have jumped in the driver's seat and taken the wheel myself."

He chuckled. "Nice to meet a fellow control freak."

"Me? I'm not a control freak." She wrinkled her nose. "Okay, maybe I am. A little. But in my house, things were a little…crazy when I was a kid and someone had to take the reins."

"Let me guess. You're the oldest? An only?"

"The middle kid, but only younger than the oldest by nine months."

"Oh, so not just the driver, but the peacemaker, too?" He tossed her a grin.

He'd nailed her, in a few words. "Do you read personality trait books in your spare time or something?"

"Nah. I'm just in a business where it's essential to be able to read people, quickly, and well."

"Me, too. Though sometimes you don't like what you read."

"True." Jack glanced over at her, his blue eyes holding her features for a long moment before he returned his attention to the road. "So, Cinderella, what has made you so jaded?"

The conversational detour jolted her. She shifted in her seat. "Not jaded…realistic."

"Well, that makes two of us. I find, in my line of work, that realism is a must."

The amber glow of the street lights and the soft white light coming from the dash outlined his lean, defined profile with a soft edge. Despite the easy tone of his words, something in them hinted at a past that hadn't been easy.

Maybe a bad breakup, or a bitter divorce? Either way, despite the zing, she wasn't interested in cleaning up someone else's baggage. *Stick to impersonal topics, Marnie.*

His cell phone started to ring, and the touchscreen in the center of his dash lit up with the word Dad. "Do you mind if I answer this?" Jack asked. "If I don't, he'll just keep calling."

She chuckled and waved toward the screen. "Go right ahead. I totally understand."

Jack leaned forward, pressed a button on the screen, then sat back again. "Hey, Dad, what's up? And before you say a word, you're on speaker, so don't blurt out any family secrets or embarrassing stories."

"You got someone in the car with you?" said a deep, amused voice on the other end. "Someone pretty, I hope."

Jack glanced at Marnie. A slow smile stole across his face and a quiver ran through her. "Yes, someone very pretty. So be on your best behavior."

His father chuckled. "That's no fun. The only thing that gets me out of bed in the morning is the potential for bad behavior."

Beside her, Jack rolled his eyes and grinned. *Parents,* he mouthed.

Seemed she wasn't the only one with a

troublesome parent. Jack handled his father with a nice degree of love and humor. That tender touch raised her esteem for him, and had her looking past the suit and tie. Intriguing man. Almost…intoxicating.

She didn't have time, or room, in her life for being intrigued by a man, though, especially since her business took nearly every spare moment. Even one as handsome as him.

She could almost hear her mother screaming in disagreement, but Marnie knew her business and herself. If she got involved with someone right now, it would be a distraction. Maybe down the road, when her business and life were more settled…

Someday when?

She'd been saying "someday" for years. And had to find the right moment—or the right man—to make her open her heart to love.

"I called because I was wondering when you'd be home," Jack's father was saying. "You work more hours than the President, for God's sake."

Marnie bit back a laugh. It could have been her conversation with her mother a little while ago. She half expected his father to schedule a blind date brunch, too.

"I'm on my way." Jack flicked a glance at

the dashboard clock. "Give me twenty minutes. Did you eat?"

"Yeah. Sandwiches. *Again.* Lord knows you don't have anything in that refrigerator of yours besides beer and moldy takeout."

"Because I'm never there to eat."

"Exactly." Jack's father cleared his throat. "I have an idea. Maybe…you should bring your pretty companion home for a—"

"Hey, no embarrassing statements, remember?"

His father chuckled. "Okay, okay. Drive safe."

Jack told his father he'd be home soon, then said goodbye and disconnected the call. "Sorry about that," Jack said to Marnie. "My dad is…needy sometimes. Even though it's been a few years since he got divorced, it's like he's been lost."

"My mother is the same way. She calls me every five minutes to make sure I'm eating my vegetables, wearing sunscreen and not working too much."

He chuckled. "Sounds like we have the same parent. Ever since my dad sold his house, he's been living with me, while he tries to figure out if he wants to stay in Boston or high-tail it for sunny Florida. He thinks that means he should comment on everything I do and every piece of furniture in my apartment."

"And what is or isn't in your fridge." Marnie's mom stopped by Marnie's condo almost every Sunday after church, but less to visit than to do a responsible child check. *You need more vegetables,* her mother would say. Or *you should cook for yourself more often.* And the best, *if you had a man in your life, you wouldn't have to do that.* Marnie loved her mother, but had realized a long time ago that a mother's love could be…invasive. "I get the whole you should make more time for home-cooked meals and a personal life lecture on a weekly basis. I think my mother forgets how many hours I work. The last thing I want to do when I get home is whip up a platter of lasagna."

"I think they go to school for that," Jack said. "How to Bug Your Adult Kids 101."

She laughed. It did sound like they had the same parent. "Maybe you should get your dad involved in something else, something that keeps him too busy to focus on you. There are all kinds of singles events for people his age. Some of them are dates in disguise, get-togethers centered around hobbies, like cooking or pets," Marnie said, unable to stop work talk from invading every second of her day.

My lord, she was a compulsive matchmaker. And one who needed to take her own advice. First thing tomorrow, she was going to look into dates for Ma and someday soon, she'd nicely tell her mother to butt out.

Yeah, right. Marnie had yet to do that to anyone, especially her mother. But she could tell others what to do. *That* she excelled at, according to her sisters.

Jack nodded. "I tried that before, years ago, but it didn't go so well. But you're right— maybe if I try again, now that some time has passed since all that upheaval, my dad will be more open to doing some activities, especially ones that get him dating again."

"And if he meets someone else—"

"He won't have time to worry about my fridge or my hours." Jack laughed. "Ah, such a devious plan we've concocted."

"As long as it works." She grinned.

Jack turned onto Marnie's street. A flicker of disappointment ran through her as the ride came to an end. "It's the fourth one on the right," she said. "With the flowers out front."

Invite him in? Or call it a night?

He slowed the car, then stopped at her building's entrance. "Nice looking place. I love these brick buildings from the early 1900s. It's always nice to see the architecture get preserved when the building gets repurposed. Not every owner appreciates history like that."

"Me, too. Coming home is like stepping into history." She smiled, then put out her hand. Impersonal, business-like. "Well, thank you for the ride."

That zing ran through her again when his large hand enfolded hers. For a second, she had the crazy thought of yanking on his hand, pulling him across the car, and kissing him. His broad chest against hers, his lips dancing around her mouth, his hands—

Wow. She needed to sleep more or get extra potassium or something.

"It was the least I could do after you stayed," Jack was saying. He released her hand. Darn. "Especially after you had a long day yourself."

Focus on the words he's speaking, not the fantasy. She jerked her gaze away from his mouth. "It was no trouble."

He grinned. "You said that already."

"Oh, well, I'm just really…tired."

"Yeah, me, too. I had a long day, made longer by someone who dropped the ball on some important paperwork. I got everything back on track, but…what a day." He ran a hand through his hair, displacing the dark locks. "Anyway, I'm sorry again about losing my temper back there."

"I would have done the same thing if my trunk looked like an origami project," she said.

He glanced in the rearview mirror and shrugged off the damaged rear. "It gives my insurance agent something to do."

She laughed. "True. Anyway, thanks again. Have a good night."

"You, too." He reached for her before she got out of the car, a light, quick touch on her arm. But still enough to send heat searing along her skin. "Would you like to go get a cup of coffee or a drink? We could sit around and complain about our jobs, our meddling parents, bad cab drivers and whatever else we can think of?"

A part of her wanted to say yes, but the realistic part piped up, reminding her of the time and her To Do list, and her no-men-for-the-foreseeable-future resolve. Besides, there was something about that zing, something that told her if she caved, she'd be lost, swept in a tsunami. The mere thought terrified her. "I can't. It's late. And I have an early day tomorrow."

"On Saturday?"

She raised one shoulder, let it drop. "My job is a 24/7 kind of thing."

He chuckled. "Mine, too. And even though every year I vow to work less and play more…"

"You don't."

He nodded.

"Me, too." Because work was easier than confronting the reasons why she worked too much. Because work was easier than taking a chance on love. Work she could control, depend upon. Love, not so much. But she didn't say any of that. She released the door handle, and shifted to face him.

Despite the fear, she didn't want to leave. Right now, with Jack looking at her like that, his eyes lit by the street light above and his strong jaw cast in a dark shadow, her resistance was at an all-time low. Desire pulsed in her veins. She wished she *had* dragged him across the car and kissed him silly when she'd had the chance. So she delayed leaving a bit longer.

"What do you do for work that keeps you busy late into the day and also on weekends?" She put a finger to her lip and gave him a flirty smile. "Let me guess. Lawyer?"

"Hell, no." He glanced down. "Oh, I get it. Pinstripe suit, power tie. Screams waiting to sue to you?"

"Well, if the Brooks Brothers fits…"

His smile widened, ending with a dimple. *Oh, God.* Dimples. She'd always been a sucker for them.

"I'm…an investor," Jack said. "Of sorts."

"Of sorts?"

"I buy and sell businesses. I find ones that need a cash infusion, and if I think they're viable, I invest. If I think they're not, I buy them and either sell them again or break up the pieces and sell it off."

A shiver ran down her back. The leather seemed to chafe now, not comfort. "You're… a corporate raider?"

"I'm a little nicer than that. And I tend to work with small to medium-sized businesses, not giant Goliaths."

The connection fused in her mind. His job. His name.

Jack Knight. Owner of Knight Enterprises. A "business investor"—a euphemism for his true identity. Jack Knight was a vulture. Feeding off the carcasses of desperate business owners.

It had to have been the exhaustion of the day that had kept her from putting the pieces together until now. How could she have misread all the clues?

And to think she'd wanted to kiss him five

minutes ago. She bristled. "The size doesn't matter to the company that gets sold off, or taken over, or destroyed in the process of that kind of 'help.'"

"I must have given you the wrong impression. There's more to it—"

"No, there really isn't. You destroy people's companies, and their lives." The words sprang to life in her throat, fueled by exhaustion, shock, and surprised even Marnie with their vehemence. She never did this, never showed outrage, never yelled. Jack Knight had brought out this other side of her, with a roar. "Do you even think about what happens to those people after you swoop in and tear their company to shreds? They spent their lives building those companies, and in an instant, you take it all away. And for what? A bottom line? A few more dollars in your pocket? Another sports car for the collection?" She let out a gust, then grabbed the door handle. It stuck, then yielded, and fresh night air washed over her. She'd gotten distracted, by a dimple and a zing. *Idiot.* "Goodnight."

"Wait. What did—"

She shut the door, cutting off his words. She'd confronted him, told him off, and told herself it felt good to finally say what she should say, exactly when she was supposed to say it. Jack idled in the space for a moment, then finally, he drove away, swallowed by the night.

Disappointment hit her first. If only she'd kissed him. If only she'd let herself get talked into that cup of coffee.

If only he'd been someone other than Jack Knight.

Then righteous indignation rose in her chest. He was the one at fault, not her. He was the one who had ruined her father's company, not her. If she'd told him what she really wanted to say to him, if she'd really let the confrontation loose, she'd have resorted to some very unlady-like behavior, and she refused to give him that satisfaction. Jack Knight didn't deserve it, not after what he had done to her father.

So she had said goodnight, got out of Cinderella's carriage, and went back to the real world, where princes didn't come along very often, and there were no mice to do the work for her.

CHAPTER TWO

"ARE YOU GOING to admit I was right?" Marnie whispered to her mother. They were standing to the side of the private dining room of an upscale Boston restaurant on a sunny Saturday afternoon. Soft jazz music filled the air, accented by the rise and fall of a dozen human voices.

A blush filled Helen's cheeks, making her look ten years younger. She had her chestnut hair up tonight, which elongated her neck and offset her deep green eyes. The dark blue dress she'd worn skimmed her calves, and defined the hourglass shape she'd maintained all her life, even after giving birth to three children. Coupled with the light in her eyes and the smile on her face, Helen looked prettier than ever, and far younger than her fifty-eight years.

"Yes, you were right, daughter dear," Helen

whispered back. "How'd I get such a smart child?"

"You gave me great genes." Marnie glanced over the room. Cozy and intimate, the private dining space offered a prime location, great parking and an outstanding menu, making it perfect for Matchmaking by Marnie meet and greets. In her experience, full and happy stomachs equaled happy people who then struck up conversations.

Today, she'd invited ten bachelors to meet her mother, and set up a buffet of finger foods on the far right side of the room. While they noshed on chicken satay and mini eggrolls, Helen circulated. Three days ago, when Marnie and Erica had proposed the idea of a mixer to Helen, she'd refused, insisting she didn't need to be fixed up, and didn't want to be, but after a while, she'd relented and agreed to "put in an appearance."

That appearance had lasted more than an hour now. Once the first man talked to Helen, and two more joined the conversation, Marnie had watched her mother transform into a giggling schoolgirl, flattered by all the sudden attention. Marnie made sure each bachelor got equal time, then stepped back and allowed the pieces to fall where they may.

She'd paved the way, then let Mother Nature finish giving directions.

"So," Marnie said, leaning in closer so they wouldn't be overheard, "is there one man in particular who you like the most?"

Pink bloomed in Helen's cheeks. "Do you see the one standing by the bar?"

"The tall man with the gray hair?" Marnie and Erica had interviewed so many eligible gentlemen in the fifty- to sixty-plus age range that some of them had become a bit of a blur. She didn't remember the details of this man, only that he had impressed her during the group interviews.

"His name's Dan. He's retired from his landscaping business, hates to golf, but loves to watch old movies." Her mother grinned, and in that smile, Marnie could see the energy of a new relationship already blossoming. "And, you'll never guess what his favorite movie is."

Marnie put a finger to her lip. "Hmm… *Casablanca?*"

Helen nodded. "Just like me. We like the same kind of wine, the same kind of music, and both of us love to travel."

"Sounds like a match made in heaven." Marnie grinned. "Or a match made by a daughter who knows her mother very well."

Helen chuckled. "Well, I wouldn't say it's a perfect match…yet, but it's got potential. Big potential. Now, if only we could find someone for you." Helen brushed a lock of hair off Marnie's forehead. "You deserve to be happy, sweetheart."

"I am happy." And she was, Marnie told herself. She had a business she loved, a purpose to her life, and a family that might annoy her sometimes, but had always been her personal rock. She gave her mother a quick hug, then headed for the front of the room, waiting until everyone's attention swiveled toward her before speaking. She noticed Dan's gaze remained on her mother, while Helen snuck quick glances back in his direction, like two teenagers at a football game.

"I wanted to thank you all for coming today, and if you weren't lucky enough to be chosen by our amazing and beautiful bachelorette," Marnie gestured toward her mother, who waved off the compliment, "don't worry. My goal at Matchmaking by Marnie is to give everyone a happy ending. So work with me, and I promise, I'll help you find your perfect match."

The bachelors thanked her, and began to file out of the room. Dan lingered, chatting with Marnie's mother. She laughed and flirted, seeming like an entirely different person, the person she used to be years and years ago. Marnie sent up a silent prayer of gratitude. Her mother had been lonely for a long time, and it was nice to see her happy again.

The waitstaff began taking away the dishes and cleaning the tables. Marnie gathered her purse and jacket, then touched her mother on the arm. "I'm going to get going, Ma. Call me later, okay?"

Her mother promised, then returned her attention to Dan. The two of them were still chatting when Marnie headed out of the restaurant. She stood by the valet counter, waiting for the valet to return with her car, when a black sports car pulled up to the station. The passenger's side window slid down. "You're like a bad penny, turning up everywhere I go."

The voice took a second to register in her mind. It had been a couple weeks since she'd last heard that deep baritone, and in the busyness of working twenty-hour days, she'd nearly forgotten the encounter.

Almost.

Late at night, when she was alone and the day had gone quiet, her mind would wander and she'd wonder what might have happened if he'd been someone other than Jack Knight and she'd agreed to that cup of coffee. Then she would jerk herself back to reality.

Jack Knight was the worst kind of corporate vermin—and the last kind of man she should be thinking about late at night, or any time. Of all the people in the city of Boston, how did she end up running into him twice?

She bent down and peered inside the car. Jack grinned back at her. He had a hell of a smile, she'd give him that. The kind of smile that charmed and tempted, all at once. Yeah, like a snake. "Speaking of bad pennies," she said, "what are you doing here?"

"Picking up my father." His head disappeared from view, and a moment later, he had stepped out of the car and crossed to her. He had on khakis and a pale blue button-down shirt, the wrinkled bottom slightly untucked, the top two buttons undone, as if he was just knocking off after putting in a full day of work, even on a Saturday. He looked sexy, approachable. If she ignored his name and his job, that was.

She didn't want to like him, didn't want to find his smile alluring or his eyes intriguing. He was a Knight, and she needed to remember that. She was about to say goodbye and end the conversation before it really had a chance to start, when the restaurant door opened and her mother and Dan stepped onto the sidewalk.

"Marnie, you're still here?" Helen said.

"Jack, you're here early," Dan said.

The pieces clicked together in Marnie's mind. The timing of Jack's arrival. *Picking up my father,* he'd said.

She glanced from one man to the other, and prayed she was wrong. "Dan's your father?" she said to Jack, then spun back to Dan. "But…but your last name is Simpson."

Dan grinned. "Guilty as charged. I'm this troublemaker's stepfather." He draped a loving arm around Jack and gave him a quick hug.

"You know Dan's son?" Helen asked Marnie. "You never told me that."

"I didn't know until just now. And, Ma, I think you should know that Jack…" Marnie started to tell her mother the rest, the truth about who Jack was, but she watched the light in her mother's eyes dim a bit, and she couldn't do it. The urge to keep the peace, to keep everyone happy, overpowered the words and she let them die in her throat.

Dan Simpson. Father of Jack Knight, the man whose company had ruined her family's life.

Dan Simpson. The man her mother was falling for.

Dan Simpson. Another Mr. Wrong in a family teeming with them.

"You should know that, uh, Jack and I met the other night," Marnie said finally. "We sort of…ran into each other."

"Oh, my. What a small world," Helen said, beaming again.

"Getting smaller every day." Jack grinned at Marnie, but the smile didn't sway her. "How do you know my father?"

She gave a helpless shrug. "It seems I just fixed him up with my mother."

"You've got one talented matchmaker standing here," Dan said, giving Helen's hand a squeeze. "You should see if she can fix you up, too, Jack."

Fix him up? She'd rather die first.

"You're a *matchmaker*?" Jack raised a brow in amusement.

"Guilty as charged," she said, echoing Dan's words.

Her brain swam with the incongruity of the situation. How could she have created such a disaster? Usually her instincts were right on, but this time, they had failed her. And she'd created a mess of epic proportion. One that was slipping out of her control more every second.

Beside her, Dan and Helen were chatting, making plans for dinner or lunch or something. They were off to the side, caught in their own world of just the two of them. All of Marnie's senses were attuned to Jack—the enemy of her family and son of the man who had finally put a smile on her mother's face. How was she supposed to tell Ma the truth, and in the process, break a heart that had just begun to mend?

Jack leaned in then, close, his breath a heated whisper against her ear. "I'm surprised you didn't try to fix me up the night we met."

"I wouldn't do that to one of my clients," she whispered back.

Confusion filled his blue eyes, a confusion she had no intent of erasing, not here, not now.

"I'm not sure what I did to make you despise me," he said, "but I assure you, I'm not nearly as bad as you think."

"No, you're not," she said just as the valet arrived with her car. She opened the door, and held Jack's gaze over the roof. "You're worse."

Then she got in her car and pulled away.

* * *

A matchmaker.

Of all the jobs Jack would have thought the fiery redhead Marnie Franklin held, match-maker sat at the very bottom of the list. Yet, the title seemed to suit her, to match her strong personality, her crimson hair, her quick tongue.

His stepfather had raved about Marnie's skills the entire ride from the restaurant to the repair shop to pick up the car the taxi driver had rear-ended, return the rental, then head home. The event had agreed with Dan, giv-ing his hearty features a new energy, and his voice renewed enthusiasm, as if he'd reverse-aged in one afternoon. At six-foot two, with a full head of gray hair, Dan cut an imposing figure offset by a ready smile and pale green eyes. Eyes that now lit with joy every time he talked about Helen.

"I never would have expected to fall for the matchmaker's mother," Dan said. "But I tell ya, Jack, I really like Helen."

"I'm glad," Jack said. And he was. His step-father had been alone for a long, long time, and deserved happiness. Just with someone other than Marnie Franklin's maternal rela-tives. The woman had something against him, that was clear.

"Her daughter's quite pretty, too, you know," Dan said.

"Really? I hadn't noticed."

Dan laughed. "You lie about as well as I cook. I saw you checking her out."

"That was a reflex."

"Sure it was." Dan shifted in his seat to study his son. "You know, you should use some of the arguments you used on me."

Jack concentrated on the road. Boston traffic in the middle of the day required all his attention. Yeah, that was why he didn't look Dan in the eye. Because of the cars on the road. "What are you talking about?"

"The list of reasons why I should go to that event—and I'm glad I did, by the way—is the same list I should give you about why you should ask Marnie out."

"I did. She turned me down."

"And?"

"And what? End of story." He didn't want to get into the reasons why he had no intentions of dating anyone right now. He, of all people, should steer far and wide from anything resembling a relationship.

He could bring a business back to life, turn around a lackluster bottom line, but when it came to personal relationships, he was—

Well, Tanya had called him unavailable.

Uninvolved. Cold, even. More addicted to his smartphone than her.

A year after the end of their relationship, he'd had to admit she had a point. When he woke up in the morning, his first thought was the latest business venture, not the woman in his life.

Then why had he asked Marnie to coffee?

Because for the first time in a long time, he was intrigued. She'd been on his mind ever since the night they'd met. Confounding, intriguing Marnie Franklin had been a constant thought in the back of his head. After seeing her today, those thoughts had moved front and center. But he didn't tell Dan any of this, because he knew it would give his stepfather more ammunition for his "get back to dating" argument.

Right now, Jack was concentrating on work, and on making amends. Jack Knight, Sr. had ruined a lot of lives, and Jack had spent the last two years trying to undo the damage his father had done, while still keeping the business going and keeping the people who worked for him employed. As soon as he'd moved into his father's office, he'd vowed he would do things differently, approach the company in a new way. He'd gone through all the old files, and had tried to apply that philosophy, one deal at a time.

Tanya might not have thought he had heart when it came to personal relationships, but Jack was determined to prove the opposite in his business relationships. That uninvolved, cold man he'd been was slowly being erased as he gave back more than Knight had taken.

More than he himself had taken.

To try his best to be everything except his father's son.

That, Jack knew, was why he kept putting in all those hours. He'd been part of his father's selfish, greedy machinations, and it was all Jack could do now to restore what had been destroyed, partly by his own hand.

Doing so felt good, damned good, but he knew the time he invested in that goal was costing him a life, a family, kids. Maybe if he could do enough to make amends to all those his father had wronged, when he went to sleep at night, then maybe the past would stop haunting him.

And then he could look to the future again.

Maybe.

It hadn't thus far, and there were days when he wondered if he was doing the right thing. Or just trying to fill an endless well of guilt.

"What do you want to do for dinner?" Jack said, changing the subject.

"You're on your own tonight, kid. I have plans with Helen." Dan grinned, and for a second, Jack envied his stepfather that beaming smile, that anticipation for the night ahead. "I'm taking her to Top of the Hub."

Jack arched a brow at the mention of the famous moving restaurant at the top of the Prudential building. "Impressive. On a first date?"

"Gotta wow her right off," Dan said.

"I must have missed the memo."

Dan chuckled. "You're just a little jaded right now."

"Not jaded. More...realistic about my strengths. I'm good at business, not good at relationships. End of story."

"Hey, you're preaching to the choir here," Dan said. "I'm the king of bad at relationships, or at least I used to be. You live and you learn, and hopefully stop making the mistakes that screwed up your last relationship."

Which was the one skill Jack had yet to master. When it came to businesses and bottom lines, he could shift gears and learn from the past. But with other people...not so much. Maybe it was because he had gone too many years trying to prove himself to a father who didn't love him or appreciate him. Jack had kept striving for a connection that never existed. That made him either a glutton for punishment or a fool. "Or just avoid relationships all together."

Dan chuckled. "What are you going to do? Become a monk?"

"I don't know. Think they're taking applications?" Jack grinned. Nah, he wouldn't become a monk, but he wasn't at a point in his life where he wanted or needed a committed relationship.

He was trying to buckle down and do the right thing where Knight Enterprises was concerned. Juggling yet another commitment seemed like an impossible task. Deep down inside, he worried more about getting too close to a woman. He'd screwed things up with Tanya, and had plenty of relationship detritus in his past to prove his lack of commitment skills. He had been his father's son in business—and a part of Jack wondered if he'd be his son in a marriage, too. The easiest course—keep his head down and his focus on work. Rather than try to fix the one part of his life that had been impossible to repair.

"When do I have time to date?" Jack said. "I barely have enough spare time to order a pizza."

Except he had found plenty of time to think and wonder about Marnie. His wandering mind had set him a good day behind on his To Do list. He really needed to focus, not daydream. By definition, the sassy matchmaker believed in destiny and true love and all of that. Jack, well, Jack hadn't been good at either of those.

"Aw, you meet Miss Right and you'll change your tune," Dan said. "Like me. Helen has me rethinking this whole love in the later years concept."

"All that from one meeting?"

"I told you, she's a special lady. When you know, you know."

Jack would argue with that point. He'd never had that all-encompassing, couldn't-talk-about-anything-else feeling for a woman before.

Well, that was, until he met Marnie. She'd stuck in his mind like bubble gum, sweet, delicious, addictive. Maybe Dan had a point. But in the end, Jack still sucked at relationships and pursuing Marnie Franklin could only end with a broken heart. But that didn't stop him from wanting her or wondering about her. And why her attitude toward him had done a sudden 180.

Had his reputation preceded him? Had

he hurt her somehow, too, in the years he'd worked with his father? Jack decided to do a little research in the morning and see if there was a connection. A memory nagged in the back of his head, but didn't take hold.

Jack pulled in front of the renovated brownstone where he lived, a building much like himself—filled with unique character, a speckled history, but still a little rough around the edges.

While his stepfather headed off—whistling—to the shower, Jack grabbed a bag of chips, taking them out to the balcony. He scrolled through his phone, past the endless stream of emails and voice mails. Work called to him, a non-stop siren of demands. On any other day, he'd welcome the distraction and challenges. But not today. Today, he just wanted to sit back, enjoy the sunshine and think about the choices he'd made.

Maybe his stepfather had a point. Maybe it was time to date again, to make a serious commitment to something other than a cell phone plan and a profit and loss statement. He'd been working for two years to make up for the past, and still it hadn't fulfilled him like he thought it would. Nor had it eased the guilt that haunted his nights. It was as if he was missing something, some key that would bring it all together. Or maybe Dan was right and Jack needed to open his heart, too. A monumental task, and one he had never tackled successfully before.

He took a chip, the fragile snack crumbling in his hand, and thought maybe he was a fool for believing in things that could crumble at any moment.

CHAPTER THREE

As soon as her mother left on her date with Dan that night, the condo echoed. Empty, quiet. Helen had been at Marnie's house for the better part of the afternoon, indulging in a lot of mother-daughter chatting and taking a whirl through Marnie's closet to borrow a fun, flirty dress. Helen's contagious verve had Marnie in stitches, laughing until her sides hurt. But once Ma was gone, the mood deflated and reality intruded.

Marnie tried working, gave up, and gathered her planner and laptop into a big tote and headed out the door. Five minutes later, she was sweating on a treadmill at the gym near her house. It had been weeks since she'd had time for a good workout and as the beats drummed in her head, and the cardio revved up her heart, the stresses of the day began to melt away.

Someone got on the treadmill beside her,

but Marnie didn't notice for a few seconds. As she passed the three-mile mark, she pressed the speed button, slowing her pace to a fast walk. Her breath heaved in and out of her chest, but in a good way, giving her that satisfaction of a hard job done well.

"You're making me feel like a couch potato."

She swiveled her head to the right, and saw Jack Knight, doing an easy jog on the other treadmill. Her hand reached up, unconsciously brushing away the sweat on her brow and giving her bangs a quick swipe. Damn. She should have put on some makeup or lip gloss or something. Then she cursed herself for caring how she looked. She wasn't interested in Jack Knight or what he thought about her, all sweaty and messy. Not one bit.

Then why did her gaze linger on his long, defined legs, his broad chest? Why did she notice the way the simple gray T and dark navy shorts he wore gave him a casual, sexy edge? Why did her heart skip a beat when he smiled at her? And why did her hormones keep ignoring the direct orders from her brain?

"I'm impressed." He glanced at the digital display on her treadmill. "Great pace, nice distance."

"Thanks." She took her pace down another notch, and pressed the cool down button. "Are you a member at this gym? I've never seen you here before."

"That's because most of the time, I'm here in the middle of the night, after I finally leave the office for the day. At that time, I have the whole place pretty much to myself."

She gave him a quizzical look. "I thought the gym closes at ten."

"It does. I have…special privileges." He broke into a light jog, arms moving, legs flexing. His effortless run caused a modest uptick in his breathing, leaving Marnie the one now impressed. She'd have been huffing and puffing by now.

"Let me guess," she said. "A cute girl at the front desk gave you a key?"

"Nope. My key comes from one of the owners."

"You?"

"I don't own it," he said. "I have a…vested interest in this gym. One of my high school friends bought it, and when he was struggling, he needed an investor, so I stepped in."

"You did?" She tried to keep the surprise from her voice, but didn't quite make it. "That's really…nice."

Not the kind of thing she expected from

Jack Knight, evil corporate raider. He'd saved the gym owned by his friend, but not her father's business. Did he only help friends? And let a stranger's businesses fall to pieces? Or was there a nice guy buried deep inside him?

Or were there a few things she hadn't accepted about her father's company and his role in its demise?

A part of Marnie had always avoided looking too close at the details, because keeping them at bay let her keep her focus on Knight as the evil conglomerate at fault. But deep down inside Marnie knew her affable, distracted, creative father wasn't the best businessman in the world. Helen refused to talk about it, refused to open those "dark doors" as she called them, to the past. And right now, right here, Marnie didn't want to open them either.

Jack leaned over, the scent of soap and man filling the space between them and sending that zing through Marnie all over again. "See? I told you, I'm not as bad as you think I am."

Her face heated. She reached for the hand towel on the treadmill and swiped at her cheeks, then took a deep gulp of water from her water bottle. "I never said you were a horrible person."

Out loud.

"You didn't have to. It was in the way you drove away from the restaurant earlier and in your stinging rejection of my invitation to coffee." He bumped up the speed on his treadmill and increased his jog pace, his arms moving in concert with his legs. "And it was just coffee, Marnie, not a lifetime commitment."

He was right. A cup of coffee with a handsome man wasn't a crime.

Except this handsome man was Jack Knight, who had destroyed her father's company in one of his "investments." She doubted he even realized what he had done to her family, and how that loss had hurt all of them in more than just Tom Franklin's bank account.

She opened her mouth to tell him what she really thought of him, then stopped herself. That urge to keep the peace resurged, coupled with a burst of protectiveness. If Marnie lashed out at Jack, the conversation would get back to Dan and her mother. She had yet to tell her mother who Dan really was, unable to bring herself to wipe that smile off Helen's face, to hurt her mother or disappoint her. Somehow, she had to tell her the truth, though, and do it soon.

Wouldn't it be smart to go into that conversation armed with information? And the best way to gather information without the other party suspecting? Dine with the enemy.

Maybe her father hadn't been businessman of the year, but she knew as well as she knew her own name that Knight Enterprises had been part of the company's downfall, too. If she could figure out how and why, then she could go to her mother and warn her away from Dan. Maybe then both Franklin women would have closure…and peace.

"You know, you're right. It's not a lifetime commitment," she said before she could think twice. "I'll take you up on your coffee offer."

He arched a brow in surprise, and turned toward her, but didn't slow his pace. "Where and when?"

"As soon as you finish your run. If that works for you."

Jack glanced at the time remaining on the treadmill's display and nodded. "Sounds good. How about if I meet you up front in twenty minutes?"

Enough time for her to hit the locker room and get cleaned up. Not that she cared what she looked like with Jack Knight, of course. It was merely because she was going out in public.

As she stepped into the shower and washed up, she second guessed her decision. Getting close to Jack Knight could be dangerous on a dozen different levels. A matchmaker knew better than to put Romeo and Juliet together—and especially not enemies like her and Jack. She had no business seeing him, dating him, or even thinking about either.

She still remembered her father's heartbreak, how he had become a shell of the man he used to be, sitting at home, purposeless, waiting for a miracle that never came. His life's work, gone in an instant. And all because of Jack Knight.

The last of the lather went down the shower drain. She'd have coffee with Jack, and in the process, maybe find a way to exact a little revenge for how he had let her father fail, rather than help the struggling businessman succeed.

What was that they said about revenge? That it was a dish best served cold? Well, this one was going to be rich, dark and steaming hot.

Seventeen minutes later, Jack stood in the lobby of the health club, showered, changed, and his heart beating a mile a minute. He told himself it was from the hard, short run on the treadmill, but he knew better. There was something about Marnie Franklin that intrigued him in ways he hadn't been intrigued in a hell of a long time.

Her smile, for one. It lit her green eyes, danced in her features, seemed to brighten the room.

Her sass, for another. Marnie was a woman who could clearly give as good as she got, and that was something he didn't often find.

Her love/hate for him, for a third. He knew attraction, and could swear she'd been attracted to him when they first met. Then somewhere along the way, she'd started to dislike him. Yet at the same time, she seemed to war with those two emotions.

He had done some preliminary research before he hit the gym, but his files were filled with Franklins, a common enough last name. Then it hit him.

Tom Franklin.

A printer, with a small shop in Boston. Nice guy, but such a muddled, messy businessman that Jack had at first balked when his father asked him to take on Top Notch Printing as a client. He hadn't realized at the time what his father's real plan was—

Well, maybe he had, and hadn't wanted to accept the truth. Buy up the company for pennies on the dollar, to pave the way for a big-dollar competitor moving into town, another branch of the Knight investment tree. Within weeks, Tom Franklin had been out of business.

Oh, damn. If Marnie was that Franklin, Jack had a hell of a lot to make up for. And no idea how to do it. Jack's memory told him that none of Tom's daughters had been named Marnie, though, so he couldn't be sure. Maybe it was all some kind of weird coincidence.

Just then Marnie came down the hall, wearing a navy and white striped skirt that swooshed around her knees, and a bright yellow blouse that offset the deep red of her hair. She had on flats, which was a change from the heels he'd seen her in before, but on Marnie, they looked sweet, cute. Her skin still had that dewy just showered look, and like the other two times he'd seen her, she'd put her hair back in a clip that left a few stray tendrils curling along her neck. The whole effect was…devastating. His fingers itched to see what it would take to get her to let her hair down, literally and figuratively. To see Marnie Franklin unfettered, wild, sexy.

"Where are we going?" she asked. "There's that chain coffee shop—"

He shook his head. "I'm not exactly a decaf venti kind of guy. When I want coffee, I want just that. So, the question is—" at this he took a step closer to her, telling himself it was just to catch a whiff of that intoxicating perfume she wore, a combination of flowers and dark nights "—do you trust me?"

Her eyes widened and she inhaled a quick breath. Then a grin quirked up on one side of her face, and she raised her chin a notch. Sassy. "No, I don't. But I'll take my chances anyway."

"Pretty risky."

"I'm not worried. I carry pepper spray."

A laugh burst out of him, then he turned and opened the health club door for her. As she ducked past him, he leaned in again and caught another whiff of that amazing perfume. Damn sexy, and addictive. "You surprise me, Marnie Franklin. Not too many people do that."

"I'll keep that in mind." She tossed the last over her shoulder, before walking into the waning sunshine.

He fell into step beside her, the two of them shifting into small talk about the weather and the treadmills at the gym as they walked down the busy main street for a couple of blocks before turning right on a small side street. Dusk had settled on the city. Coupled with the dark overlay of leafy trees it made for a cozy, peaceful stroll. For Jack, the walk was as familiar as the back of his hand.

He knew he should find a way to bring the conversation around to whether her father was the Tom Franklin he'd known, but Jack couldn't do it. He liked Marnie, liked her a lot. If she had a chance to get to know this Jack, the one who had walked away from his father's legacy and now tried to do things differently, then maybe he could explain what had happened before.

"Where are we going?" Marnie asked.

"It's a surprise. You'll see."

"Okay, but I don't have a ton of time—"

He put a hand on her arm, a quick, light touch, but it seemed to sear his skin, and he saw her do another quick inhale and a part of him—the part that had been closed off for so long—came to life. He wanted to let her in, if only for today, to have a taste of that sweet lightness, even though he feared a woman like her wasn't meant for a man like him.

"It's beautiful out. We both work hard. I think we can afford a few extra minutes to enjoy the end of the day."

She gave him a wary glance. "Okay. But just a few."

The side street led straight into a neighborhood, as if stepping into another world after leaving the hecticness of the city. Quiet descended over the area, while the constant hum of rush hour traffic behind them got farther away with each step. Elegant brick homes nearly as old as Boston itself decorated either side of the street, fronted by planters filled with bright, happy flowers. Concrete sidewalks lined either side of the street, accented with grassy strips and the minutiae of life in a neighborhood—kids' bikes, lawn tools, newspapers. Neighbors greeted Jack as he walked by, and passing cars slowed to give him a wave.

In the distance, the gold-tipped spire of a church peeked above the leafy green trees, like a crown on top of a perfect cake. His heart swelled the farther he walked. No matter how many times he came back here, he always felt the same—at home.

"How come everyone knows you here?" Marnie said.

"I grew up in this neighborhood, staying in the same house all my life, even after my mom married Dan," he said. "Even though my dad passed away and my mom moved to Florida a couple years ago, this place is still home."

"It's a pretty neighborhood. Lots of great architecture." She raised a hand to touch the black curved iron and aluminum pole of the street light. It was a replica, and a pretty darn close historical copy of the original lights that had been lit by torches a century ago. "I love these lights, too. The old-fashioned ones are my favorite."

"Much nicer than the sodium vapor and high mast ones they use on the main roads. And in keeping with the tradition that's so important to this neighborhood."

"Oh, and look, daisies." She pointed to a house fronted by the bright white flowers. "I loved those when I was a kid, so much that my dad called me Daisy-doo. Silly, but you know, when it's your dad, it's kinda special."

"I bet." His father had never been the kind for anything as superfluous as a nickname. Dan had been the one to tease, make jokes, envelop Jack with warmth and hugs. But the man whose DNA Jack shared, hadn't done so much as offer a hug.

He shrugged off the memories and pointed to the spire. "Back when this neighborhood was built, it was centered around the church. It's still pretty central to the houses here."

They rounded another corner, and as they did, the road opened up, showcasing a simple white building. The small, unpretentious church sat in the middle of the neighborhood, with the rest of the streets jutting off like spokes. Street lights blinked to life, and danced golden light over the sidewalk. "This is my favorite time of day to be here," Jack said. "It looks so beautiful and peaceful. So pristine and perfect, like a new beginning could be had for the asking."

He hadn't realized he'd said that out loud until Marnie turned to him and smiled. "That sounds so…awesome."

"Thanks. But I can't take all the credit." He gestured toward the building.

Marnie stopped walking and stared up at the church. "Wow. It *is* beautiful. Understated. Maybe because it's so…ordinary. There are so many buildings in this city that try to compete for architectural design of the year, and this one is more…wholesome, if that makes sense."

"It does. I guess that's why I like coming here."

"You go to this church?"

He nodded. "I've gone almost every Sunday since the day I was born."

She arched a brow. "Really? You?"

He leaned in again, close enough to see the flecks of gold in her eyes, the soft chestnut wave brushing against her cheek. And close enough to once again, be mesmerized by her perfume. "I told you, I'm not as bad as you think."

She raised her gaze to his, and that smile returned. "You don't know what I think about you, Mr. Knight."

He reached up and trailed a finger down her cheek, whisking away that errant hair before lowering his hand. She inhaled, exhaled, watching him. No, he didn't know what she thought about him. But damn, he wanted to know.

Was it just because she was trying so hard not to like him? Or because he was tired of being seen as the evil corporate raider, painted with the same brush as his father?

Jack just wanted time before he probed deeper, to find out where Marnie's animosity lay. Give her a chance to get to know this Jack Knight, the one who no longer did his father's bidding. Then, when the time was right, he'd broach the subject of the past. Because right now he wanted her. Damn, did he want her.

"Considering how much we have in common, Marnie," he said, "I think you should call me by my first name. Don't you?"

"And what do we have in common?"

"Besides an appreciation for good architecture, and a competitive streak on the treadmill, there's the fact that our parents are dating."

She laughed. "In my world, that's not something in common. Heck, that wouldn't even be enough to invite you to a mixer, *Mr. Knight*."

Damn. Every time he thought they were growing closer, that she was giving him a chance, she retreated, threw up a wall. They started walking again, circling past the church, then turning down another tree-lined street. They walked at an easy pace, no hurry to their step. How long had it been since he'd done that? Taken a walk, with no real hurry to his journey? Even though he had a thousand things to do, at least a dozen phone calls to return and countless emails waiting for his attention, he kept walking. Something about today, or about Marnie, made him want to linger rather than rush back to the office. Right now, he couldn't tell if that was a good or bad thing.

"So how does it work?" he asked.

They passed under a leafy maple tree, the branches hanging so low, they whispered across their heads. "What? Matchmaking?" she said.

He nodded. "Do you use some kind of algorithm or something? A computer program?"

"No." She laughed. "Most of it's instinct. We do log pertinent client and potential match information into the computer, just so it's easier to develop a list of bachelors or bachelorettes for a mixer, but when it comes to picking the best possible matches, it's all in here." She pressed a hand to her chest.

He jerked his gaze up and away from the enticing swell of her breast. He was having a conversation here, not indulging in a fantasy. Except every time he looked at her, his thoughts derailed. Especially when she smiled like she did, or laughed that lyrical laugh of hers. "Sounds sort of like buying a business. Instinctually, I know which ones will be the best choice, and which aren't going to make it, no matter how much of a cash infusion I give it."

Her expression hardened. "Yeah, I bet it's exactly like that. All guts. No logic." She cast her glance to the right and left, away from him. The warm and bubbly moments between them evaporated, and a wall of ice dropped into her voice. "So, where's this coffee shop?"

Her reaction sealed his suspicions. She'd been burned, either by Knight or someone like him. But most likely his company. Guilt churned in his stomach.

"One more block," he said, trying to redirect the conversation. "Close enough to walk there after church, which is part of what makes the location so ideal."

The wall remained, however. Silence descended on them, an uncomfortable, tense hole in the conversation. They reached the corner where the coffee shop sat, a bright burst amidst the brick and white of the neighborhood.

The door to the Java Depot was propped open, and the rich scent of brewed coffee wafted outside, luring customers in with its siren call of caffeine. Several couples sat at umbrella-covered wrought iron tables, while a trio of kids played on the small playground set up beside the shop's deck. The non-lucrative use of a good chunk of the cafe's land had been a risky move, but one that had paid off, given the number of kids and families that visited this space on a regular basis. The sound system played contemporary jazz and alternative music, lots of it by local artists who often performed on the outdoor patio.

"Cute place," Marnie said. "I never even knew it existed."

"One of those great hidden secrets in Boston." He grinned. "Though the new owner is determined to get the word out via advertising and social media."

Marnie looked around, her intelligent gaze assessing the location and décor. "I like how it's so community oriented, with the local art displays, and the playground for kids. It's almost like being at home."

The words warmed him. He so rarely saw the reaction to his work, the money he invested, the counsel he gave. Too often, he'd seen the effects of the businessman he used to be—the shuttered shops, the For Sale signs, the people filing unemployment. But the Java Depot was a success story, one of many, he hoped. Appreciation and seeing others' success was a far greater reward than any increase in his own bottom line.

"That was the idea. A neighborhood coffee shop should feel like an ingrained part of the neighborhood and reflect the owner's personality. This one does both." He waved her ahead of him, then stepped inside and paused while his eyes adjusted to the dim interior.

"Jack!" Dorothy, a platinum blond buxom woman in her fifties who had been behind the counter of the Java Depot for nearly two years, sent him a wave. She gave him a broad, friendly smile, as if she was greeting a long lost family member. Considering how long he'd known Dot, she practically was family.

"I brewed some of your favorite blend today. Let me get you a cup."

"Thanks, Dot. And I'll need a…" He glanced at Marnie.

"Whatever you're having. But with the girly touch of some cream and sugar."

"A second one. Regular, please."

"You got it," Dot said. A few seconds later, she passed two steaming mugs of coffee across the counter. "Got fresh baked peanut butter cookies, too." Before he could respond, she laid two cookies on a plate and slid those over, too, giving Jack a wink.

"You are bad for my diet, Dot." He grinned.

"You work it off in smiles, you charmer, you." She chuckled, then turned to Marnie. "Half my waitstaff trips over themselves to serve him. There's going to be a lot of envious eyes on you, my girl, because you've snagged Mr. Eligible here."

"Oh, I'm not his girlfriend," Marnie said. Fast. So fast, a man could take it personally.

"Well, you're missing out on a hell of a catch," Dot said, then gave Jack a wink. "Why this man is the whole reason I'm in business. Without Jack, there wouldn't be a Java Depot here. He helped me out, encouraged me, gave me great advice, and a big old nudge when I needed one most. Always has, and I suspect even if I tell him not to, he always will." Dot's light blue eyes softened when she looked over at Jack. "It's good to have you in my corner, Jack."

He shifted his weight, uncomfortable under Dot's grateful words. It was what he worked for, but there were days when praise for doing the right thing felt like wearing the wrong shoes. Maybe someday he'd get used to it.

"I needed a place to get my coffee," he said. "And my mom is addicted to your cookies, so if you went out of business and stopped shipping them down to her in Florida, she'd go into serious withdrawal, and I'd have hell to pay."

"Yeah, that's why you helped me out," Dot said with a little snort of disbelief. "Purely selfish reasons."

Jack grinned and put up his hands. "That's me."

Dot shook her head, then gestured toward Marnie. "He's a keeper, I'm telling you. Though you might have to beat off half the women in Boston to get him. And you—" she wagged a finger at Jack "—you need to use some of that legendary Knight charm, and win her over." Dot chuckled, then headed to the other end of the counter to help another customer.

"Legendary charm?" Marnie asked. She reached past him to pick up her mug of coffee, and give him a teasing grin. "Legendary like the Loch Ness Monster and Bigfoot?"

"Exactly." He chuckled, then picked up the second mug and the cookies and followed her to an outdoor table where Christmas lights lit the undersides of the umbrellas over the tables. A soft breeze rippled the bright blue umbrella, and toyed with the ends of Marnie's hair. His fingers ached to do the same.

He'd thought he didn't want to date anyone. That he didn't have room in his life for a relationship. A week ago, he would have sworn up and down that he had no interest in dating anyone on a long-term basis. That he, of all people, shouldn't try to create ties.

Then he met Marnie.

Maybe it was the way she ran hot, then cold. Maybe it was the way she kept him at a distance, like a book he couldn't read in the library. Or maybe it was that none of his "legendary charm" worked on her. Was it about the challenge of wanting what he couldn't have? Or something more?

Either way, he reminded himself, he was his father's son. The offspring of a womanizer who destroyed companies, ruined lives, and broke hearts. Jack had been like that, too, for too long. He'd managed to change his approach to business, but when it came down to making a commitment, would he run like his father had or stick around? Would he shut out the people he cared for, turn his back on them?

Marnie picked up one of the cookies, and took a bite. A smattering of crumbs lingered on her lips, and it took everything in his power not to kiss her. Then the family beside them got up and left, leaving him and Marnie alone on the patio. She reached for her coffee, and before he could think twice, he leaned forward, closing the distance between them to mere inches. Desire thundered in his veins, pounded in his brain. All he wanted right now was her, that sweet goodness, her tempting smile. To hell with later; Jack wanted now. "You have a crumb right—"

And he kissed her. To hell with staying away, to hell with making smart decisions, to hell with everything but this moment.

A gentle kiss, more of a whisper against her lips. She froze for a second, then shifted closer to him, one hand reaching to cup his cheek, her fingers dancing against his skin. She deepened the kiss, her delicate tongue slipping in to tango with his. Holy cow. A hot, insistent need ignited in his veins, and it took near every ounce of his strength to pull back instead of taking her on the table in front of the whole damned neighborhood.

"Uh, I think I got it," he said. Truth was, right now he couldn't think or see straight enough to tell if she was covered in crumbs.

Her fingers went to her mouth, lingered a moment, then she lowered her hand. Her cheeks flushed a deep pink and she let out a soft curse. "That…that wasn't a good idea. At all. I have to go." She got to her feet, leaving the half-eaten cookie on the plate. "Thanks for the coffee."

"Wait, Marnie—"

"Jack, stay out of my life. You've done enough damage already."

Then she turned and left. Jack leaned back in his chair and watched her go, bemused and befuddled. A woman who kissed him back yet claimed not to be interested in him. She was a puzzle, that was for sure. What had she meant by "you've done enough damage already"?

A sinking feeling told him she'd meant more than that kiss. His past had reared its ugly head again. Somewhere, Marnie was connected to the mistakes he'd made years before. He vowed to dig deeper into the files in his office, and find the connection.

Would it always be this way? Would he find his regrets confronting him every time he tried to do the right thing?

Jack watched Marnie hail a cab, get inside the yellow taxi and disappear into the congested streets. Somehow, he needed to find a way to do what he had done before. Mitigate the damage. And find a solution that left everyone happy.

CHAPTER FOUR

JACK LOGGED A hard six miles on the tread-mill, but it wasn't enough. He could have run a marathon and it wouldn't have been enough to quiet the demons in his head. He'd tried, Lord knew he'd tried, over the years.

By the time he climbed off the machine, he was drenched in sweat, but his mind still raced with thoughts of Marnie Franklin. Hell, half the reason he'd come to the gym today was because he'd hoped to bump into her.

After their walk to the coffee shop, he'd gone to the office and pulled out Top Notch Printing's file, from the piles stacked on the credenza behind his desk. So many people's lives ruined, so many businesses shuttered, their contents sold like trinkets at a garage sale.

He'd dug through Tom's file, looking for the notes he'd made all those years ago.

Owner: Tom Franklin, married to wife Helen. Three daughters. Calls them Daisy, Kitty and Chatterbug.

Nicknames. That's why Jack hadn't made the connection when he'd met Marnie. He'd never known Tom's daughters' real names, never spent enough time with the man to get that personal.

Jack dropped onto a bench outside the gym and put his head in his hands. He could still see Tom's face. Bright, hopeful, trusting. Believing every word Jack and his father said.

Jack had tried to undo the damage, but by then it had been too late. Too damned late.

He sighed and got to his feet. Instead of taking the left toward the office, he took a right and went back home.

"I thought you just left. What are you doing home so soon?" his stepfather asked when Jack stepped into the apartment.

"I'm off to a slow start today." Because his mind was far from work. Had been ever since Marnie's cab had dented his sports car. That alone was a sign he was in too deep. Then why kiss her? Why go to the gym on the off chance she'd be there, too? Why couldn't he just forget her? Was it all about trying to make up for the past? Or more?

"Maybe I need some protein or something. You want to go grab some breakfast before I head into the office? Unless you already ate."

"Even if I did, I'll eat again." Dan chuckled, and grabbed a light jacket off the back of the kitchen chair. "That's the beauty of retirement. No schedule. Lunch can come five minutes after breakfast."

They headed out into the bright sunshine and around the corner to Hector's cozy little deli. Its glass windows looked out onto two streets, while inside, business bustled along, in keeping with the city's busy pace. Hector greeted them as they walked in with a boisterous hello and a hearty wave. A gregarious guy given to playing mariachi music just because, Hector was a colorful and exuberant addition to the area. His incredible sandwiches drew people far and wide for their unique taste combinations and home-baked breads.

Dan and Jack ordered, then snagged a couple of bar stools at the window counter, and unwrapped their sandwiches. "So, what do you think of Helen?" Dan asked.

Dan and Helen had been on several dates over the last week. Dan had even invited her to dinner at Jack's apartment—and wisely ordered takeout instead of trying to cook.

They'd gone to a Red Sox game, played Bingo at a local church and taken several long walks through the neighborhood. After every date, Dan's smile grew broader, his step lighter, like a man falling in love.

"She seems really nice," Jack said. "And she definitely likes you."

A big, goofy grin spread over Dan's face. "I sure like her, too. More and more every day." Dan toyed with the paper wrapper before him. "You're okay with me dating? I mean, it's got to be kind of weird."

"You and my mom divorced years ago, Dad." Even though Dan was his stepfather, he'd been in Jack's life for so long, calling him Dad seemed natural. Jack's real father had left him the business, and not much else, letting his work keep him from seeing his son, and leaving the raising of Jack up to Dan and Helen. Probably for the best, because Dan had been a hell of a stepfather. Jack, Senior had been about as warm and fuzzy as a porcupine.

Still, there'd always been that part of Jack that had craved a relationship with his biological father. Maybe because then he could have the answers he wanted about why Jack, Sr. had walked away from his family. Why he had chosen work over his son. In the end,

Jack had realized his father lacked the capacity to love others first. And that he had been damned lucky to have Dan, who had shown him the way a good father acted.

"I want you to be happy, too," Jack said to Dan, and meant the words.

"Me, too. And hopefully, I do it right this time."

"About doing things right..." Jack sighed. "There's something you should know. Helen is the widow of one of the business owners that Knight put out of business."

"She mentioned something about her husband's company going under after some investors stepped in. I wondered about the connection."

Jack toyed with the napkin. "I was the one that talked Tom into signing with Knight. At the time I was working for my dad and—"

Dan put a hand on his shoulder. "You don't need to explain. We all make mistakes, Jack. We all screw up. The point is you learned and you changed. You're not that man anymore."

Jack nodded, as if he agreed. But he wondered how much distance he had placed between himself and the father he'd idolized. He'd tried so hard to be like him, to get past the wall between them. Had it been at the expense of his heart?

"Why did you and my mom get divorced?" It was a question Jack had never asked. Maybe because he'd been too busy working when the announcement came. Maybe because it was easier to bury himself in work than to call his mom or Dan and ask what had happened. Yet another item to add to his "not good at" list. Family relationships.

Tanya was right. He was cold and uninvolved. He'd cut off the relationships part of his life for far too long. He needed to find more ways to connect, to care. Because if he didn't, he could see the writing on the wall—Jack, Jr., was going to morph into Jack, Sr.

He'd come so close to doing exactly that. Then one day he'd looked in the mirror before the biggest deal of Knight's history, and realized he had become his father, from the mannerisms to the crimson power tie. Jack had walked out of the bathroom, quit his job and walked away.

Dan sighed. "As easy as it would be for me to blame Sarah, truth is, I was a terrible husband."

"You were a great stepdad, though." There'd been after-school softball games in the yard, impromptu weekend camping trips and annual father-son vacations. Dan had gone to every track meet, every Boy Scout canoe trip, every award ceremony.

"Thanks, Jack. You weren't so bad as a stepson yourself." Dan grinned. "But your mother and I, we just didn't have what it took. When we got married, it was a fast decision. Too fast, some would say. We married a week after we met. Crazy, but gosh, I just didn't think it through. I just said I do. By the time I realized we were like oil and water together, it was too late. I'd already started considering you my son, and I couldn't bear leaving. We tried to stick it out after you grew up, but by that time, we'd become two different people, living separate lives. If I had plugged in more, or tried harder, maybe we wouldn't have ended up that way." He sighed. "It was like our marriage died a long, slow death. We were always friends—and we still are—but that wasn't enough to make it work."

Jack had noticed years ago that his mother and Dan rarely hugged or kissed or went out alone. There'd been no drama, no fights, just a quiet existence. Jack couldn't think of anything more agonizing and painful than that. If he ever settled down, he wanted a woman who challenged him, who made his life an adventure.

A woman like Marnie?

Want if he ended up repeating his father's mistakes? Leaving his wife for one woman after another, ignoring his child, in favor of his company? There was no guarantee Jack would end up doing that, or end up a good man like Dan, but Jack's cautious and logical side threw up a red caution flag all the same.

"I'm glad your mother is happy now with that new guy she's dating," Dan said, bringing Jack back to their conversation. "What's his name? Ray? Seems like he's perfect for her."

Jack had only met Ray once, but he'd have to agree. His mother's new boyfriend was an outgoing, friendly guy who enjoyed the same things as she did—traveling, bike riding, and charitable work. "She needed someone busier than her," Jack said with a chuckle.

Jack's exuberant, spontaneous stepfather had driven his mom crazy sometimes. She was a stick-to-the-schedule, organized woman who never got used to Dan's unconventional approaches. Jack liked to think he'd taken on the best of both their traits. Some of the impulsivity of his stepfather, and some of the dependable keel of his mother. Ray's personality was much closer to Sarah's, which had made them a good fit.

"This time, I'm going to work damned hard to make sure me and the woman I marry are on the same path," Dan said. "And that I let her know all the time how much I appreciate her. Life's too damned short to spend it alone, you know?"

Jack nodded. He'd been feeling the same way himself lately. Was it just because he'd met Marnie? Because he was tired of being alone? Or because he'd glimpsed his future and didn't like the picture it presented? Workaholic, glued to his desk. A repeat of his namesake's choices. Not the future Jack wanted. "You deserve happiness, Dad. You really do."

"Thanks, Jack. That means a lot." Dan took a bite of his sandwich, swallowed, then looked at Jack and a teasing smile lit his face. "How are things going with the daughter?"

"You mean Marnie?" Jack said the word like he didn't know who Dan meant. Like he hadn't been thinking about Marnie almost non-stop for days.

"She's smart and beautiful, and a hell of a catch, according to her mother. And yes, we have been talking about you two and conspiring behind your backs. We both think you'd be a fool to let her get away."

Get away? He couldn't seem to get her to stay. "She's made it very clear that she's not interested in me."

Well, not exactly crystal clear. There was the matter of that kiss. Mixed messages, times ten.

"I think Marnie's figured out my connection to her father's business. It's no wonder she hates me. Seriously, I hate myself for some of the decisions I made back then."

Dan waved that off. "So? You make better decisions now. That's what counts. We're all allowed a little stupidity."

Jack grinned. "Either way, I won't blame Marnie if she wants to tie me to a stake and light a fire at my feet."

"Since when have you let a little roadblock like that hold you back?" Dan chuckled. "Listen, I saw the truth all over her face outside the restaurant the other day. She *likes* you."

Jack snorted.

Dan leaned an arm over his chair. "You know, there is a way to make her prove it."

"What? A little Sodium Pentothal?"

Dan chuckled then leaned in and lowered his voice. "Have her take you on as a client. When she tries to fix you up, she'll see that the best possible match is…"

"Her." Jack let that thought turn around in his head for a while. "It could work. But, I don't know, Dad. I haven't exactly done a good job of balancing work and a life thus far.

There's only twenty-four hours in a day and it seems like twenty-three of them are dedicated to the business."

Well, maybe less than that, if he counted the hours spent walking around Boston with Marnie, then at the gym trying to stop thinking about Marnie, and this morning, avoiding the office because all he could do was think about Marnie.

Distracted had become his middle name. Not a good thing right now. He had three pending deals this month, a few other recently acquired companies that still needed his guiding hand, and a To Do list a mile long. And yet, here he was, sitting with Dan and talking about Marnie. He made no move to leave.

Nor did he answer the nagging doubts in his head. The ones that said all he was doing was making excuses. Because that was easier than getting involved—and being the kind of human iceberg that had ruined relationships before.

"Chicken," Dan teased.

"I'm not chicken. I'm busy. There's a difference."

"Bawk, bawk," Dan said, flapping his arms in emphasis. "You are, too. It's time you had a life, Jack, instead of just watching from the sidelines."

He bristled. He'd had the same thoughts, but wouldn't admit it. "I do have a life. I go out, I go to the gym—"

"You *exist*. That's different." Dan clapped a hand on his shoulder, and his light blue eyes met Jack's square-on. "You deserve to be happy. Your father...well, I don't like to speak ill of the dead, but your father wasn't exactly citizen of the year. But that doesn't mean you'll turn out like him. Don't let one bad apple spoil the rest of the batch."

Jack chuckled. "How many trite phrases do you have in you?"

"As many as it takes to get you over to Marnie's office, and back out into the dating world. Who knows, maybe she'll find your perfect match for you."

"I thought the goal was for her to realize she was the right one for me."

"I'm thinking it might need to work both ways," Dan said. "Now get out of here and go over there before you *chicken* out."

"Very funny," Jack said. He got to his feet and tossed his trash in the bin, then said goodbye to his stepfather and left the deli. He stood on the corner for a long moment. To the north lay the office and a thousand responsibilities. To the east, Marnie and a thousand risks.

* * *

"What has you all distracted today?" Erica, Marnie's little sister, said. She was sitting at the desk across from Marnie, while the two of them worked on a menu for the annual client thank-you party. Erica had inherited their father's dark brown locks, but the same green eyes as the other Franklin girls. Two years younger than Marnie, she was the bubbly one in the family, filled with more energy than anyone Marnie had ever met.

"Me? I'm not distracted."

Erica laughed. "Uh-huh. Then why did you write the same thing three times on this list? Do we really need that many napkins?" She pointed to a paper sitting between them. "And you've been staring off into space for the last ten minutes. Heck, most of the day I've had to repeat myself every time I've talked to you. This is totally not like you, oh, organized one."

"Sorry. It's just been a busy day." A lie. She had been distracted by thoughts of Jack Knight. What was it about that man? He was the enemy. A man she had done a good job of despising for years.

When she went for coffee with him yesterday, it had been to gather information and come up with a plan for a little revenge. Instead, he'd turned the tables with that kiss.

And what a kiss it had been. As far as kisses went, that one ranked high on Marnie's Top Ten list. She'd gone home after the coffee, and spent half the day doing what she was doing now—daydreaming and wondering how she could be so attracted to a man yet despise him at the same time. Maybe it was some kind of reverse psychology at work.

Or maybe it was that Jack Knight could kiss like no man she'd ever met, and just the mere thought of him sent a delicious rush through her.

God, she was a mess. She needed to get back on track, not keep letting Jack derail her. If there was one thing Marnie excelled at, it was holding on to the reins. She had her business and her apartment organized to the nth degree, her planner filled with neat little squares. She made quarterly goal lists, daily agendas, and didn't go off on crazy heat-filled dates with Mr. Wrong.

Most of the time, anyway.

Then why had she kissed Jack back? Why had she let him get close? All the more reason to get a grip and get back to work.

The door opened and a burst of yellow

rushed into the room. "Oh. My. God. You guys are the *best!*" a female voice screeched.

"Oh, no," Erica whispered and rolled her eyes. Marnie sucked in a fortifying breath.

Every time she arrived, Roberta Stewart's giant personality exploded. A tall, gangly woman, Roberta's decibel-stretching voice entered a room long before she did. Marnie had known her since the first day she opened her doors, one of her first clients—and one of her least successful. Roberta was likeable, smart, and funny, but few people dated her long enough to realize that, because her first impression was so loud and busy. No matter how many times Marnie tried to counsel Roberta to tone it down just a bit, she didn't listen. And the men ran—until they were out of earshot.

Today, Roberta had on a sunny yellow dress that swirled like a bell around her hips, and a wide-brimmed matching hat trimmed with silk orchids. She let out a dramatic sigh, then plopped onto the sofa in the waiting area, her dress spreading across the brown leather like melting butter. "I just came from my *third* engagement party of the year! You guys did it *again!*" Roberta shook her head. "Amy and Bob looked *so happy!*"

"I'm glad," Marnie said, thinking of the cycling enthusiast couple she had put together a few months ago. "They're a great match."

"And now it's my turn!" Roberta jumped to her feet and clasped her hands together. "So, who do you have for me this week? Tell me, who's my new Mr. Right?"

"Things didn't work out with Alan?" Marnie had really hoped the bookish accountant would be a great counterbalance to Roberta's exuberance.

"Alan, shmalan." Roberta waved a hand in dismissal. "I need a man with verve! Life! Energy! Strength! Somebody's got to keep up with all this!" She swiveled her hips. "And poor Alan was ready to pass out before we even reached the second nightclub. Give me a man who takes his *vitamins!*"

"Maybe you should try a quiet dinner for your first date," Erica said. "Rather than all-night salsa dancing."

"But these shoes and this body were made for *dancing,*" Roberta said. "I need a man who can keep up with me. Call me as soon as you have another one. Oh, and please make sure he's had a stress test before the date. I was a little worried poor Alan's heart was going to go *kaput!*" She gave them a wave, then headed back out the door.

"Ah, Roberta. Always a memorable visit,"

Erica said once the door shut. "Who are you going to match her with now?"

"I have no idea. I like Roberta, but she needs a very special man." One that had yet to come along, though not for a lack of trying on Marnie's part. Maybe such a bachelor didn't exist in Boston. Or the greater New England area. Or maybe even on planet Earth.

No, there was someone perfect for Roberta. Marnie just hadn't found him yet. He needed to be a unique man, strong yet confident enough to be with a woman like her.

"Speaking of men," Erica said, "I have a date. Mind if I knock off early?"

"Nope. There are no appointments the rest of the day. I'm just going to finish up this menu, and then head home myself."

"Be sure you do," Erica said softly, laying a hand on her sister's shoulder. "Take a little time to let go and just be, sis. Okay?"

"I do."

Erica laughed. "No, you don't. But maybe if I tell you to do it often enough, you finally will."

CHAPTER FIVE

AFTER ERICA LEFT, Marnie sat in her office, the music cranked up on the mini sound system beside her desk, and hammered out the rest of the details for the next few Matchmaking by Marnie events. She spun around in her chair, facing the window that looked out over Brookline, tapping her feet against the sill in time to a catchy pop tune. She'd kicked off her shoes, and let her hair out of the clip that held it in its usual bun. She grabbed a half-eaten bag of chips and started snacking while she watched the traffic go by, singing along between bites, and enjoying her moment of solitude.

"So this is how a matchmaker works her magic."

Marnie gasped, dropped her feet to the floor and spun around, a chip halfway to her mouth, while several more tumbled onto her lap. She wanted to crawl under her desk and hide, or at least shrivel into a bowl. She told herself she didn't care that her hair was a mess, she was covered in potato chip crumbs, and she'd been caught signing off-key to a teenybopper hit.

"Jack…uh, I mean, Mr. Knight," she said, then covered her mouth and paused to swallow. Did she really think calling him by his last name would erase that kiss, the way he made her feel with a simple smile? That it would put up a wall he couldn't pass? She forced authority into her tone. "What are you doing here?"

Even in a dark gray suit, with his pale blue tie loosened at the neck, he looked sexy, approachable. Hard to resist. "I'm looking for a matchmaker," he said. "And you come highly recommended by a close family member. Apparently my stepfather has fallen head over heels for your mother."

"I've heard all about it, too." There was no denying the happiness in Helen's voice. Marnie had talked to her mother earlier today and heard nothing but joy. Hearing that Helen's feelings were reciprocated—

Well, that was what Marnie worked for. The cherry on top of all the work she put in, building that matchmaker sundae. Except her mother was falling for a man with ties to someone who could hurt their family all over again.

"I don't think you need my help," she said. "What was it Dot said? You've got legendary charm? I'm sure you could find plenty of women on your own."

"Whether I do or not, that hasn't brought me Miss Right yet. I think I need a professional." He came closer, then around her desk, to sit on the edge. He leaned forward, and captured a chip just as it began to tumble off her chest. Her face heated. "Someone who knows what they're doing."

She pushed the chair back, and turned to dump the rest of the chips into the trash. That was the last time she was going to eat a messy snack at her desk. "Well, I'm sorry, but I'm not taking new clients right now." A lie. She rarely turned down new clients. In her business, people came and went as their lives changed, which kept her busy year-round and left room for more. "You'll have to find another matchmaker, or maybe try one of those online dating services. Sorry I couldn't help you."

There. That had been definitive, strong. Leaving no room for negotiation—or anything else. But Jack didn't leave. Instead, he leaned in closer, his gaze assessing and probing.

"Okay, tell me." The sun shone through the window and danced gold lights on his hair, his face. "What did I do to you that makes you hate me? Yet, kiss me five minutes later?"

"For your information, that kiss was an accident. I was reacting on instinct."

Why didn't she just tell him the truth? Why did she keep hesitating, letting this flirtatious game continue?

Because a part of her wondered about the man who had helped the local coffee shop and the neighborhood gym and still knew his old neighbors. A part of her wanted to know who the real Jack Knight was.

And if there was a possibility that for all these years, she might have been wrong about him.

"An instinct?" he said, his voice low, dark. "No more?"

"Yes. No more." The lie escaped her in a rush.

"So if I leaned in now—" and he did just that, coming within a whisper of her lips, then brushing his against hers slow, easy, a feather-light kiss that made her want more, before he drew back "—you wouldn't react the same way?"

"Of course not." She stood her ground, but the temptation to curve into him pounded in her veins. To finish what they'd started back in the parking lot, to let that heady, heated rush run through her again, obliterating thought, reason.

Damn it. She didn't do this. She didn't lose control of her emotions, get swept away by a nice smile and a shimmer of sexual energy. Stupid decisions were made that way, and Marnie refused to do that.

She clenched her fists, released them, and forced her breathing to stay normal, not to betray an ounce of the riot inside her. To not let him know how much she wanted a real, soul-sucking, hot-as-heck kiss right now. Her gaze locked on his, then dropped to his mouth. *Oh, my.*

"Well, I'm glad to know you can resist that 'legendary charm,'" Jack said, then rose and went around her desk to sit in one of the visitor's chairs.

Disappointment whooshed through her. She let out a little laugh to cover the emotion, then sat back in her chair, because her legs had gone to jelly and her heart wouldn't slow. She had two choices right now. Keep denying she was attracted to him, or fix him up and get him out of her life for good. What did she care if he dated half the female population of Boston?

For a woman who craved calm and order more than chips, erasing Jack Knight from her life was the easiest and best option. No one got hurt. A win-win.

"I might be able to help you find someone," she said, clasping her hands on the desk, tight. Treat him like any other client. Act like he's simply another bachelor. "Let's start with why you think this is the right time in your life to find the perfect match?"

He leaned back, propping one leg atop the other. "I think it's time I settled down and pursued the American dream."

"Really? Right now. That's actually what you think." It wasn't a question. Jack coming to her, now, after she'd refused to get close to him, couldn't be a coincidence. It had to be some kind of game. What did he really want?

"It's true. I woke up, realized all my friends are married, have kids, houses in the suburbs. I'm the lone holdout. I guess I haven't met the right woman yet." He grinned.

She let out a gust. "Why are you really here? Because if it's to get me to go out with you, that's not going to work."

"Oh, I know. I got that message. Loud and clear."

She thought she detected a measure of hurt in his voice. Impossible. Jack Knight was a shark, and sharks didn't get hurt feelings. "Well, good."

"My stepfather was very pleased with how compatible he is with Helen, and I thought you could do the same for me."

If Marnie had anything to say about it, her mother would find someone else and stay far, far away from any relative of Jack Knight's. She had yet to find a way to make him pay for the hurt he'd brought to her family.

Confronting him and demanding answers would only backfire when Helen found out. In Marnie's perfect world, Jack Knight was destroyed and her mother never got hurt.

Marnie hadn't been able to keep her mother from being hurt after the death of Tom, but maybe she could make sure this debacle with Jack didn't impact Helen. All she had to do was find a way to keep Jack far from Helen—and that meant making sure Jack got the message that Marnie wanted him gone. She glanced over at the pile on her desk and realized there might be a way to hurt Jack and get rid of him for good—a much better and smarter way than having coffee with him and taking long walks through Boston neighborhoods. Clearly, that kind of thing distracted her too much. Brought her too close to the shark's teeth. But this way…

"Sure, I'll help you," she said, pulling out a sheet of paper from the file drawer on her desk. "Let's start with the basics. Name, address, occupation."

He rattled off his address. "I believe you know the rest. Especially my name."

Her cheeks heated again when she thought of how she had whispered his first name back at the coffee shop, of the way that same syllable had echoed in her dreams, her thoughts. Oh, yeah, she knew his name. Too well. "Uh, date of birth?"

He gave her that, too, then grinned. "I'm a Taurus, or at least I think I am. And I like long walks on the beach and moonlit dances."

She snorted. "Whatever."

"Would you rather I said monster truck rallies and mud wrestling championships?"

She laughed. "Now *that* I would believe."

"Ah, then you don't know me very well." He leaned forward, propping his elbows on his knees. "I love the beach. I couldn't move away from the ocean if I tried. There's nothing like waking up on a warm Sunday morning, and having the ocean breeze coming in through your window."

"I like that, too," she said, then drew herself up. What was this, connect with Jack time? *Focus, Marnie, focus.* "Favorite music? Movies?"

"I like jazz. The kind of music that makes you think of smoky bars and good whiskey. Where you want to sit in a corner booth with a beautiful woman and listen to the band."

A beautiful woman like her? Marnie glanced down at the sheet, saw she had written the question, then scribbled it out. That made her twice as determined to get Jack out of her life. Marnie Franklin didn't do scatterbrained or dreamy or infatuated. Damn. "Uh, movies?"

"I don't get to see many movies, and as much as I'd like to say something smart like *Requiem for a Dream*, I have to cave to a cliché. If you check my DVR, there's a lot of action movies on there." He shrugged. "What can I say? In a pinch, I opt for *The Terminator.*"

"I'll be baaack, huh?" she said, doing a pretty bad imitation of Arnold.

He chuckled. "Exactly. What about you? What's your favorite movie?"

"I cave to the cliché, too. Any kind of romantic comedy. Especially *You've Got Mail.*"

"Isn't that the one where the woman fell in love with her enemy?" Jack's blue eyes met hers, a tease winking in their ocean depths.

Did he know? Did he suspect her hidden agenda? Then he smiled and she relaxed. No. He didn't know who she really was or what she was planning for his "match." He'd been joking, not probing to see if this particular Romeo and Juliet had a shot.

She didn't care if they both liked the ocean, jazz music, and fun movies. If they'd both suffered a loss of a parent, and were still searching for something that would never be. He had ruined her life, her family. More than that, he was the kind of man who encouraged her to let loose, to become some giggly schoolgirl. She'd seen enough women make the mistake of leaping into a relationship without thinking, and refused to do the same. This wasn't a Nora Ephron movie—it was reality.

She glanced down at the paperwork. *Treat him like any other client,* she repeated. Again. "Uh, what about things to do? In your free time?"

"Running at the gym. Seeing outdoor concerts. Walking the streets of Boston."

She sighed, then put down the pen. "This isn't going to work if you keep flirting with me."

"I'm not flirting with you, Marnie. If I was flirting with you, you'd know it."

"That—" she waved a finger between them "—was definitely flirting."

"No. *This* is flirting." He got up again and approached her desk, then placed his hands on the oak surface and leaned over until their faces were inches apart. She caught the dark undertow of his cologne, the steady heat from his body. His blue eyes teemed with secrets. A lock of dark hair swooped across his brow. The crazy urge to brush it back rose in her chest.

"You are a beautiful, intoxicating, infuriating woman," he whispered, his voice a low, sensual growl, "and I can't stop thinking about you. And I love the way you look today. All…unfettered. Untamed."

Heat washed over her body, unfurled a deep, dark flame in her womb. She opened her mouth to speak, and for a moment, could only breathe and stare into those storm-tossed eyes of his. "Okay." Her words shook and she drew in a breath to steady herself. "Yes, that…that was flirting."

He smiled, held her gaze a moment longer, then retreated to the chair. "Glad we got that settled."

Settled? If anything, things between them had become more unsettled. A place Marnie never liked to be. Her concentration had flown south for the winter, and every thought in her head revolved around finding the nearest bedroom and taking her sweet time to "flirt" with Jack Knight.

Jack Knight. The enemy. In more ways than one.

She cleared her throat and retrieved her pen. In a normal client meeting, she'd let the questions flow in a natural rhythm. Her initial meetings were usually more like a chat with a new neighbor than a formal interview, but with Jack, she couldn't seem to form a coherent thought. "I, well, I think that's all I need for now. I'll be in touch in a couple days with some potential matches."

"That was easy. You sure you don't need anything else?"

You, a bedroom, more of those kisses. "Nope, I'm good," she said, too fast.

"Okay." He started to rise, and she put out a hand but didn't touch him.

She refused to let a silly thing like attraction get in the way of her goals. She needed information, and she needed Jack out of her life. Today. She could accomplish both right now.

Here was her opportunity to finally do what she'd been trying to do for weeks— find out about his business and how he operated. Maybe then she'd have the answers she needed, the ones that would close the hole in her heart and answer the what-ifs. She'd finally be able to accept the loss of her father, and move forward.

"Jack, wait a second. You know, lots of the women you'll be paired with work in complimentary fields. It might be good to get to know more about your job."

He sat back down. "Makes sense. I've told you a little about what I do. What else do you need to know?"

She had to word this carefully, or he'd realize she was looking for more than just matchmaking info. "Well, let's start with something general. Pretend we're chatting for the first time."

"Over coffee?" He grinned.

She hardened her features. The last thing she needed to do was think about that walk to the coffee shop. Or the cookie crumb driven kiss. *Keep this professional.* "Or over a desk in an office."

He nodded agreement. "Okay, shoot."

"Tell me more about how you decide which companies to invest in and which ones you walk away from."

He cleared his throat and when he spoke again, the flirt had left his voice and he was all business. "A lot of that is a matter of numbers. I look at their market share, profit and loss, balance sheets, and weigh that against future potential and opportunities. If the dollars aren't there, it doesn't make financial sense for me to invest. But, sometimes I do anyway." He shrugged. "Because of the Caterpillar Factor."

"The Caterpillar Factor?" She stopped writing. "I've never heard of that before."

"It's something I made up. When you buy a business, there's a lot of data to wade through. But in the end, I let my instincts make the final decision. That's the Caterpillar Factor." He leaned forward in the chair, his eyes bright with enthusiasm. "You know how you can look at a caterpillar and get grossed out by it? I mean, most of them are fat and have a bunch of legs, and aren't exactly something you want crawling on you."

"That's true." She gave an involuntary shudder.

"But those same caterpillars have the *potential* to be something really incredible. When you look at them, you don't know what it will be—you're judging it entirely on its current form. But underneath, buried deep inside that caterpillar, is something that, given enough time and nurturing, will be amazing and beautiful."

"A butterfly," she said, her voice quiet.

"Exactly." He grinned. "Not every business is a butterfly waiting to be unveiled, but some are. And I know that by investing in and coaching them, I can help them become something amazing." He gave a little nod, and a flush crept into his cheeks. "I know, it sounds kind of corny."

She never would have thought she'd see Jack Knight embarrassed or shy or vulnerable. But here he was, admitting that he believed in potential, that he sometimes went with his gut, even against conventional wisdom. Wasn't that how she approached her matchmaking? No computer algorithms, no formulas, just instinct?

Why did this one man—the wrong man—discombobulate her so? She'd never met anyone who could do that with nothing more than a smile, a whisper of her name.

Damn it all. She related to him, understood him, and that added another complicated layer to what she'd thought would be a simple matter of revenge. The closer they got to each other, the more she allowed him to burrow his way into her heart, the harder it became to implement her plan.

She glanced down at the paper before her. The words swam in her vision. Why hadn't Jack seen a butterfly in Top Notch Printing, her father's business? Why hadn't he helped her father more? Wasn't Tom Franklin's life and livelihood worth some time and nurturing, too?

"And what about the ones that won't be butterflies? What do you do with those businesses?"

He sighed. "Sometimes, the business is too far gone, or the owner just isn't equipped with the right skill set to help it reach the next level. We could throw millions at the company and it wouldn't be enough. In those cases, we sell off the parts, recoup our investment, and hopefully send the owner off with cash in his pocket."

"Hopefully?" The word squeaked past the tension in her jaw.

"You're a businesswoman, Marnie. I'm sure you understand that there are a million factors that can affect the decision to keep or sell a company. Some owners are great at running a business, some…aren't."

She thought of her affable, fun-loving father. He'd never been much for keeping track of paperwork or receipts. Never one to demand a late payment or argue with a customer. But that meant Tom had needed more help, not less. Why hadn't Jack seen that?

"Sometimes, despite all the due diligence in the world," Jack said, "we make mistakes, and sometimes life throws us a curveball that we didn't expect. A supplier goes under or a major customer takes their sales elsewhere. Sometimes, the companies recoup, sometimes…"

"They die," she finished. She had to swallow hard and remind herself to keep breathing.

He nodded. "Yeah, they do."

"You seem awful cavalier about this." As if there weren't people hurt in the process. As if the only thing that died was a bottom line. She clenched her hands together under her desk, feigning a calm she didn't feel.

"It's a reality. Fifty percent of businesses fail, for a million reasons. You can pump all the cash you want into them, and some just aren't destined to survive. If I got emotional about each one, I'd get distracted and lose sight of the big picture. So I don't make my decisions based on emotion. I think it helps that I don't exactly love my job, but I…respect it. Maybe someday down the road, I'll get a chance to do something else."

"And what is the big picture? Profits?"

"Well, everyone likes to make money. But for me, it's the businesses I see succeed. Like Dot's coffee shop or my friend Toby's gym. I see the placed filled with happy customers, and that tells me I did the right thing. It's not about profits, it's about quality of life. For the owners, and their clients."

"And the businesses that don't make it?" she said. "What are they to you?"

"The cost of doing business. It sounds harsh, but in the end, when there's nothing more that can be done, a failure is reduced to dollars and cents."

Under the desk, her hands curled into fists. She worked a smile to her face, even though it hurt. The smile, and the truth. "Well, I guess that's all I need."

Please leave, please get out of here before my heart breaks right in front of you.

The chips from earlier churned in her gut. She wished her day was over, because right now, all she wanted to do was go home, draw the shades, and stay in bed.

Not only had Jack just confirmed that her father's business had been a negative number in the general ledger, but his asking her to find him a match confirmed she was a negative in his personal ledger, too. This was what she'd wanted—the truth and to be rid of Jack. But still, the success had a bitter taste.

"Thanks again for taking the time to see me today, Marnie." Jack got to his feet. "I look forward to hearing from you, and seeing who you match me up with." He looked like he wanted to say something more, but all he said was goodbye before heading for the door. One hand on the knob, he turned back. "You know, you should let your hair down more often. And I mean that, literally and figuratively. It suits you. Very nicely."

The door shut behind him with a soft click. Marnie sat in her chair, watching the space for a long time. She shook off the maudlin thoughts and turned to her contacts database. Jack Knight had asked her for a match, and she intended to give him one—

A match that would challenge him and keep him far from Marnie.

Then maybe he'd stop flirting with her, and tipping her carefully constructed life upside-down. Because there was one thing she knew for sure. Jack Knight was bad for business—the business of Marnie's heart.

CHAPTER SIX

JACK KNIGHT WAS rarely wrong. He had learned over the years to read people's body language, the subtle clues they sent out that created a roadmap to their thoughts and actions. He'd used that skill a thousand times in negotiations, and in strategic meetings. But when it came to Marnie Franklin, his instincts had failed him, big time. He'd completely underestimated how angry she was—

And how far he was from proving himself as a different man than his father.

He strode into her office a week after their last meeting, waving off the assistant's offer to help him, heading straight for Marnie's desk. "What kind of match was that?"

"What are you talking about?"

"That date you set me up on. What were you thinking?"

She leaned an elbow on her chair, relaxed, unconcerned. Her eyes widened as he approached, then a flicker of a smile appeared on her face and disappeared just as fast. A smile like she knew what she had done. "I'm sorry you're unhappy with the Matchmaking by Marnie match, but we truly thought—"

"*Unhappy?* I wouldn't say that. The woman was nice and very energetic, but not my type, at all." His gaze narrowed. "Did you do that on purpose?"

"I have no idea what you're talking about," Marnie said. With a straight face.

"Marnie, I have to go to that meeting with the caterer," her assistant said. "But if you want, I'll stay awhile longer."

"I'll be fine. Go ahead to the appointment, Erica." Marnie waved her off.

Erica, Marnie's sister. His gaze skipped to her, and he saw the same leery look in her eyes as in Marnie's. Oh, yeah, they knew who he was here—or who they thought he was. Damn. How was he going to prove the opposite?

Once the door shut behind Erica, Jack winnowed the space between himself and Marnie's desk. She looked beautiful today, her hair up in its perpetual clip, her button down white shirt pressed and neat, accented by a simple gold chain and form fitting black skirt.

"I'm sure Miss Stewart will be a great match for someone, but that someone isn't me."

"You just have to give her a chance," Marnie said. "Roberta…takes some time to get to know."

"Oh, I think she's a great person. We went out dancing, and even though I run four days a week, she outdanced me ten to one. And she's funny and enthusiastic, but not my type. What did you think we'd have in common?"

Marnie shrugged. Played innocent. "Sometimes opposites attract."

"And sometimes matchmakers don't play fair. I came to you as a legitimate client—"

"No, you didn't." She got to her feet, and her features shifted from detachment to fire. He could see it in the way her eyes flashed, her lips narrowed. "You might have said you wanted a match, but it didn't take a rocket scientist to figure out your true motive. You came here, hoping I'd think you were my perfect match."

"You have made it abundantly clear that you are not interested in me. That's why I think you should put your money where your mouth is."

"What is that supposed to mean?"

"You go out with me on a real date."

"Why would I do that?"

"Because despite your strong efforts in the opposite direction—" and thinking of the mismatch she'd sent him, he wondered if it wasn't just revenge but that deep down inside, Marnie didn't want to see him connect with another woman "—I think we'd be a great match."

She scoffed. "That's my job, not yours."

"And yet you have not found the perfect man for you." He leaned on her desk and met her green eyes. "Why is that?"

"I…I work a lot. I haven't had time to date."

"Is that all? Time? Because it's the end of the day. We could make time right now."

"Go out with you? Now?"

He grinned. "Why wait?"

"I am not interested in dating you. Ever."

"What was that walk to coffee? To me, it was a trial date."

She snorted. "There's no such thing."

He leaned in closer, until her eyes widened and that intoxicating perfume she wore teased at his senses. "We don't have to follow the rules, Marnie. We can make them up as we go along."

Her mouth opened, closed. She inhaled, and for a second, he thought she'd agree. A smile started to curve up his face, when he noticed the fire return to her green eyes. "I only have one rule. To stay far away from you." She got out of her seat, standing tall in her heels and matching him in height. "Don't think another Franklin will fall for your line of bull again, Jack. You don't get to ruin any more lives in this family. We're done believing in your lies and your charming little pep talks. So stay far away from this family."

And there it was. The past he couldn't run from, sweep under a rug, or ignore. Guilt rocketed through him. If Marnie knew how much of a hand Jack had had in her father's business closing, she'd never forgive him. He wanted her to see him as the man he was today, not the man he used to be, but getting from A to B meant confronting A and dealing with it, once and for all. "Yes, we did work with your father and his shop. And I swear, I had no idea you were his daughter until you told me your nickname. He always called you Daisy when he talked about you."

Hurt flickered in her eyes. "That business would still be operating today under Tom Franklin," Marnie said, the words biting, cold. "If someone didn't destroy it."

"Marnie, there's more to it than that. I—"

"I have no interest in anything you have to say to me, or any claims you intend to make about your 'business practices,'" Marnie said.

"My sisters and I watched our father fall apart after you stepped in and 'helped' him. You. Ruined. Him. And helped him…" she bit her lip, and tears welled in her eyes "…die too soon."

"Marnie, I didn't do that." But he had, hadn't he? He'd talked Tom into signing on the dotted line, knowing full well what the true intent of Knight would be. And when Tom needed a friend, Jack was gone. *You're a cold, uninvolved man, Jack.* "I mean, yes, I did invest in your father's business, and yes, I did counsel him, but—"

"Get out of my office," Marnie said, waving toward the door, her face tight with rage. "And don't ever come back. I don't want to hear any more of your lies and I sure as hell don't want to date you."

He opened his mouth, but she pointed at the door again. "For someone who's perfected the art of matching people, you of all people should understand that some matches go well and some don't. It takes two to make it work. And sometimes only one to destroy it."

"Yeah, you."

He took her anger, and let it wash over him. He understood now why she had bristled every time he talked about his job. Why she had been so warm at first, then so cold.

And why she had set him up on a date that
was bound not to work out. "Sometimes," he
said quietly, "our best intentions can go down
paths we never saw. I'm sorry, Marnie, about
your father and his business. If I could change
any of it, I would."

Then he left, and for the first time since
he'd taken over Knight Enterprises, he wished
for a do-over. Another chance to go back and
do a better job.

Her mother had canceled Tuesday night dinner at her house, Thursday night's card game,
and Saturday's brunch. And now, the morning after the confrontation with Jack in Marnie's office, Helen was trying to get out of
her regular Wednesday lunch with Marnie.
"Ma, I haven't seen you in two weeks," Marnie said.

"I'm sorry, honey. We've just been so busy,
going to the ball games and Bingo and..."

While her mother talked, Marnie debated
the best way to tell her mother the truth. She'd
spent a sleepless night debating the pros and
cons of telling Helen the truth about Jack, but
in the end, there was only one option.

Put it out there, and let the consequences
fall as they may.

Her family had never been one to tackle the

hard topics. They'd put a sunny face on everything, and done a good job avoiding. This, though, they couldn't avoid any longer—because Helen was falling hard for Dan.

Marnie hated being in this position. Standing in the middle of two evils, both of which would hurt the ones she loved. She'd thought that standing up to Jack and telling him how she felt would make her feel better. But instead of relieving the anger and betrayal in her gut, the confrontation had left her restless, replaying every word a hundred times in her head.

No. She'd done the right thing. Now she needed to do the right thing again—

And break her mother's heart.

"Dan and I have just been having so much fun," Helen said. "Oh, did I tell you, he's taking me to Maine for the weekend on Friday? He found this lovely little cottage in Kennebunkport. If we get lucky, maybe we'll even see the former president on the beach."

That meant they were getting serious. Damn. Marnie had hoped the relationship between Dan and her mother would fizzle, saving Marnie from having to tell her mother the truth about who Dan was.

She'd avoided the truth forever, but where had that gotten her? Nowhere good. And it had given her mother and Dan time to get closer, which only added more complications. Marnie took a deep breath. "Are you free for lunch today, Ma? I'll stop on the way to get us some Thai food, if you want."

"That sounds wonderful."

Marnie said goodbye, then powered through the rest of her morning appointments, keeping her head on her job instead of what was to come. Lord, how she dreaded this. Her mother had sounded so happy, with that little laugh in her voice that they had all missed over the last few years. And now Marnie was about to erase it all.

But as she got closer to Ma's house, and the scent of the Thai food overpowered the interior of the car, Marnie wanted to turn around. To delay again. It wasn't just about breaking her mother's heart anymore, but about facing the truth herself. All along, she kept hoping to be wrong about Jack. To find out that the guy with the amazing smile and earth-shattering kisses wasn't the evil vulture she'd painted him to be.

But he was, and the sooner she got that cemented in her mind, the better.

Even if the man had asked her out. Why would he do that? Was he truly interested? Or was she just another conquest?

Helen greeted her daughter with a big hug, and a thousand-miles-an-hour of chatter about Dan. "He's just the sweetest guy, Marnie. I can't believe no one has scooped him up. He holds the door for me, brings me flowers, even sings to me." She smiled, one of those soft, quiet smiles. "I really like him."

Guilt washed over Marnie. "Ma, we need to talk. Come on, let's go in the kitchen."

A few minutes later, both women had steaming plates of pad thai in front of them, but no one was eating. "Okay, shoot. What did you want to tell me?" Helen asked.

"Dan isn't…who you think he is," Marnie said, the words hurting her throat. "I should have caught this when I interviewed him, but to be honest, I never ask about kids or stepkids and—"

"What do you mean? I've met Dan's stepson. Remember? After the mixer. He seemed very nice—"

"He's Jack Knight."

Helen froze. "Jack Knight? That's impossible. Dan's last name is Simpson."

"He's his stepfather. Jack is the owner of Knight Enterprises. The same Knight Enterprises that destroyed Dad's business. If you keep dating Dan, you'll be seeing Jack, and the reminder of everything that happened to Dad. I'm so sorry to have to tell you this."

Silence filled the kitchen, and the food grew cold on their plates. Helen got to her feet, waving off her daughter. Ma crossed to the sink, placed her hands on either side of the porcelain basin and stood there a long time, her gaze going to the garden outside the window. The rain pelted soft knocks on the glass, then slid down in little shimmering rivers.

"Ma?" Marnie said. She walked over to her mother, and placed a hand on Helen's shoulder. "Ma, I'm so sorry. If I had known, I never would have fixed him up with you."

"Dan is the best thing to come along in my life in a really long time," Helen said, her voice thick with emotion that made Marnie's guilt factor rocket upward. "Besides you girls, of course." She closed her hand around Marnie's, and gave her daughter a smile. "I'm glad I met him."

"He is a great guy, I agree, and if he wasn't related to Jack—"

"It doesn't matter. Dan and I are happy. I don't care who his stepson is." Helen turned around and placed her back against the sink. Her features had shifted from heartbreak to determination. "We might work out, we might not, but we're going to give it a shot. Life's too short, honey, and I don't want to spend any more of my time alone."

This was a new Helen, Marnie realized. A woman who hadn't been defeated by the loss of her husband, and the prospect of starting her life over again, but rather energized by it. She also showed an amazing strength that had probably always been there, waiting for the right moment to appear. Dating Dan had only emphasized those qualities, not detracted.

Her mother was happy. Taking chances. Making changes. Jumping into the unknown. All things that Marnie had held back from doing, sticking to her organized planner and her rigid schedule.

Still, the urge to protect her mother, to head off any further hurt, rose in Marnie. If Dan and Helen stayed together, it would be nothing but a constant reminder, a cut against an old scab, again and again.

"I just don't want you to be hurt again," Marnie said.

"If there's one thing I've finally learned and accepted, it's that life comes with hurt. But if you're willing to risk that, you can find such amazing happiness, too."

On the wall, one of those kitschy cat shaped wall clocks clicked its tail back and forth with the passing seconds. Helen gestured toward the black plastic body, a stark contrast to the pin-neat, granite and white kitchen. "Do you remember when your father got me that?"

Marnie smiled. "It was a joke Christmas gift. We never thought you'd hang it up."

"It made me laugh. It makes me laugh every time I see it on the wall. That's why I hung it up, and why I kept it there, to remember to have fun sometimes."

"But isn't that the problem?" Marnie said, the words tumbling out of her mouth before she could stop them. "We're always having fun, never talking about the hard stuff. You can't just keep ignoring the facts, Ma."

Helen's soft hands cupped her daughter's face. "Oh, Marnie, Marnie. My serious one. Always trying so hard to keep the rest of us in line."

"I just like things to…stay ordered."

"And our lives when you were younger were far from ordered, weren't they? But we had fun, oh, how we had fun. Your father never had a serious day in his life, bless his heart." Helen released Marnie and the two women retook their seats at the table. "Let's talk about Knight and your father. And what really happened."

All these years, they'd avoided the subject. Whenever it came up, her mother would say she couldn't bear to hear it, and they'd switch to something inane or trivial. But this new Helen, the one who had been tempered by life on her own, had a determination in her eyes and voice that surprised Marnie.

"What do you know about what happened to Dad's company?" Ma said.

"Knight Enterprises invested in the company at first, made big promises about helping him get it profitable again, then deserted him and let him fail. When the business went south, Dad sold the rest of it to them for a fraction of what it was worth." Marnie bit back a curse. "And after that, Dad just…gave up."

"Part of that's true." Helen laid her hands on top of each other on the table. She smiled. "You and I are so much alike, Marnie. We both try to keep the peace, keep everyone happy. Sometimes, you need to rock the boat and tell the truth."

Marnie knew what was coming before her mother spoke. She'd probably always known, but like her mother, found it easier to pin her anger on Jack, rather than accept the facts.

"That business was on its last legs before your father went to Knight for help. Tom had lost his passion for it years earlier, and in the last couple of years before he sold, he'd spent too many days going fishing on the boat instead of working. A business is like a garden. You have to keep tending it, or it'll die on the vine. And your father stopped tending it." She shrugged. "I knew, but I figured we were okay. And I couldn't blame him. He'd worked so many hours when he first started out and he hated being the boss. The one to hire, fire, and demand. Plus, he missed you girls' soccer games and softball matches, and weekend family trips. I think he just wanted a break, to live his life before he got too old to do so and…"

Her voice trailed off and she bit her lip. "He just wanted time. With his family. With the people most important to him. There was a lot involved in that decision, Marnie. A lot you didn't know. Your father kept things to himself, hated to worry us. All he kept saying was that we'd be fine."

"Keeping the sunshine on his face," Marnie said, repeating her father's oft-used phrase.

"That was his philosophy, right or wrong. And so I couldn't blame him for wanting time to enjoy his days. He said he had put money aside for retirement, and that we would be all right once he got some investors on board. The company would turn around, freeing him up. We'd have time together, we'd travel, we'd treat you girls to all those extras we hadn't been able to afford before. I trusted him. I'd been married to the man nearly all my life, why wouldn't I?"

Marnie's jaw dropped as she put the pieces together. The financial struggle her mother had had over the last few years, her decision to go back to work. "There was no retirement?"

Helen shook her head, sad and slow. "Your father had spent it all, investing it in some fishing charter thing his cousin Rick talked him into, and kept telling him it would pay off. Just be patient, wait, and your dad did. Too long."

Her father, a trusting, optimistic man, who had trusted a family member when he should have had his guard up. In the end, it didn't surprise Marnie as much as reveal a different side of her father.

"Rick's business went belly up before it started, and the money was gone," Ma said. "Our entire future, gone in an instant. All our equity. All we had left was the house and the company, which by then wasn't worth much at all."

"So he sold a majority interest in the business to get the money back," Marnie finished.

Helen nodded. "Your father partnered with

Knight on the agreement that they would be there to provide counsel to help him get the printing company back on track. They talked about bringing in an expert to help the operation get leaner, more efficient, hire some sales people to generate more income. Tom thought maybe he could bring about a financial miracle before I realized what happened to the retirement money. But then Knight didn't help. As soon as the paperwork was signed, the help and advice stopped. And the company, like you said, faltered. When Knight came back and offered to buy the remaining assets, your father jumped at the offer, even though it meant taking a loss. By then, he knew there was no way to rebound, and I don't think he had the heart or desire to put in the hours that might take. He wanted to be here, not behind that desk. Still, your father felt so guilty, and I think that's what broke his heart in the end. I had no idea. If I had…" She shook her head, regrets clouding her eyes. "He didn't tell me any of this until shortly before he died. I wish he'd told me sooner. Oh, how I wish he had. Communication was never the strong suit in this family, and we had…so many other worries at the time. If he'd said something—"

"We would have stepped in and helped," Marnie said. "I would have gone to work for him or loaned him some money or…" She paused as the realization dawned in her mind. Her father, sacrificing for his family right to the end. "That's why he didn't tell us. He didn't want us to do any of that."

Helen's soft palm cupped her daughter's cheek. "He was so proud of you. You and your sisters. You found jobs that you love, that speak to your heart, and he would never have asked you to give that up."

"But, Ma, we could have helped him. Done something."

"And it would have made him miserable. He wanted you girls to be happy in your own lives, not make up for his mistakes. Not to worry about him all the time."

"He wasn't perfect," Marnie said, "but he sure was a great dad."

"Before he died, he made me promise not to let hurt or anger fill my heart. That's why he got me that clock the last Christmas before he died. So I'd remember to be happy, to tick along. To not let what happened ruin our future." Her mother got to her feet, took the clock off the wall and pressed it into Marnie's hands. "Take this, hang it on your wall, and remember to be happy, Marnie. To be silly. And most of all, to forgive."

The two of them hugged, two women who

had lost a man they loved, and who shared common regrets. Outside, the rain washed over the house, washed it clean, and inside the kitchen, the first steps of healing truly began.

CHAPTER SEVEN

"TELL ME AGAIN why I'm here, besides serving as a fifth wheel," Jack said. They were standing in the lobby of a seafood restaurant located on the wharf. In the distance, he could hear the clanging of the buoys. The scent of the ocean, salty, tangy, carried on the air, a perfect complement to the restaurant's menu.

Dan chuckled. "I thought it'd be nice for you to get to know Helen a little better. And it'll do you good to eat a meal that doesn't come out of a takeout box."

Jack grinned. "You have a point there."

"Parents are always right. Just remember that." Dan arched a brow, a smirk on his face. The door to the restaurant opened, and Helen strode in, shaking off the rain on her coat and her umbrella. Her gaze met Dan's and a smile sparked on her face.

A wave of jealousy washed over Jack. Not that he begrudged Dan a moment of happiness, but seeing Helen's happiness, and the echoing emotion in his stepfather, was a stark reminder to Jack of his solitary life.

"Did you tell him?" Helen asked.

"Nope." Dan grinned again.

That didn't sound good. Jack sent Dan an inquisitive look. "Tell me what?"

Then the door to the restaurant opened again and Marnie walked in. At first, she was too busy brushing off the rain to notice Jack. She shrugged out of her raincoat, handing it the coat check. Then she turned, and his groin tightened, his pulse skipped a beat and everything within him sprang to attention. Wow.

Marnie had on a clingy dark green dress that accented the blond in her hair, made her eyes seem bigger, more luminous. The dress skimmed her body, showed off her arms, her incredible legs, and dropped in an enticing V in the front.

She smiled when she saw Dan and her mother. Then her gaze swiveled to Jack and the smile disappeared. "Why are you here?"

"I was invited," he said.

"So was I." She tipped her head toward her mother. "Ma?"

Helen took Dan's arm and beamed at both Jack and Marnie. "Our table's ready. Let's go have dinner."

"Ma—"

"Come on, Marnie, Jack." Then Helen turned on her heel and headed into the dining room with Dan, leaving Jack and Marnie two choices—follow or walk out the door. Marnie looked ready to do the latter.

Jack tossed Marnie a grin. "It is their treat, and we do need to eat. Should we call a truce, for the sake of our parents?"

She hesitated, biting her lower lip, then nodded. "If they stay together we'll inevitably see each other once in a while. So we should at least get along tonight. For their sake."

"*If* they stay together? I thought you were the best matchmaker around," he teased. "Hmmm...maybe you were wrong about who you matched me with, too."

"You were a special case."

He laughed. "Now that I agree with."

She rolled her eyes, but a slight smile played on her lips. It was enough. It gave Jack hope that maybe, just maybe, all was not lost between them. She strode into the dining room, with him bringing up the rear.

They sat across from Dan and Helen, who had taken seats together on one side of the table. Another element of Dan and Helen's strategic plan, one Jack had to admit he admired. The waiter took their drink orders, left them with menus, then headed off to the bar.

"I'm glad you both decided to join us for dinner," Helen said.

Dan draped an arm over the back of Helen's chair and she shifted a bit closer to him. "We figured it would take a miracle for you two to see you're as matched as two peas in a pod—"

"Dad—"

Dan put up a hand. "Hear me out, Jack. Marnie's mother and I are pretty damned happy. And we want to see both of you just as happy as we are. Now, maybe you two won't work out. But you'll never know unless you give it a chance."

"You had to get your matchmaking abilities somewhere," Helen said to Marnie. "Dare I suggest your mother's side of the family?"

"They're pretty obvious," Marnie said to Jack.

He nodded, a smirk on his face. "Maybe they've got something here."

Dan and Helen watched the exchange with amusement. "Like I said, you should always listen to your parents," Dan said. "We've got age and experience on our side."

"Definitely the latter," Helen said with a flirtatious tone in her voice. She flushed, then laughed, and gave Dan a quick kiss on his cheek. He cupped her face, and kissed her again.

A craving for that—that happiness, that ease with another person, that loving attention—rose in Marnie fast and fierce. Her mother had taken this leap, taken the biggest risk of all and fallen for someone else. Could Marnie do the same?

If she didn't, she knew she'd never have what her mother had right now. And oh, how Marnie wanted it. More than she ever had before.

She slid a glance in Jack's direction. Every woman with a pulse had noticed him tonight. He had on a dark blue pinstripe suit, a pale blue shirt the color of the sky on a cold morning, and a green and silver striped tie that coordinated with her dress, as if they'd planned it that way. His dark hair seemed to beg for her to run her fingers through it, while the sharp lines of his jaw urged her to kiss him.

If he was any other man, and she was any other woman, she would want him. She would probably date him. Fall for him. But even the thought of that caused the familiar panic to rise inside her chest.

Falling for Jack would be like jumping off a cliff. It was the kind of heady rush that Marnie avoided at all costs. Not to mention, his mere presence was a constant reminder of what had happened to her father's business. She couldn't do that to herself, but most especially, to her mother or sisters.

"It's very sweet of you both to think we should date," Marnie said, "but this matchmaker doesn't see the logic in that. Jack and I are too...different."

Helen propped her chin on her hands. "Really? Different? How?"

Marnie shifted in her seat. "He's a businessman—"

"As are you."

"Well, I'm in a creative industry. He's... corporate."

"That just means you'll compliment each other's skills," Helen said.

Dan nodded. "Yup. Like ranch dressing and celery sticks."

Jack turned in his chair and put one arm on the back. "There are the things we have in common, too. Like music. Hobbies."

"Not movies," she pointed out, then felt silly for even mentioning it. Really? Her strongest argument was that Jack liked *The Terminator* and she liked tissue-ready chick flicks?

Jack nodded and feigned deep thought. "There is that. Well, that settles it, then."

She breathed a sigh of relief. Good. He wasn't going along with this charade any more than she was. "Great."

"We just won't watch movies," he said, then leaned toward her. His dark, woodsy cologne teased at her senses, urged her to come closer, to nuzzle his neck, taste his lips. "We'll find other ways to entertain ourselves."

Desire roared through Marnie's veins, an instant, insane tsunami of want, as if Jack had reached over, and flicked a switch to On. Across from them, Dan laughed, and Helen gave them a knowing smile.

"I, uh, forgot. I have a meeting with a client." Marnie grabbed her purse and jerked to her feet. The only thing she could do to avoid this disaster was to leave. "I'm so sorry. Maybe we could do this another time."

Helen apologized to the men, then headed out after her daughter.

After the women had left, Dan turned to his stepson and sighed. "Sorry, son. We thought that would work out better than it did."

"It's okay. She can't forgive me for what Knight did to her father's company. I understand that." Heck, he heard it every day, as he worked to make amends, to try to undo the damage that had been done both by his father and himself.

But there were days when the task felt like pushing back a wall of water. He'd think he was making progress, then unearth another stack of files or get another phone call from a lawyer and realize how far he had yet to go. In between, he was still running Knight Enterprises, and still working on investment deals and helping the businesses he funded. A Herculean task, even with a staff working along with him.

"She'll come around," Dan said. "Look at the people you have helped. You've gotten, what, twenty companies back up and running? Invested in another dozen business owners whose companies had been dissolved? You've got a gift there, son, and you're using it to do good. I'm proud of you."

The tender words warmed Jack. For so long, he had wanted to hear them from his biological father, but never had, even when he'd modeled Jack, Senior's ruthless behavior. Now, in doing the opposite of his biological dad, he had earned respect and pride from the man who had truly been his father, with or without a DNA connection. And that, in the end, meant far more to Jack. His biological father might never have appreciated or understood or supported him, but this man did all three, and that was the mark of a true parent. "Thanks, Dad. That means a lot."

Jack's gaze went to the restaurant exit. A part of him hoped like hell that Marnie had changed her mind, but no, Helen was making her way back to the table. Alone.

"And don't you worry about Marnie," Dan said as if he'd read his stepson's mind. "You'll figure out the best way to win her heart because that's your specialty. Solving the big problems and creating a happy ending for everyone."

Jack thought of the piles of folders on his credenza. The companies he had yet to find a way to restore or repair. He had a way to go, a hell of a long way to go, in creating those happy endings. And judging by the way Marnie had looked at him tonight, he had a way to go in the romantic happy ending department, too. It was time to admit defeat and quit chasing something that didn't want to be caught.

"If there's one thing I've learned in business, it's when to walk away from the deal," Jack said, getting to his feet, and nodding a goodbye to his stepfather and Helen. "And when it's time to move on to another candidate."

* * *

Every time Marnie managed to put him from her mind, Jack Knight popped back into her world, a few days after the dinner with her mother and Dan. Marnie had just locked the door on the office and turned toward home, exhausted and beyond ready for a vacation, or at the very least a weekend away from the calls and emails and meetings, when a familiar silver car pulled into the lot and Jack hopped out of the driver's seat. The trunk had been restored to new condition, all evidence of the wreck erased by some talented body shop.

As for Jack, despite everything, a little thrill ran through her at the sight of him, tall and lean, in a pair of well-worn jeans, a cotton button-down and a dark brown sports jacket. He looked…comfortable. Sexy. Like a man she could lean into and the world would drop away.

"Leaving so soon?" Jack asked.

"It's nearly noon," she said. "On a Sunday. Most people left the office two days ago."

"Just us workaholics still in the city, huh?" He reached into his jacket and withdrew a bright pink flyer. "And people planning on going to the Esplanade this afternoon to soak up some sun and hear the MAJE Jazz Showcase."

"What's that?"

"Top scoring high school bands from around the area get to perform at the Hatch Shell every year. And this year, my cousin is playing in one of the bands that won gold at the state competition, which automatically puts the band into the showcase." He took a couple steps closer to her. "How about it? Would you like to go and support the local arts?"

"Me? Why?"

"Because I think you would enjoy it. We both like jazz, and it's a gorgeous day, one we should take advantage of and spend a few hours enjoying. And—" he took a couple steps closer to her "—because I am officially asking you on a real date."

"Jack—"

"You know, after that dinner at the restaurant, I told myself to walk away. To quit pursuing someone who didn't want to be pursued. And I did. But you know what the problem with my theory is?"

She shook her head.

"I couldn't get you out of my mind. Maybe this is crazy. Maybe this is a really bad idea." He took another step closer, and his cologne teased her nostrils, and her pulse began to race. "But I want to see you again, Marnie."

That sent a zing through her heart, and a smile to her lips. "You are a stubborn man, Jack Knight." No one had ever pursued her this hard before, and if she was honest with herself, it was nice. Very nice.

A part of her wanted to run, to retreat to her familiar comfort of organization and schedules. But the other part of her, the part that had seen hundreds of happy couples walk down the aisle, wanted to take a chance. To trust in the very process she had built her business upon.

Still, she hesitated. This was Jack Knight, she reminded herself. Going out with him would only complicate an already complicated situation. Could hurt those she loved. "I should get home. It's my only day off—"

"And yet you were working."

"Well, my only *half* day off. I have laundry and other things to do."

"Wouldn't you rather grab a picnic lunch, spread a blanket on the grass at the Esplanade, and listen to some really amazing jazz?" he said, his voice like a siren calling to the part of her that craved a break, and the need for more in her life than her work.

"Enjoy the beautiful spring day, maybe have a glass of wine, and just…be?"

God, yes, she wanted that. She relaxed far too little, worked far too much. Work kept her from thinking, though, and also prevented her from dwelling on her regrets. Oh, how tempting—and wrong—Jack's offer sounded.

Yet at the same time, he was a man who personified the very thing she avoided—taking risks. Trusting in others. Letting down your guard.

"That walk we took the other day did me some good, too, and I'm not just talking about in a cardiovascular way," he said. "Sometimes, I need to be forced out the door or I work too many hours. This weekend, the geeks are doing some maintenance on the server. That means I can't work, not while the computers are down. And my cousin is really counting on me to be there. I couldn't bear to let him down." Jack grinned.

Why did he have to keep being so nice? So…normal?

She kept waiting to see the side of him that had swooped down and shredded her father's company, and she hadn't. Now here he was, admitting he was a workaholic like her, striking yet another sympathetic chord in her heart. One who, like her, also spent far too little time in the sun and with close family. She liked him, damn it, and really didn't want to.

She shook her head even as her resistance eroded a little more. "You don't need my company to do that."

"Ah, but a day like today is so much better when it's enjoyed with someone else, don't you agree?" He reached back and opened the rear passenger door of his car. "I already have a picnic and a blanket ready to go."

"So sure I was going to say yes?"

"Quite the opposite. I wanted to sweeten the pot because I knew you'd say no."

He could have read her mind. Five minutes ago, she'd written "take some time off" on a Post-It note and tacked it onto her desk, a reminder to stop working seven days, to have some time to regroup, recharge. Except for her thrice-weekly runs at the gym, there'd been far too much work and far too little relaxation in her days. In her business, a tired matchmaker wasn't as inspired when it came to putting matches together, hence the reminder for time off.

But a picnic with Jack? How could that be a good choice? He was the kind of man who tempted her to take the very risks she'd avoided all her life. The kind of man who came with heartbreak written all over his face.

The kind of man she tried so very hard to resist. And failed.

She peered past him, and into the car. A bright green reusable shopping bag sat on top of a folded red plaid blanket. The shopping bag bulged, and the amber neck of a bottle of white wine stuck out of the top, alongside a spray of daisies.

Daisies.

Not roses. Not carnations. Not orchids. Daisies, their bright white faces so friendly and inviting.

Jack caught where her gaze had gone, and he reached inside, tugged out the flowers, and presented them to her. "I thought an unconventional woman deserved an unconventional flower."

She took them, and despite everything, her defensive walls against Jack melted a little more. "Did my mother tell you these were my favorites?"

"Nope. You did. When you told me about your nickname."

He'd remembered that tidbit. It touched her more than she wanted to admit. She fingered one of the blooms, and a smile curved across her face. "Every time I see daisies, they bring back great memories."

"Tell me," Jack said, his voice quiet and soft.

She inhaled the light scent of the delicate flowers. "When I was a little girl, there was a field near my house where daisies grew wild. Every spring, I couldn't wait for them to bloom. Once they did, I'd go and gather as many as I could carry and bring them to my mother. She'd arrange them in this big green vase of my grandmother's, set it in the center of the dining room table, and every night over dinner, we'd give one of the daisies a name. She said they have so much personality, they deserve to have their own names."

Jack leaned forward, and ran a finger along the delicate petals of one of the flowers. "And what's this one's name?"

She shook her head. "Jack, I'm too old for that."

"We both are. But it's fun to be young once in a while, don't you think? Believe me, I wish I'd taken more time to be a kid when I had the chance."

She heard something in his voice, something sad, regretful. She wondered again about the Jack Knight she thought she knew—who had ruined her father's company—and the Jack Knight she had met—a man with a definite soft spot. Which was the real Jack?

Curiosity nudged her closer to him. "Why didn't you have more kid time?"

"Long, involved, unhappy story. I'll tell it to you if I'm ever on Oprah." He shook off the moment of somberness, then plucked one of the daisies from their paper wrapper. "I'm calling this one Fred."

She shook her head, stepping away. "Jack—"

He plucked a second flower from the arrangement and held it out to her. "Let go of all those rules and regulations you live by, Marnie."

"How do you know I do that?"

"Because we're two peas in a pod, as my stepfather would say. I have kept such a tight leash on everything in my life, trying to make up for the past, trying not to be the man my father was. And where has it gotten me? Working too many hours, eating most of my meals on the run, and living the same lonely work-centered life he lived."

"I'm not..." She shook her head, unable to complete the sentence.

Jack touched her cheek, his blue eyes soft, understanding. "I see a woman who works too much and plays too little. As if she's afraid to go after the very thing she helps her clients find."

It was as if he'd pulled open a curtain in Marnie's brain. How many times had she thought the same thing? Heard those same words from her sisters, her mom? She glanced at the daisies and saw her younger self in those happy white circles. When had she gotten away from that carefree person? When had she become this woman too scared to take a chance on love?

She reached out and took the flower, caught in the game, in Jack's infectious smile, in the echoing need to forget her adult problems for just a little while. "That makes this one Ethel."

"Sounds perfect, Marnie." He closed his hand over hers, capturing the flowers and making her heart stutter at the same time. "Let's put the rest in water, and take Fred and Ethel to the concert. They'll be our table decoration, even if our table is a blanket on the ground."

It was a beautiful day, warm, sunny, the kind of day that begged to be enjoyed. She thought of the things she had planned to do at home—laundry, vacuuming, dusting. Catching up with her life, essentially, after a long week of work. Not an ounce of that appealed to her right now, but the thought of spending time outside, with Fred and Ethel and Jack, did.

He's the enemy. The one who destroyed your father. Every time you see him, it will remind you of that history.

But was that really what had her hesitating? Or was it what Jack had said, that she was afraid to go after the very things she helped her clients find?

"Come on, Marnie. Enjoy the day. Consider this your civic duty, supporting local high schools," he said, "albeit, civic duty accompanied by a glass of chardonnay."

"Oh, that sounds really good," she said, because it did, and because her resistance had been depleted when he'd named the daisy. She bit her lip, then shoved the doubts to the back of her mind. She wanted this afternoon, this moment. She pressed the Ethel daisy into his hand. "Hold these and I'll be back in two minutes. I have a vase in my office."

She ran back into the building, and up the stairs. In a few minutes, she had the daisies in some water, and had placed the vase by her desk, so she'd see them first thing every day. She was about to leave, then put a hand to her hair, and ducked into the restroom instead. She washed up, then placed her hands on either side of the sink and stared up at her reflection. Excitement and anticipation showed in her eyes, pinked in her cheeks.

Excitement and anticipation because she was going out with Jack Knight.

"What the hell are you doing?" she said to her image. "You can't get involved with him. He's all wrong for you, remember?"

Her image didn't reply. Nor did her brain rush forward with any reasons why Jack was wrong, exactly. For some reason, she couldn't come up with a single objection.

Even as she told herself she didn't care what Jack Knight thought about her appearance, she gave her hair a quick brush, then refastened the barrette holding the chestnut waves off her face. A quick swipe of blush, a little lipstick, then a quick exchange of heels for a pair of flats she kept under her desk. She grabbed a cardigan from the hook by the door, then, at the last second, she unclipped the barrette and dropped it on the counter. Her hair tumbled to her shoulders.

Unfettered, untamed.

His words came back to her, tempting, sexy, urging her to take a chance, to give him a chance. To just…be.

She stopped when she saw him standing by the silver car, holding Fred and Ethel. The last of her reservations melted away.

One day, one concert, wouldn't change anything. She'd have a good time, and be home before dark. Right?

CHAPTER EIGHT

WRONG.

The thick plaid blanket had seemed big when Marnie and Jack spread it on the grassy field that lay in front of the famous Hatch Shell. Hundreds of other families were camped out around them, armed with video cameras to capture their child's performance. The first band sat on the stage under the giant white dome, tuning their instruments while the A/V staff ran back and forth, doing last minute prep.

Marnie took a seat beside Jack and arranged her skirt over her knees and legs. She'd kicked off her shoes, left her cell phone in the car. Sitting in the sun, barefoot, with nowhere to go but right here, right now, had a decadent quality. For a while, the nagging thought that she should be doing something tensed in her shoulders. But as the sun washed its gentle warmth over her, Marnie began to relax, one degree at a time.

Well, relax as much as she could sitting next to Jack. He was so close that she caught the spicy dark notes of his cologne with every inhale. Her hand splayed on the blanket, inches from his. He had strong hands, the kind that looked like they could take care of her in one instant, and send her soaring to new heights in the bedroom in the next.

"Hungry?" Jack asked.

"Oh, yeah," she said, then colored when she realized that her hunger was for him, not food. Damn. What was with this man? Why did he draw her in so easily? She had already made that mistake with someone else. She straightened, putting a few centimeters of distance between them. "Uh, did you say you brought sandwiches?"

"Yep. Ham and cheese good with you?"

"Yes, thank you." She took one of the paper wrapped sandwiches from him and opened it. A thick pile of honey ham, topped with a generous portion of provolone cheese, as well as deep green Boston lettuce and juicy red tomato slices peeked out from between two rustic slices of sourdough bread. She took a bite, and goodness invaded her palate. "Oh, my. This is amazing. What's on this?"

"Hector's own jalapeno/cilantro mayonnaise. He owns the deli, and there are some meals that I think could get him nominated for sainthood."

Marnie took another bite. "Oh, this, definitely."

Jack chuckled, then uncorked the wine and poured it into two plastic cups, handing her one of them. "Plastic isn't exactly high brow, but I'm not exactly a fancy glass kind of guy."

"Really? You strike me as, well, as the opposite. Or at least, you have the other times I've run into you."

"It's those damned suits. They make me look all boring and dull."

She laughed. "Those are *not* the adjectives I'd use to describe you."

"Oh, really?" He arched a brow. "And how would you describe me?"

She thought a minute. "Mysterious. Guarded. An enigma." That much was true. Every time she thought she had Jack figured out, he threw her a curveball.

"Ah, the elusive guy in the shadows who never opens his heart, is that it?" He raised his cup toward hers. "To guarded hearts."

"You talking about me?"

He laughed. "You, Marnie, have the most guarded heart I've ever seen."

"Touché." She gave him a nod of concession, then a smile. "To guarded hearts. And mysterious enigmas." They touched cups, then drank. Two kindred souls, in relationships at least.

"I don't think I ever thanked you for introducing my stepfather to your mom."

"I should be thanking you for encouraging him to go to the mixer. He really seems perfect for her." Marnie didn't think she'd ever seen her mother this happy, yet at the same time, the caution flags stayed in her head. Dan came with Jack—and could her mother handle that? "He's a nice guy."

Jack nodded. "He was a heck of a stepdad, too. He married my mom when I was eight, and was one of those hands-on dads. The kind that plays catch in the yard and teaches you how to build a fire with a flint and some kindling. But the years before Dan came along were…rough."

"I'm sorry." And she was. No child should have a difficult childhood. Hers hadn't been perfect, but it hadn't been rough, either.

Jack shrugged like it was no big deal, but she got the sense it did bother him. "My father was never there. Not then, not later."

"Did he work a lot?"

Jack snorted. "My father made work a

world-class sport. Heck, I saw the Tooth Fairy more than my own dad. And when he was home, his attention span lasted about five minutes before he was off on another call or writing another memo. Eventually, my mother had enough of being, essentially, a single mom, and divorced him."

"Yet you followed your father into the family business, from the day you graduated Suffolk." When he arched a brow in question, she gave Jack a little smile. "I Googled you."

"So you *are* interested in me?"

"Cautious. You never know who you're riding home with."

Jack laughed and tipped his cup of wine toward her. "True."

She picked off another tiny bite of ham. "So if you and your father had such a bad relationship, why did you go to work for him?"

Jack leaned an arm over his knee. His gaze went to somewhere in the distance, far from the performance at the Hatch Shell, far from her. "Even though I loved Dan, I never got past that need for a father's love and attention. Pretty pathetic, huh?"

"No, not at all." Another thread of connection knitted between them. Her father had worked countless hours as he built his business. She could relate to that craving for a relationship, a connection. She too had missed out on the camping trips and ball games with her father.

Her sympathy for Jack doubled. In his eyes, she could still see that hurting, hopeful boy, and it broke her heart.

Across from them, a mother and father took turns playing peek-a-boo with a baby in a stroller. The baby's laugh carried on the air, infectious, bubbly. That was what a family looked like, she thought, the kind of family Jack should have had his entire childhood, and it added a sad punctuation to their conversation.

Jack sighed. "Anyway, I guess I hoped that if I worked for him, we'd finally have that relationship I had missed out on."

She had wondered the same thing. If she had worked for her father, would she have had a closer relationship with him? Been able to help his business? Help him? "And did you get that relationship?"

"Oh, I saw him at work. When I was getting called into his office for another 'stupid' mistake. We didn't have long, father-son talks or take lunch together or even work on projects together. Everything I learned came from the other guys who worked for my father. Many of those men still work for me today, and they're almost like a second family."

"Why didn't you leave the company?" she asked.

"I did. Took a job at another business brokerage firm, and barely had time to put my pens in the drawer of my desk before I got a call telling me my father had had a heart attack. Two days later, I was in charge. After he died, I stepped into his shoes. Well, his office." A wry, sad grin crossed his face. "I made my own shoes."

She picked at an errant thread on the blanket, hating that they had this in common, too. Of all the people in Boston, why did she have to relate so closely to Jack, and his loss?

Jack's blue eyes met hers and his features softened. "I'm sorry, Marnie. I know your father died too, a few years ago. He was a heck of a nice guy, and I'm sure that loss was hard on you."

She heard true sympathy in Jack's voice and it made tears spring to her eyes. He covered her hand with his. An easy, comfortable touch. One that eased the loss in her heart, yet at the same time it drove that pain home.

Damn him. Damn Jack for making her care. Damn Jack for caring about her. And damn Jack for being the reason behind all of this.

But he said he had quit, walked away. Then returned to do things his own way. Did that mean he had changed? That other businesses weren't being hurt like her father's? That her biggest argument against him was fizzling?

"I guess we never outgrow the need for a parent, huh?" he said.

She heard the echoes of her own loss in his voice, and it muddled the issues. She wanted to hate him—

And instead commiserated with Jack, this complex, layered man who had gone through so many of the same hurts as she had.

"Jack! Jack!" A blonde waved at them from a few feet away. A dark-haired man stood beside her, loaded down with a diaper bag, two lawn chairs and a small cooler.

Jack grinned, then got to his feet and put a hand out to Marnie. "Come on, let me introduce you to my cousin Ashley. She's the mom of the talented musician we're here to see."

"Oh, I don't think I should..." she said.

"I promise, they won't bite," he said, then took her hand and hauled her to her feet. So fast, she collided with his chest. He grinned and held her gaze for one long, hot moment. "Though I can't promise I won't."

A delicious thrill raced through her veins. Marnie released Jack's hand and bent down to straighten her skirt, and break that hypnotic connection. "Uh, maybe we should hurry because the concert's about to start." Anything to get some distance, some breathing room.

But then Jack took her hand again to help her as they picked their way among the lawn chairs and blankets and people on the lawn. He shifted his touch to the small of Marnie's back when they reached his cousin. "Hey, Ashley," he said. "This Marnie. Marnie, this is my cousin Ashley and her husband Joe."

"Nice to meet you," Ashley said, shaking hands with Marnie. Her husband echoed the sentiment, then nodded toward a little girl running across the back lawn.

"I'll be back. Have to go catch a runaway toddler." Joe lowered the things in his arms to the ground, then headed off at a light jog. Ashley unfolded the lawn chairs and placed them on either side of the cooler and diaper bag.

"I hear you have a talented son," Marnie said.

"Jack likes to brag about him, but yeah." Ashley's face lit with a mother's pride. "We think he's pretty amazing. And thank you, Jack, for making the time to be here."

"You know I'd never miss something like this."

"He'll be thrilled you came." Ashley gave Jack's hand a squeeze. "You're a great godfather." Then she turned to Marnie and grinned. "If the way he treats his godchildren is any indication, this one's going to be a great dad. Just in case you were wondering."

Marnie's face heated. "Oh, he and I, we're not…together."

"Pity," Ashley said. "Because I'd love to spoil Jack's kids rotten. Maybe even buy them a drum set for Christmas, like he did for our kids."

Jack chuckled. "Hey, that drum set led to him being on that stage."

"True. But next time, I'm letting my kids sleep over at your house when they need to practice." Ashley laughed.

The warmth and love between the cousins mirrored the camaraderie Marnie had with her own family, and again showed another dimension to Jack Knight. A man who loved and was loved, not the man she'd vilified for years. Her resistance lowered even more.

The three of them talked for a little while longer, then Jack took Marnie's hand. "They're about to start," he said. "We better get back to our spot."

Joe returned with a tow-headed toddler in his arms. "She says she wants Uncle Jack."

The girl scrambled out of her father's arms and up into Jack's. "Uncle Jack, are you comin' to our house later? Mamma made cake."

"Cake, huh?" Jack beeped the girl's nose. "Is it as sweet as you?"

She nodded. "Uh-huh. It's chocolate. With bubber dream."

"Buttercream," Ashley corrected, moving to take her daughter and hand her a juice box. "Bad for the hips and the heart, but oh, so good."

Jack chuckled. "Sure. I'll stop by tonight. And I might just have a surprise if you're good."

The little girl straightened and nodded, as solemn as a judge. "Imma good girl."

"Of course you are," he said quietly. Then he ruffled her hair. "Okay, good girl, watch your brother. I'll see you later."

Marnie and Jack walked back over to their blanket, and took their seats again. "Your family was really nice," she said. And they were. She had liked them, a lot.

"Thanks. I never had any brothers or sisters, so my cousins are like my siblings. Most of them still live in the area, and I see them pretty often. If I ever have a kid, I'm calling Ashley and Joe for advice." He sent a fond look in their direction.

"She's adorable."

"She's four. Smart as a whip, and a bottle full of sass, according to her mother, but yes, adorable."

Jack's face showed the soft spot in his heart for his cousin's children. For his family. It drew her in, even as she tried to keep distance between them. Marnie kept her hands away from his under the guise of eating, but really, it was because it had become far too easy and natural to connect with Jack. To let down that wall, to let herself...be.

To fall for him.

"How's your sandwich?" Jack asked.

She jerked her attention back to him. "Oh, uh, perfect." And it was. Low-key, easy, simple. Marnie found herself giving in to the relaxing day, the bucolic setting, the contentment of good food. Just the two of them— okay and three hundred other adults and kids—enjoying a lunch outdoors. The first band began to play, and both Jack and Marnie sat back and listened, while they ate their sandwiches and sipped the wine. As the first song edged into the second, then the third, she started to truly enjoy herself. Maybe it was the sunshine. The food in her belly. The wine. But by the time the second band came on the stage, Marnie was leaning on her elbows, with Jack so close, she could feel his shoulder brush hers every once in a while. She didn't move away. She wasn't sure she could if she wanted to.

"This is my cousin's school coming on stage now," he said, turning to speak to her.

She pivoted at the same time, which brought their mouths within kissing distance. Heat ignited in the space between them, and her gaze dropped to his mouth. Anticipation pooled in her gut.

The band launched into an up-tempo jazz selection. Marnie jerked back, clasped her hands in her lap and concentrated on the music. Not on almost kissing Jack.

The quartet played plucky notes accented by a soft touch on the drums, and occasional taps of the high hat. It was a simple group, with drums, a bass, a sax, and a piano. The players would look up from time to time, grin at one another, and then play through a complex section of the music. The last few notes tapered off and applause began to swell.

"They were terrific," Marnie said over the sound of their clapping hands. "Which one is your cousin?"

"The pianist." Pride beamed in Jack's features. "He's a great kid. Really talented. He's applied at Berklee, and he has a great chance of getting in."

"I can see why." She sat back as the band exited the stage, and made room for the next one. "I wish I had even an ounce of their musical ability. I couldn't carry a tune if you taped one to my mouth."

He chuckled. "Oh, I don't know about that. You have such a pretty voice, I bet you can sing."

She put up her hands to ward off the possibility, but the compliment warmed her. "My sister Kat, who became a graphic designer, got all the creative genes in the family."

"I think matchmaking is pretty creative, don't you?"

"True." She leaned her head on her shoulder and studied him. "What about you? Any creativity in those genes?"

He grinned. "Depends on what kind of creativity you're looking for."

Her face heated—God, what was it with this man, turning her face red all the time— as she realized the double entendre. "I meant the ones in your DNA, not the bedroom kind."

"I know." He leaned over and ran a finger

over her cheek. Her pulse skittered. "I just like to see you blush."

Oh, my. This man hit all the right buttons, and as much as part of her cursed him for doing it, another part liked it. Very much. She'd dated men, but none had knocked her so off-kilter, leaving her breathless, distracted, *wanting*.

When he looked at her, she felt beautiful. When he smiled like that, she felt sexy. And when his voice lowered like that, it set off a chain reaction of desire deep, deep inside her body.

She jerked around to a sitting position, drawing her knees up to her chest. "Oh, look, the next band is on stage."

Was she that desperate for a man in her life that she'd fall for the one man who had helped ruin her father?

Or that scared of falling for someone who turned her world so inside-out? Being with Jack was like racing down a track on the back of a runaway car. And that was the one thing that made Marnie want to bolt.

A few minutes later, the concert was over, and the attendees began gathering up blankets and lawn chairs, and start trekking back across the grassy lawn to their cars. The skies had begun to darken, and in the distance,

Marnie heard the low rumble of thunder. "We better hurry," she said, "before we get caught in the storm."

But even as she bundled up the blanket and helped gather the remnants of their lunch, Marnie had a feeling she'd already gotten caught by a storm. One made by Jack Knight.

They didn't move fast enough.

A second later, the thick gray clouds broke open with an angry burst of wind and water, dropping rain in fast sheets over the Esplanade and the hundreds of people scrambling for their cars. Jack grabbed Marnie's hand. "Come on, let's go!"

They charged across the grass, weaving through the other people, as the rain fell. Finally, they reached the car, and collapsed against it in a tangle of arms, legs and picnic supplies. "Wait!" she said. "I dropped the blanket."

"Don't worry about it. I'll get another." He fumbled in his pocket for the keys, then unlocked Marnie's door. A second later, they were both safe inside the dry car. He took the picnic supplies from her and tossed everything onto the back seat. The leather seats would probably end up ruined, but right now, Jack didn't care.

Even with the rain, the day had been one of the best he could remember having. All his life, he'd sucked at personal relationships, putting the people in his life on the sidelines while he concentrated on work. He'd worried that he'd be his father's son with women, too, that he would leave a trail of broken hearts to match the trail of broken companies.

No more.

For the first time in forever, Jack wanted to try harder, to be better, for himself and with others. He didn't want to just give back to companies, or connect with business owners, or repay those his father had hurt, he wanted to do the same turnaround with himself. He used to think that if he could just make amends for his father's choices, he would be complete. But now he wanted more.

He wanted everything his father had never appreciated. The white picket fence, the two kids, the dog in the yard. The woman who greeted him with a smile at the end of the day.

Marnie had brought that out in him. She was a challenge, a puzzle, one he wanted to solve. He had a feeling this complex, beautiful woman would keep him on his toes for a really, really long time. And oh, how he craved that.

Craved *her*.

Marnie shook her head, then swiped off the worst of the rain. Even soaking wet, she looked amazing. Water had darkened her lashes, plastered her hair to her head, and soaked the pale yellow shirt she wore, until it outlined every delicious inch of her torso. She leaned down and plucked at her skirt. "God, I'm soaked. Maybe we should hit a Laundromat and throw ourselves into a dryer." She glanced up, and caught him looking at her. "What?"

Desire pulsed in his veins, pounded in his heart. Coupled with the darkened interior of the car, the intimacy of the black leather seats, and the rain drumming a steady beat on the roof, it seemed as if they were the only two people in the world.

"You're soaking wet," he said.

She laughed. "I know. I said that."

"And still one of the most beautiful women I have ever seen in my life." That caused another blush to fill her cheeks. Damn, he liked that about her. A touch of vulnerable, mixed in with the strong. He reached out, brushed a lock of hair off her cheek. It left a little glistening trail of water, and before he could think better of it, he leaned across the console and kissed that line, kissed all the way down her cheek, until he moved a few millimeters to the left and caught her lips with his.

"We...shouldn't do this," Marnie whispered against his mouth.

"Okay," he said, then kissed her again. She tasted of wine and vanilla and all he wanted right now was more, more, and even more of her. He slid one hand up, along the smooth side of her blouse, then around the curve of her breast. The thin, wet fabric offered almost no barrier against the lace edges of her bra, the stiff peak of her nipple.

When his fingers danced over it, Marnie gasped and arched forward. *"Jack."*

He'd heard his name a million times in his life. Never had that single syllable sounded so sweet. He opened his mouth against hers, and with a groan, deepened the kiss, shifting to capture more of her breast, more of her, more of everything.

Her hands came up around his back, clutching at him, nearly dragging him over the console. Her kiss turned wild, ferocious, and that sent him into a dizzying tailspin of want, need. The rain pounded harder, thunder booming above them, lightning crackling in the sky, as the storm between them became a wild ride of hands and tongues.

His fingers went to the buttons on her

blouse, then stilled when he heard a horn honk, the rev of an engine. Damn. They were still in the parking lot, surrounded by other people. "We should take this somewhere more private," he said. His breath heaved in and out of his chest.

She drew back, her lips red and swollen, her breath also coming in little fast gasps. Her green eyes met his, held, then her breathing slowed. She shook her head. "How do you do that?"

"Do what?"

"Get me to forget all the very good reasons I have for not letting you get close. We can't do this, Jack. Not now, not ever. It's…wrong."

"It sure felt right. And explosive. And crazy, and a hundred other things."

She sighed. "That's the problem."

The rain began to slow, one of those fast-moving storms that passed almost as fast as it started. The parking lot cleared out, families going home to dinners in the oven, homework at the kitchen table. He put his hand on the ignition but didn't turn the key. "Then why did you kiss me?"

She bit her lip. "Because, for a little while, I forgot. And just…was."

"Forgot what?"

But Marnie just shook her head and asked

him to drive her home. He started the car, pulled out of the lot, and headed southwest. But as he watched the Hatch Shell get smaller and smaller in his rearview mirror, Jack had a feeling he'd lost more than just a blanket today.

CHAPTER NINE

JACK HAD RUINED HER.

Ever since the walk to the neighborhood coffee shop and the jazz concert on the lawn, she'd found her office too confining. She'd spent more time outside in the last few days than she had all year, and as the morning wore on and the sun made its journey across the sky, Marnie got more and more antsy. She paced. She hummed. She fiddled. In short, she didn't do a damned thing productive.

Erica got to her feet, and grabbed Marnie's car keys. "Okay, that's it. I'm tired of you bouncing in place. Let's get out of here and go grab something to eat. Preferably something chocolate and really, really bad for us."

"But I've got all this work—"

"To do tomorrow. It can wait, especially considering you haven't done much of it so far today." Erica arched a brow, then grinned.

"Why are you smiling about that?" Marnie ran a hand through her hair and let out a sigh. "All it does is put me further behind. I have this long list of clients waiting for me to find them a match. All these events to organize and—"

"Step out of your comfort zone, Marn, and blow off work today. There are days when you are wound tighter than a ball of yarn, which is pretty much par for the course with you, oh, control freak sister. But these last couple weeks..." Erica shrugged.

"What?"

"These last couple weeks, you've been smiling and laughing, and..." Erica put a hand on her sister's and met Marnie's gaze. "Well, it's been nice."

Marnie refused to give Jack Knight any credit for the change in her attitude. If anything, he'd made things worse, not better. Except...

The walk through the quaint neighborhood and the jazz concert at the Hatch Shell had been fun. Even running in the rain had left her breathless, laughing. It had all been a huge step out of her comfort zone and oddly, she'd enjoyed it. What had he said to her the other day?

You should let your hair down more often. Right or wrong, Jack Knight had gotten her to do exactly that in the last couple weeks. She'd slept better at night, worked better during the day, and the tension had eased in her shoulders. Maybe Jack had a point. She hated that he did, but he did.

"So...who is he?" Erica asked.

"Who's who?"

"The man who has you all atwitter. You're like a girl in junior high." Erica pointed at her sister. "There, that. You're blushing. You *never* blush."

Marnie sighed. "He's Jack Knight. The owner of Knight Enterprises."

A light dawned in Erica's eyes and she let out a little gasp. "Jack *Knight?* Of Knight Enterprises infamy? The same one that invested in Dad's business years ago?"

Marnie nodded, then explained how she'd met Jack, and what had transpired in the weeks since, leaving off the bit about kissing him.

"Okay, but that still doesn't explain why you blush every time you talk about him," Erica said.

Marnie sighed. "He kissed me."

"He...*what?* He *kissed* you? Really? Oh, my God," she said, her voice reaching Roberta-worthy decibels. "Did you kiss him back?"

"Yes, but only because he took me by surprise. And it won't happen again, I can tell you that. I reacted out of…instinct."

Yeah, right. She'd kissed him because of a reflex, not desire. *Liar.*

Erica typed something into the laptop computer beside her, waited a second, then turned the screen toward Marnie. "Oh, I'm sure it was instinct to kiss *that* hunk of yummy. Any woman with a pulse's instinct."

Marnie looked at Jack's image, one of those professional photos done for the corporate website. He had a serious, no-nonsense look on his face, along with a navy power suit and a dark crimson tie. The Jack Knight in the photo was powerful, commanding. None of the teasing looks or charming grins he'd given her. And yet, her body reacted the same, with that instant zing of desire. Curse the man for being so damned good looking. "Okay, so he's cute."

"So, what are you going to do about him? Now that you're done kissing him?"

"I don't know. I want to hate him, and I do, I really do, but…"

"A part of you is starting to like him?"

Marnie shook her head. "No, not at all."

Erica just laughed. "You do realize that when you shook your head, you then gave a slight nod? If this were an interrogation, it would totally negate your strong protests to the contrary."

"The trouble is, he seems nice. Not at all the evil corporate raider I pictured." Marnie thought of the gym he'd invested in, the coffee shop owner who loved him and raved about him, the family he adored. Twice, Jack had told her he wasn't as bad as she thought he was, yet he represented everything that had hurt her mother, her family. She shook her head. "Either way, he's all wrong for me."

"Then you better stop kissing him," Erica said with a grin. "Or next you'll end up in bed with the enemy."

Later that morning, Marnie and Erica closed up the office and headed across town to the Second Chance shelter and work counseling center. The two of them had been volunteering there for years, a good cause that helped struggling people find work.

Even though her workload had quadrupled because of the distracting thoughts about Jack, Marnie welcomed the break from the office. She'd get away from her sister's prying eyes, the ringing of the telephone, and the daisies that still sat on her desk. All reminders of Jack, and how close she kept coming to falling for Mr. Wrong.

She wanted a steady, dependable man. One who wanted a quiet, predictable life. None of this heady, crazy, spontaneity that came with Jack. He was a risk, a giant one. Hadn't she already seen how bad a risk like that could ruin someone? She had no desire to do the same.

A silver sports car glided to a stop in the lane beside her, and she flicked a quick glance at the driver. Darn it. Every silver car she saw reminded her of Jack Knight. Heck, even though she knew better, he'd been on her mind the better part of the day and nearly all night. Her hormones hadn't gotten the memo from her brain that he was No Good for Her. Maybe she just needed more time.

And less silver sports cars on the Boston roads. Because despite her better judgment, she couldn't stop from looking in the driver's side window, a part of her hoping to see a dark-haired, blue-eyed man.

Erica had dropped the subject of Jack, thank goodness, and talked on the drive about her plans for the weekend. They drove across town, then parked outside a converted two-family home that had been turned into a combination shelter and education center for people down on their luck. Second Chance had been started a few years ago by a group of local businesspeople who wanted to give back to the community, and had been successful with a large percentage of the people it served. Marnie had supported the organization from day one with monetary donations, a couple of career workshops, and clothing donations. She'd used her network to help several of the residents find jobs, and sent numerous leads to the director. It was a good cause, and one she wished every business in Boston would get behind.

She and Erica grabbed two big bags of clothes Marnie had to donate, and headed inside. Linda, the director, came out of her office to help. Linda was a tall, thin, energetic woman who always had a ready smile for everyone she met. Her ash blond hair was pulled back in a ponytail, which gave her blue floral dress and practical white sneakers a fun touch. "Oh, bless you, Marnie. The ladies here will be so glad to see all this."

"No problem. It's the least I can do. Where do you want everything?"

Linda directed her to a room down the hall that had been converted into a giant closet. "Marnie, if you could just set the items up on the hangers, then they'll be ready for after our event. Oh, and Erica, since you're here, too, can I borrow you to help with lunch service for a little bit? We're short-handed today. We had more people than I expected show up to hear our speaker today."

"Sure. I'd be glad to." Erica headed into the kitchen, while Marnie hung up the clothes and set up the shoes she'd brought. It was good, easy, mindless work that kept her from dwelling on impossible situations.

Ten minutes later, Marnie had finished. The antsy feeling had yet to go away, so she started straightening and pacing again. From down the hall, she heard a strong round of applause and the murmur of voices.

The speaker Linda had mentioned. Whoever it was, he or she was enjoying an enthusiastic response from the attendees. Linda often brought in motivational speakers, who left their listeners with a renewed enthusiasm. Might be worth popping in for a minute and listening, Marnie decided. It was better than rehanging shirts and straightening skirts, or wearing a path from the hall to the window.

She crossed into a large room that used to be a dining room, but had been opened up and turned into a mini auditorium, now utilized for speakers, AA meetings, and other events. Rows and rows of folding chairs filled the space, and not a one was vacant. At the podium stood a tall, thin man Marnie recognized as Harvey, a frequent visitor to Second Chance. He had started out homeless, addicted to drugs, and had turned his life around in recent years, becoming a volunteer and counselor at the very place that helped him. She liked Harvey, especially his positive attitude and his belief in perseverance.

"I can't thank this man enough for what he did," Harvey was saying. "He gave me a job when no one else would, he told me he believed in me when no one else did, and he became a friend when no one else was around. I'm proud as heck to introduce my mentor and good friend, Jack Knight, to all of you."

Marnie bit back a gasp. Jack? Here? Being touted as the best thing to come along since sliced bread? By Harvey of all people?

She ducked to the right to hide behind a thick green potted plant, just as Jack strode into the room, wearing jeans and a pale green button-down shirt that made his eyes seem even bluer. Her body reacted with a rush of heat, and her mind replayed that kiss in the car. God, she wanted him, even now, even when she shouldn't.

He stepped up to the podium, thanking Harvey for his warm introduction. The crowd greeted Jack with renewed enthusiasm, and several shouted his name and a welcome back. After the applause died down, Jack began to speak.

She expected one of those speeches about corporate responsibility. Or putting your best foot forward in a job interview. But instead, Jack delivered a commentary that had the audience riveted, and Marnie rooted to the spot.

"You will always have people who will tell you that your dreams aren't worth having," Jack said. "People who think their way is the only way, and that anyone who takes another path is wrong. They'll try to cut you down, or talk you out of your plans. Work to convince you that they have the right answers, or maybe even tell you to pull the plug and give up. Move on. Do something else. It can take a great deal of courage to forge forward, to keep believing in yourself. But I'm here to tell you that it's worth it in the end."

Applause, a few whoops of support.

Jack nodded, then went on. He didn't read from cue cards, or anything prepared, but rather, seemed to speak from his heart. His gaze connected with every person in the audience, and they connected right back with him. "You've heard the old adage that you have to fight for what you believe in, and that is true. But they don't tell you that the first fight you have to have is for yourself. Start by fighting for you, and fighting those doubts that keep you stuck in the wrong place, because *you* matter." At this, he pointed at the crowd, then at Harvey, then at himself. "And once you know that, the rest of the battle gets easier."

More applause, more whoops. Marnie felt a hand on her shoulder and turned to find Erica beside her.

"Oh, my God, is that Jack Knight?" Erica asked.

Marnie nodded. "I had no idea he was going to be here today."

"Wow, he's even cuter in person than he is in his picture," Erica whispered. "And without the suit and tie, he's downright sexy."

"He is," Marnie admitted. "And the people here love him. His speech is great."

"Seems to me that's a good enough reason to take a chance on him." Erica shrugged. "We could have him all wrong."

"Or he could be the greatest BS artist to come along in years."

"True. But he did bring you daisies. Doesn't that mean he deserves a second look? Or at least a chance to explain why he did what he did with Dad's business?" Erica cast another glance at Jack. "Until you do, I don't think you can truly know whether to hate him or love him."

"Love him?" Marnie scoffed. "I can barely stand him."

Erica laughed. "Oh, yeah, I can see that in the way you stare at him."

"I fixed him up with other women, Erica. I'm not interested in Jack Knight."

Except she had gone out on two, no, three dates with him, if she counted the dinner with their parents. And she'd been thinking about him non-stop for days. Kissed him twice. Desired him more than she'd desired anyone else.

"Pity. He seems like a really nice guy." Erica glanced over her shoulder, saw Linda heading for the kitchen and gave her sister a light touch on the shoulder. "I have to get back to lunch service. Just remember what Dad used to say. You can't judge the house until you see the inside. You don't know the whole story of Dad's house, and you don't know the whole story of Jack's. You don't know if Jack tried to help Dad and he refused to listen. Our father was a great visionary but not the best businessman in the world."

"All the more reason why he needed an investor who would help him, not just throw some money at him then step back and watch him drown. Regardless, Jack is a constant reminder to all of us of what happened with Dad. We don't need that in our lives."

"Maybe. But you won't know unless *you ask him about it*." Erica leaned in to whisper in Marnie's ear, with emphasis on the last few words. "Stop being afraid to look inside and find out the truth. You keep this tight little leash on everything, Marnie. Sometimes taking a risk is good for you, and your heart."

Erica left the room. Marnie debated following, but Jack's voice drew her in again. "That's the business I'm really in," he was saying, "one where I support dreams. I am honored to have been rewarded for my work, too."

Financially, the cynic in Marnie thought.

"I'm not talking about money," Jack said as if he'd read her mind. "It's the people. When you put passion and belief into what you do, it translates into the people around you, and you pay it forward with every business decision you make. For me, it's the bookstore owner who has the funds to start a literacy program for adult learners. The daycare owner who can now afford to offer a drop-in service for parents who are looking for jobs. The handyman firm that has expanded into two more cities, and hired great people like Harvey here. These are people who took a risk and it paid off. Their thank-yous arc worth more than any number on the bottom line, and at the end of the day, bring you a satisfaction you won't find anywhere else." He stepped out from behind the podium and into the audience, as far as the mike's cord allowed. "So take a chance, go after your dreams, and you'll enjoy a return on that investment that is ten-fold."

The audience erupted into applause. People got to their feet, cheering Jack and his words, reaching for him to tell him how impressed they were, thanking him for his message.

Heck of a speech, Marnie thought. Almost had her convinced he was a nice guy.

The crowd began to disperse, some people heading for the platters of cookies and coffee at the back of the room, while others opted for lunch in the kitchen. Many of the people raved about Jack's speech, clear fans of him now. Maybe her father had been sold on some "support the dream" speech, too, and been too blind to see the reality of the situation.

Except that didn't match the father she'd known. Yes, he'd been terrible at business— more of a creative than an accountant—but he'd been an incredible judge of character. Tom could pick a con artist out of a room of a hundred people, and many of the people he'd had handshake deals with over the years had turned out to be his best friends. He'd known in a minute if someone had a good heart or bad intentions.

If that was so, then why had he signed an agreement with Knight Enterprises? How could he have missed the writing on the wall? Or had Jack tried, and failed, to help Tom's business?

He brought you daisies, Erica had said. *Doesn't that mean he deserves a second look?*

Marnie lingered in the room, watching Jack interact with several of the people at Second Chance. She stayed behind her veil of greenery, her feet rooted to the spot. A woman Marnie knew well, a single mom named Luanne, stepped over to Jack. Within seconds, Luanne was crying, and Marnie's heart went out to her. She knew life had been tough for Luanne lately—not only had she lost her job, but also her home after a bitter divorce. She'd been staying at Second Chance for a few weeks now and had been the one with the idea of a donated career dress day to help the women looking for work.

"You told us to follow our dreams," Luanne said to Jack, "but I lost all mine. I don't know what to do now."

Jack's face was kind, his eyes soft. "What did you do before for work?"

"Data entry at a newspaper, working in the subscription department."

"And did you love that?"

The room had emptied out, with most of the people heading for lunch in the kitchen, a few lingering in the hall. Spring sunshine streamed in through the windows, bright, cheery, hopeful, like it was trying to coax Luanne into believing brighter days were on the horizon.

Luanne shook her head. "I hated that job. I only took it because I wanted to be a writer. Then one year turned into two, turned into ten…" She shrugged.

Jack reached into his breast pocket and pulled out a pen, one of those expensive ones, with a heavy silver barrel. He pressed the ballpoint into the woman's hand. "Take this," he said, "and write with it."

"Write what?"

"About your journey. About your life lessons. About anything you want. Back when I was young and had lots to say, I wrote novels and short stories. I even started out in college pursuing a degree in writing, before I switched to a major in business. A part of me still loves writing, the whole process of collecting my thoughts and forming them into stories." Jack shrugged. "No one will ever read what I write, but that's okay because it's just a hobby for me. You, though, you have a dream and a passion. I could see it in your eyes when I gave you the pen and said 'write.' It was as if that lit a fire deep inside you. So go, and write. The world needs more writers, especially ones with life experiences to share."

Luanne scoffed. "Who wants to hear my sob story?"

Jack held her gaze, and that smile Marnie had memorized curved across his face. "I do. And I bet the publisher at the community magazine wants to hear it, too. Send it my way when you're done, and I'll get it to him."

Tears glimmered in Luanne's eyes. She clutched the pen so tight, her knuckles whitened. "Thank you. Thank you so much."

"Don't thank me. Just take this dream, and spread it to another. Someday, you'll give someone else a pen or a kind word or some advice, and that will start them on their journey." Jack gave Luanne a gentle hug, then said goodbye and crossed to the coffeepot.

Marnie told her feet to move. Told herself to leave the room. But she remained cemented where she was, behind the plant, watching Jack approach.

Jack Knight, the demon who had destroyed her father, helping a woman down on her luck. Jack Knight, the man who kept getting her to step out of her comfort zone and let her hair down. Jack Knight, the man who had ignited something raw, urgent, and terrifying, deep inside her. Telling people to go after their dreams. Was it all a front?

A riot of emotions ran through her in the few seconds it took Jack to go from one end of the room to the other. She kept trying so hard to hate him but the feeling refused to stick.

In the end, indecision won out. Jack's blue eyes lit and his smile broadened when he spied her behind the plant. A sweet, delicious warmth spread through Marnie, and despite her better judgment, she found herself stepping out from behind the plant and giving him a smile of her own.

"Marnie."

When he said her name in that soft, surprised way, she was back in the car, the rain pounding on the roof, kissing Jack and thinking of nothing more than how much she wanted him, how he seemed to know every inch of her body so well. "I, uh, heard you talking and came in to listen. You gave a great speech."

"Thanks. I hope it touched a few people."

"It touched Luanne," she said, nodding in the direction the other woman had gone. Luanne had left the room with a lightness in her steps, a hopeful smile on her face, a changed woman. "That was really nice, what you did for her."

Jack shrugged. "It was a small thing."

"Not to Luanne. She's been through a lot, with her ex, and losing her job. I can tell that really touched her, to have someone believe in her." Marnie had to admit, that for all the bad Jack had done in the past, this moment would make a difference. She could already see a renewed enthusiasm and optimism in Luanne's features as she talked to other people in the room, showing off the pen, and spreading the words of encouragement.

"And yet, you run away every time I get close. You give me a laundry list of reasons why we shouldn't date." He took a step closer. "Why?"

She shook her head. "Jack, there's too much between us to make this work. Please stop trying to pretend there isn't."

He took another step closer, and the fronds of the plant brushed against his shoulder. "I'm not trying to pretend there isn't. But I'm willing to take the risk that we have something amazing here, something that is stronger than the past. The question is why you don't think so, too. Why you won't take a risk."

"I'm not interested in you. Or a relationship." But even as she said the words, Marnie knew, deep down inside, that they were a lie. She wanted all of that, and she wanted him—

But her wants couldn't overpower the tight hold she had on her life. If she let him in, if she took a chance—

No. She didn't do that. She didn't go off on haphazard paths, with no clear sense of direction. And that's what being with Jack was like. Insane and delicious, all at the same time. The whole thing made her want to hyperventilate.

"You make me want to take the day off, head for the Common with a bottle of wine and a picnic lunch," Jack said, his blue eyes capturing hers. "Or get in the car and drive up the coastline until we get to the tip of Maine, the edge of the country. Or just sit in a car while the rain falls and watch the way your eyes light up when I move closer and—"

She jerked away. How did he keep doing that? Every time she turned around, Jack wrapped her in his spell. Was that what he had done with her father, too? Spoken pretty words that masked Jack's true intentions? One Franklin had already fallen for Jack's words, had believed him when he'd offered a risky proposition. She refused to be the second one. "I have to go. I'm supposed to be helping my sister in the kitchen."

Then she spun on her heel and got out of the room, before temptation got the better of her. Although a part of Marnie suspected it already had.

CHAPTER TEN

JACK SAT AT his father's desk, in the office his father had spent most of his life in, and wished he could have a second chance, the very thing he'd promoted in his speech the other day. He'd told others they were possible, and had yet to find one in his own life, no matter how many hours he spent here. There were still things from the past catching up with him, nipping at his heels, and reminding him every day that he was his father's son—

And not at all proud of that fact.

The guilt of what he had done, the companies he had destroyed, the people whose hearts he had broken, gnawed at him still. The work he'd done over the last two years hadn't filled that aching hole in his heart the way he'd thought it would. It was as if he was sitting in the wrong chair, making the wrong choices. Impossible. He knew this was the right thing to do. But as he reached the end of the pile of folders, he had to wonder if that was true.

He'd told the people in that room to take a risk, to go after what they wanted. Had he taken his own advice?

He'd pursued Marnie, yes, but he'd also let her go. If he truly wanted her, what the hell was he doing here?

His assistant dropped off a stack of checks for Jack to sign. He thanked her, then began to scrawl his name across the bottom line. Each one he signed represented a new start for someone, a new chance. And another chance for Jack to make amends.

He paused on the last one. Doug Hendrickson's seed money. Jack held the check for a long time, then reached in his drawer, pulled out one of the dozens of keys stored in a box, and headed out of the office. As he left, he paused by his assistant's desk. "Cancel the rest of my appointments for today. And can you make sure this—" he grabbed a piece of paper and an envelope, then jotted a quick note on the white linen stock "—gets delivered immediately?"

"Sure," she said, then looked up at him. "If you don't mind my saying so, you look a little worried today. Everything okay?"

Jack glanced down at the note, then at the key in his hand. "Not yet. But I hope it will be."

Marnie returned from lunch, expecting the office to be empty. Erica had a doctor's appointment, and Marnie's schedule was clear for the rest of the day. But as she got out of her car, she saw a familiar car parked in Erica's spot, and her mother standing on the stoop. "Ma, what a nice surprise!"

Her mother held up a bag of cookies from a local bakery. "And I brought dessert."

"My favorite. And such a decadent treat after I just had a salad." Marnie unlocked the office door and waved her mother inside. "Let me put on some coffee."

Marnie started the pot brewing, then got them two cups and a plate for the cookies, and set it all up in the reception area. "Thanks for bringing these. This is definitely a chocolate kind of day."

Her mother laughed. "I think that goes for every day."

"True, very true." Marnie grinned, then took a bite of a chocolate peanut butter cup cookie. Heaven melted against her palate. "These are…amazing."

Marnie and her mother ate, drank and

chatted for a few minutes, catching up on family gossip. The cookies eased the tension lingering in Marnie's shoulders, a tension brought about by too many late-night thoughts about Jack, and their conversation at Second Chance yesterday.

I'm willing to take the risk that we have something amazing here, something that is stronger than the past. The question is why you don't think so, too. Why you won't take a risk.

Trust and fall. Just the thought caused Marnie's chest to tighten. She reached for another cookie and pushed the thoughts of Jack to the back of her mind. Stubborn, they refused to stay there, and lingered at the edge of her every word.

"Aren't you leaving tonight?" Marnie asked her mother. "For your big weekend in Maine?"

"About that…" Helen toyed with her coffee mug. "I'm not sure I should go."

"What? Why?"

"Because you're not okay with us being together, and the last thing I want to do is make you unhappy. You and your sisters are my world, Marnie." Ma's hand covered hers. Her pale green eyes met Marnie's. "I don't want to see you hurting."

"Ma, you were happy with Dan. He was happy with you. You deserve that."

A small, sad smile crossed Ma's face. "Not at the expense of your happiness."

In that instant, Marnie saw what her actions had cost. Not just herself, but those she loved. Her mother had given up the man she cared about—her second chance at love—to avoid hurting her daughter. Because Marnie had yet to be able to get over the past. She kept wanting to make Jack, and anyone associated with Jack, pay for something that had happened three years ago. Her mother had gotten past it, had moved on and started her life over. Marnie needed to do the same. "Here you are, protecting me, when I was trying to protect you." Marnie shook her head.

"Protect me? From what?"

"From being hurt. I thought if I didn't date Jack and you avoided Dan, that you wouldn't see Jack and think about what happened to Dad. But it's clear Dan makes you happy and that this isn't about the past anymore. It's about your future."

"Oh, honey—"

Marnie gave her mother's hand a squeeze. "You took a risk, and fell in love again—"

"Well, it's probably too soon to say fell in

love." But the blush in Ma's cheeks belied that statement.

"And I think that's pretty incredible. Because…" Marnie drew back her hand and dropped her gaze to the cookies. Cookies that hadn't erased the issues, just muted them for a few bites. "Because I've been too terrified to do that myself."

There was the truth. Marnie didn't date because she was terrified of falling in love. It was the one emotion that meant giving up control, letting go. Trusting the other person would catch you.

Ma's face softened. "Marnie, don't let fear keep you from love. Or from Jack."

"I'm not talking about Jack." Or thinking about him. Or dwelling on him. Except she was, all the time. And wondering if she took a risk on love with him, if she'd find the same happiness her mother had.

I'm willing to take the risk that we have something amazing here, something that is stronger than the past.

She realized she'd become the same thing she saw in her clients all the time, a gun-shy single who wanted love, but did everything she could to avoid a relationship. The matchmaker was terrified of matching herself.

How ironic.

"Jack's a good man, Marnie," Ma said as if reading her daughter's mind, "despite what he did in the past. He's changed, Dan said. Doing business in an entirely new way." Her mother's cell phone lit with an incoming call from Dan. A smile stole across Helen's face. The kind of smile of a woman in love, a woman who had found a man who loved her, too. A gift, Marnie realized, that not everyone found.

"Dan's a good man, too," Marnie said. She picked up the phone and placed it in her mother's palm, closing Ma's fingers over the slim silver body. "Tell him you'll go to Maine with him."

Ma hesitated. "Really?"

Marnie nodded. "He makes you smile, Ma, and that's all that's ever mattered to me."

The smile widened on Ma's face, and her eyes lit with joy. She pressed the button on her phone, and answered the call. Within seconds, Ma was giggling like a schoolgirl, and making plans with Dan. "Okay, sounds good," she said. "I'm looking forward to it, too. See you soon, Dan." Then she said goodbye and tucked the phone back into her purse.

Ma got to her feet and leaned over to give her daughter a warm hug. "You're a good daughter," she whispered, then she drew back and met her daughter's gaze with older, wiser, loving eyes. "Now take your own advice and take a chance on the man who makes you smile, too. A man like Jack, perhaps?"

"I don't know." Marnie hesitated. Jack distracted her, set her off her keel. That couldn't be a good thing, could it?

"If I were you," Ma said, "I'd make a list, just like you make your clients do. Figure out what's most important to you in the man you meet. And then use that instinct of yours to point you in the direction of Mr. Right."

Marnie shook her head. "I don't think it works on me. Too close to the work and all that."

"That's because you haven't tried." Ma wagged a finger at her. "And you never know what awaits around the next bend unless you travel down the road."

CHAPTER ELEVEN

AFTER THE COOKIE and coffee and chat with her mother, Marnie got back to work, instead of acting on her promised resolve to let Jack into her life. Erica returned from her appointment, and paused to hang up her coat, then stow her purse in the closet. When she got to her desk, she glanced across the room at her older sister. "Hey! Are those cookies on your desk?"

Marnie chuckled, and slid the plate in Erica's direction. "Ma stopped by with gifts."

"I thought she'd be halfway to Maine by now."

"She is now. She and I talked about Dan, and I'm cool with them dating. Ma is so happy, and it's nice to see. She deserves it."

Erica nodded. "It sure is. And if her being happy means we get cookies for lunch, then by all means, keep Dan around. Oh, I almost forgot!" Erica jumped up and dashed over to her desk, returning a second later with an envelope. "This came for you today when I was coming in the door. Delivered by messenger, so it must be important." She glanced at her watch. "Okay, I really gotta scoot. I'm supposed to meet with the caterer for our next event. Then I've got a date. You gonna be okay here without my astounding help?"

"Of course." Marnie tapped the envelope on her desk. Plain, nondescript, nothing more than Marnie's name and address on the front. Probably a thank you from a satisfied client. "Thanks, Erica. Have fun on your date."

Erica's smile winged across her face. "You know me, I always do. And don't forget to have some fun yourself."

Marnie just nodded, then got back to work when Erica left. After a while, she stretched, and noticed the envelope again on the corner of her desk. She undid the flap, then pulled out the card inside.

I found something of your dad's at his shop that I think you're going to want to have. Your key should still work.
Jack

Marnie held on to the card for a long, long time. She turned it over, weighing her options. In the end, curiosity won, driven by the urge to see Jack again. Ever since the conversation with her mother, her thoughts had drifted toward the what-ifs. What if she fell for Jack? What if she kissed him again? What if they took things to the next level? Would she be going around with that same goofy, blissful smile on her face?

The card had been the impetus she needed, like a sign from above that she needed to stop dithering and start acting. Wasn't it about time she found out, instead of sitting on the sidelines, giving everyone else the happy ending she wanted, too? She grabbed her keys and headed across town, her heart in her throat.

In her mind, she kept seeing the four letters of *Jack*. Not *Love, Jack,* or *Thinking of you, Jack* or even *Best Wishes, Jack*. Just *Jack*. She should have been glad he'd left the closing impersonal, business-like. But she wasn't. She wanted more. She wanted him to come right out and say what he was feeling, and then let them take it from there. Even that thought made her heart beat a little faster with anxiety.

God, she really was a mess. But as she got closer to the building, and to seeing Jack, a smile spread across her face and anticipation warmed her veins. She thought of that kiss in the car, the one at the coffee shop, and decided…

Yes, she wanted him. Yes, she'd take this risk. Yes, she would put the past behind her and open her heart.

She wove her way through the city streets until the congestion eased and the roads opened up to an area filled with small office buildings and light industrial complexes. Her father's old building came into view, a squat one-story concrete building with a nondescript storefront and a long, rectangular shape. She sat there for a long moment, staring at the building, memorizing the sign. The Top Notch Printing sign had faded, and the white exterior paint that had once been so pristine had faded to a dingy gray. Weeds had sprung up between the cracks in the parking lot. The tidy building now looked sad, defeated.

It hit her then, hard and fast. She would never again drive up here and see Top Notch Printing on the front façade. Never again see the mailbox her father had painted himself one weekend. Never again walk through the door and hear her father call her name.

In the years since her father passed, no one had rented or bought the building, and it

seemed to echo now with emptiness, disuse.
Marnie parked, got out of the car, and flipped
through the keys on her ring until she got to
a brass one. The key had been on her father's
ring for decades, and had a worn spot where
his thumb had sat, morning after morning,
when he opened the building for the day.

She slipped the key into the lock. The
lock stuck a bit, then gave way, and the door
opened with a creak. Once inside, her hand
found the light switch, and the overhead fluorescents sputtered to life, providing a sur-
real white glow in the foyer. She stepped past
the glass partition that divided the receptionist's desk from the main office. A smile
curved across her face. Her father had never
had a receptionist, but when the girls came
in after school or on the weekends, they'd
fought over sitting at that desk and answering the phones, as if it was the best job in
the world.

Marnie ran a hand over the old corded desk
phone, then let her gaze skip over the desk.
Nothing there, or on the counter where her
father would leave things for customers to
pick up. She took a right, and headed down
the hall, toward the big oak door that hadn't
been opened in three years.

Her steps stuttered and she looked up at the engraved plaque attached to the oak.

TOM FRANKLIN

That was all, no title, nothing fancy. The guys in the shop had made the sign for him one day, and he'd mounted it with the caveat that they all called him Tom, just like always. He'd been a good boss, almost one of the guys, which had made his employees love him, but had often given them license to slack on production. Still, every person who had ever worked for her father came to his funeral, a testament to his memory, his lasting relationships with people. Tom had been a good guy, a good boss, and an even better father. Oh, how she missed him.

Marnie reached up, her fingers dancing over the engraved lettering. Then she tugged off the plaque and tucked it in her purse. Doing so left a scar on the door, which Marnie liked. It said Tom had been here, and shouldn't be forgotten.

A long, low creak announced the opening of the front door. Marnie wheeled around, raising her fist with the keys in it. Not much of a defense, but better than nothing. She lowered her fist when she saw a familiar figure enter the building. "Jack. You scared the heck out of me."

"Sorry." He stepped into the foyer, and his features shifted from shadows to light. In the white fluorescents, his eyes seemed even bluer, his hair darker, his jaw line sharper. Her heart started beating double-time. "I wanted to get here before you did, but I was running behind."

She took a step closer to him, letting the smile inside her bubble to the surface. "That's okay. You didn't have to be here. I could have picked this up myself."

He took a step closer, reached up a hand, and cupped her jaw, his gaze soft, tender. "Oh, Marnie, you are so determined to fly solo."

"It's safer that way," she whispered.

"But is it better?"

She shook her head, and tears rushed to her eyes. "No, it's not."

"Then stop doing it," he said. He smiled, then closed the distance between them and kissed her. This kiss was tender, gentle. His hands held her jaw, fingers tangling in her hair. She sighed into the kiss and leaned into Jack.

And it all felt so, so right. So perfect. Falling wasn't so bad, she realized. Not so bad at all.

Finally, Jack drew back, but didn't let her go, not right away. The connection between them tightened, as the threads they had been building began to knit into something real and lasting.

It was as if in that kiss, that moment of surrender, something fundamental had shifted between them. Marnie could feel it charging the air, the space between them. The grin playing on Jack's lips said he felt it, too. From here on out, nothing would be the same. And for the first time in her life, Marnie was ready to get on that roller coaster, but still, fear kept her from saying a word.

"Before we get too distracted, let me show you what I found. I put it on your father's desk." Jack reached past her, which whispered his cologne past her senses, and opened the door to Tom's office, allowing Marnie to enter first.

She took a deep breath, squared her shoulders, then went into the office. The second her feet touched the carpet, she jetted back in time. She hadn't been inside her father's office for years. At least four, maybe more. Once she'd gone off to college, then come home to open her own business, free time had become a rare commodity and her days of playing receptionist with her sisters had ended.

Nothing had changed with the passage of time. The worn black leather chair her father had rescued from a salvage sale still sat behind the simple dark green metal desk he'd painted himself. The bookshelf held a haphazard collection of business books—gifts, mostly—that he'd kept meaning to read and never had. A stack of print samples lay against one wall, and a dish of Tootsie Rolls sat on the corner of the desk, beside a hideous green pottery pen holder that Kat had made for Dad in the third grade. Marnie's throat swelled. "It's been three years and it still seems like I could walk in here and find him at his desk."

Jack put a hand on her shoulder. She leaned into his touch, allowed his stronger, broader shoulders to hold her up. "I'm sorry you lost him," he said. "He was a really nice guy."

"Yeah, he was." She stepped away from Jack's touch, and crossed to a box on the credenza behind the desk. Her name had been written across the top, in the same precise script as the note. Jack's handwriting. She danced a finger across the six letters of her name.

"I came across that when I was cleaning

out the office," Jack said. "I thought you'd want to have it. For you and your sisters."

She pried open the cardboard. Instant recognition hit her, along with a teary wave of memories. She reached inside and pulled out the wooden photo frame, still filled with a picture of Dad and his girls, the three of them crowding the space in front of him. Ma had taken the picture, out in front of the building, years and years ago. Kat was about ten, Marnie almost nine and Erica just seven, the three of them wearing goofy smiles and matching pigtails. It wasn't the picture that caught her heart, though, it was the frame.

When her mother had brought home the print from the photo developer, Dad had showed it to Marnie and told her a special picture like this needed a special frame. He'd asked her to help him make one, and she'd leapt at the chance. Her father, who worked too many hours and came home to three girls all anxious for him to hear about school or help with homework or go outside to ride bikes, rarely had time to spend with just one daughter.

"My father and I made this together," she said, the memory slipping from her lips in a soft whisper. "He told the other girls that this was going to be a Dad and Daisy-doo project.

Kat and Erica pouted, but Dad stuck to his guns. We went out to the garage, and he and I did everything, from cutting the wood to nailing the pieces together. He taught me how to miter the corners and sand the wood filler until it was smooth. When it was done—" she flipped over the frame and ran her fingers over the letters etched there "—he showed me how to use the woodburner to put our names on it."

And there, as deep and clear as the day she'd done it, were the words *Dad and His Daisy-Doo's Great Project.*

A great project, indeed. The best one, and one of the few things that had been just between her and her dad. Her throat clogged. Her vision blurred. *Oh, Dad.*

"I didn't even know he saved it." But of course he would have. Tom had been a sentimental man, who had held on to nearly every school paper his daughters brought home, framed the weekly drawings, and made a big deal out of every life event. Tears welled in her eyes, clung to her lashes. She clutched the frame to her chest. Solid, warm, it held so many memories. "Thank you."

"You're welcome." He let out a breath, then shifted his weight. His stance changed from commiseration to serious, and she knew this was something she might not want to hear. "I've got some things to tell you, Marnie, about the way I handled your father's business."

"It's okay. It's in the past. He's gone now."

"I know, but…this needs to be said. For both of us." Jack heaved a sigh. His gaze skipped around the room, coming to rest on the visitor's chair, as if he was sitting in it, across from her father again. "When I first met with your father, I came to him under false pretences. I promised him we'd help him. It was the same line we gave all the businesses we worked with. Sometimes, yes, we did help them, but sometimes we just invested and walked away, knowing they'd fail."

"How was that a smart strategy?"

Jack took a seat on the corner of the desk. "There's a lot that goes into a buying decision, you know? Pluses and minuses, current earnings versus future. Your father might not have been great at managing a business, but he was amazing at building customer relationships, and that meant his business had incredible future earning potential. Everybody loved the guy, loved working with him, and he had a great rapport with them. But…"

"But what?"

He heard the caution in Marnie's voice, and

knew she was bracing herself for something she didn't want to hear. How he wanted to stop here, to not tell her anything. But the guilt had weighed on him heavy for years, and he couldn't keep seeing Marnie or ask anything more of her if she didn't know who he used to be.

"But there was a bigger company in town who wanted those same customers. They were a current client of my father's, and they had tried to buy your dad's business a few times, but he always refused."

"I vaguely remember something about that. My dad didn't talk about work very often."

"The competitor came to my father and I, asking us to go in, get Tom's business from him and then they could have the customers. There'd be a big bonus for Knight, of course, and a very happy client. At the time I thought it was the right thing to do. I justified it a hundred different ways. Your father was older, ready for retirement. He wasn't much of a businessman. He'd been talking about getting out of the company, having more time for himself. So I kept telling myself I was doing the right thing, that in the end, it was the best choice for Tom. But…"

Across from him, Marnie had gone cold and still. "But what?"

"But I liked your father. He was a great guy, like I said. The kind of guy you'd have a few beers with or split a pizza with. He was honest and forthright and nice."

"And trusting."

Jack nodded, hating himself for abusing that trust years ago. "And trusting."

"So you…" She clutched the frame between her hands, her knuckles whitening. "You threw him under the bus, for a bottom line?"

Jack sighed, and ran a hand through his hair. "Yes, I did all those things. I'm the one that talked to your father about Knight investing in his company. I'm the one that promised him we'd be there through thick and thin. And I'm the one who, in the end, deserted him. But, Marnie, there's more to it than what you know."

But she had already turned on her heel and headed out of the office. Before he could follow, she had rushed out. The door slammed in her wake.

Marnie ran. Her mind tried to process what Jack had told her, but it wouldn't compute. Jack had fed her father a line of lies. Then let him fail on purpose.

She jerked her keys out of her purse and

thumbed the lock. A bright green pickup truck pulled into the lot. The color triggered a memory in Marnie, and when the man in the truck got out, she remembered.

Doug Hendrickson, the twenty-some-thing son of Floyd Hendrickson, who owned a rival printing company in Boston. Back in the early days of his business, Marnie's father and Floyd had worked together, helping each other build from the ground up, trading jobs, connections, equipment. Marnie could remember going into her father's shop on the weekends, and sometimes seeing Doug when he came in with his father.

Then Floyd and Tom had a falling out, over what Marnie had no idea, and the two had stopped speaking. They'd become fierce competitors then, each trying to grab their corner of the Boston printing market. She hadn't seen Floyd or his son in years, but she knew Doug's wide, friendly face in a second.

Doug cupped a hand over his brow to block the sun. "Is Jack around? I'm supposed to meet him here, but I'm early."

"You're meeting Jack? Jack Knight?" she said, instead of telling him Jack was right inside.

"Yup. You seen him?" Doug's gaze narrowed and he took a step closer. "Hey, aren't you Tom's daughter? Uh, Kat? Or…"

Marnie worked a smile to her face. "I'm the middle one. Marnie."

"I knew you looked familiar!" He grinned. "What a wicked small world. God, I haven't seen you in years. You're not thinking of re-opening your dad's place, are you?"

She shook her head. "No."

The door opened behind her and Jack stepped into the sunshine. Damn. She should have left.

"Hey, Jack!" Doug greeted him with a smile. "Glad to see you. You got my check?"

Marnie jerked her gaze from one man to the other. "Check? What check?"

"Gee, Marnie, I would have thought some-one would tell you." Doug put his hands in his back pockets and rocked on his heels. "I'm opening up my own shop. With some fund-ing from my dad and Knight, of course. I met Jack here a few years ago and he set me up with this place and a nudge to go out on my own. This place was perfect because, well, it has all the equipment still. A little dusty, but it works." Then Doug seemed to realize what he'd said and his face sobered. "Sorry, Marnie. I know your dad passed and all, and this is probably hard."

She bit her lip. "Harder than you know. I'm glad you're the one giving this place a second life. I'm sorry if I seem short with you, Doug. It's just been a really tough day."

An ache started deep inside her chest and spread through Marnie, fast, painful, until she wanted to collapse, or run, or both. She had trusted Jack, opened her heart to him, begun to fall for him, and what did it get her? Hurt. Why had she taken that risk?

She spun toward Jack. "You did this?"

"It's complicated, Marnie. Your father—"

The anger and hurt inside her ignited. So many emotions, weeks' worth, really, bubbled to the surface. She'd kept it all tamped down, and now she wanted to explode, regardless of who was there or why. "You don't get to tell me anything more about my father. Or me. Or us. Or anything. Just leave me alone, Jack."

Before he could respond, she climbed into her car, started the engine and spun out of the parking lot. Tears blurred her vision, but she swiped them away and drove hard and fast, away from a huge mistake she'd almost made.

Just when she'd begun to think that Jack Knight was a good man, just when she was about to give him a chance, to trust that the man she'd seen at the gym and the coffee shop and the charity was the real Jack, he did something like this.

Sold the remains of her father's company to his competitor. Just like the vulture she knew he was all along.

CHAPTER TWELVE

HE SHOULD HAVE let her go. She was hurting, and like a wounded animal, Marnie wanted to escape from the person she saw as responsible for her pain. She had left the office, and run for the car, dodging the rain that had started to fall again. Her tires squealed against the pavement, spitting gravel in her wake, and then she was gone.

Jack hesitated for a half a second, shouted a *meet you later* at Doug, then he hopped in his car and wove through the traffic, darting left, right, until he saw her gray sedan ahead. He pulled in behind her, following as she navigated the city, driving against the tide of outbound traffic.

She passed her office, took a left instead of the right that would have brought her to her mother's house, and passed by the exit for her condo. She turned down Charles Street, then entered the Boston Common Parking Garage.

Jack found a space a half level above her, then hopped out in time to see Marnie heading up the stairs and out one of the parking kiosks located on the Common. She crossed Charles, then entered the Public Garden. He lingered behind, warring with letting her go and running after her. Hadn't he hurt her enough? Done enough damage?

She headed down the wide sidewalk that led to the pond and the swan boat rides. For a moment, he thought maybe that was her destination—a quiet ride on the tranquil pond while swans and ducks bobbed nearby, begging for crumbs. But her steps slowed, then stopped. She took a seat on a bench. When he saw the hunch in her shoulders, the decision was made for him. He couldn't let her hurt for one more second. Because—

Because he was falling in love with Marnie Franklin. Hell, he'd been falling for her ever since they'd met. It had been those shoes, those impractical, uncomfortable shoes that she'd kicked onto the pavement. A barefoot Cinderella who had enticed him with her fiery hair and her feisty attitude.

She might never forgive him, and might hate him for the rest of her life, but that didn't mean he wasn't going to try to rectify the mess he had made years ago. And maybe, just maybe, he'd find some peace finally. He might not be able to fix this enough to allow him and Marnie to be together, but maybe he could make it better for her.

He sat down on the space beside her on the bench. Her eyes widened with surprise. "Let me guess," he said, gesturing to the statue across from them, "favorite book as a child?"

Instead of answering, she wheeled on him. "Why are you here, Jack?"

"Because I'm trying to explain to you what happened."

"You can't. It's too late." Her eyes misted and she turned away, facing the bronze statues across the walkway. A mother duck, followed by several baby ducks, waddled from the nest to the pond. The statues were a Boston Public Garden landmark, based on the famous Robert McCloskey book about a family of ducks who had battled city traffic and rushing bicycles to settle in this very park.

"That's the statues based on *Make Way for Ducklings,* right?" he said, because he didn't know what else to say. Far easier to focus on some metal ducks than on climbing the wall between himself and Marnie. "That book's a classic."

"My father gave me the book for Christmas when I was a little girl." She turned to him, the anger still in her green eyes, the hurt rising in the bloom of her cheeks. "Do you want to know why?"

"Yes, I do." He wanted to know everything about Marnie, to memorize every detail of this intriguing woman who named flowers and blushed at the drop of a hat.

She bit her lip, then exhaled, but the tears still shone in her eyes. "Because he said no matter how far any of us girls got from him, he'd always be there to make sure we got home okay. He said he'd be there." She stopped, drawing in a breath, then letting it out again with a powerful sigh. "And he's not there. Not now, not ever again. Because of you and your investment. You ruined our lives, Jack, and because of that, he just gave up and…died."

Jack let out a long breath and rested his arms on his knees. "I know I did. And I'm sorry."

She sat beside him, still as the statues. "I don't understand, Jack. You helped Dot and your friend with the gym, and Luanne and Harvey. Why not my father? Why wasn't he worth you doing the same as you did for them?"

Jack's gaze rested on the bronze ducklings, forever frozen in their quest to tag along after their parents. "When I went to work for my father, all I wanted was a relationship with him. I thought if I became more like him, then he'd, I don't know, start to respect me. Give me an attaboy at least. So I learned his techniques, and I mastered them, and I went in there with his slash and burn and fire sale approach, and did the old man proud." He let out a curse. "I destroyed companies, sold them off like stolen car parts, and waited for my father to say I'd done a good job. He never did. He found fault where there was none, complained about my soft heart when I didn't pull the funding plug fast enough…" Jack threw up his hands. "There was no winning with that man. He was committed to the bottom line and nothing else."

"And my father's business was part of that bottom line? Because it meant more to your father gone than working?"

"Yes." Saying it to Marnie's face hurt Jack far more than speaking to any of the other business owners in that pile of folders on his desk. He wished he could undo the past, flip a switch, and change everything. "Every time I did what my father asked me to do, I died a little inside. I was so caught up in the thrill of it all, the hunt, the chase, the capture, that

I couldn't see the impact on the people, or on me."

Marnie just listened.

"When I met your father, and convinced him to sign with us," Jack said, "I liked him. A lot. And for the first time, I felt like the lowest level of scum there was because I knew I was lying and I knew what was going to happen to his business. I realized what I'd been doing and how it had turned me into someone I didn't even like, someone who lied to get what he wanted, who toed the company line no matter what it cost other people. After that, I quit working for my father. I walked away. It took me a couple weeks to find another job, and in that time, my dad went to your father and told him there was no hope. Nothing to salvage. He convinced your father to sign over the rest of the company to Knight."

"For pennies on the dollar."

Jack nodded. "By the time my father died and I was in that president's chair, it was too late. Your father had left, and didn't want to come back to the business." He still remembered that morning meeting with Tom Franklin. Regrets had haunted Jack for years. He'd been too late, then and now. Too damned late.

"Wait. You offered my father his company back?"

"His was one of the first I tried to fix. It was the one I wanted most to save, but your dad was done, and I think, glad to be out of the chief's role. He said he loved the industry, but hated the stress of being an owner. He seemed…relieved when I talked to him. I kept trying. I called him every week. But he kept saying no. Said he wanted to be retired and enjoy what time he had left. So I stopped."

"What do you mean, what time he had left?"

"He didn't tell you?"

"Tell me what?"

Oh, hell. Jack hesitated. He looked into Marnie's wide green eyes, and wondered if deep inside her, she already knew what he was going to say. "Your father had a heart condition. He'd known about it for years and I think that's what really drove him to get investors, to try to take some of the stress off his shoulders. After I lost my dad from the same thing, I tried to encourage Tom to get to the doctor, listen to the medical advice, but he was…" Jack's voice trailed off.

"A proud and stubborn man." She let out a gust and jerked to her feet. For a moment, she fumed, then she nodded. "My mother had hinted at this. That my father wanted time, and that she wanted him to have it, too. They knew. But they kept it from us."

"He didn't want you to worry, I'm sure. That's why he kept this all secret."

"Secrets are how people get hurt!" The words exploded out of her and she turned away. "If that's love, I don't want it." She waved a hand, as if brushing away a wasp. "Leave it for everyone else."

He stepped to the side, until she looked up at him again. In her face, he saw the scared woman buried deep inside her. So afraid to trust. That had been him, too, for much too long. No more. If he kept letting fear rule his heart, he was going to miss out on someone incredible. Marnie.

"Marnie, your father *did* love you girls and your mother," Jack said. "He talked about you all like his family was the best in the world. He was trying to protect you all, right or wrong."

After a long moment, realization and acceptance dawned in Marnie's eyes. "Because then we'd want to help. We'd want to talk about it. And if there's one thing my family excelled at, it was not talking about anything." She cursed and shook her head, then wrapped her arms around herself, even though the day was warm. "My whole life was like that. Things happening beyond my control. My father would keep his business worries to himself, play the jokester, the happy guy, my mother would act like everything was perfect, and I'd feel like I was missing something. Something necessary and important."

Jack rose and took her hand in his. "Oh, Marnie, I'm sure they didn't do it to hurt you."

"But it did all the same. And so I grew up, and I decided I'd control everything I could. And do the same for them. Protect my mother from...you. From love, from happiness."

"From me?"

"I was afraid that if she saw you, she'd remember what had happened to my father and be hurt all over again. But really, I was just looking for a reason to stay away from this...risk between us." She bit her lip, and finally admitted the truth to herself. Her father had lost his business and her world had been thrust into chaos. Then he died, and the chaos got worse. Both things happened outside her realm of control, and had only made her dig her heels in further. "I have my lists and my organizational things and it all gives me comfort. I went into a business where I can control people's happy endings. And you know what?" She lifted her gaze to his, and felt tears fill her eyes. "Control hasn't made me any happier. It's made me scared and reluctant. And left me alone. The only match I can't make is the one for myself, because falling in love means letting go. Taking a chance. Trusting another person. And maybe getting hurt in the process."

Jack danced his fingers along her cheek. "And would that be so bad?"

She nodded, scared even now. A part of her wanted to hold on to the comfort of that fear, but she had done that for far too long and ended up running from Jack, running from the truth, and most of all, running from the very thing she wanted.

Love.

Her gaze went to the statues again and she realized her father may not have told her everything, but in his own way, he'd always been trying to prepare his daughters for the end. "Whenever he read *Make Way for Ducklings* to me, my father used to add an epilogue. He would tell me that there would be a day when Mr. and Mrs. Mallard could no longer lead the way for the ducklings to go to the little island, and that the ducklings shouldn't worry. When that day came, that was when the ducklings knew it was time for them to spread their wings and find their own ponds. He said the Mallards knew their ducklings would be fine because they were smart and strong and would always have the love of their parents at their backs." The tears slid down her cheeks now, dropping onto her hands and glistening in the fading light. What she wouldn't give to hear him tell that story one more time. "He wanted me and my sisters to find our own ponds and not to worry about him."

"Because you are smart and strong and would always have his love."

She nodded, mute, and the tears fell, and Jack pulled her into his chest, holding her tight and strong. She cried for a long time, while pigeons cooed at their feet and the sun began to set over Boston. She cried and his heart broke for her, and he wished that of all the things he had fixed, that he could fix this one most of all. She cried and Jack envied her father, and hoped Tom Franklin knew how lucky he had been to have people love him like this.

Finally, Marnie drew back and swiped at her eyes. "I'm sorry."

He whisked away one more tear with his thumb, then cupped her jaw. "Don't be. I'm sorry I didn't stand up to my father sooner.

I'm sorry I wasn't here when your father needed me most. I'm sorry I didn't tell you all of this sooner. I'm sorry for a thousand things, and a thousand more. I've been trying to make it up to the people my father's company destroyed ever since that day, because that's the only thing that's going to let me sleep at night. I can't change the past, but hopefully I can make the future better."

"And the Hendricksons? Are they part of that?"

Jack shook his head. "That was all your father's idea. He said he wanted to see the next generation carry the company forward. He told me to contact Doug and tell him that after he got out of college, he could buy the building and its contents for a fair price."

"You held on to that property all this time? Because my father asked you to?"

Jack nodded. "It was the least I could do." He brushed back the lock of hair that had fallen across her brow. "I'm sorry, Marnie."

It was as if he couldn't say the words enough. She was the face of his and his father's selfish decisions, the mirror Jack looked into every day. But telling her and getting the truth on the table, as painful as it had been, had eased the guilt in his chest. For the first time since he'd taken a seat behind his father's desk, he felt as if he'd made a difference. Like he could stop beating himself up for the past.

"I'm glad you're helping Doug. I truly am. I couldn't think of a single soul that would take better care of my father's dream." She gave him a grateful smile. "My mother told me once that my father said he thought you were a good man when he met you."

"Really?" Jack thought of who he had been, and couldn't imagine why Tom would say such a thing.

"One of my father's skills, and I think it's something I inherited and use in my matchmaking, is seeing the best in people. He knew who you were inside, and that's what he saw. That's all he saw. That's why he trusted you."

Jack shook his head. "He must have had a crystal ball into the future because I sure wasn't a good man back then."

"But now, you are."

"Now I'm just trying to make up for the past. Going into the same office, day after day, and trying to undo the damage." He shrugged. "I'm not sure that makes me good or bad, more...doing my job."

She thought about that for a second as a trio of bicyclers sped past them, and a family paused to admire the bronze ducklings.

The end of the day brought more people to the park, their voices rising and falling like music.

"You know, you and I are a lot alike," Marnie said. "We both keep taking comfort in the things we know, the things we can rein in, rather than risk it all for the unknown. It's like what you said in your speech about taking chances. It's so much easier, isn't it, not to confront, not to upset? It's just another way to control the situation. When really—" at this, she let out a little laugh "—the one you're really not confronting is yourself. Your own fears and insecurities and worries."

How right she was. He'd gone along with his father's plans for years, because he didn't want to look in the mirror at what he'd been doing. And now, he'd avoided relationships under the guise of not wanting to repeat his family history, rather than looking at the inner demons that kept him from making a commitment. He took her hand, letting his thumb rub across the back of her fingers. Her hand felt good in his, right. "All we can do, as my stepfather says, is to live and learn, and do things different going forward."

She nodded. "That's good advice, Jack. You should take it."

"I'm trying." He grinned.

"I mean it. You should go after the things you're afraid of."

"I'm trying to go after you." He moved closer, reaching for her, but she stepped out of his grasp. "But you keep running away from me."

He reached up and cupped her jaw. He could look at her face every day for the rest of his life. Hear her say his name every morning and night, forever. After his engagement ended, he'd been afraid to risk his heart, and it almost cost him this woman. His stepfather had been right. He had been scared, terrified really, of opening his heart to Marnie because it meant taking a risk that he could turn out like his father. He was done with that. Done with worrying. The best thing to do—

Take the leap anyway.

Jack let his thumb trail along her bottom lip. "All that fire and sass, in one woman. No wonder I can't stop thinking about you."

She shook her head. "Don't, Jack. Don't do this."

She was going to bolt, and he didn't know how to stop that. Despite her words, the woman who brought people together for a living still lived in fear of her own happy ending, held that fear like a security blanket. He and Marnie were so alike, he thought, burned by their pasts and using their jobs to cover for their emotions.

"Don't what, fall in love with you? Too late, Marnie."

She swallowed hard and her eyes widened. "But we've only known each other a few weeks and we barely dated or anything."

"When you know, you know. Doesn't that happen to your clients all the time?"

"Yes, but this is different."

"How?"

"It just is."

He wanted to shake her, to tell her to take down that stubborn wall, and open her heart. But he knew she would do that only when she was ready. Pushing her would only push her away, the last thing he wanted.

His gaze dropped to her lips, trembling with the fear still in her heart, then raised his gaze to her eyes, wide, cautious. "Why are you so terrified of the very thing you tell everyone else in the world to go after?"

"I...I'm not." The lie flushed her cheeks.

"Do you know why my engagement ended?" Jack said. "Tanya left me because she said I was cold. Uninvolved. More interested in work than in our relationship. I lost her, and it was all my fault. I've kept my heart closed off ever since, and worked myself half to death, because I thought that was easier. After all, I learned that art from the master." He let out a gust and a low curse. "The irony of the whole thing is that the one man I never wanted to emulate—my father—was the man I had started to become. I won't make that mistake again, nor am I going to spend one more day alone just because I'm afraid of his legacy. I'm done running from relationships. The question is—" he took her hand again "—are you?"

"You think I'm running? Look in the mirror, Jack. You're afraid, too."

"I'm not afraid of anything, Marnie."

"Really? You told Luanne that you originally went to college to be a writer, then changed your major to business. Why? Because you wanted to make your father happy, not you. You told me yourself that you don't love your job, and you had thought about doing something else, but put it off. My question for you is why are you still working in your father's business if your first love was in writing?"

He scoffed. "Any business person will tell you that a job like that, where the sales and return on investment are almost completely out of your hands, is crazy. I've read the statistics. I know how many writers are making poverty level wages, and how many—"

"Are talking themselves out of it because they're afraid. Stop investing in other people, Jack, and invest in yourself. Then maybe…" Her green eyes met his, soft, vulnerable. "Maybe we can be."

Now she did leave, and this time, he didn't follow her. He sat back down on the bench and watched the bronze ducks marching on a perpetual journey to lands unknown. And wondered how a smart man could be so very, very stupid.

Marnie stood at her thirty-first wedding of the year and tried like heck to look happy. Instead, she suspected she had a face fit for a funeral. She shifted on her heels, slipped a glance at her watch, and bit back a groan. She'd only been here for five minutes. She couldn't make a decent exit until at least thirty minutes had passed.

This was what she worked so hard for, this was the icing on the matchmaking cake, and all the other times, she loved the moment when she saw a couple she had brought together pledge to be together forever. But not this time.

Not since Jack.

She hadn't taken any of his calls. Had refused the flowers he'd sent over. He'd even sent over a first edition of *Make Way for Ducklings,* with a little note inside that said:

The only way to get to the right pond is to take the risk and cross the street. Love, Jack.

That one word had scared her spitless, and she'd tucked the book on a shelf. Erica had just shook her head and not said anything. Marnie buried herself with work, staying late and getting to the office early, making matches until her head hurt.

Late at night, Marnie faced the truth. She was doing it again. Running from her own fears. Rather than confronting them. Was she always going to be like this? Afraid to take the very risks she encouraged her clients to take?

Her sisters and her mother had taken a leap of faith when it came to love. All three were happy as could be, and yet Marnie held back. Why?

She stood to the side of the room, watching couples kiss and dance, while the bride and groom waltzed to their favorite song. Marnie stood alone, flying solo, like she did at most of these events. And feeling miserable.

She had thought, when she walked out of the park, that she was doing the right thing. But really, she had been retreating again. All the emotions of the last few days had overwhelmed her, and brought her deepest fears roaring to the surface. So much for that resolve to go ahead and fall for Jack.

Okay, she had done that. She had fallen for him when he named the daisy Fred. But acting on those feelings—

That terrified her.

Jack had told her that people live and learn and then try to do things different going forward. Thus far, all she'd done was stick to her comfort zone. Which sure as heck wasn't keeping her warm at night.

Wedding guests tapped their forks against their wine glasses, the musical sound signaling to the bride and groom to kiss. Marnie watched Janet and Mark Shalvis giggle, then join hands and kiss each other, happiness exuding from them like perfume.

She thought of the cookie crumbs. The daisies. The picnic. The rain storm. Then she glanced in the mirror on the wall, and saw a woman who made her living creating happy endings, and had to make one of her own.

What was she waiting for? Was she going to be at her thirty-second wedding, still alone, still wishing she'd gone after what she wanted?

The only way to get to the right pond is to take the risk and cross the street.

Even if she didn't know what waited for her on the other side of the street. Or if he still wanted her. But if she didn't do it now, she'd always regret not acting, and Marnie Franklin was tired, dog tired, of living with regrets. If there was one thing her father's death should have taught her, it was that life was short. Her mother had moved on and found happiness in her golden years. What was Marnie waiting for?

Marnie drew in a deep breath, then strode across the room, over to the newly married couple. "Congratulations, you guys. I hate to leave, but I really have to go."

Janet pouted. "Can't you stay a little while longer? I really wanted to introduce you to my mom. And I have three single cousins who could use your help. They're like an advertisement for a lonely hearts club."

How tempting it would be to retreat to that default position of work, instead of risk. For a second Marnie considered it. After all, what difference would a day make?

No. She'd wasted enough days already. She shook her head, and gave Janet a smile. "Have them call me tomorrow. Right now, I have to go. I have a very important match to go make. This one needs…my personal touch."

Janet took her arm and gave it a gentle squeeze. "Good. Because no one knows what's right for another's heart like you do, Marnie."

Even her own, she thought, as she waved goodbye and hurried out the door of the ballroom. The need to be out of here, to be across town, filled her, and she couldn't move fast enough. Her heels slowed her steps, and she kicked them off, gathering them up by the straps and running barefoot across the tiled lobby. Once outside the hotel, she raised her arm to call a cab, when that familiar silver sports car glided into the spot beside her. Dare she hope?

The window on the passenger's side rolled down. "I really need to take you shoe shopping."

The deep voice thrilled her, lifted her heart. He was here. Had he read her mind? Or did he have business inside the hotel? She bent down and saw Jack's familiar grin in the driver's side. "What are you doing here?"

"Rescuing Cinderella before the clock

strikes midnight." He leaned over and opened the door. "Do you need a ride to the ball?"

"Actually, I'm leaving the ball," she said, then got inside the car and shut the door. "I was going to go look for the prince. But it appears he already found me. How on earth did you do that in a city this size?"

"Bloodhounds." He grinned. "No, I'm kidding. You wouldn't talk to me. I got desperate. So I bribed your sister to tell me where you were."

"You bribed Erica?"

"It's amazing what kind of information a chocolate cupcake can buy." Jack chuckled, then put the car in gear and pulled away from the curb. A light rain started up, casting the city in shades of gray, and reminding Marnie of that afternoon at the jazz festival. "If you hadn't come out of that wedding, I would have ended up making quite a scene."

"Oh, really? And what would you have done?"

Jack turned into an empty parking lot, stopped the car and turned to Marnie. The rain fell faster now, pattering against the glass, the roof. "I had it all planned out. I was going to march in there, daisies blazing—" he reached into the back seat and pulled out a huge spray of white daisies "—and tell the entire world that I loved you."

Joy bubbled in her heart. Once, those words would have filled her with fear, but no more. She'd almost lost him, and that realization had woken her up to the fact that she took this chance now, or lost it forever. She thumbed in the direction they'd just come. "You know, we can always go back."

"Maybe later," he said, then put the daisies on the dash and pulled her to him. "After I'm done kissing you."

She put up a hand to stop him. "Wait. I need to tell you something first."

He drew back, hurt shimmering in his eyes. "Okay. Shoot."

"I told you that you weren't facing your fears, when really, I should have said that to myself. It's just that finding out all that stuff about my father, just kicked me in the gut, and so I retreated to my default position." She let out a gust. "I buried my head in the sand, which is exactly what I blamed my parents for doing for years. Ironic, isn't it? That I did the very thing I hated?"

"Sometimes we repeat what we know, even if we don't realize it at the time."

"I put off confronting you and told myself it was because I didn't want to hurt my mother. But really, I was afraid of looking at *me*. At how I was starting to feel for you, and how much that scared me. I let what happened with my father be the reason to avoid a relationship with you because I was damned afraid of letting go."

"And now?"

"Now, I..." She paused, and the smile inside her heart made its way to her face. "Now I just ditched my clients because I wanted to run across town and tell you how I felt."

When he returned the smile, that zing ran through her, faster and more powerful than ever before. If she'd been a matchmaker with a client, she would have told the client to listen to that zing. To follow its lead. Because it always led to the heart's true desire. She raised her lips to Jack's. "I'm falling for you, Jack. You came into my life with a bang, and scared the hell out of me because you kept trying to get me to let my hair down, to be spontaneous and fun and *unfettered*." She laughed again at the word he'd used to describe her.

He brushed her bangs away from her eyes with two gentle fingers. "You are damned sexy that way, you know."

"Oh, really?" She grinned, then released her curls from the clip that held them in place. Her crimson hair cascaded onto her shoulders.

Jack let out a groan and pulled her closer. "We have got to get out of this car and behind a closed door, because I am not making the same mistake I did in the parking lot." His blue eyes darkened with desire and he leaned toward her.

"Wait. There's one other thing." She bit her lip and feigned a serious look. "Before you and I go any further, I wanted to set you up on one more match."

He groaned. "Marnie, I don't want to—"

"She's a redhead. Who loves daisies and has this silly habit of naming the flowers she receives. She loves jazz music and peanut butter cookies, and doesn't mind running through the rain, even if she often wears completely impractical shoes." Jack grinned and leaned in closer, but Marnie put up a finger and pressed it to his lips. "I have to warn you. She's complicated and scared as hell of having her heart broken. But that hasn't stopped this reluctant Cinderella from falling in love with a prince in a silver sports car."

"She sounds like the perfect match for me." The words danced across her fingers, followed by a quick, light kiss. His blue eyes lit with a teasing light. "Though she may want to think twice about getting tangled up with that prince. He's a business owner who's writing a book in his spare time. A guy who has made a few bad choices, but is doing his damnedest to make up for them. And before you get too sold on him, you should know he hates romantic comedies but loves action movies."

She shook her head. "Oh, that could be a deal breaker."

He chuckled, then drew Marnie into his arms. "Maybe we'll just watch the news instead."

"Or," she said, and a delicious smile curved up her face, "we could stay in bed and not watch anything."

"Now *that* sounds like a plan." Jack kissed her then, a deep, sweet, tender kiss that soared in Marnie's veins and filled her heart to the brim. She'd taken the risk, and found exactly what she was looking for on the other side—

Her own happy ending. And as she kissed Jack, the rain fell and the city rushed by in its busy way. But inside the car, the world had slowed to just the two of them, and the match made in heaven.

Three months later, Marnie and Jack stood at the thirty-second wedding of the year, and by far, the biggest success story for Matchmaking by Marnie. From the minute she walked down the aisle, between Dan and Helen, Jack hadn't been able to take his eyes off Marnie. She had to be the most beautiful bride he'd ever seen. She had her hair down, that riot of red curls a stark, sexy contrast to the simple satin sheath dress she wore.

"I love you, Mrs. Knight," he whispered in her ear. They were sitting at the banquet table, with her sisters on either side, while several dozen of their friends enjoyed the food and music. It had been a simple wedding, held outside on the grassy lawn of a country club, with white table and chair sets and a small portable dance floor. Beside them was a small pond, with a pair of ducks making lazy circles through the water. Nothing too fancy, nothing too elaborate. But a day he knew he'd never forget. The summer sun shone over them, like it was smiling down on their happiness. The weatherman had predicted a storm, but so far, everything had been perfect.

"I love you, too, Mr. Knight." She grinned up at him, and Jack thought there was no sight more beautiful in the world than his wife's smile. *His wife.*

He didn't know if he'd ever get used to how amazing that sounded. He hoped not. He owed that cab driver a thank-you for being a distracted driver that night.

"I hope you're ready to dance tonight," Marnie said.

"Always, if it's with you. Though it depends on what you're wearing for shoes, Cinderella."

She chuckled, then lifted the hem of her dress to reveal very sensible and very comfortable decorated tennis shoes. They'd been studded with rhinestones and featured lacy bows. He laughed. Leave it to Marnie to surprise him, even today.

"I didn't want anything to spoil our wedding," she said.

"Nothing would spoil today, not even a freak winter storm," he said, then kissed her. She curved into his arms, a perfect fit. She had been, from the first moment he met her.

"Oh! My! God! You guys are the cutest couple ever! I can't believe you invited me to your wedding!" The high, loud voice of Roberta carried across the lawn, rising several decibels above the music and the murmurs of the guests. Jack and Marnie laughed, then turned toward her. She sent them a wave, then got back to shimmying her bright pink clad self with Hector on the dance floor. The couple had been together for several months now, and had even talked about marriage. A miracle, in Marnie's eyes.

"I think she's finally found her match," Marnie whispered to Jack. "I owe you big time for introducing them. I was worried I'd never find a match for Roberta."

"Oh, and I intend to collect on that debt. For the rest of our lives." He leaned in and kissed his wife, while guests clinked their glasses and cheered them on.

The DJ shifted the music from a fast song to a slow, romantic song. Couples began to head for the dance floor, including her sisters and their dates. Jack put out his hand for Marnie.

There was a rumble, and an instant later, the skies opened up, dropping a fast, furious, soaking summer storm. Guests began to run toward the building, shrieking in the rain, and hurrying to keep from getting wet. The dance floor emptied out, the DJ pulled the plug and dashed inside, yelling that his equipment would be ruined. Even Roberta and Hector made a fast break for the cover of the country club. But Marnie stayed where she was with Jack.

"Don't you want to get inside?" he said.

She shook her head, even as little rivers of water ran down her cheeks and arms. Her dress was already plastered to her body, but she didn't seem to care. "They say that a little rain is lucky on your wedding day. And I want to make sure we have all the luck we need."

"Oh, Marnie, we already do," Jack said softly and drew her to him. "We have each other."

They kissed again, while the ducks quacked and the rain fell and the world around them dropped away. They kissed until the storm abated and the sun came out again, as if giving their marriage its own blessing. They kissed, and for the first time in their lives, Jack and Marnie put their faith in happily ever after.

* * * * *

Boardroom Bride and Groom

CHAPTER ONE

CAROLYN DUFF HAD made one major mistake in her life—a whopping cliché of a mistake in a Vegas wedding chapel—which hadn't, unlike the commercials said, stayed in Vegas.

It had followed her back here—and was working in an office just a few blocks down the street. All six-foot-two of him.

Most days she forgot about Nicholas Gilbert and concentrated on her job. As an assistant city prosecutor she barely had time to notice when the sun went down, because her days tended to pass in a blur of phone calls, legal precedents, Indiana case law and urgent e-mails. Her calendar might have said Friday, her clock already ticking past five, but still Carolyn stayed behind her desk, finishing up yet another flurry of work, even though tomorrow was the start of the Fourth of July weekend and the courts would be closed until Tuesday.

For Carolyn it didn't matter. An internal time bomb kept ticking away, pushing her to keep going, to pursue one more criminal case, to see the prison bars slam shut once more.

To know she'd done her part again.

And yet it wasn't enough. Not nearly enough.

Carolyn rubbed at her temples, trying to beat back the start of another headache before it got too intense. Then she set to work, working on a negotiation for a plea bargain with a local defense attorney who thought his client—a petty thief—merited merely a ninety-day jail stint and a small fine. Carolyn, who could see the future handwriting on the wall, one that upped the ante to a felony charge—B&E with a deadly weapon—wanted years behind bars. The presiding judge, however, wanted a fast resolution that would clear his docket of one more hassle. He'd given the two attorneys the weekend to find a middle ground.

Mary Hudson popped her head in the door. Her chestnut pageboy swung around her chin, framing wide brown eyes and a friendly smile. "Everyone's gone home," said the paralegal. "Tell me you're taking the holiday weekend off, too."

"Eventually."

Mary sighed. "Carolyn, it's a holiday. Time to party, not work. Come on, go out for drinks with me. I'm meeting some of the girls from the other attorneys' offices over at T.J.'s Pub."

"Sorry, Mary. Too much work to do."

"You know what you need?" Mary crossed to the coffeepot on the credenza, adding some water from a waiting pitcher, then loading in a couple of scoops of coffee from a decorative canister, intuitively reading Carolyn's late-afternoon need for another caffeine fix. "A killer sundress and a sexy man—one always attracts the other."

When it came to fixing Carolyn up, Mary was like a persistent five-year-old wanting candy before dinner—she'd try every tactic known to man and wasn't above shameless begging. To Mary a woman without a man was akin to a possum without a tail—a creature to be pitied and helped.

"I don't need a man, Mary." Though the last time Carolyn had gone on a date...

Okay, so she couldn't think of the last time she'd gone on a date.

Speaking of dates and men—the image of Nick sprang to mind, and a surge of something thick and hot Carolyn refused to call desire rose in her chest. What was it with that man? He'd been a blip in her life story, and yet he'd always lingered in the back of her mind like he was the one chapter in her life she wished she'd never written but couldn't forget reading. Well, she certainly didn't intend to check that book out of the library again. She already knew the ending.

One crazy weekend. One reckless decision. Four days later it was over.

Mary leaned against the mahogany credenza, arms akimbo, waiting for acquiescence. "Okay, so I can't get you to leave early, but you will be at the fund-raiser for the Care-and-Connect-with-Children program, won't you? These kids are all so needy, Carolyn. I've seen their files. Foster kids, kids living below the poverty level—they run the gamut. And don't worry about having to get too involved or hands-on. We have a lot of activities planned to keep the kids busy all day, partly to give the foster parents a break, too. It's pretty overwhelming, taking in strangers."

And overwhelming for the children, living with strangers, but Carolyn didn't say that. She kept her past to herself. When she'd left Boston three and a half years ago, she'd also left those memories behind. "I promise, I'll be at the picnic on Saturday. But I don't need a new dress. I can wear the one I wore to the office summer party last year. No one remembers what anyone wears at these things, and I can go stag because I am perfectly capable—"

"Of taking care of yourself," Mary finished on a sigh. "Yeah, I know. So are hermit crabs, but you don't see them smiling, now, do you?"

"They're crustaceans, Mary. I don't think they have smiles."

"Exactly." Mary nodded, as if that validated her point.

In the two years Mary had worked in the office, Carolyn had yet to figure out what stratosphere Mary's mind was working on. Luckily, Mary typed at an ungodly speed and filed with an almost zenlike ability. As for the rest...

Well, Carolyn was twenty-eight and didn't need anyone to tell her how to live her life. Or to tell her she needed a man to take care of her. Not when there were more important things on her desk, like a thief.

She opened the thick manila folder before her and began reviewing the facts in the case again. If she got distracted for one second, she could miss something. A guilty man, for instance. This time it was Liam Pendant, a career criminal with an unregistered firearm in the glove compartment of his truck. His lawyer wanted her to go easy on him, but

Carolyn disagreed. What if Liam had taken his crime a step further? Entered the house instead of just stolen the lawnmower out of the open garage? What if he'd taken the gun along? Used it on the homeowner who had caught him running down the driveway?

Instead of a simple burglary charge, she could be looking at another senseless tragedy, the result of a bad temper mixed with a gun.

And Carolyn knew all too well where that could lead. How a family could be destroyed in the blink of an eye. No, she decided, reviewing Liam's extensive rap sheet again, then closing the folder.

There would be no deal.

Mary took a seat on the edge of Carolyn's desk, depositing a mug of coffee before her. Carolyn thanked her and went on working. Mary laid a palm on the papers, blocking Carolyn's view. "Hon, an earthworm has more of a life than you do."

"Mary, aren't you paid to—"

"Assist, not direct you?" she finished.

Carolyn laughed and stretched in her chair. "I guess I've said that often enough."

"And I've ignored you often enough. But after two years together, I consider us friends. And as your friend, I have to say you're working too hard." She rose, crossed the room and opened the closed blinds, revealing the brightly lit city outside. "In case you haven't noticed, it's summer. People are out there enjoying the sun. Not staying inside like vampires."

For a second, Carolyn paused to turn around and admire the view. The burst of fire the afternoon sun cast over the downtown square, the busy stream of traffic leaving the city as people returned to their families or headed out of Lawford for the tranquility of the lakes that dotted the Indiana landscape.

"It's a perfect day," Mary said. "And it's going to be a perfect weekend for the program for the kids. They're going to love all the gifts and the—"

"Oh the gifts! Damn!" Carolyn rubbed at her temples. "I haven't bought a single present yet. I promised to sponsor one of those children and I totally forgot to get to the store. I'm sorry, Mary. These last few cases have been eating up every spare moment."

"There's always going to be another case," Mary said gently. "Will you please get out and enjoy the sunshine, Carolyn? I swear, all this climate-controlled air is frying your brain."

Carolyn rose and crossed to the window. For a second, she felt the warmth of the day, felt the special magic that seemed to come with summer days wrap around her heart. Her mind spiraled back to her childhood, to those first days out of school, running to greet her father when he got home from work, the endless bike rides they'd take, the times he'd push her on the backyard swing—*just one more time, Dad, please, one more time*—the games of catch that went long into the twilight hours. Once in a while they'd stay up late, watching for shooting stars or playing catch-and-release with fireflies.

Her throat caught, a lump so thick in the space below her chin, she couldn't swallow. *Oh, Dad.* How she missed him, the ache hitting deep and sharp, from time to time.

Every summer with her father had been… incredible. It had been just the two of them, after her mother had been killed in a car accident shortly after Carolyn was born. Because of that, Carolyn and her father had shared a bond. A bond she missed, missed so very much there were days when she swore she could touch the pain.

After her father died when she was nine, she'd lost that feeling of joy, that anticipation of warm days, of long, lazy evenings. She'd started staying indoors, avoiding summer because everything had lost its magic. Trying to forget the very season she had enjoyed so much.

Then Nick had come along a few years ago and reminded her of the fun she used to have. Reminded her that magic still existed.

For a while Carolyn had let loose and done something completely crazy—so crazy that it had led her to a disaster of a marriage. For five minutes she'd let go of the tight hold she'd had over her life, and when she had, the ball of control went rolling over the hill way too fast.

Thankfully, she'd fixed that mistake almost immediately, and everything was on the right path now. She was successful at her job. Sure, it had come at the cost of what other people had—a home, kids, the trappings of tradition—but for a woman like Carolyn, who had about as much experience with the traditional life as a swimsuit model did with dog sledding, it was just as well. Besides, neither she nor Nick had taken the marriage seriously, not really.

And when that face from her past appeared on the TV screen in the diner, blasting Carolyn's history on national airwaves, she'd made her choice and walked away from Nick for good.

Carolyn pushed away the memories then returned to her desk, swallowed two aspirin with the black coffee, and went back to work. "I'll leave early—er. I promise, Mary."

Mary sighed. "Okay. See you tomorrow, then. You will be at the picnic, right? Not chained to this desk?"

Carolyn smiled. "I'll be there. I promise."

"I'm holding you to it. And if you don't show up," Mary said, with a warning wag of her index finger, "you know I'll come right down here and drag you out of this office."

Mary said goodbye, then headed out of the office, already exchanging her pumps for a pair of flip-flops in her purse. Clearly, the paralegal was ready to start her holiday weekend.

Carolyn thought of the last time she'd done something that carefree. That spontaneous. And she couldn't remember. Somewhere along the road, it had simply become easier to spend weekends, holidays, Friday nights at her desk. Easier to ignore the invitations to dinners that were clearly fix-ups, the dates with men who didn't interest her, the lonely evenings at home by herself.

Mary was right. Carolyn could almost feel her father looking down on her from heaven, tsk-tsking at all the sunshine she had missed, the sunsets that had passed behind Carolyn's back as she'd worked.

Well, she *did* have shopping to do for the picnic tomorrow. What better excuse to leave early? She finished up the last few tasks on her desk, including leaving a voice mail for Liam's attorney telling him no deal, then shut down her computer. Her gaze caught on the bright blue-and-yellow envelope for the Care-and-Connect-with-Children program. She tugged it out, stuck it in her briefcase, then headed out the door.

As she headed down in the elevator, she opened the envelope and pulled out the photo of the child inside. A paper clip held a four-by-six-inch picture of a five-year-old boy to the corner of a sheet of paper.

Her stomach clenched. Oh, he was a cute little thing—blond and blue-eyed, a little on the skinny side, and in desperate need, the sheet said, of almost everything. School supplies, clothes, sheets. His dream wish list was so simple, it nearly broke Carolyn's heart: books to read and a single toy truck.

For a split second, she saw the future that could have been in the boy's eyes. If she had stayed married to Nick—if either of them had made that bond into something real.

Carolyn traced the outline of the child's face. What if...

But no. There were no what ifs, not where

she and Nicholas Gilbert were concerned. Carolyn had made her choices, and made them for very good reasons—and exactly the one that made her happy.

By the time the elevator doors whooshed open, Carolyn was back in work mode. She'd deal with this sponsorship project with her typical take-charge attitude. Clutching the envelope tight, she ran down a mental list of tasks, compartmentalizing the entire process, treating it as simply one more thing to do. Distancing herself, keeping emotions out of the equation.

That, Carolyn knew, was the best way to protect her most valuable asset—the one she'd vowed never to expose again, especially not to another lawyer—

Her heart.

The last place Nick Gilbert expected to be on a Friday night was a toy store.

Yet here he was, standing in the center of a brightly lit aisle filled with pink and lace, trying to decide between a doll that cried and a doll that burped. To him, neither seemed to offer an advantage. Burping might be a cool and very funny option—but only if you were a teenage boy looking to crack up the algebra class. Nevertheless, given the way the little girls swarming around him were grabbing the toys off the shelves, both outbursts were wildly popular.

Cry...or burp?

He may have grown up in a big family, but everything Nick knew about children could fit on the back of an ant, with room left for an entire kindergarten class. Why had he agreed to sponsor a child for the Care-and-Connect-with-Children program? What was he thinking?

He'd been swayed by a picture. By the list of needs on the sheet inside the packet of information about the child. And he'd thought, with his typical can-do attitude, that he could handle this.

Ha. He'd have been better off trying to corral a herd of elephants.

And, truth be told, he'd also thought a trip to a toy store, a few gifts thrown into a cart and an afternoon at the Care-and-Connect picnic might fill the gnawing hole in his chest. It had grown more persistent lately, like a thirst he couldn't quite quench. A crazy feeling, because he should be content. He had everything he needed. A good career. Great friends, a loving family who lived nearby. An easy lifestyle that demanded nothing.

And yet...

His grip tightened on the dolls' try-me buttons, which made them let out a simultaneous burp-cry. Two moms in the aisle turned to look at him, twin amused smiles on their face, coupled with looks of compassion. A man in the baby doll aisle. Apparently he was an object of pity.

"Trial run before I have a real kid," he joked. "I think I like the burping better. It's more entertaining."

The moms shook their heads, then laughed and walked away.

Nick tossed both packages into his cart, then swung it around and headed down the aisle. He spun to the right, intending to get out of the store as quickly as he could. This was *so* not his forte. But as he rounded the corner, his cart collided with another, jostling the dolls, who complained with another burp-cry.

Nick barely noticed. Because he found himself staring at the one woman he thought he'd managed to forget.

Carolyn Duff.

She had deep-green eyes, so wide and dark, they were as inviting as placid lakes beneath a moonlit sky. A charcoal suit hugged her body, yet gave nothing away. Sensible pumps with kitten heels, not high enough to show off the real curves of her long legs, but enough to remind him of those gorgeous, long limbs. Blond hair, put back in a severe, tight bun, but Nick knew, when she let her hair down, it would be just long enough to tease around her features and whisper along her cheekbones, her jaw.

Everything about Carolyn on the outside was delicate, and yet on the inside she was strong—like a flamingo that could weather a hurricane.

She'd been the one woman who had intrigued him more than any other in law school. Her upper-crust, stiff Bostonian attitude had been a challenge to him—because when they'd met and he'd made her laugh, he'd glimpsed the Carolyn underneath, it had made him want to peel back the layers, get her to loosen up. Tease out the fun side of the severe, break-no-rules studier.

He'd done that, then done the most spontaneous thing in his life. Taken it to the next level and married her—the biggest mistake of his life.

And now that mistake was standing right in front of him.

CHAPTER TWO

"WHAT ARE YOU DOING HERE?" Carolyn asked. Her heartbeat doubled with the shock of seeing him. She saw the same surprise reflected in the widening of his eyes, the way he seemed rooted to the spot. Nick Gilbert, the last man she expected to run into in the toy aisle.

Nick. Her...

Husband?

The thought ran through her in a rush, along with the embarrassing memory of when she'd said "I do" in a tacky Vegas wedding chapel and made promises she, of all people, shouldn't have made.

No, he wasn't her husband. Not anymore. Her ex.

Their marriage, their relationship was over now. *They* were over.

"I was about to ask you the same thing," he said.

She looked up at him, hating the disadvantage of being shorter. At six-two, Nick had always had a good seven-inch height advantage over her. Years ago she'd liked that. Liked that she could look up into his teasing blue eyes and be swept up into the humor of his smile.

But not anymore. Right now she wished she had on platform heels so she could go toe-to-toe with those blue eyes.

Blue eyes that no longer had any effect on her. Whatsoever. Despite the tingle she'd felt when she ran into him in the crowded courthouse elevator last week. And glimpsed him in the cafeteria from time to time.

She'd seen him off and on many times since their divorce, but never this close. Never had to have a real conversation with him. Even now, as she had for the past three years, she could turn away, walk down the aisle as if nothing had happened.

But something had. A little something inside her had zigged when they had zagged.

With a start, she realized he was staring at her—because she hadn't answered the question. Heat filled her cheeks, which only left her more discomfited.

Carolyn Duff didn't do discomfited. She *never* felt out of sorts.

"I'm buying toys for one of the children in

the charity—" She glanced down at his cart and saw toys. Books.

"Me, too. I think the entire Lawford legal community got onboard with this one," he said. "But maybe I should have stuck to business law. I haven't the foggiest idea what the hell I'm doing." He reached into his cart and pulled out the two dolls. "Burps or cries? Which is better? How am I supposed to know? To me, they're both losing propositions."

She laughed and when she did, it resurrected a part of her she'd thought she left behind long ago. A lightness she'd lost in the years she'd lived with her aunt Greta, then rediscovered when she'd met Nick.

A lightness she'd missed in the heavy work of being a city prosecutor.

She glanced at Nick. The poor man clearly had no clue when it came to kids—and neither did she. The two of them were stuck in the same shopping hell. What harm could come from a little talking? "I know exactly how you feel. I was standing in the next aisle with the same problem." She reached into her cart and pulled out a selection of trucks. "Fire engine or police car? Dump truck or…what is this thing? A front loader? And what is a front loader anyway? And then there's these things called transformers, but I can't figure out why anyone would want a toy that transforms, or if it's even what this boy would want." Carolyn tossed the toys back into her cart and threw up her hands. She was babbling. She always did that when she got nervous—something that only seemed to happen outside the courtroom, and apparently whenever she got around Nick, who was a six-foot-two reminder of her biggest mistake. "Whatever happened to a bat, a ball and a catcher's mitt?"

Nick chuckled. "It has gotten complicated, hasn't it? Every single thing I see here has a computer chip in it, I swear. These aren't just toys, they're technological revolutions." Nick shook his head. "Well, I'll muddle through somehow. After all, I've got a college degree. How hard can it be? Just watch me." He chuckled, showing the easy humor that had always been as much a part of Nick as his dark-brown hair and his cobalt eyes.

Did he remember that crazy decision to rush off to Vegas? The heady choice they'd made? One where they'd clearly not been thinking with brain cells, and only with the blush of lust?

Carolyn, out of Aunt Greta's house for the first time since she was nine, so desperate to cast off the strangling structure of her past, saw escape in Nick. She'd married him for all the wrong reasons and had at least been smart enough to undo it the first chance she got.

Nick leaned forward, reading the boxes that lined the shelves, studying the facts and figures, researching his purchase. He was being the detail man that made him a good lawyer, but betraying none of the funny, spontaneous Nick she'd once known. Just as well. She didn't need that man in her life. Because that man was the one who had—for a snippet of time—made her think she could be someone she really wasn't.

"This says ages eight and up," Nick read aloud, sounding as serious as a tax accountant. "I don't think that will work. My paper says the child is six."

"My—" She caught herself before she said "my child," because this wasn't her child. "The child I'm sponsoring is almost the same age. I have a five-year-old."

"Someone wasn't thinking. Giving you and me a couple of little kids like that. They should have assigned us two high school students. *That* we can handle. Buy them a couple calculators and some dictionaries. Sit them down, dispense some college advice."

"Yeah." She let out a little laugh. An uncomfortable silence filled the space between them, the kind that came from two people who used to know each other and now didn't, who were pretending everything was cool—even when a heat still simmered in the air.

Leave, her mind said. Take this pause as what it was—an excuse to go. But her feet didn't go anywhere and she couldn't have said why.

"Maybe you should try this one." Carolyn picked up a box that held a big white plastic horse designed for a doll to take galloping into the sunset. She flipped over the box, read the same age recommendation as Nick had seen and put it back on the shelf. That was all they needed—a choking lawsuit. "Forget it. Too many small parts."

He gave her a smile. "When did you get so smart about toys?"

"I didn't. It's the lawyer in me reading the fine print."

"You always were good at that part."

Carolyn let those words go, knowing Nick meant more than the directions on a box. She'd been the strict one, always playing by the rules, where he'd been the opposite.

"What's your kid's name?" Nick asked, strolling further down the aisle, toward the dress-up clothes.

"Name?" Carolyn looked at him.

"Yeah. His or her name."

"Uh…" Carolyn thought for a second. "Bobby."

Nick grinned, and when he did, Carolyn was whisked back to those college days. "Nice name. My child is named Angela."

"Your…your child? You're married?"

"Are you kidding me? Could you see me with kids?" He chuckled. "You know me, Carolyn. I'm not the kind of guy who likes to have ties."

That had been part of the attraction and part of the problem. Carolyn had gone for Nick because he'd been the complete opposite of the life she'd left in Boston, but when she'd needed him to be dependable, to listen, to be a true partner—

He hadn't been there. He'd let her down.

"No, I never married again," Nick went on. "Angela is the child I'm sponsoring."

Carolyn released a breath she hadn't even realized she'd been holding. Nick wasn't married. He didn't have kids. No other woman had laid claim to his heart.

She shouldn't care. The days when she had any stake in Nick—or in anything about Nick—were long past.

"So, nope, no kids for me. This is as close as I get." He gestured toward the basket of toys.

"A one-day commitment, huh?"

"Those seem to be the kind I'm good at." Nick's gaze met hers, and their shared history unfurled in the tension thickening the air between them.

A mother with two children, one strapped into the shopping cart's seat, the other trailing behind and whining discontent about some toy she'd been denied, squeezed past them. On the overhead sound system, someone called for a price check in aisle three. Once again, the uncomfortable silence of two people who had essentially become strangers grew between Carolyn and Nick, like a tangle of thorny vines separating once-friendly neighbors.

"Well, it was great seeing you, Nick," Carolyn said. "Good luck with your shopping."

Before she could turn away, Nick reached out and laid a hand on top of hers. Carolyn took in a breath, the air searing her lungs, awareness pumping through her veins. Nick's touch, so familiar, yet also so new after all this time apart, spread warmth through her hand. The scent of his cologne—the same cologne, as if nothing had changed, not a single thing. The sound of his heartbeat, his every breath—could she really hear that, or was it just her own, matching his?—time stopping for one, long slow second. "Wait. Don't go," he said.

"Why?"

"Why don't we shop together?"

The mother and two children disappeared around the corner, the whine of the eldest child dropping off when she apparently spied a better toy. The store's music droned on with its instrumental rendition of Seventies hits, a soft undertow of lounge melodies. "Shop together?" Carolyn repeated.

He grinned. "Do either of us look like we know what the heck we're doing?"

She glanced down at her haphazard selection of toys. A complete zoo of stuffed animals. Every type and kind of truck carried by the store. Books that featured cartoon characters, superheroes, animals and dancing vegetables. She'd pretty much bought one of everything, hoping that a scattershot of presents would result in something the child might like.

She'd already spent three hours at this toy shopping and had almost nothing that said "Wow, great gift" to show for her efforts. Every item she picked up, she hemmed and hawed over, wondering if a little boy would like this or would prefer that. The truth was, she had no idea what little boys, or little girls, for that matter, really wanted. She could barely remember her own childhood.

When it came to buying presents for a little boy, who better to ask for an opinion than a male? A male who'd been the kind to enjoy playing Frisbee and catch on the college campus? The kind who clearly knew how to have fun?

She and Nick were both adults. Their marriage—which they'd both agreed back in that diner was a mistake—was far in the past. This was a charity mission. What harm could a few minutes of shopping do?

"This is a one-time offer," he said. "One of the Lawford attorneys offering to help a prosecutor, pro bono."

She laughed again, and right there, found herself caught in the old spell all over again. The one that had made her abandon her structured life and go along with Nick's crazy Vegas plan. But this idea wasn't crazy; it was merely a partnership. "How very charitable of you."

"It's not charity. After all, weren't we always better together than apart?"

"Maybe in school, in classes, we worked well together, but not as a couple. You know that, Nick," she said. "As far as I'm concerned, we've been happily divorced for three years."

He arched a brow, cynicism written all over

his features, and she wondered if maybe the end of the marriage hadn't been the relief to him that she'd always told herself it had been. "Happily?"

"Divorce was what we both wanted. We agreed it was a stupid mistake and the best thing was to undo it as fast as possible. Tell no one, forget it ever happened. Pretend we'd never met. Remember?" Carolyn remembered those words, the argument that had accompanied that moment, and most of all, the look of pained disappointment in Nick's eyes. It had surprised her, because she'd thought Nick hadn't taken their bolt to the altar seriously at all—hadn't thought Nick took anything seriously.

"I remember our ending as being more like removing a bandage, quick and a little painful."

"Well, it's over now, and we've both moved on, right?"

"Of course. And presumably, we've matured since then."

"Have you?" she asked.

He grinned. "Not a bit."

She chuckled. "I'm not surprised."

"Ah, but that's what keeps my life fun. And makes for entertainment in the courtroom."

She just shook her head. Nick was exactly the same.

Over the years, Carolyn had managed to

avoid seeing Nick, as much as was possible in the relatively small Lawford legal community. It helped that they worked in two entirely different areas of law—criminal and corporate.

When they did see each other, they exchanged nothing more than a simple nod, a few words of greeting.

Wearing a suit, he was devastatingly handsome. Powerful. In boxers and bare-chested, he was—

Irresistible. Sexy.

Luckily, today he was wearing a two-button navy suit with a white shirt and dark-crimson tie. It fit him perfectly, hugging over the broad shoulders and defined chest she knew existed beneath the fine fabrics. As did, apparently, the rest of the female population in the store, women who made little secret of staring at Nick. And why not? Nick Gilbert was the kind of man women noticed.

Carolyn returned to the matter at hand, drawing herself up. "I'll let you get back to your shopping," she said. "It was nice to see you again. Good night, Nick."

She made moves to leave, but Nick took a step closer. "You don't want to shop together? Are you afraid?"

"Afraid of what?"

"Working together. Don't tell me the great

Bulldog of Lawford isn't up to the challenge of a little shopping trip with her ex. For a good cause, I might add."

Her chin went up a notch. "I can certainly shop with you."

"And not be at all affected by my winning personality." He grinned. And damn if that smile didn't whisper a temptation to take a dip in the pool of fun again. Just for a second.

"What winning personality?" She gave him a slight teasing smile back. "I heard you lost your last two cases."

"Are you keeping track of my career, Miss Duff?"

"Of course not."

"One might think you are. Otherwise, why would a city prosecutor care what a corporate lawyer is up to?"

Her chin rose a little higher. "Just making sure you're staying in check, Mr. Gilbert, and not breaking any rules."

He grinned. "And when have you ever known *me* to stay in check?"

The memory danced into the forefront of her thoughts. The first time she'd met Nick Gilbert. She'd been leaving the university library, overloaded and overwhelmed, books piled in her arms, preparation for a marathon study session for the upcoming bar exam.

She'd transferred to the Indiana school just a month earlier, and found the transition to be difficult, the adjustment harder than she'd expected. She'd made the best of the change, as she always had of every situation in her life—because she didn't have a choice.

She'd been financially cut off in Boston and had opted for the only school that had offered her a partial scholarship and a tuition she could afford.

But she'd had difficulty fitting in among the informal Midwesterners who didn't understand the stiff-upper-lip Bostonian. One month in, and Carolyn had yet to make any friends. As she'd crossed the campus, she'd felt the stares of the other students. Her step had caught on a bump in the sidewalk, the books began to fall—

And then Nick Gilbert came along.

He'd stood out in a sea of brown and navy like a neon sign. He'd rushed over, righted the books and done the most insane thing she could have imagined to set her at ease.

He'd made a quarter disappear.

But in that simple, unexpected magic trick, Nick had won her over and made everything Carolyn had to face seem so much less daunting.

"So, what'll it be?" Nick asked. "Tough it

out on our own in the wilds of the toy department or join forces?"

Carolyn met Nick's gaze and smiled, caught up in the old magic once again. "All right, I'll shop with you, but only because you are so clearly hopeless at this."

"Oh, I see, take pity on the man. Is that it?"

A bubble of laughter escaped her, filling Carolyn with a lightness she hadn't felt in weeks, months. How she craved that feeling, yet at the same time, felt the urge to flee. "Don't you *need* pity, Mr. Burp-or-Cry?"

"Oh, I need more than that, Carolyn."

The way he said her name, with that husky, all-male tone, the kind that spoke of dark nights, tangled sheets, hot memories, sent a thrill running through Carolyn, sparked images she'd thought she'd forgotten. But, oh no, she hadn't forgotten at all. She'd merely pushed those pictures to the side, her mind waiting—waiting for a moment like this to bring them to the forefront, like an engine that had idled all this time.

How she wished she were in a courtroom instead of a toy store. That was the world she knew, could predict. But Nick Gilbert was about as predictable as a tiger in a butcher shop.

This was a bad idea. A very bad idea.

"Playing house," Carolyn said, popping into action. "That's what we need."

Nick arched a brow. "You and me? Play house? I thought we already tried that and it didn't work so well."

"Not us. For…" Her mind went blank. Looking at Nick, thinking of playing house… oh, why had she thought she could do this? Just being here was a mistake. But she'd already made the deal and couldn't renegotiate. Not with a lawyer and especially not with this one. "I meant for the child you're sponsoring. Little girls, they like to play house. Pretend to go to the grocery store, set the table, all that."

"But not you, right, Carolyn? Or did you ever have a moment when you did play house? When you imagined being a Mrs. for longer than a few days?"

"Me?" She snorted. "You know that is so not me. I don't think I have a domestic bone in my body."

"We still have that in common," Nick said. "I've yet to become domesticated myself, though I am housebroken." He grinned. "What about you? How have things been for you over the last three years?"

Carolyn reached for the nearest toy on the shelf. "How about this broom set for Angela?"

"I recognize this avoidance tactic. Divert

attention from the personal and get back to work, right?"

"Nick, if you're not going to take this seriously—"

"Oh, I'm serious, Carolyn." He straightened, his demeanor slightly chilled. "As serious as you are."

Then he started pushing the cart, heading down the aisle toward the faux food and make-believe vacuum cleaners. Now also all business and no play. Not anymore.

Carolyn wasn't the least bit disappointed. Not the least.

"How about this for Angela?" Nick held up a pretend cooking set, plastic frying pans, spatulas, bright yellow faux eggs and floppy bacon. Little cardboard boxes of cereal marched up the side of the package, with cheery pretend names like Cocoa Crunchies and Corn Flakies.

"Perfect," Carolyn said, coming up beside Nick and holding the other side of the package. Only a few inches separated them. When she inhaled, she caught the scent of his cologne again. She could sense the heat from his body, read the strength in his hands.She focused instead on the bright happy packaging, on the images of children sitting around a plastic table, pretending they were dining at a five-star mock-up restaurant. "When I was a little girl, they didn't make toys like this. I was always taking the real thing out of the kitchen and if I didn't have any friends over, I made my poor dad sit down for pretend meals. Oh, how I made that man suffer through tea parties with me and my bears."

Nick chuckled softly. "My sisters used to try to do the same thing to me and my brothers but we were too fast. We'd steal the cookies and run like hell for the yard. Linda, Marla and Elise still think Daniel and I are the spawn of the devil because we ruined their plans to recreate the Mad Hatter's Tea Party."

Carolyn laughed. "I never did get a chance to meet your family. I wish I had. They sound so fun."

"They would have liked you."

The words hung between them. They'd been married too short a time for meeting families—not that there'd been anyone on Carolyn's side to meet. Anyone who would have cared about meeting Nick, anyway.

Had Nick told his family about her? Had he told his sisters about the woman who had stolen his heart, then broken it, all in the space of a month?

Carolyn shoved the thoughts away. She'd

had good reasons, reasons Nick had refused to see at the time, refused to listen. He'd fought her, tooth and nail, telling her it could wait, that they'd just gotten married—*stay awhile, don't go, not yet*—and not understanding at all that she'd *had* to go—

Had to get on that plane. She couldn't sit in Indiana, acting the part of the happy wife, while the man who had killed her father went on another rampage. By the time she came home, the divorce was final. Nick had done the filing, taking care of the details, cleaning up the mess.

It was all for the best, she told herself again.

"Let's get the rest of Angela's gifts," Carolyn said, returning to business. Nick seemed relieved to do the same, and they made quick work of filling the cart with toys for the little girl.

"My turn to help you," Nick said a little while later. "And for your information, little boys don't want to play house, so let's pick a different aisle."

Work again. Concentrate on the project. Not the man.

Carolyn led the way as they headed over to the aisle of trucks and cars. Nick directed her toward the larger, more indestructible options. "This is what Bobby wants." Nick hoisted up a red plastic truck large enough to transport a puppy.

"How do you know for sure? There's this one, and that one, and the one down there." Carolyn gestured all over the aisle, as confused as she had been an hour ago.

"I know because I was once a little boy. And I had one of these, except mine sported the less-knee-and-elbow-friendly metal finish." Nick turned the box over in his hands, lost in a memory. "I had a lot of fun with that truck. I remember the Christmas I got it. I was five. Daniel was three. He came charging at me, wanting to play with the truck. Cut his chin open on the coffee table and he ended up in the emergency room on Christmas day, getting stitches."

"Oh, my goodness. That must have been awful."

Nick shook his head. "My mother is a saint. She could raise all five of us and run a household blindfolded. She shot off directions to my dad and the rest of us for how to put together Christmas dinner, loaded Daniel in the car and drove to the hospital, calm as a summer breeze. We, of course, butchered dinner without her there." Nick laughed. "But when she came back, with Daniel all stitched up, she somehow made it all right and saved Christmas."

Carolyn spun the loose plastic covering on the shopping handle. She thought of how her aunt Greta would have reacted to such an event. For one, it wouldn't have happened because there'd been no big happy family around the Christmas tree. No turkey to stuff. No hectic gathering. But if there had been, Greta simply wouldn't have allowed chaos to disrupt her house. In Aunt Greta's house, chaos never, ever visited. It didn't even walk down the sidewalk. And secondly, children didn't take chances. They didn't run. They didn't ride their bikes down the sidewalk. They didn't do anything death defying. "Your family sounds like something out of a novel."

Nick smiled, then put the toy truck into the shopping cart. "Sometimes I think it was." Nick paused midstep, then met her gaze, and for a fleeting second she wondered if he was reading her mind. "Carolyn—"

"Let's get this shopping done. I need to get home. I have a ton of work waiting for me." Carolyn started down the aisle, cutting off Nick and the attraction she read in his gaze.

Then the look disappeared, gone in a simple blink.

"Yeah, good idea. We *should* concentrate on the shopping," Nick said, joining her by the race cars. "I have work waiting for me, too."

Carolyn gave him a sidelong glance but couldn't read anything in Nick's face. Maybe she had read Nick wrong. Or maybe he had changed, maybe he wasn't the man she remembered.

They finished the shopping trip, agreeing on their purchases easily. Before long, they'd found several hundred dollars worth of toys, much more than they'd expected to find or spend. The shopping spree had been fun, almost like—

Like when they'd gotten married. Never before had Carolyn gone without a plan, running by the seat of her pants, working purely on desire.

She hadn't been thinking that week, simply *doing*. And for a moment she'd thought she could do it all. Be a wife, and maybe... down the road...a mother.

What if today's toy buying hadn't been a charity mission? What if they'd been shopping for their own child?

Where would they be now? Living in a three-bedroom house in some subdivision in Lawford, kissing each other goodbye over a cup of coffee every morning? Or would they have ended up exactly where they were—divorced, scarcely cordial colleagues? Nick still acting a lot like a college frat boy, Carolyn still the stiff Bostonian?

"Those kids are going to need a truck to haul all this home," Nick said, interrupting her thoughts.

Carolyn smiled. "I think I saw some of those in aisle three."

"Don't tempt me," Nick said, and in his eyes, she read more than just the desire to buy a ride-on toy.

There was a lingering desire for her. Still burning in his gaze. Emanating from his skin, his nearness. And who was she kidding? She still felt it, too.

But the past was over. And for a good reason.

They'd made a big mistake once. Only an idiot did that twice.

"Well, I guess that's it. I, ah, can run over to the department store and pick up some clothes and sheets, if you want to take care of this stuff," Carolyn said, digging into her purse for money and then handing him half the cost of their purchases. Nick had agreed, since he had the bigger vehicle, to transport the toys to the picnic while she brought the other items. "See you tomorrow?" She tried to keep her tone as professional as it would be with a client.

As she turned to go, Nick took a step toward her, bringing them within inches of each other. Heat tingled down her spine, igniting a fire that had been dormant for a long, long time. For a second, she wondered if he were about to kiss her. Some crazy part of her wanted him to do just that. The same crazy side that had acted without thinking back in college.

Okay, probably not the best part of her brain to listen to.

"Carolyn," Nick said quietly.

"What?" The word escaped her in a breath.

"Don't go. Not yet. Grab a drink with me. Catch up on old times."

Oh, how easy it would be to let herself get caught up in him again. But no, she was older. Smarter now.

"Why, Nick? What's changed, really? You never really got serious about us. And I was always going to put my career first. Never the twain shall meet, isn't that what Shakespeare said?"

"There was more to our breakup than just that, Carolyn. Much more," he said, his eyes still on hers, his mouth inches away.

Despite her words, for a second she wanted

very much for the twain to meet. For this pounding need to be quieted.

The rational half of her said this was desire, nothing more. At the same time, the feeling unnerved her, toppled her off her carefully planned and organized pedestal. She had no room in her days for a man like him—a man who would distract her, turn her from the very work that fulfilled her sense of self.

She hadn't the time then, she still didn't have it now. Sharing a drink with him wouldn't solve that dilemma.

"You're right," Carolyn said. "And all those reasons are still there, Nick."

The temperature in the aisle dropped a few degrees. "As always, you make a compelling case, Counselor. Well, tomorrow then." He turned to go, heading for the cash register.

As she watched him disappear, Carolyn told herself she was glad she'd turned down Nick's invitation. Because Nick Gilbert was a much-too-appetizing bowl of chocolate and cherry ice cream, and Carolyn was definitely feeling lactose intolerant.

CHAPTER THREE

NICK STOOD IN THE KITCHEN of his three-bedroom house and wrestled with the iron, cursing whoever had invented the damned thing. "Remind me again why I'm going to this shindig."

"Because you're a guy who cares about kids," said his brother, Daniel, who was making his regular visit to Nick's house. He'd already raided the fridge, complained about the dearth of acceptable meal choices, flipped through Nick's DVD collection twice and taken two of the newer flicks, as if Nick's house was Blockbuster. Nick didn't complain. He liked the company, and tolerated his brother's intrusions. Most of the time.

A writer, Daniel had the same dark brown hair and blue eyes as most of the Gilberts, but preferred a more relaxed approach to clothing, meaning anything fancier than jeans didn't exist in his closet. "And you better,"

Daniel added. "You grew up with four brothers and sisters."

"I didn't mean about the kids, I meant, why am I attending an event where Carolyn's going to be?" Earlier, he'd told his brother about running into Carolyn at the toy store.

A coincidence? Or a second chance with the woman he had never really forgotten?

Nick cursed the iron again as the steam sent globs of water over his shirt. "What is it with these things?"

"Didn't Mom teach you how to take care of yourself before she released you into the wild?" Daniel slid into place beside his brother. "Here, let me do it. For Pete's sake, you're making a mess of it."

Nick stepped back, amazed that his younger brother could wrangle the machine into doing his will. In five minutes Daniel had the golf shirt pressed and ready to go. "How do you do that?"

"It's called being a bachelor and being too poor to afford dry cleaning." Daniel grinned and held out the shirt, then waited while Nick slipped it on. Then he unplugged the iron and set it on the ironing board to cool. "And *I'm* not distracted by thoughts of a woman right now."

"I'm not distracted."

Daniel arched a brow.

"Okay, maybe I am. A little." Nick picked up his keys, slid them into his pocket, then faced his brother. "I thought I was over her. Over the whole damned thing. Then I see her last night at the toy store and—"

"It was *Love Story* all over again?" Daniel hummed a snippet of the movie's famous theme song.

"Not at all. More a remake of our worst moments together." But there had been one moment when he'd remembered why he'd been attracted to her. Why he'd married her. They'd had fun—for a few minutes—and then Carolyn had gone back to being the stuffy city prosecutor, the woman who was about as much fun as a bag of rocks, and Nick was reminded all over again why they'd broken up.

Yet guilt pinged at him still. She hadn't been the only one at fault, and he knew it. He hadn't exactly been Joe Sensitive, nor had he been Husband of the Year.

"I'm just glad I got out of that marriage after a few days instead of a few years," Nick said. "Carolyn was always too damned straight-laced for me. I want a woman who can have a good time, make me laugh, live a little. Not drive me absolutely insane. And when I think of Carolyn Duff, driving me crazy is the term that comes to mind."

Daniel bent down to pat Bandit, Nick's German short-haired pointer. The spotted dog wagged his tail with furious joy, nearly knocking over the scraggly ficus tree beside him. A shower of dry leaves littered the floor. "There were some good times, too, from what you've told me. Some *very* good times."

An image of one particularly good memory—with the neon lights of Vegas shining on Carolyn's peach skin while they made use of every surface in their suite at the Mirage—flashed in Nick's mind. He saw her smile, heard her laughter, could almost smell the scent of her raspberry bubble bath.

"Okay, maybe one good memory. Or two." Another one popped into his mind, followed quickly by a third, slamming with a sting like pellets into his chest. Nick shook his head. As good as those times had been, the end had been fast and unforeseen, like a sneak guerrilla attack that came and ripped him apart in the middle of the night.

Carolyn had been stubborn about leaving him in that diner, adamant about ending the marriage as fast as it began, claiming he hadn't cared, he hadn't been listening.

And back then he probably hadn't. But she hadn't given him much of a chance, either.

Just as well. They'd been totally unsuited for each other.

Since the day of the divorce, Nick and Caroline had become nothing more than strangers, albeit strangers who had once shared a bed. And yet last night he'd sensed a vulnerability in her, a chink in the Carolyn armor, that made the lawyer in him see a flicker of doubt in the witness's case.

He wondered—could he have been wrong in letting her go? Could they make it work if they tried again now?

Nick shook his head. He hadn't changed much in three years, and from what he'd seen, neither had she. "We were insane to get married in the first place," he said to Daniel. *Definitely insane.*

Still, at odd moments, Nick thought the exact opposite. Crazy thoughts, the kind that hit him in the middle of the night when he awoke from a dream that had featured a lot of neon lights and left him pacing the floors. He'd raid the fridge or pour a scotch, and still the memories would tickle at the edges of his mind.

He was a lawyer. Even though he'd had a lot of evidence, and a whole lot of facts in the case of his marriage, he knew when someone was hiding the truth. Carolyn most definitely had been keeping a tidbit or two in check when she'd handed back the plain gold band, sliding it across the table of the diner, then walked out of his life.

Until yesterday.

Nick shrugged it off. They were totally different people—and they were over. Two very good reasons to put Carolyn out of his mind.

Daniel straightened. Bandit let out a whine of complaint, then trotted off to find a toy for fetch. "Maybe this wasn't just serendipity, you two running into each other. Both of you getting kids to sponsor for that picnic thing. Maybe it was a sign from the Fates or whatever."

"Will you let it go?"

"Only if you tell me what made you two start talking to each other after all this time apart."

"Desperation." Nick chuckled. "We were both stuck in the toy aisle, me with a girl to buy for, her with a boy, and we didn't know what we were doing. Forced allies, nothing more."

"Uh-huh. You couldn't have asked any of the moms there? Or called your sisters?" Daniel said. "All of whom would have willingly given you advice."

"I, ah, didn't think of that."

"Told you. You were blinded by the pretty woman who still gets your car engine racing."

Nick rolled his eyes. "If you weren't my brother, I would stop talking to you. I've told you a thousand times that Carolyn and I aren't any good together. You know that old adage about the bird and the fish?" Daniel nodded. "Well, try imagining that same fable with a hawk and a shark."

"With you being the shark, I presume?" His brother gave him a good-natured jab in the arm. "Corporate lawyers, you're all the same."

"Hey, I take offense to that. You know I'm not like other lawyers. I'm more...unconventional. Fun."

"You're looking pretty conventional right now." Daniel gave his older brother's pressed golf shirt a light pat. Bandit took the opportunity to bound over and deposit an orange plastic bone at Daniel's feet.

"Oh, but I'm still unconventional underneath." Nick raised the left sleeve, baring his arm and the tattoo he'd had for the last three years. The still-vivid image of a cartoon shark—a joke he'd had put on his arm back in law school—never showed under Nick's suits, but usually peeked out from under the hem of his short-sleeved shirts.

"Of course. I expected nothing less. And I still think that's the most apropos image for you, big brother. You do realize, though, that both hawks and sharks are predators? That puts you two in the same class of animal." Daniel grinned, then tossed the bone down the hall. Bandit took off after it, running too fast and skidding past the vinyl squeaky toy before scrambling back around to snatch it up. "So what are you going to drive this time? What was it for the senior prom? A backhoe? Took out a damned tree on your way home, I might add."

"It was a tractor. My date about died, but no one forgot my entrance." Nick took the toy from Bandit, repeating the same scramble, miss and skid pattern as before. "That dog never learns."

"Neither do you," Daniel pointed out. "You're still as crazy as when we were kids. Sending your assistant on an impromptu trip to Jamaica—"

"To boost office morale."

Daniel went on, ignoring Nick's interruption. "Karaoke singing, without the musical accompaniment—"

"Just having fun."

"In *court*?"

Nick shrugged, pleading no contest to the charges. "I won the case, I might add. Proved my client's jingle was not offensive."

"And hosting a birthday party for your nephew, complete with pony rides and a petting zoo in your backyard, for God's sake. You know that you about made our sister have a heart attack. She is not the pony ride type." Daniel shook his head. "It's like you thrive on fun."

Daniel was right. He did indeed thrive on having fun. After growing up in a hectic family, fun was what he knew. It was as familiar as his own face, and it gave him an odd sense of comfort. And it helped him feel like he hadn't become too much of a grown-up yet.

But lately it had grown tired. He had a house—an investment property—but it was empty, except for Monday nights when his friends came over to watch the game. He'd dated women who laughed, women who were…fun. But not serious.

Carolyn Duff had been serious. The one serious girl on the Lawford U campus. So serious she'd offered a challenge, an exciting allure to Nick, who'd set out to make her smile, laugh. After their first date he'd found something in her he hadn't found in other women, a depth of character that made him want to try harder. Be more than he had been up until then. She'd brought a sober touch to his life, the kind that had him toying with the idea of settling down, becoming a grown-up. And so he'd had that crazy idea of running off to Vegas and getting married.

Because he'd thought he could have it all.

But no.

Nick swallowed the bitter taste of disappointment. He was happier this way anyway. Unencumbered. Free. Answering to no one's drum but his own.

He slid the directions to the picnic into his pocket, then checked again to be sure he had his keys and wallet, along with a deck of cards. "Well, I'm not doing anything like that today. I've had enough surprises for a while."

Daniel walked with his brother to the door and waited while Nick locked up, leaving a dejected Bandit inside. "Where you and Carolyn are concerned, I think the surprises are just starting."

"No, we're over. Have been since she dumped me on the drive home from Vegas three years ago."

"Uh-huh," Daniel said, clearly not believing a word. "I'll believe that when I see you two together and there's no more electricity between you than two clods of dirt. Remember the day I stopped by for lunch last year? I saw the two of you in the hallway of the courtroom. I'm lucky I'm still alive."

"What do you mean, still alive?"

Daniel clutched his heart and faked gagging. "The way you two looked at each other, it was like a couple of light sabers going at it. She wants you. You want her. If the math was any simpler, it would be preschool."

"You forget everything else that goes into that equation. Like the fact that she ditched me to go off and put herself into the middle of a hostage situation, even after I begged her not to. That she also realized she didn't have time for a marriage, not that and a career, too. That this had all been some crazy impromptu decision she made and just wanted to forget. Like buying a pair of shoes that didn't match her dress."

Daniel chuckled. "Aren't we the jaded one?"

"Come talk to me when you make a commitment to something other than a car lease."

Daniel raised his hands in surrender. The two men headed down the stairs of Nick's front porch and paused at the end of the walkway. The July sun had already raised the temperature to the mid eighties, making Nick glad he'd opted for light khaki shorts to wear with the cream shirt. The event organizers had put "casual attire" on the invitations, not "business," and for that, Nick was grateful. There was nothing worse than standing around all day in the heat in a suit.

"So, you're still claiming you have no interest in her?" Daniel asked.

Nick shook his head. "There's nothing between us. Not anymore."

Daniel tick-tocked a finger at him. "Don't lie to me, big brother. I grew up with you, remember? I know the signs of you getting ready for a date."

"It's a benefit picnic. For needy children."

Daniel laughed. "And the children really needed you to wear cologne, trim your nails and press your shirt?"

"I wanted to look…" Nick cut himself off before he said the word *good*, which would imply that he cared what Carolyn thought of his appearance. And he didn't care. At all. "Professional."

"Let's see how 'professional' Carolyn looks in your eyes today." Daniel winked. "And like I said, how long the two of you resist each other."

Carolyn sat at a picnic table on the fairgrounds of the Lawford City Park, surrounded by busy, chattering children, and did her best to keep her gaze off the park's gaily decorated entrance and on the task at hand. The problem was, she wasn't very good at either.

She'd bought a new dress—darn Mary and her suggestion—just that morning. She shifted on the bench, acutely aware of the bright-blue-and-white dress and how she had gone to an awful lot of work on her appearance for something that was supposed to be casual.

"Geez, Miss Duff, can't you make an eagle?" a little girl with a name tag that read Kimberly asked. "I learned how to make birds in kindergarten."

Carolyn cursed whoever had come up with the craft for this table. A bald eagle paper bag puppet, AKA a torture marathon with paper. There were wings and talons and a beak to make. Little pieces of construction paper to glue all over the place. One side had to be the front, and Lord forgive if she got it wrong because then, apparently, the eagle couldn't eat.

The kids had already informed her, with a look of disdain, that her first eagle attempt would have died of starvation. So now Carolyn was making her second lunch bag bird.

And clearly mangling the thing into a version of roadkill. "There aren't any rules decreeing we *have* to make an American eagle. What about a Monarch butterfly? Or a nice little robin?" She gave Kimberly an encouraging, work-with-me smile.

Kimberly returned a blank stare. "Isn't this a birthday party for *our* country? And isn't the eagle our country's bird?"

The kid had her there. Darn, these third-graders were awfully smart.

This was one more reason why Carolyn hadn't had children. Because she wouldn't know what on earth to do with one after delivery. Why she'd been assigned to this table, she'd never know. It had to be one of Mary's brainstorms.

Speaking of whom, Mary waved to her from across the field. Carolyn gave her a grimace back. Mary either didn't see the facial gesture or chose to ignore it. She just went back to blithely setting up the food. The younger children were attending a puppet show put on by a local bookstore. The performance was due to end any second and thus the children would be arriving soon. Then the rest of the festivities would get underway. The third-graders at Carolyn's table had pronounced themselves too "old" for such a babyish activity, so Carolyn had been asked to oversee them and keep them busy in the meantime.

A flutter of nerves ran through Carolyn at the thought of meeting her sponsored child. She chided herself. She was an attorney. She'd faced down threatening criminals. Blustering defense attorneys. Stern-faced judges. She shouldn't be nervous about meeting a five-year-old, for Pete's sake.

"Uh, Kimberly, let's forget the eagle. And create another display of patriotism." Carolyn crumpled the lunch bag into a ball and reached into the craft bucket for new supplies. "Here we are, children. Flags. The perfect Fourth of July symbol." She handed each child squares of red, white and blue paper, then cut out red strips. This she could do. She hoped. Carolyn began gluing, drizzling the white Elmer's along the edge of the red strips, then laying them on top of the white squares. The glue smeared out from under the red strips, turning it into a messy puddle, dampening the construction paper and turning the tips of her fingers pink.

Kimberly, who had already completed a flag and whose paper was neat and nearly perfect, just shook her head.

Carolyn sighed. Too much glue. Geez, what had she been doing during her childhood years? She'd forgotten the simplest of crafts. And then she remembered why with a pang in her chest. She knew the exact minute she stopped being a little girl and turned into a grown-up.

The day she'd watched her father die. No, not die—he'd been murdered. Shot right in front of her.

Because he'd sacrificed himself for her.

The memory sliced through Carolyn with a sharp ache, like a break that had never healed properly. She drew in a breath, sucked the pain back to the recesses of her mind. Carolyn had lost her father, lost her entire world, and been sent to live with her aunt Greta, who didn't believe in bringing children up with tea parties and construction paper, but with discipline and hard work.

She'd been nine, probably the same age as the kids around her. And much too young, she knew now, to quit working with construction paper.

Carolyn shook off the maudlin thoughts and returned her attention to the half-dozen kids and the stacks of red, white and blue paper. The children were all busily making their versions of Fourth of July festivity, seemingly unaware that many of them lived with families whose income fell in the shadows of poverty level. Hence, the benefit picnic. For the kids, at least, Carolyn would do her best and make a flag.

Oh, for Pete's sake. A flag was about as simple as crafts got. Then one glance at the crumpled roadkill eagle project reminded Carolyn looks could be deceiving, particularly when there was craft glue involved.

"I've passed the bar exam. I can do this," she muttered. She wasn't going to let a third-grader show her up. She'd do this—and do it even cooler than her young charges.

And it would keep her mind off expecting to see Nick at any moment. If she was lucky, he'd just drop off the toys and skip the main event, especially after their earlier exchange at the toy store.

Carolyn reached into the center of the table, grabbed a ruler and a fresh sheet of red paper, traced exact lines from corner to corner, then cut out new stripes. Kimberly watched her for a second, then elbowed the other little girl beside her, Veronica, according to her name tag. The two of them stopped their flag construction to watch as Carolyn measured a perfect rectangle of white, then carefully applied dots of glue to her stripes, marked their placement with the ruler and affixed them.

"My teacher would like your flag," said a

little boy with tousled brown hair. His name tag, placed upside down on his chest, read Paul. "She likes everything neat. I'm messy." He held up his flag, which looked so much like Carolyn's first attempt, it was embarrassing.

"She's getting better," Kimberly said to Veronica.

"At least this one doesn't look dead." Veronica pointed at Carolyn's first beakless eagle.

Carolyn didn't spare her peanut gallery a look. She simply went on with her project, adding a perfect square of blue to the upper left corner. Kimberly slipped her the packet of silver stars. "Thank you," Carolyn said.

"There should be fifty of them, in case you didn't know. I know because Miss Laramie told me. She's really smart."

"And I can see that you are quite intelligent, too," Carolyn said.

Kimberly beamed.

Carolyn withdrew the first stars from the packet and was about to stick them on when she realized exactly why Mary had sat her at this table. So Carolyn could interact with the children.

Work with them.

Get to know them.

Duh. She'd done about as much interacting as a potted plant. She probably had more experience with philodendrons, too. Once again, Carolyn slapped on a smile. "Kimberly, Veronica. Would you two assist me in affixing the stars?" Carolyn gestured toward the pile of shiny five-pointers. "And then Paul can finish the task?"

"What's 'affix'?" Veronica asked. "Is that like a kind of glue?"

"I think it's a color," Paul suggested. "Isn't it?" He gave Carolyn a confused look, then worried his lower lip.

"*Affix* means to fasten, to attach," Carolyn explained, then noticed she was still surrounded by blank looks. "Yes, glue."

"Uh, Miss Duff, those are stickers," Veronica said, then peeled off the paper backing and stuck one of the stars on her flag. "See?"

"Oh. Of course. Well, will you help me stick them on, then? Please?"

At that, the girls brightened. They dug into the package and started slapping them onto the blue square, not in the neat rows that Carolyn would have preferred, but in a slipshod fashion that soon took the shape of a flower. Carolyn smiled and praised their creativity, telling herself that she was here to relax, not become an anal-retentive craft woman.

And as Paul added his stars at the bottom, forming "grass" for the flower, Carolyn had to admit the new version of the flag was cute. Different. A true melting pot of other people. "This is perfect," she told the kids. "You've managed to capture the spirit of democracy in America. Excellent attention to detail."

The kids just blinked, jaws slack.

"I see you've managed to make some friends," said a familiar voice.

Nick.

Carolyn turned around, trying to stay aloof, cool as an ice cube. Not an easy feat, considering Nick managed to look both handsome and boyish in shorts and a golf shirt.

Then she caught a glimpse of his tattoo, peeking out from under the sleeve of his light cream-colored shirt and a hit of desire slammed into her so hard, she had to hold her breath to keep from betraying the feeling. He still had it. Well, of course he would. A tattoo was a permanent kind of thing.

The memory careened through her mind. Meeting him that first day, her gaze sliding to that left arm, seeing the unconventional, unexpected adornment on his upper arm, and immediately being intrigued. Attracted. After his magic trick, they'd talked, and she'd done something she'd never done before—

Asked him out on a date, a date that had lasted long into the next day. Not because they'd slept together, but because they hadn't stopped talking. For days they'd talked, about everything under the sun. In him she'd found someone so different, so open, she'd become a human conversational waterfall. Three weeks later they'd been married.

Four days later, divorced.

And three years later, she still couldn't forget him. Or that tattoo. "Here to join in on the crafts, Mr. Gilbert?"

"Uh…no. I'm not exactly crafter material." He glanced at the table of children, now arguing over the supply of scissors and paper. "Besides, I think you have it under control."

Carolyn laughed. "That's an illusion."

He cleared his throat. "Actually, I came over to see if you'd seen Mary yet. I know the younger children are due to arrive soon and I was looking forward to meeting Angela."

Why did disappointment ripple through her when he didn't mention anything about seeing her? Noticing her dress? That she'd left her hair down, instead of putting it back into her usual chignon? She didn't want Nick to be interested in her again. She didn't want to relive her past. "Mary was over at the food table, last I saw her."

Instead of glancing in that direction, Nick considered Carolyn for a long second. She felt as if he could see past every wall she'd constructed, every bit of armor she'd put in place over the years.

He leaned down, until his mouth met her ear, his breath whispered past a lock of her hair. "You look beautiful today, Carolyn."

Something hot and warm raced through her veins. She refused to react to him, though her hormones didn't seem to be riding the same resolve wagon.

"Thank you."

He was still close, so close she could see the flecks of gold in his eyes. If she leaned a few inches to the right, she could touch him. Feel his cheek against hers.

"Oooh, Miss Duff has a boyfriend," Veronica sing-songed. "Miss Duff and Mr. Stranger, up in a tree—"

"*K-I-S-S-I-N-G*," joined in a chorus of young voices.

What were they teaching these kids in school nowadays? A lot more than reading and writing, that was for sure. Carolyn turned her Evil Eye on the group, the one parenting trick she'd learned from her aunt. "We're just colleagues. And we're *not* kissing."

Not now. Not later. Not ever again.

"I thought a collie was a dog," Paul said, his face scrunched up in confusion.

"It is, Paul." Nick slipped onto the wooden bench and took a seat beside Carolyn. "Now, what are you making here?"

"A flag."

"A flag, huh? Cool." He glanced at Carolyn. The tension of the day knotted her shoulders, surely showed in her face. Nick gave her a grin—the grin that said he had read her and her unease with both her charges and the task as easily as the newspaper—then turned back to the kids. "You want to know what else is cool?" He withdrew a deck of cards from his pocket, slid them out of the box and laid the stack on the table. "Who wants to see a little magic?" All three kids raised their hands. But Nick turned to her. He held her gaze for a split second, long enough to communicate that it would all work out, if she would just trust him. "Miss Duff, do you want to do the honors and pick a card?" He pushed the deck in front of her.

Just trust him.

Carolyn hesitated. She glanced at the kids. They stared at her. Her stomach clenched, and she looked back at Nick, suddenly terrified he'd leave her alone with them and more of those stupid paper-bag eagles. "Okay, Nick," she said, then she reached forward, cut the deck and picked one of the red-backed cards. She showed the three of diamonds to the children, keeping it from Nick's view. Then she slipped it back into the deck.

Paul's eyes were wide with excitement. "Oh, did you see that card? It was the—"

"No, don't tell me," Nick said, putting up a finger. "I'm going to read Carolyn's mind and tell all of you what her card is." He squeezed his eyes shut, making a big production out of the whole trick. He put out a hand, touched his fingertips to Carolyn's forehead. "I'm seeing…something red."

Veronica and Kimberly gasped. Carolyn smiled. Paul's jaw dropped.

"And in diamonds."

The kids looked at each other, shock and awe written all over their features. Carolyn kept a bemused smile on her face, giving nothing away. This was Nick at his best, taking center stage, working a group, creating his magic.

Nick pretended to concentrate more, his fingers fluttering over Carolyn's face. He drew back, opened his eyes. "Is your card… the three of diamonds?"

The kids exploded in wonder. "How did you know that?"

"That's cool!"

"Oh, my goodness! He really does know magic!"

And just like that, Nick had the children at Carolyn's table chattering with him, laughing and showing off their flags and eagles. He marveled over each one like they were the next Picasso. In an instant he'd accumulated a Nick fan club. And Carolyn, who hadn't managed any of that, was left feeling like the lunchroom lady dispensing the broccoli.

On the other side of the park, a big yellow bus pulled up, announcing the arrival of the younger children. Mary signaled to Nick and Carolyn. "You ready?" Nick asked.

"Sure." Though she felt anything but. Her success rate thus far had been zero.

Nick laid a hand on hers. "I'm sure you and Bobby are going to get along just fine."

Nevertheless, a quiver of doubt rose in her stomach. As the other children dispersed to find their sponsors, Carolyn rose to clean up the mess on the table. Before she could protest, she found Nick by her side, helping. She scooped the scraps of paper into a nearby trash bag. Nick did the same, and for an instant his hand brushed against hers.

A surge of want rushed through her, as if she'd been denied water for a month and had just come into contact with a pool of it. It was only because she hadn't touched him in three years. That was all.

Damn that Nick Gilbert. Being around him was always like this—distracting, crazy.

He made her forget. Forget her priorities. Forget what was important. And most of all, forget that when she needed him, he wouldn't be there.

If there was one thing Aunt Greta had drilled into Carolyn's head, it was this: Losing focus created mistakes. And mistakes led to people getting hurt, to losing the ones you loved. It led to showdowns in convenience stores, with men who should have been behind bars instead of holding guns to people's heads.

No. She wouldn't get involved with Nick. Not again.

Carolyn yanked her hand back, opting to stack the pile of scissors instead. If she were smart, she'd poke Nick with one and make him go away. But in a park full of lawyers, assault with a cutting implement probably wasn't a good idea.

"Carolyn…"

The way he said her name, in the same soft, hushed tone he'd used years before, made her pause. She didn't move, didn't turn around.

Didn't look in those blue eyes. Because she knew if she did she'd be a goner. "What?"

"Today will go just fine. You'll be okay."

The man knew her too well. Knew her past. Knew her secrets. And that gave him an unfair advantage that choked her throat.

Carolyn finished clearing the table, avoiding his gaze. She loaded the containers into her arms and turned to face him. "Of course it will. And for you, too. Enjoy your day, Nick."

The temperature between them dropped.

"You as well, Miss Duff." Then he turned on his heel and walked away.

The bus carrying the younger children emptied out, spilling children into the park like water emptying from a pitcher. In a second Bobby would be here. Carolyn would give him the presents, they'd eat lunch and then the picnic would end. Nick would go home and so would Carolyn, their temporary association over. Just as well.

She knew she'd made the right choice, then and now. Nick was spontaneity personified; she was the one who stayed on the straight and narrow path. She'd learned that was where her talents lay—working in an environment she could control. Predict. Reason with. It was how she had survived her childhood after her father died. It was what she knew and understood, a world as comfortable as a blanket.

Nick Gilbert, on the other hand, she couldn't predict. Control. Or reason with. And that was exactly why she was going to make sure everything about him stayed in the past—as soon as this day was over.

CHAPTER FOUR

NICK LOST THE STARING CONTEST before it barely began.

"Okay, so I've done this before," Angela began, her green eyes assessing him. "And you don't have to, like, hang out with me or even pretend to be nice. I know you're just here because you have to be."

Nick bit back a grin. "Same as you, right?"

She nodded. "Exactly."

He put out his hand, waited for her to put her much smaller one into his and shake on it. "We're agreed. Not to be friends, just—"

"Stuck together. Until another Madeline thing is over and I go back to the fosters."

Nick released Angela's hand, then gestured toward a bench beside the playground. Children climbed in and out of the brightly painted equipment, laughing and happy, while the sponsors stood around in little chatting clusters with foster parents and real parents.

Angela, however, acted as if she was years and years beyond such games.

How sad, Nick thought. Sadder than anything he'd seen in a long time. He didn't have much experience with kids, heck, any experience besides his brothers and sisters and their children, but even he knew this wasn't what kids should sound like. Jaded. Bitter. Like they could care less.

"Okay, *I'm* new at this, so you'll have to translate. Madeline thing? Fosters?"

Angela rolled her eyes. "You know *Madeline,* the book? The one that makes being an orphan look like one big adventure?"

That struck a memory in him of something he'd read as a kid. "Oh, that one. Full of nice nuns and cute dogs."

"Exactly." Angela nodded. "Except real orphanages aren't like that."

"I'm sorry."

Angela picked at an invisible piece of lint on her denim shorts. They were clean but worn, and Nick wondered if they were hand-me-downs. From an older child in the family where she was staying? From another foster child? From her old life? "The fosters aren't so bad," Angela said. "Most of 'em."

"Your foster parents."

She nodded. Her blond curls bounced with

the movement, framing her face in a light halo that reflected the sun in a golden cloud. "These ones are kind of nice. Better than the ones before."

Nick didn't want to ask about "the ones before." Those five words were enough to tell him that this girl had been through more in her six years on earth than he had been in his twenty-eight. Suddenly he wanted to draw her against him and promise nothing bad would ever happen to her again.

But he couldn't. So he didn't.

"Are you happy there?" Nick asked. This was an odd position for him, being a sort of pseudoparent, even on a temporary basis. He wasn't used to being the grown-up, at least being any more grown-up than he had to be in the courtroom, and it forced him to think in new ways. Forced him to look at the world differently than he ever had before.

To see a world outside the two-parent, mostly ideal one he'd grown up in, too.

"Yeah." Angela shrugged. "The fosters say they want to adopt me." She pointed toward a tall, friendly looking couple across the park, who looked as if they had stepped out of a magazine for perfect parents. They waved and smiled at Angela. Nice, happy, trying to include her in the family. "I'm waiting. See what they do."

Hedging her bets, Nick was sure. Not committing her heart until the ink was dry. He saw a flicker of hope in Angela's eyes, then she popped off the bench, smoothed her shorts again.

"I can go play with the other kids, and you can go with *them*, if you want." She gestured at the other lawyers.

Nick looked down into Angela's eyes and thought he'd never seen anyone look as lonely and in need of a friend as she did. He could do "friend." "Parent"…probably not so well. "Nope. I'm fine right here. I'll let you in on a secret. Lawyers are totally not fun. And they don't know any good jokes."

A smile flitted across her face, then blew away like a candle in a windstorm. She shrugged. "Okay, whatever."

A tough cookie, this one.

Nick reached into his pocket and pulled out a quarter. "Do you believe in magic, Angela?"

She eyed him. "Not really. It's for little kids." But he could see a part of her still really wanted to be a little kid.

And that, at least, Nick could give her. He was good at that.

As Nick bent down and began working magic with a quarter and swift fingers, making the coin disappear and reappear in Angela's ear, behind her head, under her chin—every time eliciting a smile and a gasp of surprise from the girl who'd given up on magic—Nick's gaze strayed across the park to Carolyn. Even from here he could see her stiff posture, the frustration on her face as she struggled to connect with Bobby, her sponsored child.

And he realized he had, indeed, seen that look of loneliness and of being lost, in another's eyes once before—and noticed it lingered still, all these years later.

Once before, he'd taken on the challenge of getting her to loosen up, and had had fun winning his own personal bet. Could he do it a second time? This time, not with the intention of winning her back—he'd already been down that road and knew where it led—but to help her make some inroads with those kids today. He didn't know who looked more uncomfortable—Carolyn or poor Bobby.

But as Nick crossed the field toward the table, one nagging doubt in his chest told him this time around getting past those walls Carolyn Duff had in place was going to take more than a simple magic trick.

* * *

He came up behind her, so quietly she almost didn't notice. But Carolyn knew Nick could have been as silent as the wind and still she would have sensed his presence, felt him there.

"Do you need some help?" he said.

Did she need help? She needed an army battalion of it. Carolyn hadn't felt so over her head since she'd prosecuted her first criminal case alone. Bobby Lester had stopped talking after exchanging a total of three words with her—"hi" and "thank you." She'd earned a few smiles for the gifts, which had let her know she'd at least made good shopping choices, thanks to Nick's advice, but the boy was as closemouthed as a clam. Now, he was off eating lunch with the other children, which was supposed to be followed by a short film in the park's pavilion. Carolyn had volunteered to set up the games. Anything to avoid another trip into a conversational No Man's Land. "No, I'm fine."

"And elephants are parading in the sky today, too." Nick put a hand on her shoulder, the touch searing through the light cotton of her dress, and turned her gently to face him. "It's not such a bad thing to ask for help, Carolyn."

"Really, Nick, this thing with the kids, it's nothing. A few games with some children." Children who wouldn't talk to her. Children who were as foreign to her as Martians.

She could do this. Heck, she could command a courtroom. Could get the toughest criminals to confess. Could win over the most jaded juries. So what if she had all the homemaking skills of a monkey?

"Why won't you let me help you?" he said. "Or let me get someone to—"

"I can handle this, Nick."

Frustration sparked in his eyes and he took a step back. "Of course. I forgot. You're Carolyn Duff, the bulldog who works alone. Doesn't need anyone."

She pivoted away from him. "Don't…don't call me that. It sounds…" The words trailed off, caught in her throat.

"Sounds what?"

"Sounds so cold coming from you." The nickname she had taken pride in because it meant she was doing her job—the very job that had broken them apart.

"How about if I call you Carolyn the Yorkie pup?" A tease in Nick's voice, erasing all offense.

She laughed. "Marginally better."

He moved closer. Every ounce of her went

on alert, even though they were still a very respectable distance apart. "You're not okay. I can tell."

"I am."

"You couldn't lie if your life depended on it, Counselor."

"Then it's a good thing I'm not on the witness stand."

He watched her, his gaze sweeping over her features. "How have you been, Carolyn? *Really* been since we broke up?"

She started to say fine, but before she could get a word out, Nick interrupted her with another question.

"Do you still sleep with the lights on?" he asked, his voice quiet, concerned.

One question. That's all it took to remind her that ninety-nine percent of the time, her life was completely in control. That everything was exactly as she wanted it. But there was that one percent that once in a while—when night fell—remembered a moment in her past that had turned everything from wonderful to terrible.

She swallowed, but her throat remained parched. "He's in jail, Nick. It's over. And I'm fine." She turned back to the games, getting to work. Stay busy, stay on task. Stay organized—and stay away from Nick. Who, even if she had told him all the details of her past, had never really listened. Not really.

"Well, if you need to talk, I'm here, you know. We're still friends."

She wheeled back to face him. "Come on, Nick. We're not anything anymore. And if I needed someone to talk to, it wouldn't be you."

He let out a gust. "Why not me?"

"You don't take anything seriously. That was half the problem. And that's fine, that's who you are. Makes you good with kids, at parties, not so good with relationships. So stop trying to perform an instant therapy session at a picnic, Nick. Just let it go." She moved away, inserting distance. As much distance as she could, with the intensifying heat, the baking sun, the fenced-in area where all the games would be held, all of it seeming so much more enclosed with Nick here.

She cast a glance in the direction of the pavilion, but the children were all sitting on blankets, watching a mermaid dance and sing on a projection screen. No saved-by-the-bell help to distract Nick would be arriving anytime soon. "I don't have time for this, anyway. I have to get these games set up. The kids will be done anytime now, and if we don't keep them entertained they'll run rampant, and you know that will just drive Mary crazy. Just imagine a whole slew of little ones…" Carolyn kept rambling as she laid out rows of bean bags for the tic-tac-toe toss, then reached for a series of bright rainbow-colored beach balls and yellow plastic bats. "…and if we're not ready, they'll just run roughshod over—"

"Hey, don't be the game martyr here, Carolyn," Nick said, interrupting her, laying a hand on hers, taking some of the toys out of her grasp. "Let me help."

"I've got it under control."

"Of course you do," Nick said, then ignored her completely, moving down to the next set of games and reaching into the boxes to set up the fishing poles and magnetic fish that went along with the six-foot, round plastic pool that had been filled earlier. "Didn't you just say, though, that I'm the one who excels at games? Let the master be of assistance."

She may be the one with the nickname of bulldog, but she knew she wasn't the only one with the canine's famous tenacity. What if Nick had been like that about their marriage? What if he had fought that hard to hold on to her? To get to know her, really know her. Not just play at being married, like it was a game of fetch.

But he hadn't. He had argued with her that

day, of course, but then he had signed the papers and let her go, never saying another word.

He'd given up on them as quickly as a man giving up on a sport he couldn't master. A part of her had been relieved, and a part of her had been disappointed. Heartbroken.

Realizing that Nick may have spoken a good game about wanting her, loving her to no end—

And then in reality, not really meaning any of it. He'd done what Nick did best—chased her until he had the prize, then let her down when she needed him most.

Carolyn spun around, the beanbags rustling in her grasp. "Why are you *really* here, Nick?"

He paused. "Same as you. I sponsored a child, so I'm doing my part. Delivering the toys, interacting with my sponsoree."

"No, I meant here with me. You can interact at the food table. The craft table. A million places other than here. You really don't need to help me...or keep trying to prove whatever point you are trying to prove."

"Here come the kids," he said.

And indeed Nick was saved from answering by a rising tide of excited voices, their high-pitched squeals coming at Nick and Carolyn like a chorus of dolphins.

"Brace yourself," Nick whispered in Carolyn's ear, so close, so very close. And her resolve to stay away from him weakened.

Just a bit.

"Nick!" A little girl barreled forward, out of the crowd, straight into Nick's legs, the force of her greeting breaking Nick and Carolyn apart. The little girl clasped him tight. With a laugh, Nick reached down and swung her up, into his arms.

"Hey, Angela. Did you have fun?"

She nodded. "Uh-huh. Did I tell you about the movie we saw after lunch? It was a mermaid movie. I love mermaid movies. Especially mermaid movies with lots of fish. I love fish. 'Cuz I love to swim. Except I've never had a pool. I really wish I had a pool. Do you have a pool?"

"Nope. But I like to swim, too. Swimming's pretty fun, especially when there's a slide or a diving board involved."

Carolyn scanned the crowd, seeking the face of Bobby. All the while, she listened to the excited chatter of Angela and Nick's enthusiastic responses. How had he done that? Struck up such an immediate rapport with the child?

"Hi, Miss Duff."

Carolyn looked down. Bobby stood before her, as solemn as a judge about to sentence a serial killer. "Hello, Bobby. Was your excursion entertaining?"

"Uh-huh."

"And the film? Did you find that enjoyable?"

Bobby toed at the grass. "Uh-huh."

Carolyn scrambled for another subject, something, anything. "Wonderful. Is that because you enjoy films with mermaids?"

Bobby's face scrunched up, and his shoulders rose and dropped. "They're girls."

Carolyn took that as a negative. Okay. So she'd asked all the same questions Nick had, and received four words in response. None of the instantaneous best-buds stuff. What was she doing wrong?

"We've been instructed to pair up for the games," Carolyn said to the boy, indicating the first race, where other volunteers had slipped into place to man the stations. "Would you like to be on my team? For potato-sack races and the bean-bag toss?"

Bobby glanced up at her, dubious. "Miss Duff, you're a…"

"A what?" Carolyn prompted when he didn't finish.

"A girl. I don't know if you'd be a good racer."

"I ran track in high school, Bobby. I assure you, I'd be a wonderful racer." Since Carolyn hadn't done anything like this in what felt like a thousand years, she couldn't be really sure. And her experience with children was nil, so her comfort level was in the negative digits. Still she put on a bright smile. "What do you say, want to give it a shot?"

Bobby gave her a look that said he'd rather be sentenced to a lifetime of community service. "Do I have to? Can I just sit on the bench over there? And watch?"

"Oh, yes. Certainly." Carolyn watched him go, trying not to feel like a complete and total failure.

She was surrounded by laughing, happy pairings. Sponsors and children who were slipping legs into potato sacks, talking as if they'd known each other for years. And here she couldn't get one five-year-old to think she had any game ability at all.

"Seems you're one leg short of a sack race."

Nick's voice. Carolyn turned around, to find Nick and Angela behind her. For a moment, she considered not admitting the truth, then decided that if she didn't get some help with this kid thing, Bobby's entire day would be a bust. And the most important thing here was Bobby—not her pride. "I lost my partner. He doesn't find me very...fun," she said, lowering her voice, "because I'm a girl."

Nick chuckled. "Now *that* I understand, being the older brother of some not-so-fun sisters."

"Girls can be fun. I'm...fun."

"You are." A smile curved up his face. "Or at least, you were. From what I remember."

A heat brewed between them, built on past memories, but Carolyn knew they were as fragile as tissues, and nothing to build a future on. She brushed it off. "Well, apparently, Bobby doesn't agree."

"Want to trade, for the race? Angela won't mind, I'm sure. Once she came out of her shell and began to trust me, she really opened up. She's a great sport."

"Nick, I'm not so good at this kind of thing." Carolyn shifted from foot to foot, suddenly uncomfortable with the whole idea of racing in a sack in front of her colleagues. Possibly falling on her face. Making a fool of herself. Carolyn the Bulldog losing control, being silly? So not her. "I should probably sit out the games and—"

"How will you ever get good at being with kids if you don't try?"

"And why would I want to get good at being with kids?"

"Because someday, Miss Duff, you might just want to try marriage again." His gaze met hers, and something hot and dark burned in their depths, something she couldn't read. "There may be a man who captures your heart. A man you want to stay with. A man you want to make a future with. So why not take a taste of the future today?"

"Because—" She cut off the sentence. She couldn't finish it, not here. Not in front of all these people. That was a little more information than the entire Lawford legal community needed to hear.

And besides, the days when she told Nick Gilbert her plans for her romantic future were way in the past.

"Angela," Nick said, waving the little girl over. "I want you to meet a friend of mine."

Angela bopped across the grass, her blond curls springing up and down with her steps. She beamed up at Carolyn. "Hello. I'm Angela."

"This is Carolyn," Nick said.

"Miss Duff," Carolyn corrected.

"Miss Duff?" Nick arched a brow.

"Well, children should learn to be respectful. And formal. If boundaries aren't put in place—"

"For Pete's sake, Carolyn, this is supposed to be a casual event. And we're making friends here, aren't we, Angela?" He bent down and smiled at the girl. She nodded, curls bouncing like they were on a moonwalk. "Friends go by first names."

"But—"

"This isn't a court case, Carolyn. It's a picnic. Loosen up."

Was that the problem? She'd been too stiff? Too formal with Bobby? But she knew no other way. Had no experience with anything but court. There, she excelled. Here...

She couldn't be more out of her element if she'd been swimming with sharks.

"Here," Nick said, thrusting a potato sack at her. "You and Angela take this one, and I'll go make friends with Bobby. And us boys will challenge you girls."

Angela laughed, the sound tinkling in the summer air like coins dropping into a jar. "Oh, the girls will win. Girls always win."

"Want to bet a piece of pie on that?" Nick said.

"Sure!" Angela turned to Carolyn. "We can beat 'em, can't we, Carolyn? Oh, I mean, Miss

Duff." Her little face sobered, the mirth wiped away with those two last words.

Carolyn had never felt more like a party pooper in her life.

"Sure we can, Angela," Carolyn said, holding out the sack so that they each could step inside. "And…call me Carolyn."

CHAPTER FIVE

NICK REACHED THE FINISH LINE, breathless and in a big pile of arms, legs and laughing small children and uncomfortable lawyers. He bent over, helped Bobby to his feet. "Not bad for a couple of amateurs, huh?"

The little boy beamed. "That was fun. I never did that before." Bobby's chest expanded with pride. "And we won. You must be really good at this."

"Nah, just lots of experience. My dad and my brother are the true reigning Lawford potato sack champs." Nick winked at Bobby.

"Your dad does this with you?" The boy's face fell six inches, and something clutched at Nick's heart.

"Well, he did, but now he's too old. And frankly," Nick said, pressing a hand to the ache in his back, "I think I might be, too." That struck him—that he was getting past the age where he should be doing this kind of thing, and yet it didn't bother him as much as he'd expected it would. He'd had fun with Bobby, and for a second it felt like Bobby was his nephew. A cousin. Maybe even his own kid.

Now *that* was a weird sensation. Never before had Nick imagined having kids of his own. That had been one of those thoughts a million miles off in the future, like retirement planning. He shook it off. He wasn't the kind to raise a family. He'd tried marriage once, screwed it up and had no intentions of going there again.

Bobby and Nick started to walk toward the grandstand, where Mary was holding a trio of trophies for first, second and third place. Across the line of sack racers, Nick caught sight of Carolyn and Angela. He chuckled. Poor Carolyn. She looked about as comfortable out here as a porcupine at a balloon factory. She was back to being the stiff, strait-laced Bostonian he remembered from college. Getting her to loosen up had been half the fun of dating her. But apparently, Carolyn had gone right back to who she used to be—and that rigid persona didn't mix well with kids.

"It must be nice," Bobby said.

"Must be nice, what?" Nick asked, drawing his attention back to the boy.

"To have a dad who shows you how to race like a sack of potatoes."

Nick's gaze strayed to Carolyn again, and he could have smacked himself upside the head. Of course. Everything about the day made sense. Her discomfort around the children. Her difficulty connecting. Her reluctance to join in on the crafts, the games.

It wasn't just that she'd lived in Boston. Or that she wasn't used to being around kids. Carolyn had much, much more going on than that.

Nick may be clueless when it came to what little girls might like for toys, but he had at least grown up in a two-parent family. Two parents who were still alive, still sitting at either end of the Thanksgiving table.

He hadn't watched his father get gunned down buying a gallon of milk. Then been sent to live with a woman who'd hated his existence.

He hadn't forgotten that hole in Carolyn's past, but he hadn't quite realized the impact of it on her, not until today. How hard it must be for her to be around children who'd experienced similar tragedies, to listen to other kids and parents who were working hard to maintain their families against tough odds. And then to see all these kids who were lost souls in foster families, being brought up by strangers?

Regret ran through Nick with a stab. How could he have been so cavalier as to suggest Carolyn was being formal? Lawyerish? Damn, he was a moron. Later, he vowed, he would apologize. Find a way to make it up to her. And most of all, help her make the whole day run much easier.

"Oh, look, Nick. Ours is gold. Do you think it's real?" Bobby was asking.

Nick followed where Bobby was pointing at the six-inch trophy, simply a gold-embellished pillar. He doubted it was anything more than real aluminum, and that the sheen came from gold spray paint. But he'd been a kid, too, and knew what it meant to a boy of that age to believe in the impossible.

He bent down to Bobby and smiled. "Absolutely. It looks real to me."

"I wish my mom could see it." Bobby sighed. He squinted against the bright sun as he looked up at Nick. "She was too sick to come today. So she stayed home. Lots of days she's too sick. But maybe when I bring this home, she'll feel better?"

Another slam into Nick's chest, that brought him up short. Drew him a thousand miles away from this being just fun and games and into something so much more. Something that could—

Have an impact on this kid's life.

An awesome sense of responsibility weighed on Nick's shoulders, a weight he'd never felt before. He tried it on, sure at first that being so used to not reporting to anyone, not being in charge of anyone but himself, that he'd resist the feeling of being needed by anyone.

But…

He looked at Bobby, at the kid's wide eyes, waiting for an answer, for someone to reassure him that his world would be okay, and decided he could do this. For this one day.

"I'm sure she will," Nick said. He might not be able to make up for Bobby's ill mother, for the boy not having a father—or for the potato sack races that Carolyn and all the girls like her had missed—but he could make one boy's day shine. Shine as bright as that trophy.

If there was one thing Nick was good at, it was showing somebody how to have fun. And maybe, in doing that with Bobby, he'd find a way to fill that weird hole in his own life, too.

Last place.

Carolyn had never come in last in anything in her entire life. From the sullen looks Angela kept sending her way, her partner in the potato sack race never had, either. "That was fun, wasn't it?"

"Where's Nick?" Angela said in response. Apparently that was a no.

"He's on the stage. He and Bobby came in…first."

"*And* they got a trophy." Angela shot her an accusatory glare.

"You still get a ribbon for participating," Carolyn said, trying to keep an upbeat tone. "And there are other games. Lots of chances to win yet."

"Here comes Nick!" Angela broke away from Carolyn and dashed toward her knight in shining armor.

Mary wove her way through the crowd and up to Carolyn. "How's it going so far?"

Carolyn groaned. "I'm getting my tubes tied."

"That bad, huh?"

"I am so not cut out for mothering. I don't think I could be trusted with a puppy at this point. In fact, don't even send me home with a houseplant. I'd kill the thing with boredom."

"Oh, it can't be that bad."

Carolyn gestured toward Nick, who had Bobby mounted on his shoulders, and Angela trotting alongside. Two people, apparently

Angela's foster parents, had joined them. Angela was proudly making introductions. "See the Pied Piper of children. Note the lonely old maid who drove them away."

Mary laughed. "Maybe you should join forces with Nick. After all, the whole point of today is to engage the kids. And if it all works out, you can take it a step further."

"A step further?"

"And sign up for the Be-a-Buddy program." Mary made a sweeping gesture, indicating the crowd of children and adults. "That's what this is all about. A trial run of sorts. If the day is successful, we're hoping to get a lot of the sponsors to be a part of the buddy program and continue interacting with these kids. So many of them really need a strong role model in their lives. Someone who can see them on a regular basis and do enriching, fun activities."

Enriching? Fun? Strong role model? With *kids*? Mary had her confused with someone else.

Carolyn put up her hands. "I am the last person who should be involved in that. You know my schedule, Mary. You know what my life is like."

"I do," Mary said gently. "And that's exactly why I think you should be a part of this. I think you need it more than the kids do." She gave Carolyn's arm a squeeze, then walked away.

It should have been easy to walk away.

The picnic had broken up. The children had begun boarding the buses or getting into cars to go home, loaded up with toys and cookies, their faces filled with delight—and disappointment that the day was over. Nick had earned a tight hug goodbye and an explosion of gratitude from both Angela and Bobby, then noticed the little boy gave Carolyn a stiff handshake.

He could read the longing in her eyes, though, the moment of hesitation when he'd thought she might reach out and pull the boy into a hug. Then Carolyn had drawn back into herself, the moment of softness gone. She'd become the bulldog again.

The woman he'd known so briefly back in law school disappeared as quickly as a feather in the wind. Disappointment slammed him in the chest. He'd hoped maybe Carolyn could have loosened up, had a good time, but then again, he hadn't exactly helped a whole lot in that area, had he?

He'd had good intentions and gotten distracted by activities with the other kids. Leaving Carolyn to fend for herself. He'd let her down again, even though he hadn't meant to.

"Oh, look, she came."

Nick turned to find Mary, the event's organizer, who had come up beside him. For a second he expected Mary to be talking about Carolyn, then realized that wouldn't make any sense. He really needed to clear his head. Every other thought was about Carolyn Duff, for Pete's sake. "She who?"

"Bobby's mother. Bobby said she hadn't been feeling well this morning, and I didn't think she'd make it to the picnic. He was so disappointed. But she's here. She knew how much this mattered to Bobby, so she came." Mary smiled. "She's one tough lady."

Bobby darted across the field toward the woman, just as Carolyn wandered over and joined Nick and Mary. She shaded her eyes against the sun. "Is that Bobby's mother?"

"Yep. Oh, look, he's waving at us," Mary said. "I think he wants to introduce you to her."

"Oh, I don't think—" Carolyn began.

"I think you should," Mary interrupted. "It'll only take a second."

Nick could see Carolyn's hesitation, sensed it in the set of her shoulders, the tension in her jaw. He remembered what she had told him about her childhood, about the years she had spent with her cold, unforgiving aunt Greta. Alone in a big, empty Victorian house, with no other real family. Carolyn, Nick knew, would feel uncomfortable in a family situation. Even though she'd said earlier that she'd wished she'd met his family, when they'd been together, she'd always found an excuse not to meet his parents, his siblings. The very idea had seemed to scare her.

The bulldog of Lawford could take on criminals, put them behind bars for years, but when it came to barbecues and holidays, she backed down and turned tail.

"Come on, it won't be so bad," Nick said, slipping his hand into hers. To offer support… friendship. Nothing more. But her delicate fingers were cool against his broad palm, the feel of her as familiar as a sunrise.

She looked up at him, defiant and brave. "I never said it would be. Let's go." Despite her words, Carolyn didn't let go of Nick's hand until they were across the field.

There they met up with Bobby and a small, thin brunette woman who looked tired but happy. Bobby stood before her, one arm holding on to hers, the other clutching his trophy. Pride shone in every inch of his face. "Nick, Miss Duff, I want you to meet my momma."

"I heard wonderful things about you both." The woman smiled. When she did, ten years were wiped off her face, and the difficulties of her life, so clear in her face, in the threadbare floral shirt and worn jeans she wore, seemed to be erased. "I'm Pauline Lester." She extended a hand. The trio shook and exchanged introductions.

"They bought me toys, Momma," Bobby said. "So many, I don't think I can fit them in my room. Do I have to give them back?"

His mother laughed. "No, you can keep them all, sweetheart." She drew her son against her, his wiry body cradling gently into her thin frame, her arm a shield and comfort. Then she met Nick and Carolyn's gaze. Tears of gratitude welled in her eyes, but didn't spill over. "Thank you. I can't even begin to tell you how much this means to my son, to me."

"It was nothing," Carolyn said, wishing now that she had spent even more on Bobby, that she could afford to buy this mother and her son a whole house, furnish it from top to bottom. Pull an entire extreme makeover for this struggling family. "We just tried to get him something he'd like."

"Oh, you did, and then some. Bobby's a

wonderful boy." She ruffled his head. "He doesn't need much."

"Just you, Momma," he said, burying his face in her shirt, as if inhaling her perfume. Imprinting her memory.

Carolyn's throat swelled shut. Why had Mary paired her with this boy? The one who brought up everything from her own childhood? The parents she had lost—one she'd never known, the other that had been stolen from her. Her heart broke for Bobby—because she'd been where he was, wanting so hard to hold on to someone who wasn't guaranteed to stay.

She felt a touch against her and looked down. Nick had slipped his hand into hers again. He gave her palm a squeeze.

Whoa, there was a surprise. He'd been paying attention and he not only knew, he understood. And was telling her he was there. Twice now he had done this. Gratitude flooded her and she sent him a smile.

"Did you see my trophy, Momma? I think it might be real gold." Bobby hoisted up his first place trophy, beaming with pride. "Nick and I won the potato sack race. He said he and his dad were the potato winners all the time."

"Is that so? Well, you picked a good partner, then."

"And Nick said that I'm his buddy." Bobby's smiled widened. "I never had a buddy like that before."

"That's wonderful, Bobby." His mother drew in a breath, then let it out in a shudder. She coughed, and Carolyn could see exhaustion claiming her. "Let's go home now."

"Are you okay, Momma?"

She patted his shoulder. "Just fine, Bobby. Just fine."

But all the adults could hear the lie the mother told her son.

"Thank you again," Pauline told Nick and Carolyn. "It's really nice to see Bobby smiling again."

Then she turned and left, with her son at her side, his hand on her arm, protective and doting.

A family, no matter how small, but a family all the same. In a two-person cocoon.

"What is it with you two?"

After Bobby and Pauline Lester had left, Nick hung around to help finish cleaning up. He was just about to leave when he turned to find Mary Hudson, the event's organizer, standing beside him. She had her arms crossed over her chest, and though there were faint shadows of exhaustion beneath her eyes from the long day, he could see the sharp look of inquisitiveness in her hazel gaze. "Us two who?" he asked.

"Oh, please. Like you don't know. You and Carolyn. Everyone within a three-county area can tell there's unfinished business between the two of you." She picked up a stray piece of trash on the ground and tossed it into a nearby barrel. "And I know, because I work with Carolyn every day. She refuses to talk about you. Whenever Carolyn is silent, that's a sure sign she's hiding something big."

Carolyn wouldn't talk about him with other people. Nick didn't know whether to take that as a compliment or an insult. "It's all in the past."

"Not that far in the past, from what I can see."

"Carolyn has moved on, I'm sure." Nick was probing and he knew it. Shamelessly probing.

"No, she hasn't. She spends every minute of her day working. Stuck in that office, poring over her computer, or in court. She has no love life, no life at all, really. She needs a man."

And from the way Mary was eyeing him, giving him a visual résumé read, he'd apparently already been interviewed and hired for the job. But Mary didn't know the history between Carolyn and him. There were some roads that couldn't—and definitely shouldn't—be traveled twice.

"I'm sure she'll meet someone," Nick said, then turned away, tearing his gaze away from Carolyn, even as doing so seemed to tear something in his gut.

But it was better this way. He knew it, knew it so well he should have written the words on the walls of his house. They were already scrawled all over his heart. He'd screwed up when he'd married Carolyn, rushing into a marriage he'd had no business proposing, because he was after the chase more than the big picture.

Even now, he didn't have the desire to settle down fully. Really become a fully functioning grown-up who mowed the lawn on Saturdays, changed diapers on a regular basis and paid into a college fund. Until then, he should steer clear of women, especially women like Carolyn, who made getting serious into an art form.

"Nick, wait."

He pivoted back.

"I promise, no more talk about your love life," Mary said, holding up her hands in surrender. "This is about the kids. You did such a great job today."

"Thanks."

"You're going to make a great dad some-day."

"I'm leaving that job to my sisters and brother. Plenty of Gilberts to go around already. I'm better in the indulgent uncle role."

"Too bad," Mary said. "Because I saw true parenting genius. You brought Angela out of her shell, got her talking her head off all day. Bobby had fun. It was incredible."

Nick didn't reply. If he was such great parent material, he'd have been married and had kids of his own by now. But he'd totally messed up his one attempt at marriage, and he wasn't about to go running down that heartbreak hill, not again. "I should get going. Thanks for a great day. You pulled off a hell of an event."

"Don't go, not yet. Would you mind talking with Jean Klein? She works for the Lawford Department of Child Services. She and I were wondering if you could do us a favor," Mary said. "Well, not us so much, but Bobby."

"Bobby? Sure, just tell me what you need."

"It's easier if Jean explains." Mary led him over to one of the picnic tables, where Carolyn was already sitting and chatting with another woman, whom Mary introduced as Jean. Nick slipped into a seat opposite the two women. Mary sat down beside him.

"First," Jean began, "I wanted to say I appreciate your time and the time of all the other attorneys today. It was wonderful to see the kids so happy, but especially Bobby. He had a great time, engaging with other people. He hasn't been adapting so well to the challenges of the last few months. It's been really hard on him since his father died."

"His father died?" Nick asked. He glanced at Carolyn, and saw a deep well of sympathy in her eyes.

Oh, damn. Of all people, Carolyn was the last person who should be sitting here, hearing this. Not after all she'd gone through as a kid. It had to be bringing up some awful memories. The sudden urge to shield her rushed over him. But she was an adult, and had made it clear that she didn't need him—or anyone else. So he sat where he was and returned his attention to the conversation.

Jean nodded. "It was tragic. A drive-by shooting last year."

Poor Bobby. What an awful thing for a little boy to have to go through. The urge to reach out to Carolyn again doubled. His hand snuck across the divide between them on the bench, there if she needed it, or not if she didn't.

"To compound the boy's difficulties," Jean

went on, "his mother has been in and out of the hospital."

"He mentioned she's sick."

"Breast cancer. Though the worst seems to be behind her now, or we hope so. I think part of what's making it so hard for her to win this battle is worrying about her son. Money was tight before Bobby's father died, but afterward, there wasn't any insurance, and with his mother sick, they've been living paycheck to paycheck in this tiny little apartment you can barely call a home. And when his mother gets sick, he sometimes doesn't have anyplace to go."

Jean drew in a breath, let it go. Her concern for the child was clear in her voice, her mannerisms. Nick's respect for the case worker multiplied. He could only imagine how hard it must be for her to deal with this kind of thing every day, when all he worked with was business law. None of this heavy, emotional baggage.

"All the other times, Bobby's grandmother was able to take care of Bobby, but now his grandmother is simply too old and recently had to be moved to a nursing home. The last time Bobby's mother was hospitalized, we had no choice but to send him to foster care."

"Foster care?" Carolyn repeated. "Living with strangers?"

Nick's gaze slid again to Carolyn. He could see she understood far too well what that must have been like for Bobby. He read it in her face, in the concern in her voice. Although he knew, from what she'd told him, that life with her aunt Greta had been awful, he began to realize, just in what was etched in her eyes, how much he hadn't known about his whirl-wind wife, how much of her past he'd missed, in the rush to the altar. He hadn't been paying attention then—but he was now.

"I'm sure Bobby didn't do well there," Carolyn said.

Jean shook her head. "Too many changes, too quick. It's been incredibly difficult for him. He wants his family back, and well, that's not going to happen. It's hard for a child that age to understand that the world is never going to go back to the way it used to be."

Nick swallowed hard. "Yeah. I understand."

Carolyn was mute. But Nick could read, in the set of her shoulders, that she empathized with Bobby, probably more than anyone at this table. His hand snaked closer, inching across the rough pine surface, but still he was too far away from her, and she had drawn into herself, her body stiff, everything about her saying she was a sole sentry in her feelings.

"That's why I was so amazed to see him smiling today," Jean continued. "When I say I haven't seen that boy smile in months, I mean it."

"I had no idea," Nick said. "So many of these children today have such difficult lives and yet they were happy, as if nothing had happened."

This was a world Nick had never seen. It had always existed; he'd just been going along blithely with his life, never really seeing how others lived right alongside him. But now, to have it presented in person, with big brown eyes, made him sit up and take notice.

"They're resilient," Jean said. "And determined. The kids are the ones that make my job rewarding."

"Hey, Mary, can I get a hand over here?" One of the volunteers shouted, her arms overloaded with leftovers from the food table.

Mary rose. "Sorry, I have to go clean up."

"I'll help," Carolyn said. The two of them headed off to catch a teetering pile of bowls just before it came tumbling down. Nick suspected Carolyn had left the table, not so much to help, but because the subject matter was hitting a little too close to home.

He watched her for a minute and saw her

slip back into being efficient, strong Carolyn. The woman who betrayed no emotion. Nick brought his hands together in a tight knot and let out a sigh.

Carolyn and her walls. If only she hadn't had so many of them, maybe there would have been hope for them. For their marriage to survive.

Hell, who was he kidding? He hadn't tried so hard to scale those walls. Doing so would have meant buckling down, getting serious. Being the kind of man who really worked hard at his marriage. He'd gotten married on a lark. Then, when faced with the reality of what he'd done, taken the easy way out. Even now, three years later, Nick didn't feel any more ready or prepared to make that leap than he had before.

"Anyway," Jean said, interrupting Nick's thoughts, "back to the reason I wanted to talk to you. I noticed that Bobby seemed to latch on to you. He opened up. Had fun." Jean smiled. "That's also something Bobby hasn't done in months. We were hoping that for this weekend, maybe you would consider being his buddy."

"Buddy?"

"It's part of the Be-a-Buddy program," Jean explained. "Sort of like the Big Sisters/ Big Brothers program." Nick nodded his understanding. "You'd hang out with Bobby, like you did today, and take him places. Have fun. Let him be a kid. His mother's not feeling well and having a rough time of it lately, so this could be the break she needs for a few days. Plus, Bobby needs a strong male role model. And, most of all, he needs to laugh."

Nick shifted on the hard wooden picnic seat. He splayed his hands across the table. Strong male role model? Him? Ha, if only they knew him. He wasn't anyone's role model, more a model of how to be a cut-up in the classroom. "Jean, I'd like to help, but—"

"Don't say no. He needs you." Jean laid a palm atop his. "Mary told me you've undergone a criminal background check because you're involved with a youth basketball program at the YMCA. That clears one hurdle for us already, and allows you to get started with Bobby immediately. And if it's too much for you to do alone, feel free to ask a friend or family member to help you out. Sometimes that makes it easier to make that bridge with a child."

Unbidden, Nick's gaze sought out the one other person left on the picnic grounds who would understand Bobby Lester. Someone else who had lost a father…had her childhood ripped away. And someone who could…

Maybe be the ying to his yang. He'd always

been the clown, where she'd always been the serious one. Maybe together...?

He watched Carolyn finish the clean-up of the food table, her movements stiff and severe. What had happened to the Carolyn he had met so many years ago? The woman he had managed to get to loosen up, to laugh, and then finally fallen in love with? The woman who had, for one brief moment in time, made him consider growing up, maybe take life a little more seriously?

Could he—if he helped her find her way back to those days—find where he had lost that thread in their marriage? Make up for the way he had messed things up? And maybe if he repaired that damage, ensure a better future down the road, for both of them?

He thought of Bobby. Of the laughter that had bubbled out of that boy today but had not entirely covered the deep dark sadness that lingered behind his eyes.

Nick might be the one who could provide the fun and games, but to truly touch Bobby's life, he knew only one other person in the world who would understand that world. Who could reach into the gloomy spaces in that boy's heart and really draw him out.

"I'll do it," he said. "But on one condition."

CHAPTER SIX

"NO WAY."

Carolyn stood in her office on Sunday morning, hands on her hips, refusing Mary for the four hundredth time. "Absolutely not."

"One holiday weekend, Carolyn. Not a lifetime commitment. Think of it as a vacation."

Carolyn turned away and sank into her leather chair. "With Nick? That's not a vacation, Mary. That's like one big—"

"Ball of temptation. I've seen him up close, Carolyn, and he is a hottie, in all capital letters."

Carolyn shook her head. "And you are an incurable romantic. Seeing happy endings where there aren't any. I have work to do. Tell Nick to find someone else. Surely the man has friends. And I know he has family."

"He wants you." Mary arched a brow and grinned. "Wants *you*," she stressed again.

"I don't want him."

Liar, liar. Everything within Carolyn had wanted Nick yesterday. It had taken a supreme act of willpower not to give in to the desire to touch him. To feel the warmth of the sun on his arms. To curve against his chest, just as she had years before. Because her body didn't forget. Her mind remembered every inch of that man's body. Even if the rest of her knew better.

Knew getting involved with him, especially a second time, was a bad idea.

"Either way, you're too late," Mary said. "Because—" she paused a beat, long enough for Carolyn to hear the familiar ding of the elevator "—he's here now."

"He's *here?* How could you do that? I told you—"

"Overruled, Counselor." Mary grinned, then headed out of Carolyn's office, leaving the door ajar.

Before she could react, Nick entered her office, and Carolyn's breath left her. For a long second she didn't see Bobby, didn't see Mary pass by, wave and head downstairs, didn't see anything but the vibrant blue of Nick's eyes and the familiar curve of his grin.

He was here. Just when she'd thought he was out of her life again for good. And damn if her heart didn't react as predictably as a moth to a bug light.

"Nick. I'm sorry. I just found out about—"

"Miss Duff…uh, Carolyn," Bobby cut in. "Nick told me we're going to the fair today. You're coming, right? Nick said you're really good at the games and he said you can win a prize for me."

The boy's eyes were wide, his smile full of hope. And Carolyn was caught in Nick's already woven web. She shot him a glare. She thought of everything Jean had told them yesterday, and guilt rocketed through her. Bobby was relying on them, counting on Nick and her to provide a few of the good times his life had been so devoid of lately. There was no way out of this.

Still, she stalled. "A little pre-event disclosure would have been nice, Mr. Gilbert."

"I didn't want you to ready an objection, Miss Duff."

"My docket is already full," she said, indicating the pile of work on her desk. "I don't have room in my agenda for extraneous field trips."

Bobby looked from one adult to the other, completely confused.

"Counselor, I think you need a recess. It is Sunday, after all, and the courts are closed."

Carolyn ran a hand over her face. Nick was not making this easy. Why wouldn't he listen? Didn't he understand? What if something went wrong? What if something happened? Didn't he read the statistics about holiday weekends? The drunk drivers, the partyers starting fights, the fireworks accidents, the looters taking advantage of closed stores—

The nightmares ran through Carolyn's mind at double time. "Nick, I don't think you're taking into account all the criminal element variables."

"It's a simple field trip, Carolyn. Not a foray into the depths of Sing-Sing."

Her heart began to race, her lungs pumping faster. She rocketed back two dozen years, unable to stop the comparisons to her own life. What if?

What if something went wrong? What if she couldn't stop it? What if Bobby got hurt?

Bobby stood there, wearing a short white T-shirt decorated with a flag, and little navy shorts. His hair was freshly combed, his old, nearly worn-through sneakers neatly tied. Trusting. Innocent. Again, she thought, what if?

"Nick, I really can't," Carolyn said.

Bobby's face fell.

"Counselor, I request a sidebar. On behalf of my client." Nick gestured toward Bobby.

Carolyn knew she wasn't going to be able to get rid of Nick easily. That persistence had been what had worn her down all those years ago in college. She refused to let him win again this time, though. She laid her pen on her desk. "Bobby, would you like to sit at the desk outside my office? It's Mary's desk and she has candy in the dish. You can have two pieces."

A grin spread from one ear to the other, then halted. Bobby looked up at Nick, as if he was afraid someone would tell him no. Nick gave Bobby a nod, then bent down to whisper in his ear. "Go ahead. And if you take three, I won't tell anyone. By the way, I bet that chair spins pretty fast."

Bobby hurried through the open door and climbed onto Mary's leather chair. A second later he was swiveling in a circle and sucking on a peppermint.

"Nick, I don't have time for this. I have a plea bargain to work on, a bunch of depositions to review…" She waved a vague hand at her desk. Excuses, she knew, but valid ones. "You'll do just fine with Bobby on your own."

"We both know it's not about your workload, Carolyn. What's the real problem?" He leaned closer. "Don't you want to spend time with me? And Bobby?"

She let out a gust. "Not everything in my life revolves around you."

"Then what is it?"

"Don't you read the paper? Aren't you worried something might go wrong?"

"Something…" He stared at her. "What could possibly go wrong?" His old devil-may-care smile curved up his lips. "What, some rogue carousel horse might run amok?"

Carolyn paced her office, frustration pushing her steps. "I'm not treating this as a joke, Nick. A thousand things could happen."

He got in front of her, preventing her from wearing any further path in the carpet. "You can't live your life around the possibility of what might happen. You have to take risks."

"With someone else's child? What if—"

"And what if everything goes just fine? What if we all have a good time? What would be so wrong with that?"

She shook her head. Nick didn't understand. He hadn't lived through what she had. He hadn't had a childhood where he woke up in the middle of the night, screaming from nightmares. She knew the dangers, understood what could lurk in the world. "You don't need me to go."

"That's where you're wrong. Bobby *does* need you. You specifically."

"Me? Why? He's barely said three words to me since we met."

"You know why," Nick said quietly. His gaze met hers, and a beat passed between them. "Because Bobby's father was murdered, just like yours. You are the only one, Carolyn, the only one who can truly understand what it's like for him."

The words slammed into Carolyn, words that she thought would have no effect on her, not anymore. She'd been over that for so long, but now she glanced out the door, at the little boy spinning in the chair a few feet away, his head downcast, his shoulders hunched with a weight that only a few, a select group that Carolyn was part of, none of them by choice, could recognize. Her eyes blurred and then she no longer saw Bobby.

She saw herself.

Her mind rocketed back to that day—that day in the convenience store, when she'd cowered, sobbing, by the milk, thinking if she could make herself really, really small, maybe the bad man wouldn't notice her and he'd just go away. He'd leave, leave her and her father alone. He'd stop yelling, stop asking for money no one had.

But he hadn't stopped. And when her father had tried to stand up to him, tried to make him go away, because he'd been scaring Carolyn—*telling her to shut up, shut the hell up*—his gun in her face, and then her father was there, and the gun had gone off, the explosion so loud Carolyn thought she'd never hear again.

And her father falling, falling, falling, so slow, she had run forward, trying to catch him, thinking if she could catch him, she could stop it all. But she hadn't been able to stop him from falling. Stop the blood. Stop his life from leaking onto the tile floor, into a sticky, copper-smelling puddle beside her. Even when the policemen had come and taken away the bad man, and then her father, Carolyn hadn't wanted to believe it was over. Hadn't wanted to leave. She'd just stared at that crimson spot on the floor, willing it to go away, for all of it to disappear.

She sucked in a breath, tried to steady herself again, clutching her desk, the scent of copper so strong again in her nose she thought she might be sick. But no, it was over. It was over. Breathe. Breathe.

She had been nine. Bobby had been four. Was there ever a good age to hear that someone had stolen your father?

"He needs you, Carolyn," Nick repeated.

She shook her head and spun away from Nick, away from the sight of Bobby, the memories his presence evoked, to face the window, her gaze going to the sunny view of Lawford below her. The city was quiet, the downtown area empty as a cemetery. "Not me, Nick. Please, not me."

Nick came up behind her, his hands going to her shoulders, a light touch, but so heavy inside her. "I think you need him, too. Mary says you work all the time. You have no life. This might be exactly the right thing for you."

She wheeled around, out of his grasp. "How do you know what I need?" she whispered, keeping her voice low, so Bobby didn't overhear. "We were only married four days, Nick. Knew each other for, what, three weeks? You think you really got to know me in that time? You didn't. Not really. Let's not kid ourselves."

"No, I guess I didn't." A shadow dropped over his face and he took a step back. Then it was gone, and he cleared his throat. "This isn't about us anyway. This is about him. It's one weekend. A fair, some fireworks. Let's put our differences aside for two days, for Bobby's sake. And maybe, just maybe, we can make a difference in his life." Nick's gaze met hers. "You used to tell me how awful it was living with your aunt Greta. How cold she was. How would things have been different for you when you were a kid, if someone had stepped in and played mom and dad—or simply played fairy godparents like we would be—for you, just for a weekend?"

Aunt Greta. She'd tried to forget the icy aunt who had raised her after Carolyn's father's death, a woman so devoid of emotion she might as well have been a stone.

Tears sprang to Carolyn's eyes, and a lump wedged so thick in her throat, she didn't think she'd ever get it dislodged. She shook her head, her fists clenched together. "That's not playing fair, Nick."

"I'm not playing anything, Carolyn." He reached up and cupped her jaw, his touch tender and gentle. "I've made my case, Counselor. While I await your verdict, I'm going to go join the rest of the jury in the outer office before he turns into the Tasmanian devil on a serious sugar high."

Nick told himself not to be disappointed. That Carolyn had every right to say no. He'd sprung the idea on her at the last minute, when she'd had a stack of work on her desk and—

And damn it, he could give a thousand reasons why she might be justified in saying no, but that didn't mean he liked a single one of them.

"How's come Miss Duff didn't want to go?"

"She had a lot of work to do," Nick said. He and Bobby wandered the noisy, brightly lit midway of the Lawford Fourth of July Weekend Festival, a stack of tickets for rides in one hand and the remains of a sticky cotton candy poof in the other. Little blue sugar crystals coated Bobby's lips and dotted his T-shirt, but he had a smile on his face and a belly that looked full enough to burst.

"Can we ride the Roaring Dragon ride next?" he asked, taking the cotton candy from Nick and devouring the rest. "Dragons are my favorite thing in the world."

"Why don't we let that candy settle first? I don't think we want your snack to make a reappearance." He might not know a lot about kids, but he did know enough to know mixing sugar and fast movement too soon would be a disaster.

"Okay." Bobby tossed the empty cotton candy stick into the trash then stopped in front of one of the carney stands. Stuffed animals in a range of sizes marched across the front of the stand, swinging tantalizingly in the light breeze.

"Come on up, take your chances!" A skinny man, dressed in jeans and a bright-red T-shirt advertising the fair sat on the edge of the booth, leaning out, waving at all who passed. "Throw the balls into the basket, win a prize. Get in all three, win your choice."

"Can we do it, Nick?" Bobby tugged on his sleeve, practically jumping up and down. "Can we? I really want that stuffed dragon. *Dragon Tales* is like my favorite show ever. And I really love dragons. Only not the kind that breathe fire. Fire is kind of scary, but dragons are cool."

Nick chuckled. How could he resist that? Earlier this morning, Bobby had been morose, worried about his mother, who had been so sick, Jean said, that she'd still been in bed when Jean had picked Bobby up and brought him to meet Nick at Carolyn's office. That had had Nick worried. He was good when a kid was bubbly. Full of energy. Ready to play. But dealing with an emotional, moody child—

Not his best suit. Which was why he'd called on Carolyn. She was the one he'd hoped could handle the tough stuff. Thankfully, once he and Bobby had reached the fair, the somber mood had lifted, and now Bobby seemed to have left all his troubles behind. He and Nick had had a blast so far, riding tons of rides, stopping in at some of the exhibits and wandering through the petting zoo. If it meant keeping Bobby in the good humor Nick was comfortable with, Nick would play any game at the fair.

"Think you can win it, Nick?" Bobby asked again.

"Sure, I can try. But I have to warn you, this one is not my area of expertise."

"No, it's not. It's mine."

Nick turned, sure he'd imagined the voice. But no, there she stood, a smile on her face, wearing shorts and a T-shirt, her blond hair back in a ponytail, looking so much like the Carolyn he used to know back in college that he couldn't believe she was the same woman he'd seen in the office a couple hours earlier. It was as if stepping outside the doors of the county prosecutor's office had made her shed the skin of the strict, tough Carolyn and brought her back to the woman he had fallen in love with all those years ago.

"Miss Duff!" Bobby exclaimed. "You came."

"Call me Carolyn," she reminded gently, then bent down to his level. "And yes, I came, because Nick here is no good at winning these games and I couldn't let you go home empty-handed."

She glanced up at Nick and their eyes met, held. For one long heartbeat, Nick knew. She was here for more than giving this boy a stuffed animal. It was about giving him the experience he was missing because he'd lost that half of his family so critical to normalcy.

Because despite all her worries about safety, just like Nick had thought, she understood what Bobby was going through, and didn't want him to miss out on what she had in her childhood. For once, Nick had read Carolyn right, and he wondered whether if he had done it once, he could do it again.

"So," Carolyn said, rising and brushing her hands together, "shall we do this?"

Bobby nodded. "Can you get the dragon?"

"Anything you want, Bobby."

Nick slapped down a five-dollar bill and the man placed three balls before Carolyn. He explained the game, then stood to the side and demonstrated with one swift throw how easy it was to land a wiffle ball in the wooden basket, the kind usually used for gathering fruit. "He makes it look easy," Nick whispered to Carolyn.

"They always do, but if it were easy, everyone would win and the fair wouldn't make any money." She bent down next to Bobby. "Okay, I'll share the secret with you on how to win, but you have to keep it a secret. My father told it to me and now I'll tell it to you."

Bobby's eyes widened with excitement at being let in on a secret. He nodded solemnly. "Okay."

Keeping her voice low, Carolyn demonstrated with the ball in her hand. "You need to get as close as you're allowed to, according to the rules. You want to toss underhanded, put a little spin on it and don't throw too hard. The basket isn't very deep and your goal is to aim for the lip of the basket, where the sweet spot is."

"What's a sweet spot?"

Carolyn smiled. "The best spot to hit, so that the ball will drop right into the basket." She rose, juggling one of the balls in her right hand. "Watch."

Nick watched, amazed, as Carolyn stepped up to the booth, leaned forward, but not so much that she extended over the counter, and tossed the ball. The white sphere rose upward in an arc, spinning as it arched toward the basket, pinging off the rim, then dropped lightly into the basket and settled in the bottom.

"You did it!" Bobby jumped up beside her. "You did it!"

Several people who had stopped by the booth to watch Carolyn shoot applauded her success. Nick, however, wasn't impressed so much with her aim as he was with the change that had come over Carolyn when she'd leaned down and talked to Bobby. Her entire demeanor had relaxed, and she had become someone else. Someone who reached out, extended a thread, then knotted that connection into a rope.

It was an entirely new side of her. A side he realized he liked. Very much.

"Do it again," Bobby said. "All three gets to pick any toy."

Carolyn shot Nick a smile. "Nothing like a little pressure."

"You can do it," he said, taking a step closer.

Carolyn wavered for a moment. Nick's breath, warm against her neck, sent a wave of desire rushing through her. She forgot all about the carnival game. The fairgoers. Why she was there. All she wanted to do was lean into Nick's touch and see where that particular game of chance got her.

Then Bobby tugged at her sleeve and brought her back to reality. "Can you do it again?"

"Sure, sure." Carolyn shot the second ball, then the third, sinking both of them into the basket. Around them, the crowd erupted into applause, the bell was rung announcing a winner, and Bobby sported the largest smile a child could. He chose a bright-green-and-red stuffed dragon that was nearly half his size and thanked Carolyn several times as they walked away.

"Wow! You are really good at that. Did your daddy win you a dragon, too?" Bobby clutched the dragon to his chest, as proud of the stuffed animal as a new parent.

"No, a bear. I still have it."

Bobby plucked at the dragon's scales, his fingers pulling at the yellow triangles, his gaze downcast. "Is your father still alive?"

"No, Bobby, he isn't," Carolyn said. She drew in a breath. This was harder to talk about than she expected—because she *never* talked about it. She'd put it behind her after that day, moved forward—charged forward, really, determined not to let one day become the moment that defined her life.

Yet, there had been moments when she'd been growing up when she had wished *someone* would have talked to her. Mentioned her father. Told her a story, told her it was okay to talk about what had happened. Aunt Greta had refused to mention the death of her brother, had buried the topic along with him at the cemetery. Leaving nine-year-old Carolyn to stuff those feelings inside, with nowhere to vent that volcano of fear, worry and hurt.

What Carolyn had needed most back then was a friend. A friend who understood. And as she looked down into Bobby's eyes, his fingers clutching that dragon as if the stuffed animal could ward off all the rest of the evil in the world, she knew he, too, needed a friend. "My father—" she swallowed "—he was killed by a bad man when I was nine."

Bobby bit his lip, clutched the dragon tighter. "A bad man hurt my daddy, too," he said, the words slow in coming. His teeth tugged at his lip some more, then he went on. "My daddy is in heaven now. And my mom, she has to go to the hospital a lot, sometimes for a long time. My grandma's too old to watch me, so when my mom is gone, I have to live with other people. Did you have to do that, too?"

Carolyn nodded, her voice lost in a swell of emotion. Oh, how she knew that life. Knew it too well. Poor Bobby. Carolyn's heart squeezed so tight she thought it might never beat properly again. Her throat closed, her breath caught, then she forced out a gust, extended a hand and—

Reached out. Tentative, she captured Bobby's free hand in her own. He hesitated, then the little palm warmed hers, fingers curling between her own, tightening into her grasp, holding on to her as firmly as he did the dragon. Now her heart swelled to bursting with compassion and she whispered a single wish to the heavens. That this boy would be safe forever, that the road ahead would be easy for Bobby Lester, because the one he was on had already been too hard. "I'm sorry, Bobby. I'm so sorry."

He looked up at her and nodded, understanding extending between them like a web. "Me, too."

Nick's arm stole around Carolyn's waist, strong, secure, *there*, and she let herself lean into his touch, needing him right then as much as Bobby needed her.

Then the three of them stopped and simply stood there, pretending they were watching the Ferris wheel make its slow spin. But really, not seeing anything at all but a blurry circle of lights.

CHAPTER SEVEN

JEAN MET NICK and Carolyn, along with Bobby, outside the fair at nine that night, on the dot. She looked harried and overwhelmed, but grateful to see Bobby sporting a smiling face and arms full of prizes. "I take it you had a good time?"

Bobby nodded. "Uh-huh. It was really fun," he said. "Can we go every day?"

Jean laughed. "Sorry, Bobby, but the fair moves on to another town tomorrow."

The little boy swallowed, and accepted that information without complaint, disappointment clearly something he was used to. Nick's chest tightened. Once again Bobby's world and the one he'd grown up in were a thousand miles apart. He may not have been rich or spoiled, but he sure had been privileged, and indulged with happiness and family. Guilt rocketed through Nick, and in a weird way he wanted to give some of those years back, if only so that Bobby could have them instead.

Bobby shrugged, as if he didn't care, the bravado back in place. "That's all right. The fair was just okay anyway."

It wasn't okay, not by a long shot, not in Nick's book, but he was powerless to make the fair stay in town. To change the circumstances of one boy's life.

Carolyn met Nick's eye and he saw her bite back a sigh, just as he did, at the sound of Bobby's too-old speech. "Bobby won this mirror all by himself," Nick said, clapping the boy on the shoulder with the change of subject, hoping it would restore the child's good humor. Not really knowing what else to do. "He hit three balloons with the darts. He's got some seriously good aim. Probably see him in the Major Leagues someday."

That earned a smile. Hurrah.

"Good job, Bobby," Jean said.

"Thank you." Bobby, however, still didn't seem much happier. Nick looked to Carolyn for help.

"Tomorrow, Bobby, will be quite the adventurous evening. We'll be reconvening and attend the fireworks celebration."

Nick sent Carolyn a sidelong glance. *Reconvening? Celebration?* Bobby also gave her a baffled look. Carolyn just stood there, stiff as a board. What was wrong with her? It seemed like every time the boy got close to her, she put up this wall of formality.

She did it with Bobby; she did it with Nick. Here he'd thought they were making such great progress and that he could finally read her, understand what made her tick.

Obviously, he'd gotten it just as wrong this time as he had three years ago. Maybe she was right. Maybe he didn't understand her.

Or maybe he just needed to try harder.

"We'll have fun tomorrow, Bobby, I promise," Nick said, ruffling the boy's hair.

Bobby's smile spread so far across his face, Nick was sure it reached from one ear to the other. "You mean it? You're not just saying that? A lot of people make promises and then they have to break them. And…well, I'll understand if you can't come." He toed at the dirt beneath his worn sneakers, then looked up again. "I bet you're real busy."

Bobby stared at him, waiting for the answer. Nick knew what the boy was really asking. Would Nick be there—beyond this weekend. This fair. The fireworks tomorrow.

Would he be a real friend? And not just a guy making an empty promise?

Nick's gut tightened. He wasn't used to this.

People expecting anything of him. Sure, there were expectations at work, but those ended when he walked out the door. In his personal life, he answered to no one, unless he counted Bandit, and all the dog wanted was a can of food every morning, a walk every night and a reliable ball-throwing partner. Not exactly a major commitment.

Except for his whirlwind marriage to Carolyn, he had never really settled down with anything or anyone, and even then, four days wasn't any kind of commitment. Bobby was looking, Nick knew, for more. Not a lifetime, but more than Nick Gilbert had ever given before. He looked to Carolyn for a good answer, but she had already inserted that distance that she was so good at.

Why had Mary ever put the two of them in charge of children, specifically this one? Neither of them had what it took to connect, not over the long haul. Nick thought he could do this, but…

Damn, it was a lot harder than he'd thought.

"Sure," he managed finally, because what else could he say? When the boy looked at him like that, with such hope in his eyes, it made Nick want to run for president and change the world. "I'm your buddy, for as long as you want."

"Come on, Bobby," Jean said. "Time to go home." She took him by the hand, seeming to read the tension in the group. "Your mom is waiting and I'm sure she wants to hear all about your day. Plus, it's bedtime. You'll see Nick and Carolyn tomorrow for the fireworks."

Then Jean was gone, with Bobby in tow, leaving Nick and Carolyn alone.

"I should go, too," Carolyn said. But she didn't move. Her gaze caught his, and again he wondered if maybe one of the problems between them hadn't been that he hadn't read her right, but that he hadn't tried *hard enough* to read her.

He'd seen another side of her today, in the way she'd reached out to Bobby, let herself be vulnerable. A side he wanted to explore more. Letting her go now didn't seem like an option.

Nick turned and took Carolyn's hand, falling into touching her, relying on her, just as he always had before. His world had been rocked, and he sought the closest mountain he knew. "Stay," he said. "Please."

"I—" She cut off the sentence. "Okay. But let's get out of here. It's so busy. And noisy."

Nick nodded. "I know just the place." Still holding hands, he led her to his SUV, then held the door for her. She brushed by him as she moved to sit in the passenger's seat, giving him a hint of her perfume. Sweet floral notes, an undertone of jasmine. He leaned forward, unable to stop himself from getting close to her, and pressed his lips to her neck, inhaling the scent and leaving a long, lingering kiss along the delicate skin that curved beneath her blond tresses. Oh, so familiar. So sweet. He was tempted to do more, to let his fingers walk along the same path, to take her in his arms, but he didn't. Carolyn paused, tense for one second, then she drew in a breath, let it out, along with his name. "Nick, what are you doing to me?"

"I don't know," he answered honestly. He stood there, inhaling that perfume, his mind rocketing to the past, wanting to kiss her so damned bad. Then, with a sigh, he let her go and rounded to his side of the car. He got inside, put the Ford in gear. Neither of them said anything as he drove out of the fairgrounds and across Lawford to a small jazz club on the north side of the downtown area. When he stopped the car, Carolyn turned to him and smiled. "You remembered."

"I did."

He hadn't forgotten much at all about Carolyn, as much as he'd tried. He still knew her favorite type of music. Her favorite meal. The scent of her perfume, and most of all, how she would feel in his arms and in his bed.

That, most of all. But even he knew a relationship couldn't be built on attraction. If it could, they'd still be together. Three years ago, they'd missed laying the foundation, and he wondered if it was possible to find the building blocks they needed this far after they'd undone what little of a relationship they'd had.

He came around the SUV and opened her door, taking her hand as she stepped out of the vehicle and onto the sidewalk. He didn't *need* to take her hand—he knew Carolyn was the kind of woman who could take care of herself and didn't expect him to be a gentleman—but he took her hand because he wanted to touch her, and not let go. Electricity sizzled between them, with a low hum of awareness. Again the desire to kiss her rose in Nick. But he knew if he did that now—

He wouldn't stop.

They entered the club, a cozy little place decorated in cranberry and gold. A trio comprised of a pianist, saxophonist and singer stood on the stage, singing an old Billie Holiday song. Only a few other people were sitting inside, so Nick and Carolyn had their choice of seating. They opted for a booth tucked in the back, providing privacy, a quiet little nook.

They hadn't been to this place in more than three years, but he remembered this booth. Remembered sitting across this very table from Carolyn, watching her laugh, sway along with the music. Remembered falling for her.

As if she could read his mind, her gaze broke away from his and she surveyed the room. "It's not very busy tonight."

"Probably because of the holiday. Most everyone went out of town." He studied her, reading the faint shadows beneath her eyes that spoke of exactly what Mary had told him—Carolyn worked far too many hours. She was, as she had been back in college, pouring herself into her career. They were still complete opposites. Nick, the guy who worked just enough to live and have fun, and Carolyn whose whole life was work. "Why are you in town? You could have gone off to some exotic island or a spa for the weekend."

"You know me. I don't do that. If I had my choice, I'd be in the office, working."

"You're still like that, Carolyn?" He'd hoped for more. He'd hoped she would have changed. That maybe he'd have had some influence on her.

"You say it like you're disappointed."

"I thought maybe…"

"Thought what? That I would get a life? Move on? Find someone else?"

The image of her with another man caused a surge of jealousy to wash over him. "No."

"You know why my job is important to me. Why I work so hard."

Because of what had happened to her father. Because she didn't want to let another murderer walk the streets. So she put in every hour she could to ensure no crime was left unprosecuted, no piece of evidence missed. "Your father wouldn't want you to spend your whole life behind a desk, either, Carolyn."

She turned away and he knew he had hit a nerve.

"So, what can I get you folks?"

The waitress's friendly voice interrupted them. She stood at the side of the table, a dozen gold bracelets jangling on her skinny wrist as she poised her hand over the order pad.

"Cosmo, with a lime twist."

"Dewar's on the rocks," Nick said. "And thank you, Regina," he added, reading her name tag. "It must not be a very busy night tonight for you."

She shrugged. "I kind of like it this way

once in a while. Lets me rest up for those crazy Friday nights when it seems I run off twenty pounds between here and the bar."

Nick laughed. "We'll do our best to keep your bar running to a minimum so you get a chance to put your feet up."

The other woman grinned. "Thanks. I think you'll be my favorite customer all week." She gave Nick a friendly tap with the order pad, then headed off to the bar.

Carolyn's gaze swiveled back to Nick's. "How do you do it?"

"How do I do what?"

"Make friends with everyone. The kids. The waitress. Jean. And I'm this major social misfit."

"You're not a social misfit."

"Nick, those kids barely said three words to me at the picnic. I only got Bobby to talk to me when I was winning him a prize. You were the one all the children wanted to hang around with. You're their buddy. I'm just the fifth wheel that they put up with because they had to."

"Aw, Carolyn, you're not that bad."

She arched a brow.

"Well…" He hesitated. "You might want to try not using multisyllabic words like *re-*

convene and *celebration*." He shrugged. "Just loosen up a little."

Carolyn groaned and dropped her head into her hands. "I was totally awful, wasn't I?"

"Not totally…" Nick paused. "Okay, yeah."

"It's just so hard for me."

In college, Nick had seen Carolyn—the stuffy Bostonian—and seen a woman he thought just needed to relax. Learn to be spontaneous. But now as he looked into her eyes and saw the glimmer of tears, the strain of how hard she had tried today written in her tensed muscles, her worried features, he realized her struggle to connect with people didn't stem from which side of the country she'd been raised on, but from all the facets of her background brought together.

"Aw, Carolyn, don't let it bother you so much. You're doing fine."

She arched a brow of disbelief.

"Was it always this hard for you?"

"Yeah, I guess." Carolyn toyed with her napkin. "It was so hard to fit in, being the only kid in my class who was an orphan, and the only one whose parent's murder had been all over the news. Then, on top of that…"

"You lived with an aunt who made antisocial into an art form."

"I survived."

Nick reached across the table and peeled her fingers away from her napkin, taking her hands again in his, wishing he could make everything easier for her. Wishing she would let him be Sir Galahad and knowing that was exactly the opposite of what Carolyn Duff wanted. "I know you did, Carolyn. I know. But it was still hard."

She had survived—and thrived. Built strength on top of her scars.

"It's just…I forget how to be a kid, if I ever really knew. I'm so uncomfortable around them."

"They don't bite, you know." He pretended to think about that for a second. "Most of them, anyway."

Carolyn laughed. "What's the secret?"

Just the reward he'd been looking for— Carolyn's smile. "It's easy. Just think of the most immature thing you can. And then say it or do it. Works for me."

Another smile crossed her face, blasting Nick with a beam of sunshine. Damn, when she smiled, he had a hard time remembering his own name.

"Nick, you lived like that. I never did. I had to grow up too fast. And you…"

"I had the apple pie childhood."

But how had all that apple pie benefited

him? He'd had it easy, really, and in turn become the easy, fun-loving guy. The one who hadn't really realized how much he wanted something more—

Until he'd had it for a second, then lost it.

Was there a chance of getting it back? Or should he simply learn his lesson once and for all, and accept what was and wasn't in the cards?

"Me, I lived with Aunt Greta," Carolyn went on, "who made Mommie Dearest look warm and fuzzy."

The waitress came back with their drinks and dropped them off, sending a smile Nick's way. "Here you go. I made sure the bartender gave you a little extra."

"Thank you."

"Oh, it serves me, too," she replied. "Saves me a trip back."

Nick chuckled as the waitress headed away. Since no one else had entered the club, she slipped into a booth with another waitress and the two of them started chatting.

He returned his attention to Carolyn. "You can connect with these kids if you want to, Carolyn. All it takes is opening up. You did that before."

"That whole opening up thing is easier said than done." She shrugged. "Look at you.

You have an instant friend in the waitress, for Pete's sake."

"You have friends. Mary, for instance."

"I do, but it's harder for me. I just don't do this as easily as you do."

"Because....?"

"Because I missed something in Friendship class." Carolyn smiled, then took a sip of her drink and shook her head. "I don't think I did the homework."

"You made friends with me."

"*You* were different."

"How? What made me different?" Maybe, if he could reassemble the pieces of their relationship, see where it fell apart, he could insert the missing parts. Make it work again. With time, could they be together again?

Would it be better the second time around?

Looking at her now, feeling like he could drown in those emerald-green eyes, he wanted it to be better. Wanted it to work. Wanted to prove to her that he had changed, become a different man than the one she remembered from college. Wanted to take her in his arms and promise her—whatever it took, whatever she wanted.

"You made it so easy, Nick. Just like you do with everyone."

If he was so good at making people like

him, why couldn't he have made her fall in love? He realized now, with the passing of time, that they'd rushed into marriage, some kind of heady without-thinking decision that hadn't been based on love at all, just a powerful cocktail of infatuation and lust.

If he'd given their relationship more depth...

Where would they be now?

He shook his head. "It wasn't me. It was you."

"Me?" She toyed with the rim of the martini glass. "Your memory is a little faulty."

"I'm serious, Carolyn. There was something about you. Something that made it so easy for me to be myself. But I don't think I ever really opened up, not like I should have."

"Nick, you're one of the most open people I know."

He picked up the scotch, knocked a little back. "I'm not. Not really. Not with most people. I talk, yes. I joke. But...I don't *really* talk. I haven't buckled down and gotten serious about anything besides my career, and even that hasn't been as satisfying as I expected it to be. I never even got that serious about us."

"No, you didn't." Crimson rose in her cheeks and she dipped her gaze to study her drink.

Guilt sat heavy on his chest. "I'm sorry, Carolyn."

"It's okay, Nick. It's in the past."

"Yeah. Where it should stay, right?" His breath held while he waited for her answer, even as he knew he shouldn't. Getting involved with Carolyn again would probably be a mistake. Had he changed all that much? Really?

No.

Could he honestly give her now what he hadn't been able to give her then?

No.

Then why wrap himself in the same mistakes…knowing they'd have the same outcome? Because he'd gotten distracted by the feel of her in his arms, the scent of her perfume, the very nearness of her.

"Why did you really do it, Carolyn?"

There was no need to explain what he was asking, because they both knew the real question. The massive elephant nobody had wanted to discuss, but had been sitting on the table between them all this time. They'd talked around it for days, but neither had wanted to poke at the beehive that had been their divorce.

Well, Nick was tired of letting it lie dormant. He wanted to rile up the hive. See what happened. Because, despite everything, despite knowing he was better off without her, he still wanted Carolyn—and if there was any chance that she still wanted him, too, he was willing to put up with feeling that sting again to see where it might lead.

"You know why. Because Ronald Jakes got out of jail again. Those idiots on the parole board thought he was rehabilitated. That a few years in jail without any trouble meant he was safe to let loose on the public. But he wasn't," Carolyn said, studying the drink again, as if it were a crystal ball to the past. "I couldn't stay with you and pretend to be happy while he was out there, going after someone else."

The band segued into a popular Frank Sinatra compilation. Their waitress got up to refill another table's drinks, then sat back down. But at the booth where Nick and Carolyn sat, the tension tightened.

"But once he was caught again, back in jail for good, Carolyn, why didn't you come back? Why couldn't we have tried again?"

That was the question she had never answered. She had used the parole and re-offending of Ronald Jakes, her father's murderer, as an excuse to let their marriage slip away, and never fought to reclaim it. The weeks had passed, turned into months, then years, and Nick kept thinking that one of these days Carolyn would turn around, rethink her decision. He'd given her time, space, all the things he thought she needed, and then realized he'd given her so much time and space—

She wasn't coming back.

"Why didn't *you* come after me, Nick?" She met his gaze with her own. Clear, direct and honest. "You don't have to answer me, because we both know why. We rushed into a marriage, but neither of us were ready for what being married entailed. Buying a house, having kids. Look at us." She gestured between them. "We can barely handle taking a kid to a fair for an afternoon. Never mind a lifetime of that. You're not so bad at it, but if anything, these last couple of days have shown me how un-apple pie I am."

"The way you grew up doesn't have to dictate how you live the rest of your life."

"Don't be giving out advice when you're not following it yourself."

He sat back in his seat. "What is that supposed to mean?"

"You're still acting the way you did back in college. You're not growing up. You're not settling down. It's all a game." She let out a gust. "*I* was part of the game."

He leaned forward, caught her hands. The cozy restaurant provided a dark, intimate cover, leaving them nearly alone, while the sultry jazz music played on in the background. Her breath fluttered in and out, her pulse ticked in her throat, and no matter how frustrated he got, all he could think about was kissing her, damn it. "You were not."

"Oh, yeah? Tell me the truth, Nick." Carolyn closed the distance between them even more. "Did you want me because I was a challenge, that cold Bostonian girl who turned down every guy at Lawford U, or because I was truly someone you loved?"

"I…"

She tugged her hands out of his grasp, grabbed her purse and slid out of the booth. She paused by the table. "Just the fact that you're hesitating answers the question."

Then Carolyn left. Something in her broke as the door shut behind her, muting the sound of the music. And Nick.

Carolyn stood on the sidewalk, waiting for a cab. She inhaled the warm, humid summer night air. A slight buzz of traffic filled the streets around her. A few cabs passed, but all had their lights off. Occupied.

The door to the club opened, releasing a

burst of air-conditioned air, a snatch of a song. And Nick.

"You think that settles it?" he asked. "You think the only reason I wanted you was to add some kind of silly conquest to my list?"

"Yeah." Now that she had said it, the truth became a sharp edge slicing along her heart. She'd thought she couldn't hurt over Nick Gilbert anymore. She'd been wrong.

"I wanted you for a hundred different reasons, Carolyn. And I still do."

"Nick, there's nothing between us except past history." She turned back toward the street. Where was a cab when you needed a really good exit?

"Nothing, huh? Why don't you try this for nothing?" Then before she could react or think, Nick took her in his arms and pulled her to him.

And kissed her.

Three years had passed since the last time she had been kissed by Nick Gilbert, but it felt like three hundred. Carolyn's entire body surged forward, responding like a starving traveler who'd stumbled upon a feast. Her arms reached around him, locking in on familiar muscles and planes, fitting into the same places as before, drawing him closer. Closer still.

His lips knew hers as well as the musicians inside had known their notes. At first his mouth drifted over hers, soft, easy, gentle—a prelude to what was to come—then, with a note of urgency, his hands splayed against her back and his mouth opened against hers. And everything within Carolyn opened in return.

He tasted of scotch and old memories, of everything she had denied herself over the past three years, and everything she had dreamed about and ached for, when the regrets crept in and shared her bed at night. Her fingers slid into his hair, then down his neck, along his shoulders, as if she couldn't get enough of touching him now—

As if she knew she'd better memorize this kiss because there wouldn't be another.

Nick pulled back, but his arms remained holding her tight to him. "*That's* what we still have in common, Carolyn. And if you'd start with that, *then* we could move forward."

She swallowed hard. How easy it would be to let that kiss be enough. To pretend everything was fine. But she knew better. And in her heart she knew Nick did, too. "It wasn't enough then, Nick. And it's still not enough. I wish it was. Oh, how I wish it was."

He broke away, a gust of frustration escaping him. "What is it with you and these emotional walls? Getting close to you is like trying to scale Alcatraz."

She looked at the man she once thought she'd known better than herself and realized she'd been wrong. It had taken two to end this relationship—and it was now taking two to keep it from blossoming again. "Don't talk to me about putting up walls, Nick Gilbert. Not when you've thrown up just as many emotional bricks as I have."

A cab came down the road, its top light on, and Carolyn raised her hand. In the kind of luck that only seemed to happen in the movies, the yellow cab stopped. Carolyn got in and left.

Before she could be wrapped in Nick's spell again.

CHAPTER EIGHT

JEAN'S FACE SAID IT ALL. But Nick still forced himself to ask the question. "Where's Bobby?"

"He can't come today. We're looking for a temporary placement for him." A heavy sigh escaped Jean, seeming to weigh down the air around all of them.

Not that the air had been all that light to begin with. As promised, Carolyn had arrived at the city park where the best fireworks viewing could be found, but hadn't said much to Nick. They had planned to spend the late afternoon at the park, have a picnic dinner, then let Bobby play before the fireworks started late that night. Nick wondered how they were going to get through all that time with him and Carolyn barely speaking, because it seemed pretty clear they'd gone back to being—what was her word?—cordial colleagues.

"A temporary placement?" Carolyn asked. "Why?"

"His mother had to be admitted to the hospital this morning. She's not doing well. They think she has pneumonia, and after just battling breast cancer, the doctors didn't want to take any chances, so they had her checked in."

Carolyn put a hand to her heart. "Is she going to be all right?"

"The doctors think so. And she'll probably only be there for a few days, at most. She needs an IV, some antibiotics. She's been feeling ill for a while but resisted going to the hospital because she didn't want Bobby to be put into foster care again."

"I understand that," Nick said. "It's clear how much she loves him."

Several other families passed by, heading for the small public barbecues set up by the picnic tables. The scent of grilled meat filled the air, coupled with the sound of laughing children and barking dogs.

"Right now," Jean said, "Bobby's at a residential child care facility, until I can find him a foster family. It's a holiday weekend, so I'm having a hard time. Everyone's away on vacation."

"But surely, you have lots of families to choose from."

Jean indicated the picnic table beside them and gestured for the two of them to sit. "Can I be frank?"

Nick and Carolyn nodded in tandem and settled onto the opposite bench.

"We don't have a ton of foster parents to choose from. There's a long program to go through to be approved. Finding a temporary home at the last minute, especially on a holiday weekend, can be a challenge." Jean placed a hand on Carolyn's, met Nick's gaze. "I don't want you two to worry about Bobby. We'll find someplace for him until his mother is out of the hospital. He'll be fine."

"But what if you don't?" Carolyn said.

Jean's eyes were sad, filled with a reality she knew, but didn't really want to share. "He'll stay at a residential facility. It's not our first choice. And the upheaval for Bobby has already been so hard."

"Isn't there any other option?" Nick asked. He thought of Bobby's eyes, of the sadness he had seen in the boy's face. Damn, that kid had already faced enough. When would he catch a break?

"Well…" Jean paused. Looked from one of them to the other. "Bobby's mother and I did discuss one other possibility. And I wouldn't bring it up if I wasn't completely out of options."

"What?" Carolyn and Nick said at the same time.

Jean steepled her fingers. "Bobby responded really well to the two of you. He *smiled*. He *laughed*. You have no idea how huge that is. This is a boy who has had nothing but tragedy for the last year of his life. His mother liked the two of you. She said Bobby did nothing but talk nonstop about the picnic and the fair."

"We had a great time with him, too. He's a fabulous kid," Nick said.

"He is," Jean agreed. "Pauline said she hasn't seen her son this happy in ages, and she'll do about anything to keep him that way, especially while she's in the hospital."

"I can understand that," Nick said. He thought of his own mother, how she'd put her family ahead of virtually everything. The Gilberts had been blessed with a happy home, free of what Bobby had gone through, but they had one commonality—mothers who deeply loved their children.

Jean bit her lip, then went on. "Because of that, she'd much rather see him stay with friends than strangers."

"Friends?" Carolyn asked. "As in…?"

"You two."

The words hung in the air. No one said anything for a long moment.

"You want *us* to watch Bobby?" Carolyn said.

"It's an idea."

Carolyn's gaze met Nick's. Held. They each knew how being in a foster home had affected Bobby. They'd seen it in the boy's eyes. Heard it in his voice.

Carolyn thought of her own childhood. Of being ripped out of the only home she'd ever known, and being sent to live with a cold, dictatorial woman, essentially a stranger, who had never extended a warm hug or a kind word. What difference would it have made to her to have had even a few days with someone who had made her laugh? Made her smile? Given her the memories of potato sack races and cotton candy?

Would she have been able to forget what had happened to her father, if only for a little while, and felt like a normal child? Could it be possible to give that same gift to Bobby?

"Are you thinking what I'm thinking?" Carolyn asked Nick, wondering whether she could even do this, because this was completely not her area of expertise. *Out of her comfort zone* didn't even begin to describe it. "I mean, it's a crazy idea, but you said before, you and I are better—"

"Together than apart," he finished, reading her mind, slipping into the familiar patterns from three years ago as if no time at all had passed. "It's only a few days. I'm sure we could do it."

"I can rearrange my work schedule." Carolyn smiled, suddenly feeling like this was the perfect choice. Helping Bobby—what better way was there to spend her time? "Mary would be thrilled to help me do that."

"I'm owed some vacation time on my end, too." Even as the plan took place between them, Nick couldn't believe they were considering such a crazy idea.

But then he thought of Bobby. Of the wonder he had seen in the boy's face over simple things like a stuffed dragon, a ride on the Ferris wheel, a new truck. He'd appreciated everything—and asked for nothing.

Nick had been so incredibly fortunate in his own life. This would be a chance to give back, and see a direct result of his efforts. He'd enjoyed the toy buying, the picnic, the fair, so much more than he had expected. He looked to Carolyn again and nodded.

"Jean," Carolyn began, "Nick and I would

like to take Bobby in, until it's time for him to return to his mother."

Then an awful possibility occurred to Nick. What if Pauline never got better? What if Bobby eventually had to leave and go into permanent foster care? Could Nick let him go then?

He'd have to. He certainly couldn't take Bobby on as a son. Nick was a single man—a man who worked an incredible amount of hours—a man with few responsibilities, who hadn't even managed to hold on to a marriage. Heck, he'd barely grown up himself.

Clearly, he wouldn't make a good father, and especially not a good single father. Surely, if something tragic were to happen, Jean would find someone to take Bobby. Someone who would love him and want to give the boy a permanent home.

"I was only throwing the idea out. You two don't have to do this," Jean said. "It's a terrible imposition, on such short notice, and—"

"We want to," Nick said, thinking again of the boy and of the way his face had lit up at the fair, of how a simple thing like winning a stuffed toy had changed his outlook for hours. "That way, he can still go to the fireworks, still have the fun that we promised him, and his mother won't have to worry. He'll be in a stable home, with two people."

Relief flooded Jean's features. "Are you really sure?"

Once again, Carolyn and Nick locked gazes. An electric thrill of connection ran between them, hot, fast. This was what had brought them together in law school, this energy, this shared passion for changing the world. They each nodded, then turned back to Jean. "Yes, we're sure," Carolyn said.

"Forgive me for getting personal," Jean said, "but you two aren't married and...don't live under the same roof. How are you going to make this work?"

Ah, the one detail they had overlooked in their rush. They'd both only been thinking of the child, not each other. In that moment, Nick saw Carolyn realize what their hasty offer entailed—the two of them being together.

Entirely together. Under one roof. For the next few days.

It had only taken them three weeks the last time they'd been together on a continual basis to make the decision to run off and elope. How long would it take, the second time around? Or would they realize this time in a matter of days instead that they were meant to continue on their separate paths?

"We'll figure it out," Carolyn said. "For Bobby's sake."

"Of course we will," Nick added. But at that moment, with every one of his senses on heightened Carolyn alert, he wasn't sure what he was supposed to be figuring out—

How to love Carolyn again, or how to forget her again.

The overnight bag sat in the foyer, a blaring announcement of Carolyn's insanity. She stared at the small brown suitcase, wondering if it was too late to back out. To come up with another plan.

Then she thought of Bobby and reconsidered. Hadn't she known what it was like to be shuffled off to someone she didn't know, someone who didn't really want her?

For him, she could do this. She'd just avoid Nick. Not look at him when he woke up in the morning, his hair slightly mussed from sleep. Steer clear when he stepped out of the shower, his skin warm and steaming from the heat. Keep an entire floor between them when he went off to bed and sank beneath his covers, wearing—

"Do you want me to show you to the guest room?"

Nick's voice, low, husky, behind her. Carolyn tensed, then relaxed, steeling herself again before turning around. She would not react. Would not show him that hearing his voice, seeing him here—in the most intimate of environments, his home—had any affect whatsoever on her.

Whoa. He looked good. Wearing only a simple blue cotton T-shirt and cutoff shorts. His feet were bare, the muscles of his arms exposed, and the tattoo, that silly shark tattoo, peeked out from under the sleeve, teasing at the edge of her vision.

Bandit skidded in, plopped down beside his master, then nosed forward, sniffing at the new guest. He offered up a slobbery greeting on Carolyn's hand, then sat back and panted happily. She'd won the dog over with nothing more than a smile.

"Sorry, I'm a mess," Nick said, grabbing a towel from the counter and wiping his hands. "I was doing a little yard work before you got here. Trying to clean up out there so Bobby will have some room to play. The weather's so nice and—" He cocked his head, studied her. "What? Do I have grass in my hair or something?"

"Oh, oh, no." Shoot. She'd been caught staring at him. Well, what woman in her right mind wouldn't? Nick Gilbert gave *handsome* a new definition. And it had been way too long since she'd been on a date. "I just got lost in my thoughts."

He took a step closer. "Were any of those thoughts about me?"

He knew she'd been staring at him, darn it. "No," she lied.

"Too bad. Because a few of mine lately have been about you." Another step closer.

"Just a few?" she said, trying to tease, but the words just sounded panicked.

He caught the strap of her sundress beneath his finger and Carolyn froze, unable to think, to hear, to do anything but stare into Nick's eyes and think about those few days they had been married. How wonderful the days had been. How much sweeter the nights had been. His touch was light, almost chaste, yet the sensation of skin on skin sizzled along her nerve endings, sparked her memories.

Had it been this good three years ago? No, this was better. Hotter. More tempting. Because she *knew*. She knew what pleasure awaited her in Nick's arms.

"I've had more than a few thoughts about you," he said, his voice low and dark with a mirror of her desire. "In fact, every other thought ever since that kiss outside the jazz club has been about you. Maybe we shouldn't have agreed to move in together. Even for a few days." Another step, closing the gap. "Why can't I forget you, Carolyn?"

"Uh, because you once told me that you have a photographic memory?" The words were a squeak, her senses off-kilter, her normal equilibrium gone. Good thing she'd never faced Nick in court, because she'd have lost every time.

"Maybe," he said, his voice lower, darker now. "Or maybe it's because I never forgot this." And then he leaned down and kissed her.

This kiss wasn't like the one last night. It wasn't sweet, it wasn't quick. It didn't tease her, or make her wonder where they stood.

This kiss rocked her to her very core, and stamped every cell in Carolyn's body with the message that Nick Gilbert still wanted her. He cupped her jaw, then opened his mouth against hers, tasting her, holding her captive with the desire that still ran so strong in her veins that ignoring it would surely have made her fall apart.

Her arms circled around his back, her fists bunching the cotton of his T-shirt, lifting the fabric until she could touch his back, feel his warm skin against her palms once again. She ran her hands up those hard planes, tracing the ridges of his spine, then over the tips of his shoulder blades, down again, over every inch of his skin. She had missed him. Missed this. Missed everything about Nick.

Nick's kiss deepened and he groaned, then his hand slipped between them and cupped her breast. Every one of Carolyn's senses erupted into a fire that had been lying dormant for so long—too long—and she arched against him, pressing her breast deeper into his palm. His name slipped out of her mouth, half moan, half whisper. Nick's other hand tangled in her hair, fingers dancing along her neck.

The grandfather clock in the hall gonged the hour and Nick pulled back, his fingertips sliding around and releasing her jaw last, as if he wanted to linger there for as long as he could. Then he smiled. "I think about *that* most of all."

"Me, too." Why bother lying? He'd only read the truth in her eyes, the quickening of her pulse, her rapid breathing.

He studied her, his eyes dark. "If we're going to stay here together, we might want to have a few ground rules."

"Ground rules?"

Nick traced along the edge of her lips.

"Because if we keep doing that, I'm going to break every rule of gentlemanly conduct known to man, and with a child around, that's probably not a good idea."

Carolyn took a step back. Putting some distance between them helped her clear her head, find her footing again. "You're right. Bobby will be here in a few minutes, and although we want to be one big happy family for the next few days, we don't exactly want to go too far."

"Or pretend to be something we aren't." Nick's gaze met hers, penetrating, searching for answers. "Like happily married."

The truth. Right smack-dab back between them again. Why did they always have to circle back to this?

The dog, apparently disappointed that none of this concerned him, turned around and left the room, picking up a plastic bone as he left. He gave the toy a squeak-squeak of indignant protest at being left out of all the fun.

"You're right," Carolyn said, picking up her bag. All business again, any trace of what might have been between them a moment ago gone. Nick had a point. Pretending to be happily married—or pretending to be any kind of couple at all—could only lead to trouble and broken hearts down the road.

Where did she expect their kisses to go, really? After Bobby went home, she and Nick would return to their lives, to their careers. The impasse they had reached three years ago still as wide as ever. Nick was still the devil-may-care playful guy he'd always been, the one who couldn't see how important Carolyn's career was to her. He hadn't listened to her then; he wasn't listening to her now.

And either way, they wanted different things from their futures. Nick came from a large family. He'd told her that someday he wanted the same thing for himself. The three-bedroom house she stood in was in-your-face evidence of that. She was still the woman who wouldn't take that chance, partly because of the hours she worked and partly because she was no good at mothering. If ever two people weren't meant to be together, it was Carolyn and Nick.

"Maybe I should just get settled in," Carolyn said, "and then, when Bobby comes, we can concentrate on him. And forget that kiss ever happened."

His jaw tensed. "We're very good at that, aren't we, Carolyn? Pretending things never happened between us."

Before she could answer, Nick took the suitcase out of her hand and charged up the stairs.

CHAPTER NINE

THE TROUBLE WITH ACTING on impulse was where it got you. All Nick could think about now was the way Carolyn had felt in his arms. How she had moved against him, touched him, kissed him back. How for one long, sweet moment she had been his again.

And then reality had intruded and brought them right back to square one. Fellow attorneys who used to be married. Now she was using the convenient Bobby wall to keep from even coming near him. Everywhere they went, it was Nick-Bobby-Carolyn, so that Carolyn didn't even have to get close to Nick.

Fine. That was probably just as well. He didn't need to court temptation more than once to know it was a bad idea.

They were at the park with Bobby, killing time until the fireworks started. The minute Bobby had arrived, Carolyn had announced that they should have a picnic at the park, as if she wanted to get out of the house as quickly as possible. They'd packed up a cooler with some food, grabbed a blanket and set out for the park, leaving a dejected Bandit at home.

Now, with the food eaten, Nick had put the cooler back in the truck and they were wandering the park, looking for the perfect location to view the fireworks. The sun had nearly set, casting everything around them in a dark-purple haze of twilight.

"I missed the fireworks last year," Bobby said quietly as they walked down a grassy hill. "That was when my daddy died."

Nick and Carolyn exchanged a glance. He saw tears well in Carolyn's eyes—of sympathy? Of understanding? Or of her own memories? She looked away first, and he wanted to reach out to her, but again she withdrew, putting up that damned wall.

Instead, Nick laid a hand on Bobby's shoulder. "Let's hope these fireworks are extra great." It was a wonder the words even made it past the lump in Nick's throat.

Bobby nodded. He thought for a minute, then he turned to Carolyn. "Do you think my dad can see them, too? In heaven?"

She seemed taken aback by the question. A shadow washed over her face.

She had to be wondering the same thing.

426 BOARDROOM BRIDE AND GROOM

Was her father watching from above? Had he watched all the milestones in her life? Her graduation from law school? Her first case? Her short-lived marriage?

How lucky Nick had been to have a two-parent cheerleading team for everything he'd done, while Carolyn hadn't had anyone. She'd forged forward, essentially on her own, through all the milestones in life. No one sitting in a cramped seat in the too-hot assembly hall of the elementary school, a tissue pressed to a face, beaming with pride over a screechy rendition of "Hot Cross Buns." No one who would hang every A-plus test on the refrigerator front and center, layering the achievements one on top of the other with the pride only a parent could have.

Carolyn turned her face up to the sky, then met Bobby's inquisitive look. "I believe he can, Bobby. And I bet he has the best seat in the house."

"Yeah." Bobby smiled at the thought. He had on a brand-new USA sweatshirt that Nick had bought him from a street vendor, and wore a neon necklace around his neck— a Carolyn purchase. Nick had no doubt that before the night was over, Bobby would be decked out with at least one item from every vendor staked out around the park. "Do you think your dad watched them from heaven with you, too, when you were little?"

Carolyn fiddled with the fringe on the edge of the blanket in her arms. "I don't know, Bobby. I haven't watched fireworks since I was eight."

"Really?" Nick gaped at her. "Your aunt never took you?"

Carolyn shrugged like it was no big deal. "She didn't see the point. Thought they were a waste of the city's money. And the show was put on after my bedtime, anyway."

"But surely one night out of the year—"

"You had to know my aunt Greta, Nick. There was no 'one night out of the year' with her. Not for anything." The pinched look on Carolyn's face told him the subject was closed.

"I like to stay up late," Bobby said, interjecting a change of conversation with the timing only a kid could have. "My momma says it's okay, as long as I'm reading."

"What kind of stories do you like to read?" Carolyn asked, clearly grateful for the subject switch. Once again, treading anywhere near her past had her building up the walls so fast, Nick could practically hear the bricks knocking into each other.

Bobby shrugged, and for a second Nick

thought he wouldn't answer, would refuse again to connect with Carolyn. Nick was about to intervene, when Carolyn started talking again.

"When I was a girl," she said, the memory leaving her lips in a quiet stream, "my father used to read me adventure stories. Books with pirates and lost treasures. Knights who had to slay fire-breathing dragons, things like that. Those were my favorites."

Bobby brightened. "I like those, too! I don't have very many, though. When my momma is sick, we don't get to go to the library because it's a long walk. And pirate books are expensive to buy. But it's okay. Sometimes I just make up pirate stories in my head."

Carolyn smiled. "Well then, tomorrow how about we go to the bookstore and buy you lots of pirate books? That should keep you busy reading for a long time."

"You will? Promise?"

She nodded. "Nick and I will read as many of them to you as you want, too. One of the things I did to pass the time when I was a girl was read. I still love reading."

"I can't wait!" Bobby grinned. "I love bookstores. And books."

"That's great."

Bobby's grin spread further. "Can I go play

for a while? Until the fireworks start?" Carolyn and Nick nodded. Bobby ran off to the playground, swinging his arms and humming to himself.

When Bobby was gone, Nick closed the gap between himself and Carolyn. "I think you've made a buddy now."

"It was easier than I expected."

"I hate to say it, but—" he grinned "—I told you so."

"At least he'll have some wonderful memories to take home with him."

"Yeah. Memories and toys." That was all they could give the boy. It wasn't anywhere near what Nick had had as a kid, but hopefully it would be enough.

Carolyn watched Bobby head over to the playground, then begin to climb on the jungle gym. Only a hundred yards or so separated them, but a feeling of panic rose in Carolyn's chest. "Do you think he's okay? Not too far away?" She glanced around the park at the swarm of strangers. "I don't think there's enough security here."

"He's fine, Carolyn. Nothing's going to happen."

"Maybe we should call him back. There are an awful lot of people here. Do you see that guy over there?" She gestured with her head. "I think he looks suspicious."

"The one who is helping his daughter climb the monkey bars?"

"No, the other one. The one on the bench. Watching the kids. What's he doing?"

"Watching his own kid." Nick took Carolyn's hand, rubbing a thumb over the back. "It's okay. Not every human is a criminal. And besides, we're right here."

She shook her head, not convinced, her gaze darting from person to person, assessing every one of them as if she were a judge determining guilt or innocence. "Bobby's not ours. I couldn't bear it if something happened."

"Carolyn, look at me."

It took a lot of effort, but she tore her gaze away from the boy and turned toward Nick. "What?"

"Everything will be fine. What happened to you isn't going to happen to Bobby." He reached over, brushed a lock of hair out of her eyes. "When you learn to let go, you'll have a life, too. The one you've always deserved."

She shook her head and busied herself unfolding the blue plaid blanket in her arms. Nick grabbed the opposite end and helped her spread it on the ground. "It's not that easy, Nick."

"It's exactly that easy. It always was."

Carolyn settled on the blanket, back to watching Bobby, the concern etched again in her face. "You always thought so."

"What's that supposed to mean?"

She sighed. "To you, everything is black-and-white. One and one makes two. But for me there are other variables, things you never considered. I don't blame you, Nick. You can't consider what you haven't experienced."

His temper flared, a burst of leftover frustration from years before, rising to the surface. "I can't consider what you've never told me, either."

"I've told you everything about my past."

He let out a chuff. "You've told me like you were a witness on the stand, Carolyn. Relating facts in a case, not giving me your heart." He gestured toward Bobby, who was holding on to the bars and swinging back and forth. "You told Bobby more in the last five minutes than you ever told me."

She followed his line of sight, considering his words for one long moment. "I suppose you have to ask the right questions, Counselor, to get the right answers."

Nick swallowed hard. Had that been the

problem? He'd never asked the right questions? Never delved deeply enough with Carolyn?

They didn't say anything for a while, just watched Bobby play. "He looks kind of like you, don't you think?" Carolyn said softly.

Nick glanced at the boy. A towhead, yes, but Bobby did have some similar features. Same eye color, lanky build. "A little, yes."

"It makes me wonder…" Carolyn cut off the sentence, shook her head.

"Wonder what?"

"Nothing. Never mind."

"Oh, no fair, leaving me in suspense. Here, let The Great Nick read your mind." He turned her toward him and placed a palm on her forehead. The whole thing started out as a joke, a tease—one of the parlor tricks he'd pulled a hundred times in college—but then, as he paused long enough to think of what Carolyn might have been thinking, the truth hit him hard. His palm dropped away. The tease left his voice. "You're thinking what if…what if we had a child. What if Bobby was…ours?"

"Of course not." She inserted some distance between them. "You know I'm not the kind of person who should have kids."

"Why?"

"You know why, Nick. I work a million hours a week, so that rules me out right there."

Nick settled on the blanket, pretending to watch Bobby slide down the slide, dart back to the steps, climb up again and make the swooshing trip down again. "And why is that, Carolyn? Your work schedule can be shifted, you know. There are plenty of attorneys who have families and careers."

"I'm fulfilled the way I am now."

"If you're so fulfilled, why did you kiss me back?"

"If you're so happy, why did you kiss me?" she countered.

He let out a laugh. "Always the lawyer. Answering a question with a question. Am I going to have to get a bailiff and a Bible, Miss Duff, to get a straight answer out of you?"

A burst of white light exploded over their heads, arcing outward in a scatter of stars. "The fireworks have started, Nick."

He caught her gaze, defiant, strong. Sexy. Despite everything, he still wanted her. "Yes, Carolyn, they most certainly have."

Carolyn tried to keep her gaze on the explosions in the sky, the vibrant colors blasting outward in heavenly flowers. But every time another bloom of sparks soared overhead, Carolyn found herself glancing at Nick. Thinking of their conversation—

And of where they were going as soon as the fireworks show was over.

Back to his house. Back together. After all she had done for the past three years to stay away from Nick Gilbert—away from the temptation of his eyes, his smile, his touch— she had offered *voluntarily* to spend the next few days with him.

Crazy, absolutely crazy.

The humidity draped around them like a thick, heavy blanket. Carolyn had worn a sleeveless shirt and shorts, as had Nick. What had been a great decision weatherwise, however, only gave her a heightened awareness of Nick. Despite their conversation, their differences, differences that seemed to get less and less resolved the more time they spent together, she couldn't stop thinking about kissing him earlier, and about what it would be like to kiss him again.

Beside them, Bobby went on watching the fireworks, completely enthralled and utterly unaware of the adult tension right behind him.

Nick's fingertips brushed against Carolyn's bare shoulder and she flinched, then turned, a thousand nerve endings standing at attention. "Just brushing away a mosquito," he said.

"Oh. Thank you."

"Anytime." That familiar grin, the one she could have drawn blindfolded, curved once again across his features, and something tripped inside her chest. The switch that was always waiting, as if the light inside her had gone dark years before, and now here he was, the only one who could turn it back on. "Anytime at all."

Now, she wanted to say. And the next second after that. And the one after that. But she didn't say any of those words. Instead, she returned her attention to the sky—

And didn't see a single thing.

"How do they make these?" Bobby asked her.

"Well..." Carolyn began, then stopped. "I don't really know. Nick?"

He took the opportunity to scoot closer, and Carolyn drew in a breath, so very aware of his presence, of how they made a little family, and how if she let herself, she could believe this was real, that they were real, and together again. "They're made out of lots of things, Bobby. Gunpowder makes them explode, but it's the colors that are the cool part. Certain colors are made by different chemical compounds. Blue comes from copper salts, for instance, gold from aluminum and magnesium."

"That's pretty cool," Bobby said. "So the people that do this job gotta know how to mix all those chemicals, huh?"

Nick nodded. "And especially how to light the fireworks safely."

"When I grow up, I'd love to have that job. It would kind of be like being a dragon."

Carolyn chuckled. "Yes, I suppose it would be."

"Except, my momma says I should go to college." He crinkled his upper lip.

"You should," Nick agreed. "And when it comes time, you look me up. I'll write you a recommendation. Help you find a good school."

"You will?" His eyes widened, the blast of red and green above reflecting in his gaze, his smile. Then his smile drooped and he dropped his head. "Maybe I will."

Carolyn could have read the body language from a mile away. Bobby had been disappointed so many times in his life he didn't want to put any hope into the future. He'd rather let the dream go now than hold on to it for the next dozen years and then find out Nick was only making an offhand comment—and didn't really mean it.

"Bobby—" Carolyn began.

"I want to watch the rest," Bobby said, then he turned back and tipped his head upward, wrapped again in the show in the sky.

The hall clock was chiming eleven when Carolyn entered Nick's dimly lit kitchen. She raided his refrigerator and assembled a midnight snack of cheese slices and fresh fruit. Nick had gone all out with Bobby's arrival. Considering virtually everything in the refrigerator was new, Carolyn suspected Nick didn't usually stock four different kinds of cheese, three kinds of grapes and every other type of fruit grown in the United States—and a few foreign countries, too.

As she loaded decaf grounds into the coffeepot and set it to brew, she thought about Nick. When she'd first known him, he'd seemed so easy to read, as clear as crystal. But now there were facets to him she couldn't read. Had she been wrong about him before?

Or had she only seen the surface Nick and not looked for the deeper man?

"How's Bobby?" she asked when Nick entered the kitchen.

"Still zonked out. He never woke up, from the minute we got in the car, and never even stirred when I carried him upstairs. He's all tucked in, and he's got that stuffed dragon right under his arm."

Carolyn laughed. "He's pretty attached to that thing."

"I think he's pretty attached to us."

"He is, isn't he?" Carolyn said. "Maybe we shouldn't have done this. Knowing he has to go back home and someday maybe go to other foster homes, if his mother gets sick again. We won't always be there for him, Nick. It's not like Bobby is a neighbor's puppy we can take back and forth whenever we feel like having him over."

"At least we're giving him some really fun moments that he'll remember. That's got to count for something, right?"

"It's not enough. Not nearly enough." She shook her head and paced a little.

"Carolyn, you worry too much. I'm sure Bobby will be just fine."

She wheeled around. "And you worry too little. You're doing it again."

"Doing what again?"

"Pulling out just when someone needs you most."

"I'm not doing that."

"You are. Just like you did with me." She shook her head. "You know, I was an adult.

I handled it okay, but Bobby's a kid. Don't let him down."

He scowled. "I'm not planning on doing anything of the sort."

But she could see, in the way he turned away, how he put some distance between them, that she had nailed his intentions. Disappointment sank heavy in her gut. For once in her life, Carolyn didn't want to be right. "Maybe you're not, Nick. But just keep Bobby's needs at the top of your list. I know what it's like to be him."

"And what is it like, Carolyn?" Nick asked, taking a step closer, the gap between them narrowing in the small kitchen. "Tell me."

"You know. I've talked about my past often enough."

"Talked, but not *told* me much. You accuse me of not getting involved, but how can I do that when you don't let me in? You've only let me glimpse the inside of you, Carolyn."

Carolyn didn't answer him. Instead, she handed Nick a cup of coffee, then followed him as they walked through the kitchen and out to the screened porch. Bandit stayed behind, gnawing happily on a new chew toy.

Outside, the night birds called softly to each other, and far in the backyard, bugs hummed. The moon hung low over the trees, and stars sparkled in the sky, like leftover fireworks. "I don't understand you, Nick."

"What don't you understand?" He shot her a grin. "I'm a guy. I'm a pretty simple creature."

"Why do you own this huge house but have no kids of your own? You never married again."

He didn't say anything for a long time. The birds filled the silence with their own chatter. "I haven't found anyone I wanted to settle down with, and either way, I'm not exactly the settle-down kind. Despite my temporary record to the contrary."

"But…why buy the house? I mean, most people buy homes after they get married."

"Yeah, they do. I guess I did it all wrong, huh?" He shrugged. "I saw this place as an investment. It's in a great neighborhood, corner lot. Nice acreage. When it became available, it made sense to buy it. Someday I'll sell and make a tidy profit. Like I said, it's an investment, only with windows and doors."

"That's all?" It was the kind of logical argument a lawyer would make. Full of justifications, facts. But…it sounded so sad. So… empty.

"Yep. That's it."

"Why didn't you ever remarry?"

The question, coming out of left field, did what she had expected—surprised him. But Nick recovered quickly. Clearly, like her, he was used to questions that rocked the boat a little. "Same reason as you, I'm married to the job."

"Perjury is a crime, Mr. Gilbert."

"I wasn't aware I was on the stand."

"And I never thought you'd lie to me."

He turned away, cupping the mug in both his hands and straying to the screened windows, staring out into the deep darkness beyond them. "I'm not lying, exactly. Like you, I've chosen my job instead of a relationship."

"But why?" Carolyn said, coming up behind him, so aware of their closeness. Of them being alone. Of the intimacy of darkness. She caught the scent of his cologne, inhaled it into her lungs, breathed until it was part of her. Her hand reached out into the darkness of the porch, but stopped inches away from touching Nick. "That wasn't the way you used to be. I mean, you were never Mr. Career."

"It's the way I should be. I'm fine for this kind of temporary gig, but maybe I shouldn't do it on a permanent basis." He turned to face her, his catching a glimmer from the light inside. "In fact, I think it was best that we broke up."

"Best?" Even though she had been the one to deliver the words across that diner table three years ago, hearing him say that now, stung in ways she hadn't expected. Her hand dropped away. Cold air invaded the space between them. "How can you say that?"

"How can you be so surprised? You know me, Carolyn. I might have tried my hand at it, but deep down inside, I'm not a commitment guy, a family man. I'm the guy who makes people laugh, the one who has a good time, then gets out before things become too serious. Right?"

"And is that what you're going to do here, with me? With Bobby?"

"Bobby staying here is temporary, though I'm sure we'll still see him afterward from time to time."

"You didn't answer me." Her gaze met his. Direct. Not allowing him room to escape. "Is that what you're going to do with me?"

"Isn't that what you want? Just like you did before?" He took a step closer. "You were the one who called it all off. You barely gave us a chance, Carolyn."

"And how would we have worked out, Nick? Now you're telling me that we would have come to the same destination regardless of what I said that day."

"We probably would have. Don't you agree?"

She wanted to scream in frustration. Nick couldn't have been sending more mixed messages if he was a Morse code operator with broken fingers. "What is wrong with you? One minute you're kissing me, the next you're telling me the best thing we ever did was break up. What do you want, Nick?"

"What do *you* want, Carolyn? I can ask you the same thing you're asking me. You're here with me now, but why? Where do you see this ending?"

She saw the intensity in his gaze, how he sought hers for the truth, and knew she couldn't demand it from him without giving it in return. But was she ready to admit how she felt? Doing so would mean traveling a road she couldn't backtrack.

But, oh, how easy it would be to just give up this fight. To close the distance. Her heart raced, her skin tingled with awareness and her hand curled at her side, fingers itching to touch the bare skin on his arms, the exposed vee above his shirt.

Instead she took a step backward, into the shadows. "I'm here for Bobby."

"Perjury, Miss Duff," he reminded her.

"I'm not lying." Entirely.

"You're not here out of curiosity? To see what might have been?"

"Is that why you're here?" she countered.

A grin curved across his face. "Never have a love match between two lawyers. There are no answers, only one-upmanship in questions." Then he paused and met her gaze again. "Tell me the truth, Carolyn, where is this going?"

Nick's pulse ticked in his throat, a constant beacon, drawing Carolyn forward. She laid the coffee mug on a nearby table and closed the distance between them. The wildlife had gone so quiet, it seemed she could hear Nick's heartbeat—or was it hers? She could measure his every breath, hear her own escape in ragged jerks.

And then she stopped resisting, stopped fighting a battle she wasn't going to win, not while she and Nick were under the same roof. She reached out and touched him, her hand on his arm—warm skin, so warm—then his shoulder, then his neck, pulling him closer. "Maybe only here."

She leaned forward, raising on her toes and kissed him, because it was a lot easier to do that than to tell Nick the truth.

That she had already started falling in love all over again.

CHAPTER TEN

NICK DIDN'T SLEEP.

He stared at his ceiling, then got up and paced the floors of his bedroom. Moonlight sent a slash of white across the hardwood floors.

He was in deep. Too deep.

In the morning he'd have to find a way out. Somehow he'd have to end things—sever the ties completely—with Carolyn. Find a way back to the life he'd had before, to a place with no commitment, no expectations. It was the only way to protect them both. To keep him from making the same mistake twice.

That day in the diner, when she'd left for Boston, it had taken him about five seconds to decide to go after her. He'd missed her in the airport and ended up on a separate flight. When he'd arrived in the city, however, he'd seen Carolyn in a different mode: the passionate, crusading spirit that would end up defining her career.

And he'd realized at that point that he would never be that serious about anything. That she was someone who dug in with both heels and held on tight. He had yet to find anything that mattered that much to him.

Back then, not even their marriage. They barely knew each other, had married on a lark. So he let her go. Didn't fight her on the divorce. He'd simply cleaned up the debris of their marriage and moved forward.

Carolyn was right. What had changed between them, really? He hadn't become any more serious now than three years ago. It was simply his own selfish heart still wanting her.

The best decision, Nick decided, climbing back into his bed, was to call it quits. Before anyone got in too deep. And hearts got broken.

Because his own was already beginning to ache.

On Tuesday morning the paper arrived with a slap on Nick's front porch. Carolyn retrieved it, thinking how odd it felt to wake up in his house. As she made a pot of coffee and opened up the paper, she decided she would tell Nick that this grand experiment was over.

What had she been thinking last night?

Kissing him? Entangling them even more than they had been before?

Today she'd move out. She'd still be here during the day for Bobby, but at least remove herself from the temptation of spending every night in Nick's arms. Last night had been torturous. After that kiss, going to bed—without him—had been nearly impossible. She'd barely slept, acutely aware of his bedroom just down the hall. Worse, she'd been filled with the knowledge of what it had been like the few days they had been married. Her mind had teased her with images of how it could be again, if only she'd journey those few feet.

But no. Nick and she were as different as two people could be. He still didn't know her, still didn't listen. She'd reached out to him once during their marriage, asked for his help, asked for him to support her—

And he hadn't heard her. She couldn't risk her heart again. Only a fool did that twice when the answer was already there, right in front of her.

She redoubled her resolve. As much as she cared about Nick, the best decision was to walk away.

Nick entered the kitchen, fully dressed, with faint shadows beneath his eyes. Apparently she hadn't been the only one missing a few winks last night. "Good morning." He reached for the pot of coffee and poured himself a cup. "Thanks for making this."

"No problem." She sipped at the hot beverage, then decided to tackle the difficult subject before the day—and her courage—got away from her. "Nick, we need to talk."

Bandit, who had followed along behind his master, a squeaky bone in his mouth, heaved a sigh of long-suffering doggie patience and slid under the kitchen table. The bone dropped to the floor by his paws.

"I was about to say the same thing." Nick toyed with his mug. "This isn't working out."

"I agree. Us under the same roof—"

"Is too tempting."

"Especially when we both know it isn't going to lead anywhere."

"Are you sure, Carolyn?"

With one word she could undo this. She could be back in Nick's arms, just like last night. Longing ran through her, swift and painful, tempered by common sense. The urge to reach out, lay a hand on his shoulder and feel that strength beneath her palm, had her curling her fingers. "Yes, I'm sure."

This was what she wanted. What she had always wanted. She would be back at work in a few days, and all of this would be nothing more than a memory. Just like before.

A wave of regret washed over her. But she brushed it off, forced it away. She had already survived a breakup with Nick once before. She could do it again.

She could.

The front door opened, which sent Bandit scrambling to his feet and running down the hall with a flurry of barks. In walked a man who looked like a younger version of Nick. "Knock, knock. I bet you forgot our golf game this—" He stopped short, one hand patting Bandit, his mouth agape, eyes wide, staring at her. "Whoa. You have company. I'll come back later."

"No, no, I'm not—" Carolyn felt her face heat "—company. I'm…Carolyn."

"*You're* Carolyn?" The other man stepped forward, a grin spreading across his face. "Well, hello. I've heard quite a bit about you. And I have to say, you are probably the last person I expected to see here, but—"

"My brother is going to shut up now," Nick interrupted, "if he wants to keep his jawbone intact."

The other man chuckled, then extended his hand. "I'm Daniel. The younger and cuter

Gilbert son. And the one with all the manners, apparently."

Nick shot his brother a glare.

"Carolyn Duff," Carolyn said, shaking hands with Daniel. "And really, there's nothing going on here. Nick and I are just helping out one of the kids from the picnic, Bobby Lester. His mom is in the hospital for a few days and he has no other family, so she asked us to take him in. Nick and I being together is just a temporary partnership." Damn. She was babbling again. Take her out of the courtroom and she was a social mess.

Daniel arched a brow. "Temporary. Uh-huh."

"Didn't you have a golf game to get to?" Nick asked.

Daniel hopped over the side of an armchair and settled himself into the seat. "Kind of hard to play a golf match against myself. Besides, I'm not in the mood for golfing now. I found something much more interesting to watch."

Nick groaned. "You are a pain in the neck."

"That's what makes me kin," Daniel said, giving his brother a teasing grin.

Bandit began whining and running circles around Nick's feet. "The dog needs to go out. I'll be right back."

"Take all the time you need." Daniel waved Nick off. "I'll chat with Carolyn while you're gone. Bring her up to speed on all your bad habits."

Nick muttered a few choice words under his breath as he rounded the corner.

"Okay, so give me the straight scoop," Daniel said, turning to Carolyn. "Are you and Nick getting back together? Because without you, the man has been as miserable as a monkey in a pool."

Carolyn laughed. "No, we're not. This is just for a few days."

"I've seen the way you look at him. And the way he looks at you. What's stopping you from getting together?"

"For one, we're divorced. For another, Nick's looking for different things out of life than I am. He always has been." She shrugged as though it didn't matter. As if it didn't disappoint her that nothing had changed. "He's not the settling-down, getting-serious type and I'm…well, I'm as serious as an encyclopedia."

"Whoa, whoa." Daniel put up his hands. "Where did you get the idea that Nick isn't the settling-down type?"

Carolyn slipped into the second armchair and ran a hand over the faded tapestry pattern. "Daniel, everything about Nick screams not settling down. You know him."

"Well, yeah, I do. And granted, he's not exactly Commitment Charlie, but I like to think that's because he hasn't had enough incentive." Daniel gave her a knowing grin.

"Don't look at me. Nick and I already tried the marriage route and failed the test."

"You guys were students. Immaturity comes with the territory." Daniel waved a hand in dismissal. "You should try it again now. Considering you're older and wiser."

"Exactly. We're older and wiser, which is why we shouldn't do this."

"Oh, please. You're both just scared."

"We're not scared. Just…smart."

Daniel glanced over his shoulder, then returned his gaze to Carolyn, his voice lower now. "Did you ever think that maybe the reason the two of you broke up had less to do with what you did or didn't have in common and more to do with what you two didn't talk about? You were only together for, what, three weeks? And I bet not a lot of talking happened in that time."

"Well, no…" Carolyn's voice trailed off and heat filled her cheeks. Then she realized Daniel might be right. That was where you got when you married a man you'd known for three weeks. You made a lot of assumptions and didn't work with a lot of facts. Because they had, indeed, probably spent more time exploring each other's bodies than minds.

She'd always thought they had broken up about her decision to put her career ahead of their marriage. Had she missed a piece of the puzzle? Given up too easily? "Why? What did he tell you about why we broke up?"

Daniel leaned back in the chair. "Not for me to say. You ask Nick, if you want to know. Seems to me, the real problem standing between you two is a lack of words." Daniel chuckled. "What do you know? Two lawyers who are talking *around* the problem instead of talking it *out*."

Bandit came skidding around the corner, panting, as if afraid he might have missed a little fetch while he was outside. A few seconds later Nick entered the room and sent a suspicious glance at his brother. "What were you two discussing?"

Daniel chuckled, then got to his feet and headed to the door. "See you on Thursday night, Nick?"

"Of course."

"And should I tell Ma to set an extra place at the table?" Daniel gestured toward Carolyn. "You'll make her year."

Nick scowled. "You were *leaving*, weren't you?"

They could still hear the sound of Daniel's laughter, even after the door shut behind him.

"Clearly I'm not the only one with a determined matchmaker butting into my love life," Carolyn said.

"He's usually not this bad. I think he's just trying to take advantage of his younger-brother irritability factor." Nick's gaze met hers, and for a second her heart seemed to stop. "I hope he wasn't too hard on you."

"No, not at all." She considered asking Nick about what Daniel had told her, but then she heard the sound of footsteps on the stairs. Bobby was coming down. Deep conversations would have to wait.

Just as well. Because the answers might not be something she wanted to hear.

"Are you sure you've got this under control?"

Carolyn laughed. "Contrary to what you might think, I'm good at more than just practicing law."

Nick raised a teasing brow, but Bobby stood on the sidelines of the living room, beaming with cheer. "Okay."

Bobby had come downstairs, and instead of wanting breakfast right away, he'd asked immediately about the pirate books. Since the bookstores weren't due to open for a couple more hours, Carolyn had suggested they instead organize a treasure hunt. She'd made the two guys wait inside for fifteen minutes while she set everything up in the backyard.

"Okay, I'm ready." She handed Bobby a crudely drawn map on a slightly crumpled piece of paper. Bandit danced around Bobby's feet, almost as excited as the boy. "Your map, sir."

"Is it real?" His eyes were wide as he puzzled over the directions.

"The only way to know is to follow it." Carolyn leaned down and pointed at the different drawings on the paper. "You have to watch for all these landmarks and take the exact number of steps to get to the treasures."

"Treasures?"

"Yep. There's more than one." Carolyn grinned. "What's a good treasure hunt with only one surprise at the end?"

Bobby beamed. "Can I start now?"

Carolyn opened her mouth to say yes, then glanced down at the dog, his tail waving wildly. "Wait. There's one more thing you need." She reached into the box of supplies she'd gathered from inside of Nick's house earlier, and pulled out a bright-red bandanna.

"You need a partner in crime." Then she bent over, tied the bandanna around Bandit's neck and gave the dog a pat.

"Oh, he looks so cool! Like a real pirate!" Bobby tugged on the cloth and gestured toward the map. "Come on, Bandit, we need to go find some treasure!" The dog yipped, and off the two of them went, heading for the first stop on the map, the elm tree at the back of the yard. Bobby stopped by the tree, then started measuring ten paces to the nearby shrub. Soon he was rewarded with the unearthing of a small yellow ball.

Nick sidled up beside Carolyn. "Wow. I'm impressed. How did you come up with all of this?"

"One thing I learned to do while I was at Aunt Greta's was entertain myself." Carolyn leaned back against the patio table and crossed her arms over her chest. "I reread those pirate books from my dad over and over again and used to come up with all kinds of imaginary stories. Then I'd hide things all over the house and make maps for myself to find them later."

"I take it Aunt Greta never joined in?"

Carolyn chuckled. "No, definitely not. But...I think she supported me in her own way. I'd come home from school, and sometimes there'd be a little bag of toys. Small things, like jacks. Or crayons. And when I'd run out of drawing paper, there'd always be a new pad." Carolyn turned to Nick. "And every month, for years, there was a new pirate book. She never talked about my father. Never talked about what happened, and she wasn't the best parent. But those pirate books..." Carolyn smiled and a glimmer of tears showed in her eyes "—those pirate books made all of it bearable."

"They told you she cared. At least a little."

Carolyn nodded, mute.

Nick's arm stole around her, and he drew her against his chest. She pressed her face to the soft cotton of his T-shirt and allowed a couple of tears to dampen the fabric before pulling away.

"Ah, enough of the past. There's a pirate's treasure out there," she said. "And a pirate to attend to, who seems to want our assistance." Bobby gave them a wave from his place by the swing. "Are you going to help me search, matey?" Carolyn put out her hand, a smile on her face, the fun Carolyn he knew and remembered firmly back in place.

He laughed, so damned glad to see this woman that right now he'd have followed her to the ends of the earth if she asked. "Aye, aye, captain."

* * *

The doorbell rang in the middle of waffle making. Nick was cooking, Carolyn was threatening to get the fire extinguisher, Bobby was laughing and Bandit was running yipping circles around them all, hoping to get lucky with the rejected burnt attempts at breakfast.

To Nick, it felt exactly like a real family. Ever since Bobby had come downstairs and they'd started the pirate game, Nick had forgotten exactly why he'd thought it was a bad idea to get involved with Carolyn again. In the past hour he'd seen a side of her he hadn't expected.

Heck, the whole last few days he'd seen other sides of her he hadn't even realized she had. And he was longing for more.

More laughter to fill his house. More waffles—as awful as they had turned out. More treasure hunts in the backyard.

Suddenly he didn't want to return to the way things had been before. He wanted only for it all to stay exactly the same as it was right now.

"At least Daniel didn't just walk in this time," Nick said. "How about we all go out for breakfast and give up on this?"

"I vote for that," Carolyn said, thrusting a hand in the air. "Bobby?"

"Me too! If we can bring home a doggy bag for Bandit."

"Of course." Nick chuckled, then left the kitchen, heading for the front door.

When Nick was gone, Carolyn started cleaning up the mess. Bobby slipped into place beside her, eager to help, scraping the remains into Bandit's bowl, then helping her put the flour, butter and milk away. "I think it's safe to say Nick isn't the chef in the family," Carolyn said to him, and Bobby laughed.

She froze. Had she just said those words? "In the family?" And why was she surprised? For a while there, they *had* felt like a family. A regular mother, father and child, sitting down for a breakfast on an ordinary day. She'd grown comfortable here, with Nick, with Bobby, and had, somewhere along the way, lost the severe, strict courthouse Carolyn, along with the pins that had held her hair in place. She'd relaxed. Had fun. Forgotten about the disasters that could be looming around the corner. And found, as Nick had said, that it wasn't as hard as it looked.

It had been...wonderful.

"Maybe we should only let Nick make cereal with milk," Bobby was saying. "And peanut butter sandwiches. And—"

"Good morning."

Carolyn stopped washing dishes and turned around. Jean stood in the kitchen, trailed by Nick, whose face held the downturn of disappointment. "Jean."

"Hi, Carolyn." Then she smiled and turned to Bobby. "Hi, Bobby. How's it going?"

"Great. We're making waffles. But they're terrible. So Nick is taking us to a restaurant and letting them make the waffles."

Jean laughed. "Sounds like a good idea."

"Can I get you some coffee?" Carolyn asked, and as the words left her, she realized how much she had become at home in Nick's house, if she was already playing hostess.

"No, I'm not staying. Actually, I came by to deliver some good news." She bent down to Bobby's level. "Your mom is home from the hospital. And she's ready for you to come home, too."

He popped out of the chair, eyes wide with excitement. "She is?"

Jean nodded, laughing. "Absolutely. And I've arranged for a home health aide for a few days so she doesn't wear herself out. Plus there'll be a visiting nurse stopping by to make sure she's healthy and following doctor's orders."

"I can go home, right now, and see her?"

"Absolutely."

"Let me get my stuff!" He started toward the stairs, then spun back. "Is that okay, Nick? Carolyn? I mean, I really wanted to get waffles, too, but she's my mom and she's been sick and I want to see her real bad."

How could Carolyn feel one iota of disappointment at that face? But she did. She didn't want him to leave, didn't want this perfect bubble to burst.

All these years, she'd gone without a family, and now for a few days she'd had one, as oddly assembled as it had been. To lose it again, as quickly as she'd gained it—

Hurt.

But she knew she couldn't be that selfish, not when Bobby was overjoyed at being reunited with his mother. She glanced over at Nick and saw he seemed to be working as hard as she was at holding a smile on his face.

"If it was my mom, Bobby," Carolyn said, meaning the words and trying hard to force cheer into her voice, for Bobby's sake, "I'd be rushing out the door, too. I'm so glad she's better."

He smiled. "Me, too."

"Here, let me help you pack," Nick said. The two of them went up the stairs, the little boy talking the whole way, his joy so clear it shone like the sun.

"Kids like him remind me of why I do this job," Jean said. "It's nice to see a happy ending once in a while."

"Do you think his mother is going to make it?" Carolyn asked.

Jean nodded. "Her doctor told her as long as she takes care of herself, she should be fine. She's young. She caught the cancer early. And she's got a lot to live for."

Carolyn cast a glance toward the stairs. "Yeah, she does." She was sure Pauline knew just how much, especially after losing her husband. Caroline offered up a silent prayer that the days ahead would be filled with nothing but happiness for Bobby and Pauline. Then she went back to the dishes because her vision suddenly seemed awfully blurry. "I hope it all works out for him."

"And what about you?" Jean asked. "How will the story end for you?"

"Me?" Carolyn loaded the dirty dishes into a sinkful of soapy water. "My story will just keep going on as it has. I'll go back to work, go back to prosecuting cases. Putting bad guys in jail. Doing my part to change the world."

"Have you ever considered you're trying to change the world from the wrong end?"

Carolyn dried her hands and turned to face Jean. "What do you mean?"

"You were obviously great at this. Maybe," Jean ventured, "if you became a social worker, you could change these children's lives, *before* they grew up and became part of the criminal justice system."

"Oh, no, I don't think—"

"Just think about it," Jean said. The telltale sound of little footsteps coming down the stairs echoed through the house, announcing Bobby's return. "Together, you and Nick have a magic touch with children. And that kind of magic doesn't come along every day."

Bobby was leaving. This little fantasy world was coming to a close. Carolyn might have been able to fool herself into thinking she could have this world, that she could make this work, but she needed to get real. These past few days had been temporary. A vacation from reality. Nick hadn't changed, hadn't become Mr. Two-Point-Five-Kids overnight, and neither had she, even if part of her had flirted with the idea for a little while.

The magic Jean had thought she'd seen between Carolyn and Nick was really all an illusion. And the sooner Carolyn accepted that, the better.

Empty.

The house seemed emptier than ever before. Nick stood in the kitchen, at a loss. He could go into the office—but he'd already taken the day off. He could call Daniel, but the thought of suffering through a golf game—and his brother's questioning—was too much.

Or he could go to Carolyn.

But she had run out of here, practically on Bobby's heels, pleading a heavy workload even though she'd already taken the day off. He'd known it had been much more than that. She was avoiding him. Avoiding being alone with him. Because whenever they were alone, all those unanswered questions from the past came bubbling to the surface.

He had what he wanted—his life back to the way it used to be. No one expecting anything of him. No one to be responsible to or for. He should be happy. Instead, a strange sense of loss kept invading his thoughts.

Bandit started barking and darted out of the kitchen. A second later the barks stopped and Bandit returned, sliding under the table for a ball. Daniel brought up the rear. "Don't you ever answer your door? Or is Bandit the new butler?"

"You're awfully determined to get a golf partner today."

"No, I gave up on the golf game. I came by to borrow your jet skis. I'm heading to the lake with a few of the guys."

"Sure." Nick waved a hand in the direction of the garage. "Keys are on the hook."

"Whoa. You're just letting me take them? No questions asked? And no, 'Can I come to the party, too?'"

"I'm not in the mood for a party."

"Not in the mood for a party? You? Since when?"

Nick scowled. "Don't you have a lake waiting for you? And probably a date, too?"

A knowing grin spread across Daniel's face. "This is about Carolyn, isn't it? Speaking of which, where is she? And the kid?"

"The kid has a name—Bobby."

Daniel's grin only widened, which sparked Nick's temper even more.

"Bobby's mother came home from the hospital, so he went back to his own house. And Carolyn went to work. As usual."

Daniel let out a low whistle. "So she left you."

"She didn't leave me. She went to work."

"Uh-huh." Daniel swung one of the kitchen chairs around and sat down, draping his arms over the back. "So, are you just going to stay here and be the grumpy dwarf or are you going to go make things right with her this time?"

Nick crossed to the coffeepot and poured himself and Daniel each a mug, then sat down at the table. "There isn't anything to make right."

"I don't understand why not. Just this morning you were doing the happy family thing. And doing it pretty well from what I could see."

"It was an illusion," Nick said. "Like the card tricks I did when I was a kid. We pretended we believed it for a little while, and it seemed real. But it wasn't. Now we both go back to our lives."

"Oh, and such great lives they were, too." Daniel rolled his eyes. "For the oldest one in the family, you can be pretty stupid."

"What was wrong with my life?"

"What was so *good* about it?" Daniel countered. "You live in this big empty house all by yourself. Like you want to get married again, have a family, but you're afraid to go after what you want."

Nick scowled and got to his feet. "I'm not afraid of anything."

Daniel just sipped at his coffee, silent.

His brother was good at that. Playing the silent card, waiting for Nick to fill the gap in conversation. Nick refused to play that game, refused to give Daniel the satisfaction. "Do you want some lunch?"

"Not especially." Daniel leaned back, stretched, patient as the Cheshire cat.

"Well, I do." He didn't—it was still too early for another meal—but Nick needed the distraction. He opened the fridge, the door practically bouncing off its hinges, pulling out ham, cheese, mustard. He grabbed a loaf of bread and slapped together a sandwich but didn't eat it. He tossed the butter knife into the sink and turned around. "I screwed up with Carolyn before. What if I do it again? I married her for all the wrong reasons, didn't think about what I was doing, then didn't take the whole thing seriously enough and lost her. What kind of idiot does that make me?"

"A pretty big one." Daniel grinned. "But what if you go for it…and you don't screw up? What if the best thing ever just walked out your door today and you lost her twice? Now that would make you an idiot of Guiness World Record proportions."

Nick ran a hand through his hair. "Is there a reason I keep you on my Christmas list?"

"Yeah, I'm always right."

Nick paced the kitchen, the sandwich untouched on the counter, his coffee growing cold. "All my life I thought I didn't want to have a family. I grew up with all that, and figured once I was an adult, I'd finally have me time, you know? I'd wait until I was, oh, I don't know, Methuselah's age to have kids. But then, these last few days, I realized..."

"That the whole family thing is a little more fun than the bachelor life?"

"Yeah. Maybe."

"Then go for it. Take a chance. Dive headfirst into the marital pool again."

Nick put up his hands. "I never said I wanted to run off to the nearest church."

"Bawk, bawk, chicken-boy." Daniel rolled his eyes. "Go after Carolyn and quit being so damned scared that you'll make the same mistake a second time. Talk to her. You'd be amazed what can happen if you do that."

"It's not that simple, Daniel." Even Nick could hear the weakness of his protest.

Daniel shot to his feet. "Hell, yes, it's that simple. You're looking for something that does exist if only you'll take a chance.

You've been playing it safe, my brother. Playing games instead of taking things seriously."

"I am not."

His brother shrugged. "It's your life. You want to waste it, fine. But you're letting the best thing that ever happened to you get away. Because you're being too damned stubborn." He put his mug in the sink. "Thanks for the coffee. One of these days you'll thank me for the advice."

His brother walked out the door. Bandit trotted beside him, a ball in his mouth. Ever hopeful. Just like Daniel.

Nick glanced around his kitchen, all neat and tidy again, the traces of Bobby and Carolyn erased. It was as if they had never been there. He put his mug in the sink, then, as he did, a piece of paper caught his eye.

He picked it up, flipped it over. The treasure map.

X marked the spot for the biggest prize. The one that had lit Bobby's face—an old book on dragons that Carolyn had found in Nick's study, along with a ship in a bottle Nick used to keep on the mantel. When Bobby opened the shoebox and found those two prizes, he squealed with the joy of someone unearthing a pot of gold.

What if Nick could see that look of joy

every day—on his own son's face? And share that joy, as he had today, with Carolyn by his side? See her smile, so content, so relaxed, so full of joy. For that one moment, Nick had felt as if the entire world was perfect.

His finger traced along the dashes, weaving along the 2-D version of his backyard. Maybe Daniel was right. Maybe it was as simple as following the path of his heart…

And seeing what lay at the end of that road.

CHAPTER ELEVEN

LATER THAT AFTERNOON, Nick stood in his office but didn't get a lick of work done. He was working the phones but didn't pursue a single client. The pink message slips piled up on his desk, his persnickety assistant's face looking more and more concerned every time she slipped into his office and added another one to the stack. But he waved them off.

There wasn't a thing in that pile that couldn't wait until tomorrow. He had something far more important to handle.

In front of him he had the treasure map, filled with its dashed lines, all leading to one big *X*. Beneath that he had his own treasure map of sorts, though whether he'd end up finding a prize at the end or getting seriously burned still remained in doubt.

"Come on, Jerry, give me something better than that. You know you have a gold nugget sitting right in front of you that will work."

Nick paused, listening to the other man. "That sounds perfect. Okay, what do you need from me on my end?" Another pause. "Consider it done."

Nick hung up the phone, then headed down the hall to the senior partner's office. Within a half hour he had called a meeting of the top partners of the law firm. He pleaded his case, laid out all the facts and, to his surprise, swayed every last one of them into supporting his project.

"I have to tell you, Nick," said Graham Norbett, one of the oldest senior partners, as he exited the room and clapped Nick on the shoulder, "that was one of the best arguments I've ever heard you make. You had such passion. Such…belief in what you were saying."

"Thank you, sir."

"It's nice to see you becoming so excited about something. So committed. Not that you aren't committed to your job, of course, but—" the gray-haired man tipped his head "—a man your age needs a passion in life, and I think you've found yours." One more clap on the shoulder, then Graham walked away.

"Mr. Gilbert," his gray-haired assistant, Harriet, said, leaning inside the room. "I hate to bother you, but you've got someone waiting in your office."

"On my way."

"All right." Harriet, who hated to get behind at work, had stress written all over her face. Nick chuckled to himself. His assistant always had her hands full keeping him on track. Whenever he went off the beaten path of how things should work, Harriet's blood pressure rose twenty points. He made a note to give her another vacation day. The woman was going to need it after this week.

As Nick started working the phones again, this time using his cell, he wondered about Graham's remarks. Finding his passion. Maybe he had. Or maybe it was just a one-day enthusiasm for something new. No way to know…at least until he proved he could pull this off. Nick kept on talking, making use of every second on the walk back down the hall to his office. "Yeah, Marty, that sounds good. I can—"

He stopped, midconversation, when he saw who sat in the dark-brown leather chair opposite his desk. "Marty? I'm going to have to call you back… Sure, two o'clock works great for me. Thanks."

He slid the phone into his pocket, entered

his office and shut the door. "Carolyn. What are you doing here? Is Bobby all right?"

"Bobby is fine. I wanted to talk to you about us." She smoothed her hands over her skirt, then glanced up at him. "I realize I ran out of your house this morning without much of an explanation."

Already, he could tell by her stiff language and demeanor that this wasn't going to go well. "You did."

"I know I said I had to get to work, but really…" she smoothed her skirt again, then laced her fingers together and met his gaze head-on "—I was avoiding being alone with you. These last few days have…resurrected old feelings, and I came by to make sure that you knew there is nothing between us."

He took a seat on the edge of his desk. "Nothing. At all? Between us?"

"There's some attraction, sure, but—"

"Why are you doing this?"

"Doing what? I'm being honest."

"You're breaking up with me again. For no good reason. Again."

"I had good reasons the first time. And now."

He crossed his arms over his chest. "Okay. What are they?"

"I already told you. We can't have a relationship based solely on attraction."

"I agree. And you, Carolyn, are just talking, but nothing is coming out. What do you really want to say?"

Carolyn popped out of the seat and crossed to the window, as if she couldn't look at him anymore. She stared out at the same city that ran below her view a few blocks away. "I can't be with you, Nick. It doesn't matter if I want you or not, if we had a few days that were fun. Us being together is just not a good idea."

"And you had to come all the way over here, in person, to tell me that?"

She nodded.

He came up behind her, pausing a moment to inhale the floral notes of her perfume, then he reached out and took her into his arms, holding her to his chest. She resisted at first, then leaned into him. "Perjury," he whispered.

"No, Nick." She turned and twisted out of his arms. "It's self-preservation. It's what I do best."

"Self-preservation? Or fear?"

"Maybe both. Either way I don't get hurt. And I keep on putting the bad guys in jail. Win-win, right?"

"I only see you losing." He wanted to shake her, to force her to see what she was giving up. Frustration rose in his chest, tightening his heart. "In these last few days, I saw a side of you, Carolyn, a fun side, a laughing, happy side. You deserve that happiness. And you can balance that with your career. You know you can."

But she was already shaking her head. "I'm already happy."

"Working a million hours a week? Living alone? Come on, don't give me that. I'm living that lie and I'm not happy."

As the words left him, he realized how true they were. He wasn't happy. He hadn't been happy in a long time.

Three years, to be exact.

He had everything a bachelor could want. The problem? The bachelor didn't want that life. He wanted the woman he'd married.

She let out a gust. "You're asking me to do the impossible, Nick. I can't."

"What's so impossible? We try again?" He closed the gap between them, cupped her jaw. "Was it that bad, Carolyn?"

Tears shimmered in her gaze, then she shook her head and they were gone. "No. But that's what made the end so much worse. I'm not going to open my heart to you and be vulnerable and have you let me down. I *needed* you, Nick, and I never need anyone. Do you have any idea how much it cost me to ask you for help that day?"

He opened his mouth, then shook his head. "I never lived your life, Carolyn. I'm not going to pretend to say I know. But if you'll let me in—"

"No. I did that and you let me down."

"I—" He cut off his sentence, then breathed out a sigh. "I did. I was young and stupid and didn't realize what being a good husband was all about. I'm sorry, Carolyn. I'm really, really sorry."

She stared at him, her lips parted in surprise. "It's all right. It's in the past."

"No, it's not all right. You needed me to understand why you had to go to Boston. I should have done that, and moreover, I should have gone *with* you. Stood by you. But I was too damned selfish, too damned focused on myself to see what you needed." He took her hands in his. "When Ronald Jakes got out of jail, and you saw his face on the screen, I don't think I realized what that did to you. I grew up with everything, Carolyn, and that made me blind. Cavalier. Insensitive. I don't think I realized fully what you went through until this week. I should have. I'm sorry."

"I…" A smile flitted across her face. "Thank you."

He cupped her jaw, his fingers trailing along her face. "You've had a hell of a life, and I admire you for what you've done with it. How you've turned a tragedy into a passion. I just don't want to see you do that at the expense of everything else."

She broke away from him, crossed her arms over her body and headed for another window. Everything about her again spelled distance. Nick couldn't understand why. "There's something else that's been bothering me ever since I saw you again. Something that's bothered me ever since I walked out of that diner, and you…you let me go. Never fought for the marriage. For me."

"What?"

"I've prosecuted a lot of cases, Nick." She turned, put her back to the window. "I know when a defendant is holding something back. When there's that little tidbit he's left out. What aren't you telling me? Why did you give up on us so easily?"

He swallowed, and knew he had to be honest, to tell her everything. If there was ever going to be any hope of getting Carolyn back, they would have to start their relationship with good, strong honest bricks this time. "I followed you."

He watched the pieces fall into place, the numbers adding in her emerald gaze. "To Boston. When I went after Ronald Jakes again."

A faint smile crossed his face. "You asked me once if I was trying to play Lancelot when you wanted to go to Boston. I guess that's what I was doing. When I told you not to go, it was because I wanted to protect you. But you went anyway. I thought if I followed you, I could still protect you. I wanted to stop you from doing anything rash." He'd known that she'd gone out there, charged with the fire of vengeance and worry for the people Jakes had gone after, and Nick had hoped to head off Carolyn's rush to justice. "But—"

"But when you got there, I was already in the middle of the situation."

"Why did you do that, Carolyn? Risk your life with that maniac?"

She backed up, turned away and went back to the window, her breath escaping her in a long whoosh. "I thought I could help. I thought I could tell the police something about how the man thought. I thought I could stop him, bring about some miracle Hollywood ending."

"And you didn't."

"I never thought he'd do that. I never thought—" Carolyn cut off the sentence, then drew in some strength, and finished it "—he'd kill himself."

"And leave you without the closure you went there looking to get."

"I didn't go there for closure. I went there to help."

He shook his head, wishing he could get her to stop lying to herself, too. "You went there to fill those empty spots inside you. I saw it in your eyes. Saw it when you ran past the police barrier and insisted they let you help. I thought I was doing you a favor by letting you go, letting you pursue your passion, because I knew what it meant to you. I kept thinking you would find the missing pieces left by what you went through with your father. I thought if I let you go, you'd come back eventually, but all that did was allow you to bury yourself further in a hole you've never climbed out of."

"I'm not in a hole, Nick." But she looked away as she said the words.

"Oh, yes, you are. I know because I'm in the same one. For a different reason. My life is empty, Carolyn. Literally and figuratively. I live in a big empty house, a house that I now see means nothing without you in it. After you left today, I realized I didn't want to go back to what I had before. I want more."

He stayed close to her, not touching her, but close enough to inhale those floral notes, to see the tendrils of blond hair that danced around her jawline, the tears that pooled in her green eyes. "All these years, I've been searching for what I lost that day in the diner, just like you. But after this weekend, something changed for me, and now I'm prepared to make the leap and go after it. While you're still too afraid to make any changes."

She shook her head so hard, little wisps of hair escaped her bun. "I'm not afraid."

"You're more afraid than anyone I know, honey."

Her chin came up, determination setting her jaw. "Don't you understand? Every time I let someone get close, they get hurt. Like my father. I can't risk that." She shook her head, backing up, away from him. "No, Nick, it's safer this way. Safer if I just keep living my life the way I always have."

"Safer for who? For you? Because I sure as hell don't mind taking the risk." He saw her throwing up the walls again, building them so fast she was blocking any chance of them ever being together again. "Don't do this a second time, Carolyn."

"Nick, I have my career to think about. I'll be buried under cases, motions to file, briefs to prepare—"

"There will always be cases, Carolyn."

"Maybe someday down the road, we can…" She shrugged, her face crumpling a little.

And then he knew, all the pieces of this weekend, of the past three years piling on top of one another rushing at him—this wasn't just about them, it wasn't about her leaving for Boston that day. It was some bottomless debt she had never let herself finish paying.

"Oh, God, Carolyn, don't you think you've atoned enough for that day?" he said, his voice gentle, low.

She tried to hold his gaze, tried to keep her chin up, but then her lips began to quiver, her eyes filled and she had to look away. She shook her head, her fists balling at her side, Carolyn the Bulldog working so damned hard to maintain her composure, her walls. And every one of them began to fall a little at a time. "That's not what I'm doing."

Nick went to her, taking her arms, his hands sliding down to those determined fists, peeling back those fingers, slipping his hands into hers. "Oh, sweetheart, you can't stop them all."

"I'm not..." And then she was crying, really crying, and she stumbled into his arms, her tears soaking his shirt, drowning the silk of his tie. "I have to try, Nick, I have to try."

Nick just held her tight, letting the grief pour out. The realizations that the Ronald Jakeses of the world would just keep coming, day after day after day, in convenience stores and playgrounds and houses, and all Carolyn could do was try to put a finger in the dike and hope to stem the rising tide. "Carolyn, you can't stop them all," he murmured into her hair.

She shook her head, trembling in his arms. "What if I miss one? What if another child gets hurt? What if—"

Nick drew back, meeting her watery green eyes with his own. "What if you stop for one minute and live your own life? Will *that* be such a crime?"

"Look what happened to Bobby's father. That guy should have been in jail, not out on the streets with a gun. If he had been, Bobby's father would be alive today."

He stepped back, frustrated. "That's not even rational and you know it. Things like that happen everywhere. Every day. You can't stop the whole world."

"No, but I can control my corner of it." She swiped away the tears on her face. "And that's why I came here today." She swallowed, straightened her spine, resolve becoming her starch. "To say goodbye. Once and for all. I can concentrate on my job, like I always have." She drew up, shaking off the emotion, slipping into her old self as easily as a coat. "It's what I have to do."

"What?"

He hadn't seen this blow coming. Hadn't expected it at all. He'd thought he'd call her on the carpet, tell her they needed to make a choice, finally go forward or decide to grow apart, and she'd see the light and dive fully into a relationship with him. After all, they were older now, and surely, after all that had happened in the past few days, she'd seen that they could have a future. "Goodbye? But—"

"I'm sorry, Nick. I really am. But it's the smartest thing to do." She gave him a half smile. "After all, someone's gotta slay the dragons, right?"

Then she turned and left.

Telling Nick exactly what he hadn't wanted to hear. That he'd been dead wrong about Carolyn a second time.

But that didn't make losing her twice go down any easier.

CHAPTER TWELVE

EMPTY.

Carolyn went to work, buried herself in her job, came in early, stayed late every day, put in so many hours that three days passed without her seeing the sun rise or set.

And still it wasn't enough. Not nearly enough.

To wipe Nick Gilbert from her system.

She asked her boss for more and more cases, until he started refusing her. "I'm ordering you to take a vacation," he said.

"I can't, Ken. I need to work."

"No, you need to take time off. I know what you're doing." His light-gray eyes filled with concern. "I've seen it in myself. You're trying to burn out."

"I'm not—"

He put up a hand. "Don't argue with me. You're hoping that if you put in enough hours, you'll stop hurting over whatever it is that's got you in pain. I did it myself when my marriage started falling apart. And you know what happened? Things got worse. My wife left me, my kids stopped talking to me. Now I live with a dog that sees me only as his primary supply of food." He ran a hand through his hair, prematurely gray at forty-five. "Don't make my mistakes, Carolyn. Take some time off and fix your life. So you have one when you're my age."

She opened her mouth to argue, then saw the regrets and loneliness in his eyes. For the first time since she came to work at the city prosecutor's office, Carolyn took a look around Ken's space and noted the pictures. His ex-wife and two sons, happy and smiling on ski trips. On vacation in sunny locales. All this time, Carolyn had thought that these were family photos from Ken's life, but now she realized Ken wasn't in a single one of the pictures.

The truth slammed into her like a medicine ball to her gut. She was staring at her own empty, solitary future.

The other day she'd walked out of Nick's office, said goodbye, and chosen exactly what she was looking at right now. These pictures—it wasn't what she wanted.

But how to balance a life with the work that

she loved? The work that meant so much? The work that had defined her very self?

And in doing so, take the biggest risk of all?

Nick had taken some big risks before, but now he stood on the steps of the courthouse, about to argue the most important case of his life and convince the most difficult juror ever.

A juror who had already made her decision and might not even be open to an appeal. But he wasn't the type of lawyer who liked to lose, especially when it came to his own life.

Carolyn came through the double doors of the courthouse, a briefcase in one hand, a stack of files in the other. Mary flanked her on the right, chatting about where they should go to get a late lunch. Nick stepped in front of Carolyn and blocked her. "Miss Duff?"

Damn. Just seeing her had him ready to ditch his whole plan, take her in his arms and kiss her right here. He was sorely tempted to loosen her hair from the tight bun and run his fingers through those golden tendrils, to see the light in her eyes change from a bright green to the dark emerald of desire.

Carolyn drew up short and stopped. "Nick? What are you doing here? I thought—"

He grinned. "I'd like to present some testimony to you."

"Actually, I'm leaving court for the day. I'm going on vacation."

He blinked. "Vacation? You?"

"Boss-ordered." A faint smile crossed her lips. "But I thought it was a good idea, too."

"Do you have time for one more case?"

She took a step down, coming closer to him, sending his thoughts once again on a wild ride. "What kind of case?"

"I'd like to plead the case of you…and me."

Her face fell, frustration rising in her features. "I thought we settled that one."

A small crowd of lawyers had stopped what they were doing and were watching, making no secret of their eavesdropping. "Not to my satisfaction."

Carolyn's eyes widened, and for a second Nick thought she would protest, bolt, do whatever it took to upset his careful plan. But then the smile on her face expanded, just a little, and he knew he had a chance. "What evidence do you have, Counselor? Because I'm willing to consider an appeal, if it has merit."

"First, this." He stepped forward and stopped waiting to do what he really wanted to do. He took her in his arms, lowered his mouth to those sweet crimson lips and kissed her. She tasted of peppermint and coffee and of everything Nick dared to hope he could have again in his life.

The spontaneous gesture took her by surprise, and at first she didn't respond, which made Nick wonder if he'd done the wrong thing. Then, just when he worried he should step away, should give up on this insane idea, Carolyn melted in his arms and kissed him back.

He kept their kiss short, relatively chaste, considering they were in front of the courthouse and surrounded by most of the Lawford legal community. "May I enter that into evidence?"

Carolyn grinned. A faint redness filled her cheeks. "I'm, ah, not sure how to classify that."

He chuckled. "We can debate it later."

"Sounds like a good idea."

"My second argument," Nick said, trailing a finger down her chin, wishing he could kiss her again, "requires a field trip."

She arched a brow. "A field trip?"

He stepped back, put out a hand. "Do you trust me, Carolyn?"

A long second passed, and Nick wondered if he had lost her again. They still had a lot of unanswered questions between them. But he hoped that if he could show her this one thing, she'd understand everything about him, about what made him tick and about what was most important in life. And through that, maybe she'd find the answers to her own questions, too.

"Here, let me take these," Mary said, stepping between them and unloading all the files from Carolyn's hands and then slipping the briefcase out of her grasp. "That'll make it easier. For you to *go*, Carolyn."

"Well?" Nick asked.

"Okay. But…"

"No, buts, Carolyn. Trust me."

She hesitated a moment longer, then put her palm into his. The feel of her hand in his was like heaven, but Nick didn't count on it. Not yet. Nothing, he knew, was set in stone.

Together they walked down the courtroom steps and over to his SUV, parked in front of the courthouse. Illegally, but Nick figured one ticket was worth what he was doing today.

"Are you going to tell me anything about where we're going?" she asked.

"Not exactly." He fished in his suit pocket. "But there is a map." He handed her a piece of paper.

"What's this?"

"A treasure map, of sorts. Only it leads to someone else's treasure."

She gave him a quizzical look, then scanned the document, terribly drawn, considering he had all the art skills of a duck. "This doesn't tell me anything. There is a rule about evidentiary disclosure, you know." She buckled her seat belt and gave him a curious glance.

"You can appeal later."

She laughed. "You're breaking the rules."

"That's my specialty," Nick said, then put the vehicle in gear.

They wound through the streets of Lawford, soon leaving the downtown area behind. Nick's gut remained tight, tension holding its knot. He had no idea if everything he had worked on would pan out all right or not. Or how Carolyn would react. He'd worked solely on instinct with this particular feat of magic, pulling it all off in a matter of days.

But if he knew Carolyn the way he thought he knew Carolyn—

Then this would be what she'd been searching for. What they all had been searching for. The closure she needed, the way home.

Finally they turned down a tree-lined street and stopped in front of a small Cape-style house with a detached garage. A lush green lawn marched up a small sloping hill. A trio of pink azaleas flanked one side of the front door, a row of hedges the other. It was a simple house, as far as houses went, but perfect in so many other ways. Only one other car sat in the driveway.

"Where are we?" Carolyn asked.

"At X." Nick pointed at the treasure map, at the large capital letter that sat in the center of the paper, gave her a grin, then got out of the SUV. He came around the other side and opened the door for Carolyn. As he did, the occupants of the second car also got out. Jean Klein, Pauline Lester and Bobby.

"But...what is this?" Carolyn looked up at Nick, confusion knitting her brows.

The knot in his stomach doubled. Here went nothing. Either this impulsive plan went off without a hitch—or it all blew up in his face. During that weekend, he thought he'd gained insight into Carolyn. Insight he hadn't really had in college because he hadn't truly been paying attention. Back then, it had cost him—cost him dearly because he'd lost her.

This time he hoped he'd gotten it right, that what he had read in her, in the pockets of time when she'd opened up and let him see inside her heart, had allowed him to read what she truly needed. He took Carolyn's hand, then led her up the small walkway to meet the other trio by the front door. "We have a ceremony of sorts to attend."

"Whoa." Carolyn stopped walking and jerked Nick to a halt. "You aren't springing another elopement on me, are you?"

He studied her face, his breath caught in his chest. "Would you say yes?"

"Nick, that's not even funny. What's going on?"

"Trust me, Carolyn."

Her gaze swept over his features. Then she looked to the house, to the other people waiting for them. "All right. But if I see a minister—"

"Would it really be so bad to marry me again?" he asked, leaning forward, whispering in her ear. Thinking of the first time he had proposed—badly, he thought—on one knee in the student union of the law school. Just thinking of that clumsy, hasty proposal had him cringing. The next time he asked Carolyn to be his wife, he'd make sure he did a much better job.

She turned to face him, so close they could have kissed. His heartbeat accelerated and everything within Nick surged with desire. Damn. What was it about this woman? She drove him crazy, absolutely insane. Yet he wanted her. More with every passing second, more than he had three years ago, more than he'd ever thought possible. He must be one hell of a glutton for punishment, because she'd just broken up with him for good four days ago.

"Let's go see what's behind door number one," Nick said, then started walking again before he gave in to the urge to take her in his arms and kiss her. There were, after all, people waiting.

"Hi, Nick! Carolyn!" Bobby said when they reached him and his mother. Jean smiled at the two of them. "My momma is all better now. The doctor says she's going to be okay."

Nick and Carolyn looked to Pauline, who gave them a nod, her eyes filled with tears. Happy tears. Even Jean's eyes were misty.

Relief surged through Carolyn. A happy ending. The one she had prayed for, the one she hadn't even quite dared to hope would really come true for these two. "I'm thrilled for you," she said to Pauline, then bent down to Bobby's level. "And for you."

"And she said this year, she can be my room mom in my classroom. That means she can come have lunch with me every Thursday. That's pizza day. I love pizza."

Carolyn laughed. Such a simple thing, an ordinary, everyday kind of thing, and now, this little boy would be able to have that gift. "That's great, Bobby."

He paused, then looked up at his mother. She smiled at him and nodded. "Go ahead, ask her."

He turned back to Carolyn. "Carolyn, umm… would you come to my class someday? My teacher lets us have special people come and talk and well…" Bobby hesitated, toeing at the concrete for a moment, then his big brown eyes met hers. "Well, since your daddy died, too, I wondered if you could come when I talk about my daddy. Be my special person for that day. Because you know what it's like to not have a daddy."

The air around Carolyn stilled. Her heart squeezed. Then tears welled in her eyes and she reached out to Bobby, at first only taking his hand, but then that wasn't enough, not nearly enough to tell him how much he had touched her, opened a part of her heart, her life, that she had thought was closed, and her arms went around him. Even as the tears began to fall, to finally fall, she pulled him into her chest, holding him tight, this kindred spirit who had helped heal that last scar in Carolyn. She nodded, her tears dropping onto his T-shirt, leaving fat droplets on the cotton. "I'd love to, Bobby. I'd love to."

"Thank you," he said, but his voice was a little muffled by the hug.

A long moment passed, filled with some sniffles from all the adults, before Carolyn rose. Nick cleared his throat. "Well, I bet you're all wondering why we dragged you out here today."

"Jean said it was something to do with the Buddy program," Pauline said.

"In a way. Much more than being a buddy, though." Nick reached into his suit jacket and pulled out a large manila envelope that had been folded in half. He opened it up, then handed the package to Pauline. "This, I believe, is yours."

She looked down at the envelope, then back at him, confused. "Mine? But…what…what is it?"

"A deed."

The two words hung in the air, light as butterflies. Then they gradually filtered into her consciousness. Her eyes widened, her jaw dropped, her body froze, as if she were afraid she'd move and the whole thing would disappear. "A deed? To…" She pivoted, one inch at a time and looked at the little white house with the dark-green shutters and the wide bay window. And she started to cry. "For me? And Bobby?"

Nick nodded, a grin spreading across his face. "Yes."

Her hands went to her mouth, fingers shaking, shock all over her features. "Oh, my, no, no, you can't be serious."

Carolyn stared at Nick. A house? An entire house for Pauline and Bobby? This was way bigger than a few toys, some books from the bookstore. How had he done this and in such a short period of time? This wasn't a magic trick. This was the *impossible*.

"Look in the envelope," Nick said. "And find the keys to your new front door."

Pauline's hands were shaking so badly, Jean had to help her. The two of them reached inside, then slid out a keyring, with two silver keys hanging off it. Beside Pauline, Bobby finally started to realize what was happening. "Do we own a house, Momma? A real house? Just for us?"

Carolyn didn't even realize she was crying until the tears choked her voice. "It seems you do, Bobby. This one right here." She stared at Nick, who wasn't providing any answers. He just grinned, lighting up the spark in his cobalt eyes and emphasizing the crinkles around them. She noticed something new in his face, something she hadn't noticed before.

"It's ours?" Bobby said. "Forever? We don't have to give it back?"

"Yes," Nick said. "It's all paid for."

"*Paid for?* All of it?" Pauline's mouth opened. "How? Why?"

"My law firm, and a couple others in town, wanted to do a little more than contribute to a picnic or buy a few toys. So I made some calls."

"But this is too much," Pauline said, trying to hand the envelope back to Nick, force the keys into his hand. "We can't accept this."

Bobby stood before his mother, not saying a word. Holding his breath.

"You've been dealt a difficult hand in life, Pauline," Nick said, refusing to take the envelope or the keys. "Accept this gift and make a new start. For you and your son."

She shook her head. "There are so many other families much more deserving than I. I can't do this, knowing that they need the money, as well. I'd much rather see you take what this costs and divide it among them."

Nick smiled. "I figured you'd say that. And I already have an argument ready. You see, my law firm makes a lot of money. Too much. And they'd like a way to offset some of those taxes. What better way to do that than help other people?"

"That's incredible, Nick," Jean said, her face wide with shock. "Just so incredible that…I don't even have words for what that's going to mean for so many families in this area."

Carolyn now realized what she was seeing in Nick. The passion he had in law school. That change-the-world belief that had attracted her to him. This was the Nick she remembered. This was the Nick she had fallen in love with.

This was the man she had been looking for over the last few days, and the man, she suspected, he had lost. He'd been merely looking for a purpose.

It was what he hadn't found in corporate law. It was what he'd always wanted. And it had taken one little boy to bring it out in him.

"You did it," she said quietly. "You changed the world."

"Not the world." Nick chuckled. "More like one square of one street. Same as you, kind of. There's still a long ways to go."

She slipped her hand into his and gave his palm a squeeze. "You've gone miles already, Nick." Then she pointed toward Pauline and Bobby, who were inserting the key into their new house, chatting excitedly about the future, about their new life. A life that would forever be based on hope and joy. And would no longer be rooted in tragedy.

"All I need now is for you to make the journey with me, Carolyn." He turned to her. "What do you say? Are you ready to take that chance?"

CHAPTER THIRTEEN

CAROLYN HAD NEVER been very good at magic. She'd tried a thousand times to memorize the little tricks that Nick had tried to teach her years before, but didn't seem to have the sleight of hand that he had. Couldn't remember the steps to the card tricks or the disappearing balls. But this time she was determined.

She'd left the new house after Pauline and Bobby had taken time to exclaim over every stick of furniture, every plant in the backyard, and asked Nick to meet her at the park that night. She'd needed some time to think, a moment to come to terms with the changes in her life.

"You have me intrigued."

Carolyn turned at the sound of Nick's voice. He strode toward her, tall, handsome, a man she now realized that she could lean on, depend on, make a partner in her life.

"That was part of the plan. Keeping you on your toes."

He grinned. "This is a new side of you."

"A good side, I hope."

He closed the distance between them, and Carolyn inhaled, for a second forgetting what she wanted to say. Forgetting everything but Nick.

"Every side of you is a good side," he said.

"You showed me something today, something that made me realize there's a way to have everything I want."

"I did?"

"When you gave that house to Pauline and Bobby, I realized I could put together what I've been doing in law with helping kids like Bobby. Jean had told me I was working the wrong side of the justice system. That maybe I'd serve society better by helping these kids before they end up in the courts."

"You…want to work with kids?"

Carolyn laughed. "Yeah, I know it's insane, isn't it? I can't even make a paper bag eagle, and I'll have to learn a whole new vocabulary, but…" She smiled. "I saw what a difference it could make to a kid like Bobby. You were right."

He grinned. "Did I just hear what I thought

I heard? A lawyer admitting the opposing counsel was right?"

"There aren't any witnesses to my admission so it'll never hold up in court," she teased. "But, yes, I did. You kept telling me that someone like me, someone who had been through the same experiences as Bobby, would be the perfect person to help him. To get through to him. And today I realized I had. I saw me in him, and he, in his own way, helped me, too."

"Helped you heal the wounds of your past."

She nodded. "What if there had been someone who had talked to me about what I went through? Who had taken me out of Aunt Greta's house, even for an afternoon, and given me a bit of normalcy? Or let me know that it was okay to feel guilty about the day my father was killed? Maybe I wouldn't have grown up so afraid, so worried about the Ronald Jakeses of the world. And so convinced I had to keep repaying my father for making a sacrifice any father would have made."

Nick took her in his arms, holding Carolyn to his chest, the smile that crossed his lips telling her he approved, very much approved, of this new idea. "Not that you weren't a great bulldog, but I truly think you have a message, Carolyn, and it's been stuck inside you far too long."

She tipped her chin to meet his gaze. "We could make a good team, you know. You could do the charity end, spreading keys to houses far and wide, and I could help put together counseling and buddy programs."

"That sounds like the ideal package." His smile widened, and he dipped down to brush a kiss across her lips. "But there's only one hitch. For it to work perfectly, we'd probably have to be together all the time."

She grinned. "I thought of that. After all, haven't you always said we were better together than apart? And—" a hint of a tease appeared on her face "—since we're both lawyers, we'd need a contract for something like that, wouldn't you agree?"

"A contract?" His face fell.

But her grin only got bigger. Oh, how Carolyn was going to delight in this new side of her life. She hadn't realized until these last days with Bobby and Nick how freeing fun could be. Not until she'd stopped having it and gone back to work-only mode. But now, being able to tease Nick, actually having found a way to have it all, everything about herself felt lighter, as if she was walking on a cloud.

Carolyn stepped out of Nick's arms and waved her fingers in front of his face. "Perhaps I should try to produce a contract out of thin air?"

"Produce a contract. Out of thin air. Here in the park?" He arched a dubious brow.

She waved her fingers again, making a big production out of the movement. "I want you to know I'm serious, Nick. That this time I'm not hopping on any planes. Not running out of a diner. Not hiding in my workload." Then she slid two fingers of one hand up her sleeve in a quick, nimble movement and produced the tiny black velvet box for the engagement ring he had given her all those years ago. Not a big magic trick, as far as tricks went, but hey, she would leave the great hocus-pocus to Nick. "This is the first half of the contract. I believe you have the rest. The part that fills in all the blanks?"

His eyes widened. "You saved this?"

She nodded, a glimmer of tears slightly blurring her vision. After she had given back the rings in the diner, she had held on to the box, never able to part with that little remnant of their past. "You're not the only one who still had dreams, Nick. Who didn't give up. I just put all that away, in the back of my dresser. And pretended I didn't still hope."

"Oh, Carolyn," Nick said, sweeping her into his arms again, the box crushed in her grip. "I love you. I always have."

"And I love you, too." She lifted her lips to his, and they kissed, sealing the deal the only way Nick and Carolyn ever had. This kiss was sweeter than any before, because it brought their love full circle, had the taste of forever etched in their joining.

Then Nick leaned down and picked Carolyn up, sweeping her off her feet. He pulled her to his chest, holding her tight, his smile wide and happy.

"What are you doing?" she asked, laughing.

"This time, I'm taking you to meet my family, because once you do, they're not going to let you get away, either. First, though, we'll stop at my house and pick up that ring. You're right. I did save it. You're not the only hopeless romantic here." He grinned, carrying her all the way back to his SUV. "And I want to do this before you have time to file an appeal, Counselor. Just in case."

"I second that motion," she said, kissing his neck, his lips, every part of Nick that she could reach. Then she noticed something and put a hand on his chest. "Wait, Nick, there's something I forgot."

"What?"

"Can we stay here and watch the sun set? I don't want to miss the beginning or end of another day for as long as I live." She twined her arms around his neck. "And I want to see every single one of them with you."

"Of course." He set her down and found a good place on the grassy knoll for the two of them to see the day come to an end. Carolyn curled into the cocoon created by Nick's arms, and as the sun's last rays cast their warmth over her skin, she opened her heart the rest of the way to the overwhelming evidence of how absolutely wonderful true love could be.

* * * * *